Dark Matter

Alyssa Huckleberry

Core

I always knew it would be me.

Don't ask me to explain how I knew—I won't be able to.

As far back as I can remember, there was talk of colonizing outer space. I didn't grow up freaked out by the idea. Maybe I should have been—my parents were.

The year I was born, the United States celebrated its one hundredth anniversary of the successful establishment of a colony on the moon. Venturing into outer space was never foreign to me, it never carried fear the way it did for the adults around me. I learned about the solar system in school like every kid through the generations…but I also facetimed with the scientists stationed at headquarters and had a third-grade pen pal who lived on the moon.

But that was when the earth was only *thought* to be dying…before scientists put an expiration date on earth's existence. That news changed everything: disbelief melted into panic, which boiled to cold-blooded terror when the drafts were instated.

But maybe I'm getting ahead of myself. I forget that not everyone is fluent in space-talk; that my everyday reality is startling to some. My mom in particular reminds me of this all the time. She accuses me of being intentionally abrupt just so I can elicit shocked reactions from people around me.

It isn't true. I just don't see the point in sugar-coating situations. I'm blunt because it's an efficient form of communication…it's only noticeable because the rest of the world seems eager to bury their heads in the sand and tiptoe around anything and everything sparking discomfort.

If it were my way, I'd outline the current state of affairs with bullet points and roman numeral subpoints...but I'll play nice and cater to the delicate nature of humanity these days. Ms. Anderson, if you're reading this, I hope you'll note that my ability to embellish a written piece and elaborate on an idea have greatly improved since the ninth grade.

My name is Selina Alois. If I'm going to be thorough, I should mention that Selina means *moon* in Greek, and Alois speaks to my German roots— it was the name of a famous warrior in the German culture. My dad's particularly proud of this heritage, although I don't know that I've seen evidence of heroism in my paternal line deserving of such a moniker. There I am being blunt again.

I swear I keep most of these thoughts to myself—I'm very good at only voicing those tidbits that serve a productive purpose. But I figure you deserve the full story, and if you're going to understand what happened, you should know it all.

I was named in honor of the moon, and, while my parents would never admit it, I suspect it was also a superstitious ploy to keep me from being sent from earth.

My parents have a lot invested in me. I'm their only child—and they're lucky to have one at all. There are strict rules about reproduction now: couples have to apply to the federal bureau and undergo invasive procedures to establish a clear bill of both physical and emotional health before they're even entered into the interview process and tasked with IQ tests. In a world with an expiration date and increasingly-limited resources, it's irresponsible to let just *anyone* populate the world. Or that's the thought.

My parents sat in the queue for four years before they were approved—just in time, because my mother's age would have barred her from eligibility when she turned thirty. You know, to protect against an "old" egg being fertilized. So, at age 29, my mother and my slightly-older father welcomed me into the world.

According to the extensive nurse's report, I was a "strong and remarkably silent baby." I like this part of the report—I memorized it a long time ago. I'd like to think that much has stayed the same—I pride myself in my resilience and fortitude.

And then, I grew up—that part hasn't changed with the evolution of the world. Because it's always been noted as an important distinguishing indicator among humans, here's what I look like: my hair is long (halfway down my back), thick (think horse mane), and the color of burnt toffee. The highlights are completely natural—I'm asked all the time what I do to my hair (the answer is, nothing). My skin is pale with yellow undertones. I blush easily, and my high cheekbones seem to accentuate any embarrassment or unwanted attention.

My eyes are wide and large: almond-shaped orbs of chartreuse green with a ring of thick amber surrounding them. I'm blessed with thick, midnight-black lashes that I'm told make for a startling contrast—my eyes are my best feature. The rest of me is rather unremarkable: medium height, medium build…although I'd like to note that my figure is strong and athletic—not slight and waifish, like so many of the other girls. I like physical activity…the real kind, not the simulation (more on that later).

History accounts I've read describe a time when children were allowed to venture out into the neighborhood unsupervised, a time where they were safe to play and explore in the local park, a time when physical books were still in existence, and when you went to an actual place to buy groceries for baking.

I've seen the pictures of families packed on the beach or of children gleefully gripping the steel links of public swings—*public swings, can you believe it?*—as their parents pushed them back and forth.

The pictures of children curled up with books are the ones that get me the most. A simple snapshot of a bookcase stacked with volumes of beautifully-bound and wonderfully-colored books makes my heart catch a little: I'm nostalgic and heart-sick for a past I never experienced. There's something magical about seeing all the books stacked and organized at the discretion of the owner: arranged by color? Author? Height? Subject matter?

I can only imagine the thrill of tracing fingers across a thick page of paper and inhaling the smell of glue and nutmeg and pine…at least, that's what I imagine the books to smell like. I got a book-scented candle for Christmas, and that's what it smells like. But who knows if the candle-maker ever smelled a book.

So, what does my world look like? Let me see if I can illustrate it for you using the most superfluous descriptors and tidbits.

Children don't play on playgrounds (too unsanitary) or in the neighborhood (unsafe, and too many toxins in the atmosphere), but they connect with their friends digitally to play video games and even to exercise together.

Excursions to the beach or to the mountains are special events requiring vaccination; books are unsanitary relics that have long ago been recycled to free up much-needed room (and to reduce emissions leaked into the atmosphere from printing presses, AND to reduce exhaust from transportation required to physically connect would-be readers with their tales). It's much more efficient to consume literary content digitally…and that's the only means available to the reader today.

There are no physical "grocery stores"—all food items are purchased online and delivered by drone.

Physical exercise is important to maintain the health and fitness of the human race, but conditioning is achieved through family-owned exercise equipment and electro-magnetic stimulators that activate and stimulate muscles and organs without actually taxing them (it's safer that way).

The one place that all children congregate is school. For a few years, even this small concession was taken away—but the lack of socialization and personal human interaction was so detrimental that "education in a building" was deemed a necessary risk for the health and progress of humanity. I don't think I need to tell you how thankful I am for that.

And then there's the general state of the world. Earth's been dying for a long time—I know that's not new. I've read the reports. We've studied the unheeded warnings and scientific reports that came out during your time. A world with an ever-increasing population, and no black plague or yellow fever to naturally keep numbers in line with the natural resources available in the world.

Scientific breakthrough and medical advances have elongated life expectancy—a gift to humanity at the detriment of the earth's health—but we've not advanced so much to reverse or slow the damaged ecosystem exacerbated by carbon emissions and greenhouse gases.

Hence, the population limit.

If you feel that the many obstacles my parents had to bypass in order to have a single child are ridiculous, you should know that they're considered the lucky ones. Only 9.3648% of the population is cleared to reproduce.

In your time, sixteen-year-olds celebrated the acquisition of drivers' licenses, stressed about SAT tests, and planned outfits for prom. None of this applies in my world.

Humans driving? I can't even imagine it. In a rare departure from our modus operandi, I have to agree with my mother that the thought of a human driving a machine is terrifying. No, that was abolished a long time ago—all transportation craft is powered by sophisticated technology.

High-stakes tests are still in existence, but they are hardly the marathon exams scratched out using those canary-yellow graphite instruments I've seen pictures of. It's much more efficient now: they just hook your brain up to a special machine that reads and interprets brain wave activity.

In four minutes flat, you have your score. Before you feel too jealous, I should point out that this also mitigates any opportunity to artificially boost your score using tips and tricks of the trade—there's no way to study for something like this.

And while society did decree that physical attendance in a building for learning was necessary for humans in their formative years, they did not go so far as to reinstate dances or sports teams or after-school clubs. Too dangerous, too risky, too unpredictable. We can still pursue these interests, but through community technology platforms…never in the flesh.

The thing we get that you never had? Sterilization. You think *you* felt pressure taking the SAT test? HA! Moments after we receive our scores, a doctor comes in with an injection that either boosts our vitals and encourages reproductive health, or ensures that we will never, *ever* procreate. It only takes a minute for the technology to run a sophisticated algorithm rating an individual's projected capability to contribute to society. From there, it's the Darwinian approach of selective breeding and survival of the fittest.

All of this probably sounds terrible to you, but it's what I've grown up with. We're indoctrinated with these ideas early, so none of it seems egregious or horrifying. Still, I realize that it's a grand departure from the way of life you know. Like you, we find our junior year of high school to be stressful. There's just less we can do about it.

I'm not sure if it makes it better or worse knowing that your future is literally out of your control. There's no guilt attached to a poor performance, but there's massive anxiety surrounding the physical exams. So maybe that's a natural place to start…the week leading up to *the* exam.

Seven Days Until Testing

"Selina, did you add turmeric to your avocado and flaxseed toast?" my mother asked from across the table. Her voice was calm but pinched—I suspected she was even more nervous about the impending assessment than I was.

I hate turmeric. I'd been dutifully ingesting blueberry and kale smoothies, spinach salads with pumpkin seeds and walnuts and salmon, and green tea every day…all part of the regimen my mom had spent a small fortune procuring. All foods supposedly beneficial to the brain and heart health; all foods I'd faithfully eaten from a young age (you can never start preparing too early). I'd obediently eliminated even dark chocolate from my diet (the one dessert allowed in our household because of its antioxidant benefits) due to the caffeine content…but I couldn't bring myself to adopt turmeric.

I looked to my dad for back-up, but he chose to take an exaggerated swig of tea in just that moment. I knew he supported my mom's health campaign, but he was also the one I could usually count on to administer balance.

"Mom, we've talked about this. I'm eating all the health foods except for turmeric," I told my mom honestly, bracing myself for the inevitable fight.

My mom already knew I wasn't taking any turmeric. I'd never eaten turmeric. Still, she laid her fork down on the carefully-pressed cloth napkin in front of her and sighed heavily.

"Selina. You're only going to get one chance at the exam," my mom warned, eyebrows rounded like golden McDonald's arches.

"Mo-om! I know. Why do you think I've eaten all those other foods? I didn't even fight you over the chocolate," I pointed out, trying my best not to get defensive. I'd read somewhere that when you become emotional, you respond irrationally and inhibit your best thinking.

My mom didn't respond. I didn't have anything more to add. My dad gulped his tea and changed the subject. "How are your friends feeling about the test, Selina?"

"I don't know—we don't really talk about it," I answered honestly, grateful to redirect the focus off of me.

"It's a pretty big deal, not to talk about it at all," my mom cut in, voice tight. She was still trying to make a point that she'd clearly communicated a dozen times.

"There's not really anything we can do about it, you know?" I answered, speaking more to my dad than to my mom. "I'm sure they're all nervous and stressed about it," I added quickly before my mom could make a snide comment about turmeric consumption.

My dad hummed his agreement and wisely saw fit to change the subject once again.

"We're working on new programming that will allow for smell to be transmitted through technological communication," my dad told his mildly-interested audience. This wasn't really that new—he'd been talking about this for months now. But every time his team was able to send through a new scent, he got excited.

"What's the latest scent?" I asked agreeably.

"Citrus! We started with the obvious fruits, but yesterday we were able to pin down the pomelo. That was a tricky one—we kept getting too close to a grapefruit," my dad explained.

I smiled. This was what we were groomed and protected for: careers meant to explore and attain perfection in discretionary products.

"That's nice, dear. Your team has been working on that scent for a while— it must feel good to have that breakthrough," my mom sang her predictable praise.

We didn't discuss anything else noteworthy. My mom rarely chose to talk about her work, preferring instead to focus on micromanaging the lives of those she loves. My dad doesn't mind…perhaps because it's been a part of his routine for so many years. I didn't grow up feeling annoyed by the attention, but everything's been amplified this past year.

The evening passed agreeably. For all the technological advances we've made, students are still loaded up with homework: exercises meant to build brain matter and equip us for the big exam. I don't really mind—this offers structure to my day and gives me an excuse to bow out of mundane conversation with my parents before too much time has passed. And I don't mean to brag, but I'm pretty smart. So the work doesn't feel that hard.

I'm not brilliant-smart, like a few of the kids I take classes with. I'm pretty sure there are a few kids who aren't worried at all about the exam. But I'm smart enough that I don't seriously worry about being sterilized or relegated to a meaningless profession.

Three and a half hours later, I was ready for bed. I aimed for a solid 8 hours of sleep a night, and most nights, I got it. This was not one of those nights.

It was a dark, dark place. Heavy, oppressive wooden beams lay on the perimeter of the open-raftered building that extended into a back patio covered with dirt mixed with rock and peanut shells. Wide, cafeteria-style picnic benches sat on the patio, evenly spaced and covered with a thin layer of debris.

A restaurant, I somehow knew before my eyes rested on the charcoal barbecue and condiment station off to the side. There were white paper plates and a jar of yellow mustard and the flicker of sepia-hued firefly lights, but the entire scene struck me as dark. Darkness marked not by the monochromatism of black but rather the absence of light.

The patrons themselves were swathed in palettes of gray and brown and black—all covered in grime. Many wore hats; none wore smiles. Conversation was muted, and the hunched shoulders and beleaguered expressions on the faces of the men and women somehow warned of intensity, of a threat I could not see.

Cast-iron lanterns hung from shepherd's hooks that creaked and protested as a warm breeze blew through. A strong wind—one that propelled me forward into the scenery I'd been quietly surveying with much trepidation.

What was it that tipped them off? What was it about me that was different? As my feet struggled to find purchase on the sooty gravel beneath me, all eyes turned to rest on my figure. Suspicious eyes; eyes that seemed to look through me and warn me and despise me all at the same time. Lasers that penetrated my nerves and turned my blood to ice. I had been noticed, and I had to move forward.

The warm breeze that had swept through stopped abruptly. I feigned nonchalance and took steps towards the establishment. If it were possible, the pigmentation of the structure darkened even more.

Very aware that my presence had caused some sort of disruption, I slid onto the edge of the nearest bench and kept my gaze down. I was aware of the eyes on me; eyes that had never left me.

"Where is she?!"

The voice was cold, authoritative, and gravelly. IT had arrived, and it had come for me.
I woke abruptly, covered in sweat and out of breath. This was always how I woke from *the* dream. It didn't always end in the same place: sometimes, I stood up from the table, both palms pressed flat against the splintered-wood surface of the table, my gaze directed towards IT.

IT, with face shadowed and obscured—I could never make out any features of IT, but I knew instinctively what IT wanted. That was pretty straight-forward: me.

In some small way, this dream contributed to my conviction that I would be chosen. When I think back to how I knew, I always come back to the dream. I didn't need to know where I was or what it meant—my subconscious had already worked it out. The same way you can dismiss a dinosaur nightmare, I knew the dream to be a prophetic warning. Of what, I hadn't quite figured out.

Six Days Until Testing

"Selina, are you ready?" my mom called from the kitchen.

Of course I was ready. I was always ready…but this was part of our morning routine, the daily song-and-dance. It was just one way my mother told me she loved me, since the specific words infrequently left her mouth. I was smart enough to know this and rolled my eyes but never complained or commented on my mom's silly ritual.

Instead of answering, I walked out into the kitchen and peered out the expansive, floor-to-ceiling window to the street below. The pod hadn't arrived yet, but it would within the minute.

My mom smiled at me, then handed me the carefully-crafted lunch she'd prepared the night before. "Have a great day, Selina." Her words were sweet, but the tone of voice never matched. This wasn't to be held against her—very few people were blessed with warm, affectionate voices. It wasn't a feature natural selection necessitated for modern-day survival.

"You too, Mom, Thanks for the lunch. Bye, Dad!" I called over my shoulder before walking out the door. A muffled response was my cue to leave.

The moment the door clicked shut behind me, I exhaled. It was a habit I'd formed years ago, much by accident. There was some small freedom in leaving the "haven of protection" to venture outdoors.

A plexiglass elevator took me down the four levels to the street; this was where I caught the pod to school.

The pods were always exactly on time—that was the beauty of machinery and equipment run by computers and not humans. The self-driving vehicles were carefully colored for function: yellow pods were made specifically to transport students in place of the school buses of days past.

A pressurized door registered my approach and whirred open to reveal ten stools encapsulated by what you would probably describe as test tube cylinders. No seatbelts; the cylinders guarded against unexpected movement. There were no accidents or crashes.

Various other students were collected along the way, but there was no conversation yet. The pods were silent zones.

The commute to school wasn't long. When the doors opened, I took familiar steps to the front of the school and then inside.

Our schools look a little like history's hospitals. Sterile, simple décor, and bright. Advanced technology. Large. Oversized white travertine tiles on the floor; mosaic, rainbow-colored murals on the walls lauding the tenets our society holds most dear: progress, opportunity, and sustainability.

The first time someone visits, they're blown away by the beauty and intricate workmanship of the place, the tiles that sparkle in the glint of the four o'clock sunlight and cast dreamy, spectral light across the flooring comparable to that of stained-glass windows. I've walked through the doors 563 times…so I tend to just pass by.

On this particular day, I did glance at the murals—if only to reassure myself of their presence. The upcoming exam had everyone in a tizzy, and as much as I wanted to claim immunity from the anxious frenzy, it affected me, too. I found comfort in familiar, tangible objects.

"Selina!"

I was torn from my thoughts. Glancing up, I saw Clarice waving me over, waddling full-speed in my direction.

My parents approved of Clarice because she was clean and studious and ambitious and musically-inclined. Her silky, jet-black hair swished back and forth over her shoulders as she juggled her saxophone, tablet, and lunch. I know—not much compared to the baggage students used to have to lug around school. But in my day, anything more than a simple bag looked out of place.

I shook my head fondly. "I hope you count this towards your daily phys-ed goal," I teased, gesturing towards her many belongings. "That has to count for at least ten pounds."

Clarice rolled her eyes. "Right. My phys-ed goal. My number one worry."

I opened my mouth to banter back but saw Clarice's cinnamon-brown eyes cloud over. She was worried about the exam, and she would be annoyed by any attempt to redirect the conversation. Wisely, I kept my mouth shut and cocked my head to the side, inviting the verbal dump I knew well enough was about to come.

"Please tell me you saw Mr. Boothe's tweet," Clarice rushed on, eyes narrowed as she scrutinized my face for an expression.

On unspoken cue, my palms oozed sweat and my heartbeat quickened. Clarice would notice my pupils dilate, but still I worked to present an appearance of composure. Mr. Boothe? Tweet?

He wasn't a prolific presence online, but any communication from Boothe's handle carried influence. As the director of The Organization he also served as Secretary of Education, and he was responsible for every scholastic matter pertaining to the youth. I worried that this latest announcement might relate to the exam.

"I haven't," I answered directly, opting for honesty. "When did he post?"

"Just minutes ago," Clarice told me breathlessly, cheeks flushed with excitement. "I'm guessing he didn't want our parents to freak out and keep us from coming to school today. Which is, of course, brilliant—and also terribly sneaky."

It was clear from her response that she was euphoric over the recent turn of events…if for no other reason than because of the drama she imagined unfolding in households across the country.

"Clarice! What did he say?" I demanded.

"So you know how the first people to colonize the moon were teens, like us?" Clarice asked, leaning in close and lowering her voice. I smelled coffee on her breath—her mom would be livid if she knew Clarice was cheating on her exam diet. I wondered why she was insisting on such secrecy when the communication in question was a public broadcast. But that was Clarice.

I nodded my head to encourage her to continue, silently wondering what this was all about. Were they ready to send the next wave of citizens to the moon? The first expedition had been initiated by a group of high school juniors (our age precisely) who had established base camp with virtual assistance from senior astronauts. It had been a major feat for mankind: since then, thousands had flocked to the moon as a haven from the ever-increasing population of earth.

Population on the moon was heavily controlled, and spaces rarely came available. Scientists adhered to a strict schedule: every two to five years, a select number of spots were released…and they were snapped up within the minute.

Earlier generations played the lottery for money, hoping to win a million-dollar jackpot. My generation didn't care a bit for money—it was no longer the most precious commodity. Today, it's all about land. The lottery has changed from coin currency to property ownership… the dream is to secure a safe place in the universe. This doesn't mean an acre or two on earth, as once might have been the case.

"Did he announce new slots for the moon?" I asked impatiently, wishing to high heaven that Clarice would cut to the chase.

"No," she told me, eyes wide as teacups as she shook her head back and forth. She was genuinely shocked by whatever news she had heard—I'd never seen her so stunned.
A cold wave of dread washed over me. Unable to wait any longer, I pulled my tablet from my bag and stared at the wheat-gold notification that glowed in the backlight of my device.

In this year's exam, juniors will be screened for inter-galactic colonization of Venus and Heidel. More to come in tonight's state of the union address. #intergalacticcolonization @AdamBoothe

I stared at the screen. I blinked. The sky-blue scrawl burned my eyes as my brain worked to make sense of the Helvetica type. After what felt like an eternity, I pulled my eyes from my device and met Clarice's gaze.

"Can this be for real?" I asked, stupefied. My mother would have been horrified by my poorly-phrased question *(how you speak is how you think, which is what the exams measure!).*

"I waited to see if there would be an immediate retraction," Clarice answered knowingly. "It's been in cyberspace for almost seven minutes now. It's for real."

For a long moment, Clarice and I stared at each other. No words; just looks carrying the weight of twelve tons.

Venus? Heidel? *Colonized?!*

I couldn't begin to fathom it. I knew there'd been probes and drones sent out, but human life? Sustained on Venus? Heidel? My mind reeled, a marquee of questions scrolling through my brain like a chorus line in a Broadway musical. It was note-worthy that The Organization had chosen planets from both the Milky Way and Andromeda galaxies.

"Selina!"

Once more, my attention snapped back to my petite, lily-skinned friend. I could tell by the look on Clarice's face that she'd said my name more than once.

"Homeroom. We're going to be late," she warned, nodding her head towards the clock. "They'll have to tell us more about it," she added, guessing at my thoughts.

Clarice was right. I'm sure our homeroom teacher had plans for our class period, but they were never addressed. The room was buzzing even before we made our way inside; students were reluctant to take their seats, and even then those seated stretched limbs across aisleways to speculate with peers. It took Mr. Macken three times to be heard.

"I know. I know," Mr. Macken repeated in a placating tone, almost as though he were working to convince *himself* that everything was going to be okay. "I know," he said a final time, for good measure. "I saw Mr. Boothe's tweet, too. And I have an update."

This final remark silenced any last murmurings. Apparently, we were all starved for news. Information was a precious commodity, and none of us wanted to miss out.

"I'm just as shocked as you are," Mr. Macken went on. I worked hard not to cry out to Mr. Macken to *just get to the point!* We didn't care what his response to the news was—we just *wanted* the news! "And apparently Mr. Boothe is coming here this morning to speak with the junior class."

I blinked, then looked across the classroom for Clarice. I wasn't sure I'd heard Mr. Macken correctly…Mr. Boothe was coming *here*? To *our* school? Nothing like that had ever happened before…

"He wanted to address you in person," Mr. Macken explained. "We're all to report to the auditorium in fifteen minutes. Before we line up, a few reminders…"

I half-listened as Mr. Macken reviewed etiquette and best practices, then stumbled into line without really paying attention to what I was doing. I sat obediently in the auditorium, waiting for Mr. Boothe. My brain hummed like a swarm of bees had taken up residence inside.
There was a quiet reverence in the auditorium that was unnerving. We weren't a disrespectful bunch, but I'd never seen so many of my classmates in one place with so little noise.

When Mr. Boothe walked out, I felt the hair on my arms prickle in anticipation. My mouth went dry. My eyes went dry.

"Good Morning," Mr. Boothe greeted the junior class without looking up at them. He didn't expect a response, and he didn't get one. "By now, many of you have seen my tweet from this morning and are likely curious to know about the intergalactic exploration I referenced. Your parents are, as many of you likely guessed, 'freaking out'." He laughed, and there were some hesitant chuckles from the audience that quickly died out.

"It's no secret that earth is dying—and we've long angled to set up permanent residence on the moon to alleviate the burden mankind has made on earth. These efforts have been largely successful," Mr. Boothe began, summarizing years of painstaking labor and scientific achievement into a simple sentence. "And yet…they're not enough. We've known this to be the case for decades, and scientists have been working on the solution.

"Our research has progressed to the point where we now feel we can successfully transport humans to Venus and Heidel—and we've tested some incredible machinery and outfitting that should protect mankind from otherwise inhospitable living conditions. The key word in those phrases is, of course, *should*.

"What your parents don't know—what the world will soon know—is that we've already sent two chimpanzees to both Venus and Heidel. Our satellite imaging and technological records show that transport to the planets was without issue, and the chimps were able to land on each planet and move about the atmosphere." Mr. Boothe paused, then added, "Neither chimp survived the return trip to earth, but that is an entirely different matter.

"The point is, we're ready to move forward—we're ready to colonize Venus and Heidel."

As Mr. Boothe appeared to have finished his speech, dozens of hands shot up in the air. Mr. Boothe put his palms up and waved their hands down.

"I'm not finished. You probably guessed at this next part—the individuals who will initiate contact with these planets are going to come from the junior class. The individuals will be determined in conjunction with the exams," Mr. Boothe finished rather anticlimactically.

"How long will the mission be?" one student called out, not bothering to follow protocol.

I watched Mr. Boothe carefully: as a political figure, he would be extremely careful and measured in his responses. We couldn't necessarily count on him to be truthful: I needed to observe his nonverbals for any sign of dishonesty or half-truths.

Mr. Boothe paused. I wondered if he was thinking through his answer or if he worried about encouraging misbehavior and calling out from the audience. He smiled, cocked his head to the side, and rubbed the side of his neck in a way that suggested he was stressed. My gaze traveled to the half-empty coffee cup that sat atop the podium. Lukewarm, by now. I wondered why he'd brought it at all—it was a discouraged habit among the youth, and he hadn't taken a single swig. *Must be his security blanket.* There for comfort, and little more.

As if reading my thoughts, Mr. Boothe looked directly at me for a prolonged, intense moment before taking a half-hearted swig of the muddy-brown liquid. He grimaced at the taste, looked down at the contents of the cup with disappointment, and then looked back up at the junior class.

"That depends on the success of the mission," Mr. Boothe answered directly. "We've never sent humans to these plants before. Although we hope for and have prepared for success, we don't know for sure what will happen once you leave Earth's atmosphere.

"We've tested technology that resists the augmented effects of aging, if that's your concern," Mr. Boothe added. "We've harnessed machinery that allows for time to pass in equivalence to Earth. But the amount of time spent on the planet, and the prep work and voyage…that's impossible to say."

I chewed the inside of my cheek. An honor—the *highest* honor, to be chosen for such a mission. The exam would test for additional factors and only select an individual deemed to be an exemplary specimen. To be selected would mean certain glory, privilege, and esteem to the family for a lifetime. Longer than a lifetime, if you considered the narratives that would grace the history texts.

Also, grave danger, That's what the individual would certainly face, and without choice in the matter. The exam had just become exceptionally more complicated: the stakes were no longer a matter of whether you agreed with the potential the exam read in you…now, the exam would be responsible for deciding whether or not you would live your days out on Earth.

"I can't even believe this is happening," Clarice whispered into my ear, her breath warm.

I nodded without looking over at my friend. It was pretty incredible.

More students yelled out questions to Mr. Boothe, but this time, he declined to answer. He left his tepid coffee on the podium without thought: nodding once to Mr. Macken, he took measured, purposeful steps off the stage.

It could have been my imagination (I *was* pretty paranoid at this point), but as Mr. Boothe glanced over his shoulder and into the audience one final time, I felt sure that his gaze rested on me.

"SO random. Venus and Heidel? Of all the planets, why those two?" Clarice asked, stuffing a stalk of celery in her mouth and chomping away as she searched her friends' faces for a reaction.

I attempted a smile that came out as a grimace, then looked to the other girls sitting around the plexiglass lunch table (the most sanitary surface, as tested in 1500 variable-controlled laboratory experiments).

Our group of friends had been intact for the past 4 years. Research showed that optimal levels of happiness and contentment are reported with 3-5 close friends, so that's what I had been encouraged to cultivate. I found the study subjective and ambiguous—were family members included in that number? What was the level of intimacy in each relationship?—but I made myself compliant with the findings. I knew well enough to pick and choose my battles…and this was not my mountain to die on.

Clarice was my best friend, and the others—Madi, Andra, and Tessa—were perfectly nice and kind. That was good enough for me, and for Clarice. But Clarice seemed to thrive off the drama and spotlight, while I tended to shy away. Our differences were punctuated as Clarice hummed with excitement and talked a mile a minute…and I wanted nothing more than to process the news in silence.

"I agree," Madi chimed in. "Venus is at least close, but Heidel? That's so far out. It's not even in our home galaxy."

"Totally different technology, too," Tessa pointed out. "They've clearly been working on this for a long time. It would take entirely different equipment to transport a human closer to the sun than farther away. Makes me wonder how many other experiments they've run that we don't know about."

The inside of my cheek began to bleed. Tessa was right—I hadn't thought about that. There were a thousand details I wanted immediate access to…

"Our parents have to be freaking out," Andra added. "*Freaking* out."

"Which do you think is more dangerous?" I asked abruptly. I wasn't keen to fan the flames of the drama—I wanted to get back to Tessa's point. "Depends on if you want to freeze or burn," Clarice exclaimed before covering her mouth with her hand. "Sorry. Inappropriate, I know. But isn't that kind of what it comes down to?" she asked uncertainly.

"Heidel is the longer trip," Tessa agreed. "And you have to cross galaxies, and you're soooo far from the sun. But Venus is too close to the sun—I can't guess at how they've managed to protect against the sunspots and flares."

"And probably being that close to the rays causes cancer," Andra agreed.

"Everything causes cancer," Clarice rolled her eyes. "Cancer is the lowest concern."

"Not if it's like an A-bomb," Tessa pointed out. "It could make really nasty or horrible things happen."

"I didn't even think of that," Clarice exclaimed, eyes wide as she gnawed on another piece of celery. "So true. Oh my gosh, they're both terrible."

"Makes me glad I'm not meeting the phys-ed standards," Andra announced. "You know they'll pick someone in peak physical condition."

"Or not…" Clarice countered. "They might choose someone mediocre so they don't waste a 'prime specimen.'"

"Yeah right. We both know they're too proud to send anyone less than best. It won't be me, either," Tessa winked.

"I always forget about your eyes," Madi gushed.

"Well, she had the surgery when she was five," Clarice pointed out. "We didn't even know her then. And she sees perfectly fine now."

"20-20," Tessa agreed. "But I'm technically genetically imperfect. So that leaves the three of you," she finished, wiggling her eyebrows suggestively towards Clarice, Madi, and I.

"Don't even say that!" Madi exclaimed. "That's my worst nightmare. I'm nauseous just thinking about it. They couldn't *make* me go, could they? What if I get sick and miss the exam? I'm sure they're looking to pick the candidates soon—I would automatically be disqualified."

"That's an interesting point," Andra agreed. "I wonder what extra criteria they added to the exam…what are they looking for?"

I thought back to Mr. Boothe and his lingering gaze. "They already know who they want," I heard myself say out loud.

Clarice coughed on her celery and Madi gasped.

"What are you saying, Selina?" Tessa asked, voice lowered.

Heat crept into my cheeks—I hadn't meant to voice my thoughts out loud. But I had, and there was no sense in backtracking now. The girls would know I was lying and only wonder what I was trying to hide.

"I just feel like they already know what they're looking for—probably even *who* they're looking for," I explained. "We just agreed that they've been plotting this mission for a long time…they've probably been watching our junior class for just as long."

There was a long, uncomfortable silence.

"Well, that's creepy to think about," Clarice finally said for all of them.

"Sorry," I apologized, not sure what else to say. "I wasn't trying to be creepy."

"Riiiight," Clarice teased in an exaggerated voice that said she was working hard to neutralize the situation. Clarice was emotionally intelligent that way: she could read the emotional atmosphere and come up with the perfect response in a snap. It was one of the things I loved most about her.

The girls offered up tinkles of laughter, hesitant giggles that spoke to their anxiety. No further conjectures were made.

Five Days Until Testing

I sat in fourth period, unable to focus. I was supposed to be taking careful notes in organic chemistry class, but instead found myself surveying the rows of students. I was eyeing the competition; scrutinizing each peer to determine his or her chance of selection for the intergalactic mission.

There hadn't been any new news put out regarding the mission. I'd waited for more—I'd expected The Organization to put out details: how many juniors would be selected, the date of scheduled departure, and a bit more context behind why the mission had been dreamt up. But Mr. Boothe's social media presence had gone silent, even as the millions and then billions of comments and questions piled up under his account.

I'd feigned nonchalance with my parents after school—normally, I had an hour or two to myself before my parents arrived home from work. Yesterday, I'd arrived home to find both of my parents nervously twittering about the house: my mom already working on an extravagant dinner at 4 PM, my dad "working from home." I watched him refresh his newsfeed obsessively every minute— he wasn't getting any work done.

Surprisingly, it was my dad who finally brought it up.

"I heard Mr. Boothe came to school today."

My heart had skipped a beat at the mention of the announcement, but I took a controlled sip of water. "I was wondering how long it would take for us to talk about it," I answered neutrally, looking from my mom to my dad.

"Did he give any details?" my dad asked, brows furrowed in concern. I didn't even look at my mom—I knew her face would be wrought with worry.

"Not much. He didn't tell us anything that he didn't tweet. A couple of kids tried to ask questions, but he didn't answer much. He did say that they've developed technology to allow humans to survive on Venus and Heidel, but that was already implied, right? He seemed to intentionally avoid sharing particulars," I added as an afterthought.

"What do you mean?" my mom was quick to ask.

"He didn't want to commit to anything. He seemed cagey. I guess that's how he always sounds," I thought aloud.

"Hmmm," my dad muttered. My mother stuffed a forkful of oven-roasted brussel sprouts into her mouth.

"It's an honor to be picked, right?" I asked nervously, picking at the food on my plate.

"Of course!" my parents were quick to gush.

"A huge honor," my dad added, raking his fingers through his hair. I looked from his taut face to my mother's forced smile and made an effort to look congenial. If we were all going to fake it, then fine. I could read between the lines well enough.

Now, in fourth period, I found it impossible to focus. My teachers, to their credit, had shown exceptional grace in the matter: most had allowed for questions and conversation (mostly fruitless since none of the teachers knew any more than the students, but it was still nice), and a couple had even modified their curriculum to focus on Venus and Heidel.
 Calculus, for example, was completely centered around physics calculations of inertia, velocity, and potential energy on and to Venus. This made some students nervous, but I appreciated the gesture—it felt like an acknowledgement of our situation.

"Hey, are you ready to start the experiment?"

Blinking away the competitive daydreams of intergalactic selection, I turned my attention to my lab partner, Max. His mousy-brown hair lay across his forehead in a swoop that required frequent head tosses to clear the line of vision for his eyes. Even still, his hazel-green eyes studied me, and I felt myself blush.

"Sorry. I was distracted. I'm ready," I answered with eyes averted.

Max was the analytical type—he could study someone's face and know what they were thinking (or so I imagined) and it made me uncomfortable. He was bold that way: he would stare and openly assess when others would bow to social propriety and look away.

"You sure?" Max asked, handing me a beaker.

"Yep," I answered, allowing my hair to fall beside my face as a barrier between us. "What do you want me to do?"

A long pause. I wondered if Max was *trying* to make me uncomfortable— if the prolonged silence was an intentional effort to try to get me to say more. My stubborn side kicked in; I would not say a word.

"Why don't you hold the bromine?" Max finally suggested, his words slow. "I'll get the eugenol from the front."

I raised my eyebrows in agreement, still with eyes downcast as Max handed me the solution and angled up to the front. Once his back was to me, I sighed in relief.

"What is going on with you and Max?" Andra hissed from behind, her whisper raising the hackles on the back of my neck. I whipped around so fast that I felt a spasm in my neck.

"What do you mean?" I demanded in my own aggressive whisper voice. I was keen to have the discussion end well before Max returned.

"He can't stop staring at you," Andra huffed in exasperation. "And you won't look at him. Why are you two so weird? Did he tell you that he loves you or something?"

"Ohmygoodness," I interrupted, eyes bulging as I gestured for Andra to stop talking. "You're crazy. Nothing is happening!"

"If we do the experiment right, we'll notice a carbon-carbon double bond between eugenol and bromine," Max disagreed, walking up to hear the last of the conversation.

Andra giggled, and I blushed. The blushing would *not* help my case—I was immediately annoyed with Andra, frustrated with Max, and exasperated with myself.

"Don't you have your own lab partner?" I asked Andra pointedly, voice a bit more surly than I'd intended. Andra made a face but turned away. The exchange was certain to be the topic of conversation during lunch.

"That was harsh," Max laughed, setting the materials on the table.

"You don't know Andra," I snapped. Inwardly, I cringed at the sound of my voice. Defensive. I sounded defensive.

"I don't," Max agreed matter-of-factly.

I rolled my eyes. For all the progress of mankind...

"Did you just roll your eyes at me, Alois?" Max laughed.

"I did," I answered, surprised both by my candor and Max's use of my last name.

"Ouch. You're really on a roll today, aren't you?"

"Depends on who you ask. I'm not in the mood to be silly and flirtatious."

"Flirtatious? Who said anything about flirting?" Max teased lightly.

Even though I knew he was joking, the heat rushed to my face. I didn't need to explain; I shouldn't have had to explain. It would probably even be better if I *didn't* try to explain. But, of course, the next words out of my mouth were an explanation.

"I'm not flirting! I just want to do the science experiment," I snapped, busying myself with the instruments.

"Right. Your interest in the bromination of stilbene has been duly noted," Max quipped sarcastically. "It was immediately evident at your rapturous response to our teacher's instructions."

He was pushing my buttons, and I couldn't let it go. My pride. It was always my pride.

"Do you mind?" I huffed, tucking my hair behind my ear and lifting my gaze to look Max directly in the eye. I hoped I looked intimidating. "I'm a bit distracted."

Max held my gaze; his eyes smiled at me. I realized too late I had probably been baited into that very moment and inwardly kicked myself, cursing my pride again.

"We're *all* a bit distracted," Max pointed out. "We all got the same news, Alois."

There was something about the way he called me by my last name that felt intimate and familiar—I couldn't decide if I liked it or if I wished he would stop.

"But not everyone is going, smartass."

The words were out of my mouth before I had time to think through the weight they held. My left hand flew to cover my mouth at the same time my right hand held the bromine in place.

To his credit, Max just laughed. It was a hearty, genuine laugh—it took some of the edge off my nerves. But they came back in a hurry with his next remark.

"So, you think you're going?"

The heat crawled up my spine like sails being raised on an open sea. What was there to say? Was it worth denying? It was such a presumptuous thing to believe!

"I'm going," were the words that ended up coming out of her mouth. I offered no frills or decorative packaging to my words—just the bald, naked weight of my gut instinct.

Max studied me for a long moment, then nodded. "Yeah, I know. I'm going, too."

Four Days Until Testing

"Physical education has never been more important," Mrs. Crick announced, clipboard tucked underneath her sizable bicep. "The limited opportunities for organic movement and exercise in our daily life make these lessons crucial, and the announcement of the intergalactic missions only add to this importance."

"I still prefer the muscle-stimulation machines," Clarice whispered to me under her breath.

A smile tugged at the corners of my mouth as I shook my head in unspoken acknowledgement of Clarice's comment.

"The muscle-stimulation machines may keep the body from atrophying, but the rigid, structured movements do not prepare the body for extemporaneous movement," Mrs. Crick added pointedly, looking directly at Clarice as she spoke.

"For that reason, this afternoon's exercises are meant to challenge the body and the mind in unison," Mr. Tyre cut in, stepping forward to stand beside Mrs. Crick.

My brain lit up like a Christmas tree in anticipation of the task to come—my heart beat quickly as I waited anxiously to hear what the challenge would be. My competitive nature determined that I would excel at the task, whatever it might be.

"Not competitive at all, right, Alois?" Max teased.

My body tensed; I turned to find Max standing just behind me, arms across his chest in nonchalance I doubted he felt. Since when was Max so interested in my every move?

"What is it to you?" I asked, voice thick with annoyance.

"He's eyeing the competition," Chris joked, nudging his friend. Chris was the top-performing junior in…everything. His name was synonymous with unrealistic expectations and perfection in many conversations.

"You would do well to do the same," I snapped without thinking.

Chris looked taken aback, and Max laughed heartily. I felt Clarice's incredulous gaze penetrating the back of my neck. What had gotten into me? Why was I picking a fight with the most popular and successful guy in school? Especially since Chris had always been pleasant with me…

Mercifully, Mrs. Crick spoke, ending the chance for me to embarrass myself further. My gratitude ended abruptly when I heard Mrs. Crick's next words.

"Selina, you must be feeling confident. Why don't you start us off?" Mrs. Crick suggested, her voice cranky.

"I'd rather not," I answered bluntly.

This time, my boldness was met with a sharp elbow in the ribs (Clarice) and a stifled guffaw (Max). Something about Mr. Boothe's announcement had changed my demeanor entirely. I wasn't afraid of authority, and I certainly wasn't intimidated by my instructors. The consequences they could mete out fell far short of the probable outcome of travel to Venus or Heidel.

"I don't believe that was a question," Mr. Tyre groused, his voice low in warning as he stepped alongside Mrs. Crick in a show of support.

With a heavy sigh, I rolled her shoulders back. "What do you want me to do?" I asked, my cat-like eyes direct and unblinking.
"If you'd been listening, you would know," Mrs. Crick couldn't help but point out.

I didn't say anything, but I raised my eyebrow in a veiled challenge. I would obey, but I would not reduce myself to the point of apology. It was Max's fault that I'd gotten into trouble—I wasn't going to accept the blame, even if I had to suffer the consequences.

"You're to hold a plank for five minutes, then push up to a headstand—a controlled ascent, no momentum. Your descent should be measured to a five-count. From there, you'll run a timed mile, climb the obstacle wall, and end in a final five-minute plank," Mr. Tyre announced matter-of-factly.

My heart thudded in her ears. The sequence would be challenging—it had been organized to target the major muscle groups, test cardiovascular strength, measure strength and flexibility, and assess grit. In short, the instructors were looking for a read of overall fitness—a read that would hint at suitability for a trip through space.

Adrenaline coursed through my veins. I wasn't sure how my body would fare in the tasks, but I was eager to find out. That my pride was on the line meant I would push myself to the limit.

"Am I to have a training partner?" I asked.

In most such simulations, students were paired with a same-gender, similar-fitness-level peer with which to compete…the idea being that the individuals would each push themselves a bit more.

"Do you want one?" Mr. Tyre asked, eyebrows raised.

"Yep. Max, let's go," I snapped. Rolling my shoulders back and stretching my arms across my chest, I took a step forward.

There were chortles, a gasp, and the buzz of whispers as I requested a male partner. That had never been done before.

Not to be shamed or cowed, I turned around in mock surprise to see Max's face frozen in an expression of surprise and hesitation.
"You're not intimidated, are you, Max?" I asked, green eyes flashing in an open challenge.

"Selina—" Mrs. Crick began to protest, but Max cut her off.

"It's okay, Mrs. Crick," Max told her. "I don't mind partnering with Alois."

I bristled at Max's continued usage of my last name but straightened up and smiled politely.

"Great. I'm not going to go easy on you, just because you haven't competed with a girl before," I warned.

There were more giggles that I ignored. Whatever—I was already in over my head. There was no sense in pulling back at this point. Clarice would skewer me later, I was sure. I had just secured my position as the main talking point during lunch, too.

"Of course not," Max replied evenly.

Without another word, he knelt down on the ground and settled into a plank position. I noticed his arm muscles ripple and looked away. Competing with Max was supposed to push me, not distract me.

"You're not getting extra credit for holding a plank longer," Mr. Tyre pointed out.

"He knows," I snapped before Max had a chance to respond. "He's just trying to intimidate me and show off."

"Is it working?" Max asked, voice smooth even with his core contracted.

"Nope," I lied as I lowered down into plank position. "Mrs. Crick, whenever you're ready."

Mrs. Crick rolled her eyes and shook her head disapprovingly before clicking the timer.

"Begin."

The first two minutes were easy; the next two minutes hard, and the last minute a significant challenge. I refused to show any hint of discomfort: I stood stock-still, spine level and eyes cast directly downward. No one was going to accuse me of cheating or engaging in any funny business.

I forced herself to breathe evenly: in through my nose, out through my mouth. I didn't hear any noises from Max, but I wasn't expecting to. I knew better than to look over at him—he wouldn't show any evidence of fatigue, either. This was a physical challenge, but it was really a battle of wills.

"Five minutes," Mrs. Crick called.

I knew better than to collapse onto my knees—to do so would have been a sign of weakness. I held the plank, waiting for Mrs. Crick's next cue. Max did the same.

"Headstand," Mr. Tyre called out in a gruff reminder.

I walked my feet forward slowly, forearms glued to the ground in front of me. This was going to be the hardest part. My upper body had always been my weakest part…and a controlled ascent meant I was going to have to tap into shoulder muscles I wasn't sure I had. Muscles I was *sure* Max had, judging from the bulges coming from the sleeves of Max's shirt.

Max made it up in the air first.

I worked to ignore the wolf whistles and cheers that clearly indicated my opponent's success; I needed to worry about my progress only.

With forearms pressed firmly into the ground and arms wrapped behind my head, I contracted my core and walked my legs in even closer. When I could go no further, I cautiously lifted my left leg up into the air. Mrs. Crick had warned against using momentum, but I was betting on her allowing a one-legged kick up.

Here goes nothing.

With silent resolve, I lifted my right leg to meet my left. Teetering in mid-air, I held every last muscle fiber in tight and bit my lower lip until it bled in a fight for control. My foundation was anything but firm, but I was desperate to stay inverted and steady.

Ten.
Nine.
Eight.

I counted each breath and willed my body to hold on.

Seven.
Six.
Five.

I vacillated back and forth like seaweed in a current but stayed upside down.

Four.

Three.
Two.
One.

Max had nailed the posture; I had barely scraped by. But when Mrs. Crick called time, I had passed. My body folded like an accordion in a speedy-but-controlled descent. When my feet touched the floor, I exhaled in relief and stood to my feet.

For the first time since the competition began, I looked over at Max. He was studying me, too—with what looked to be admiration. Max was clearly more athletic than me, but I was holding my own. I wasn't worried about the mile—I wouldn't beat Max, but I knew I was fast.

We didn't have the luxury of running outdoors often—more often than not, exercise took place on a treadmill or using electromagnetic impulses that stimulated muscle movement…this would be a treat.

"What's your best mile time, Alois?" Max asked when we were crouched next to one another on the starting line.

I shook my legs out in a simple warm-up and felt my excitement mount. I smiled at Max but said nothing. Max's best time was sure to be faster than my best time—but I was planning to set a new record. There was no use in sharing old data.

"Let's just race," I suggested, eyebrows raised in challenge.

Max's grin back was genuine. "You got it."

When Mrs. Crick shouted the start of the race, I was ready. Pushing forward with long, even strides, my body seemed to come to life.

Max took the lead early on with a powerful surge that I didn't try to compete with: I knew how to run my race, and I wasn't going to be put off by anyone. That was the benefit of my phys-ed program; the routine I had established that ran counter to what most of my peers engaged in.

With the invention of the muscle stimulators, most of my peers opted to hook up to machines that exercised each major muscle group in isolation without any physical exertion. It was how most people met their fitness goals without ever actually engaging in any physical activity. This was not—and had never been—my method.

As my body fell into a steady rhythm, I lengthened my stride and inhalations before increasing the revolution of footfalls. After the first lap, I picked up the pace, arms pumping as I closed the gap between us.

I wasn't going to beat Max; I didn't expect to. But I wanted to make it close. Max maintained his pace, but my speed continued to increase. I was vaguely aware of excited shouts from my peers who clearly appreciated my performance and seemed impressed by my athleticism.

The final lap,

I came within fifty feet of Max. He crossed the finish line a solid ten seconds before me, with a time of 5:24. My heart did cartwheels when I heard my own time of 5:34…I'd beaten my personal best by a solid twelve seconds.

I kept my ecstasy bottled as I slowed to a walk. It was better to pretend that the run had been typical. I kept my breaths measured and was thankful when my heartbeat returned to neutral quickly: another benefit of my rigorous training regimen.

I sought Clarice's face in the crowd and flashed her a quick smile of excitement—Clarice shook her head and rolled her eyes fondly.

"That was pretty close, Max," Chris commented, clapping his friend on the back.

"She's fast," Max agreed, and my heart swelled with pride. "We're not done yet," he added, a hint of irritation in his voice.

I didn't acknowledge either comment as I walked towards the obstacle wall.

The wall was tall: over forty feet in height. Set above lightly-padded flooring, the spongy wall had rubber protrusions that served as grips and ledges for hands and feet in a climb to the top. The outcroppings were unevenly spaced (Max, with his long limbs, would have an advantage here) and varied in size (with my smaller hands and feet, I would have an easier time establishing a grip).

Strategies in climbing the wall varied, but I planned to rely on momentum to make it to the top. While the protrusions changed position to keep the challenge fresh, I had tackled enough sequences to know that my chances of making it to the top were about 6 in 10…when I had the wall to myself, with someone spotting me.

The rules for a competition were different. I maintained a neutral expression as Mr. Tyre explained that both Max and I would climb the wall at the same time, without a spotter. We would have ten minutes to make it to the top.

Rolling out my neck, I studied the placement of the bulges as Mr. Tyre spoke. My brain worked to highlight a path to the top, although there was no obvious route. My lower body was stronger than my upper body, so I looked for grips that I could wedge my feet into—from there I could push my body upwards. It wouldn't work to try to pull myself up using my arms.

Just before the start of the competition, I glanced over at Max. He appeared at ease: with languid movements he rolled his arms in exaggerated circles to stretch. He caught my gaze and wiggled his eyebrows playfully.

"You ready?" he asked.

"Of course," I announced flippantly, shrugging my shoulders for good measure. Truthfully, I wasn't confident about this leg of the competition, and Max had picked up on it.

"Whenever you're ready," Mrs. Crick announced, pulling me from my thoughts.

Pushing any doubts or thoughts of Max to the side, I took a deep breath and wiped my palms on my shorts before chalking my hands and reaching to my right for the first hold. I always started slow: testing the shift of weight as I moved my center of gravity; testing the strength of my grip as I pulled myself onward and upward. I took pains to keep my breathing even so as to establish a rhythm—after a while, it felt like second nature.

On some level, I was aware of Max's presence: I knew he was climbing alongside me, and I could see him out of my periphery. But I focused on my own climb, and our trajectories didn't seem to intertwine. That was a good thing.

As we made our way higher, however, the number of grips diminished…and our paths closed in on one another. I fought to focus and maintain my cadence as I subconsciously guessed at Max's intended path and potential moments of intercession.

When Max's foot slipped out of the hold just seconds later, I didn't think before reacting. My own left foot jutted out and pushed his foot against the wall and down into a more secure grip.

It was only after Max was stable that I realized what I'd done. It wasn't a bad move—it was certainly sportsmanlike—but it defied my competitive nature and didn't fall in line with the tone of the task at hand.

Max didn't say anything. I didn't expect him to. We were thirty feet above the ground: it would hurt a lot to fall, and it went without saying that there would be injuries sustained. There was no room or space for conversation, however brief. 'Thank you' could wait.

Not a minute later, Max returned the favor. My eyes were set on a grip just out of reach—I'd determined to launch myself upward to make a grab for it. My left fingers made connection but couldn't make purchase…my fingers curled desperately for some sort of traction without success.

Max's hand snapped out like a crocodile lunging for dinner: his firm grip encircled my left wrist and guided me to the hold I'd aimed for. This time, I established the grip I'd intended to make.

Heart racing wildly, I pressed my body close to the wall and waited for my breath to return to normal. Time limit or not, I would not do myself any good trying to advance on frayed nerves.

Wholly unaware of the passage of time, I only knew we were marching closer to the ten-minute time limit every moment. Max made it to the top of the wall and tapped out; not long after, I achieved the same feat. Both under ten minutes.

Safely perched on the wooden ledge above, I turned to face Max. Wiping the sweat from my forehead using the back of my hand, my lips turned up in a hint of a smile.

"Thanks for that," I offered.

Max studied me for a moment before answering. "Why'd you help me?" he asked without acknowledging my expression of gratitude.

"I don't know," I answered honestly. "I didn't think about it. I guess I didn't want you to fall."

Max nodded.

"Why'd you help me?" I asked back. "Because I helped you first?"

"Maybe," Max shrugged. "I didn't think about it, either. I didn't want to see you fall, either, I guess."

I nodded, then blew out a deep breath. I wanted to leave the heavy moment behind us.

"One more challenge left...are you ready?" I asked playfully.

Max smiled, but it was clear the ferocity of competition had died out. Somewhere in the last challenge, we'd switched from acting as competitors to teammates...and I wasn't sure how I felt about the new dynamic.

The last plank was more painful than the first, but we both held it until Mrs. Crick's final pronouncement of time. Among much fanfare, I found a seat with which to watch the rest of my classmates compete. It was only after I was seated that I noticed Mr. Boothe's presence.

Far away, watching from behind the comfort and obscurity of a tinted window, Mr. Boothe stood watching the phys-ed performances.

I rankled, realizing that no one had alerted us to his presence or observance. What was he there to see? How much had he *already* seen?

I had a slippery, slimy feeling that I already knew.

Three Days Until Testing

People were looking at me differently. I could feel it; I sensed it before Clarice announced it during lunch.

"It's not just because you challenged Max," Clarice explained, as though I didn't already know.

"But I still can't believe you did that," Andra gushed.

"Total badass move," Tessa agreed. "I would never have had the nerve."

"I wish I had seen Mrs. Crick's face. Or better yet, Mr. Tyre's." Andra giggled, her hand covering her mouth to show the extent of her surprise.

"Who cares what the teachers looked like? I would have paid serious money to see the look on *Max's* face," Madi chimed in. "What did he say to you?"

I looked over at Clarice in exasperation...she *had* to have anticipated that response from our friend group. Clarice shrugged innocently, but the wisp of a smile played on her lips; Clarice knew exactly what she had started, and she wasn't one bit remorseful.

"He didn't say anything," I answered, trying to keep my voice neutral. I didn't want the girls to think that anything was amiss...I was having a hard enough time explaining my behavior to myself. There were so many ways to explain away my actions...but what was the truth?

I hadn't been sleeping well, for starters. The recurring dream; now joined with others that were no less disturbing. I knew better than to dismiss these narratives of the night: they were more than mere shadows of my subconscious mind. They were telling me something. *Warning* me of something. Somehow, they were linked—but I hadn't unearthed the connecting tissue just yet.

Then, there was the stress of the exam. There was nothing I could do to prepare, and yet the exam stood like a monolith in the back of my mind, competing for space and attention and prominence. I could look around the monolith and pretend it didn't exist for a time, but it didn't remove it. At the end of the day, or in a rare quiet moment, I was forced to recall that the most important moment of my life was mere days away.

I'd increased my phys-ed training, and my appetite diminished. My mom had noticed both aberrations immediately; since, she had followed me around with healthy snacks and nagged me to rest and take care of my body. I wasn't sure which one of us was more stressed.

But the physical release felt good—it was the only thing that could calm my nerves and loosen me up. I longed to run outside, like I had during the competition....

"Selina, you have to give us more than *that*," Madi protested. Even the seniors are talking about your nerve...we have to know the details!"

"I don't know what to say," I muttered, at a loss for words.

"Selina's liked Max for a couple of years now, and it appears that he likes her, too," Clarice began, her voice full of authority.

Heat flashed through my body and irritation sparked, sending a wave of electrical energy up my spine. I gawked and opened my mouth to protest, but Clarice held up an open palm. "If you can't explain what happened, then *I* will."

"I—" I began, mouth open like a fish. But I couldn't find the words to continue, so my mouth closed; my brain willed Clarice to be kind.

"Neither of them have admitted this, of course," Clarice explained, "but it's obvious to everyone around them. It's anyone's guess why Selina chose to challenge Max publicly in phys-ed—I doubt Selina herself knows. But she did, and they competed. And we all learned that Selina is an incredible athlete, Max is an incredible athlete, and Selina isn't always as competitive as she let's on. Which is to say that she would rather help her crush than destroy him, when it's all said and done."

My face was fire-engine red. I could feel it. Clarice smirked smugly, eyebrows raised in silent appraisal. Tessa, Madi, and Andra stared at me, then to Clarice in wonder.

"I don't like Max," I muttered, shoving the last of a carrot in my mouth before swooping my lunch bag off the table and walking away.

It wasn't that I was mad—I just wasn't sure I could handle one more complication in my life at the moment. I didn't know if I had the energy to try and unpack what exactly *had* happened yesterday.

"Selina!"

I froze in place before turning around carefully, afraid of who I might find behind me. Relief flooded through me when I found it was only my calculus teacher, Mrs. Armand. I stood in place, a hesitant smile on my face as Mrs. Armand walked up.

"Where are you headed?" Mrs. Armand asked.

When I struggled to answer, she waved her hand. "It doesn't matter. I'm glad I caught you," she added, eyeing me closely. "The incident yesterday generated a lot of attention...among staff, too."

I cleared my throat and looked at the floor uncomfortably. So far, my parents hadn't caught wind of the incident—which was surprising, considering how news spread. My luck was likely a result of most parents' unwavering focus on the upcoming exam.

"I'm not sure what made you do it...and it doesn't really matter," Mrs. Armand went on. "I did want to talk to you about your calculus test, if you have a moment."

I looked Mrs. Armand in the eyes for the first time. "Did I do poorly?" I asked, genuinely surprised.

"Not at all. But you seem to have misinterpreted a couple of the questions," Mrs. Armand said smoothly.

Too smoothly. It seemed as though she'd already had the answer prepared. Puzzled and intrigued, I matched her countenance and smiled politely.

"How kind of you to offer your time to my education and understanding," I responded a bit mechanically. "Do you have some time now?"

For all of my supposed strengths, patience was a virtue absent from the collection. I didn't want to wait to find out what Mrs. Armand was talking about...I wanted answers that moment.

"I thought this might be the opportune time," Mrs. Armand agreed, stifling a chuckle. "Let's go to my office."

The walk down the hallway was quiet. I knew very little about Mrs. Armand—the conversation we'd just had outstripped the sum total of every other interaction we'd ever had together.

We reached Mrs. Armand's office space, I followed my instructor inside and waited for an invitation to sit that never came. As soon as the pressurized doors whooshed close, Mrs. Armand spun on her heel and faced me squarely.

"The calculations we've been using in math, to project the inertia and feasibility of life and momentum and all that—" Mrs. Armand began, spitting the words out in runaway train fashion. She paused to catch her breath, and I could only nod, wide-eyed.

"They're incorrect."

I stared, eyes darting back and forth in confusion. What was Mrs. Armand telling me? I didn't understand. The calculus calculations had all been theoretical, based on data collected by teams of scientists, satellites, and sophisticated computer algorithms. It had been an engagement strategy, meant to harness students' newfound interest in Venus and Heidel in order to hook their interest in abstract, advanced math.

"My math is incorrect?" I asked, struggling to make sense of the urgency in my teacher's voice.

"Your math is sound," Mrs. Armand told me firmly, eyes intent on my face. Her pupils seemed to bore holes into my forehead, so intense was her gaze.

"So—" I croaked.

"The formulas are sound, the conceptual foundation is sound, the process is sound. The numbers are incorrect," Mrs. Armand said flatly.

My eyebrows furrowed. I was still missing what Mrs. Armand was trying to tell me. The numbers were taken directly from the scientists—they were data points that went uncontested; assumed to be sound as the gospel.

"Venus' vitals are close enough," Mrs. Armand prattled on. Beads of sweat began to collect around the perimeter of her heart-shaped face; her fine gray hair began to curl just at the crown of her head. Pink spider legs of stress materialized on her forehead and cheeks, and I finally caught wind of what my calculus teacher was trying to tell me.

"The intergalactic mission," I said dumbly.

Mrs. Armand nodded.

"Venus is just a bit off, but Heidel..." I looked up at my teacher to clarify.

"Is very off," Mrs, Armand finished without offering any details.

I stared at Mrs. Armand, eyes wide and lips drawn. I had no idea how Mrs. Armand came to possess the information she'd just shared, but I knew well enough from my instructor's anxious fidgets and discomfort that it was top-secret information, not meant to be shared. The ferocity behind Mrs. Armand's behavior suggested that she'd just put herself in great danger.

Mrs. Armand met my gaze: for a moment, we shared a look of deep, unspoken understanding. The mission to Heidel would fail. What that meant, I didn't know—and I knew better than to ask. I wasn't even sure if Mrs. Armand knew.

The mission to Venus had no guarantees, but it was the safer bet. Mrs. Armand had put herself at risk in sharing this information with me. Which meant...

Mrs. Armand somehow also knew that I would be picked for the mission.

I swallowed hard. My mouth felt dry and tasted like a mixture of dust and Elmer's glue. My palms leaked sweat and my vision grew blurry. My life was becoming a dream; my dreams were coming to life.

"Will I have a choice?" I managed to croak.

The bell rang, signaling the end of lunch. Mrs. Armand bit her lip and sighed heavily, her eyes sympathetic. She didn't say anything. She didn't have to.

In a daze, I walked to my next class.

Two Days Until Testing

My life was becoming more confusing by the moment.

I'd never had many secrets, and now I didn't know where to pocket all of the tidbits I wasn't supposed to share. Some weren't necessarily secrets, like the phys-ed challenge with Max, but it wasn't something I was keen to discuss with others (especially my parents).

Others most certainly were—like the confusing and concerning information Mrs. Armand had shared. And still other information didn't fall under either category, like the fact that Mr. Boothe seemed to be popping up more and more frequently, and that his watchful eyes always seemed to find me.

It could have been my imagination. Mr. Boothe hadn't been on my radar in any significant way before; now he was. I reasoned that it was possible I was only *noticing* Mr. Boothe now, that nothing had really changed. I rationalized this way, but I knew in my heart that it wasn't true.

These were the thoughts bouncing around in my head when Chris chased me down in the hallway.

"Hey, Selina," he tried to say casually. I caught the slight uptick in tone that told me he was not quite as comfortable as he'd have me believe.

"Hey." I turned to face him. Whatever he was about to say, I was sure it wasn't about the weather.

"Do you want to get some phys-ed in after school?" he asked.

To his credit, Chris maintained even eye contact. I tried to control the widening of my eyes but was sure the surprise registered loud and clear.

"You want to train together?" I asked, eyebrows raised.

My mind worked rapidly to try to figure what Chris was up to: was he trying to normalize opposite-gender phys-ed sessions? Doubtful. Working to redeem the honor of Max? Max hadn't really lost any face in the interaction (that I knew of). He couldn't possibly believe that I could push him as hard or as far as some of his highly-athletic friends…

"Yes," Chris agreed, his face blushing just a bit.

If I hadn't been so busy working out what was *really* taking place, I would have enjoyed the fact that the most popular junior in school was squirming in my presence. When Clarice heard about this exchange, she would pump me for every last detail.

"I'll explain after school," he mumbled under his breath.

I didn't say anything at first. Enough bizarre things had happened over the past week to account for prudent pause: I needed to set myself up for success, but more importantly, I needed to avoid any situation that could lead to disaster. I was a caged canary released into the wild of the Amazon jungle: I wasn't sure what I could trust, what was real, and what outcomes might follow from seemingly-straightforward requests.

Chris looked highly uncomfortable as he waited. He shifted his weight from side to side, glancing over his shoulder and past mine to see who was watching. Whatever had driven Chris to ask was a powerful force, indeed—and my curiosity was difficult to deny.

"Okay," I agreed, gaze still locked onto the model specimen standing before me. If nothing else, it would give me an opportunity to run out on the track again…I much preferred this to the treadmill.

"Thanks. 4PM," Chris blurted out before scurrying down the hallway.

"Aaaand what was that all about?!" Clarice asked, materializing out of thin air like I knew she would.

I turned and rolled my eyes at her. "Nothing. Although, I'm not sure I would tell you if there *was* actually something happening. Did you forget what it means to be a best friend?"

"I was waiting for that." Clarice accepted the criticism and pushed her lower lip out in an expression made to incite sympathy. "You can be mad at me for saying what I did in front of the girls, but please don't deny that what I said was true. We're better friends than that."

I opened my mouth to protest, then closed it. I didn't want Clarice to be right, but the truth was, I didn't know how I felt. A week ago, I would have sworn up and down and left and right that Clarice was wrong; but the previous week had called into question most everything I held as absolute truth.

"I'll take it!" Clarice blurted as soon as she saw my hesitation.

I had to laugh at the dramatic response as I pushed Clarice away playfully.

"I don't care how right you are—and I'm *not* saying you're right, by the way—you are not allowed to make public pronouncements regarding my personal life," I lectured.

Clarice held up an open palm and stretched her eyes wide as she nodded up and down. "Sooo…all is forgiven?" she asked carefully.

"I'm not forgetting anything anytime soon," I warned. "You're not getting off that easy. But I don't want to fight with you, especially not this close to the exam."

"What exam?" Clarice joked; a feeble attempt to lighten the mood. As I shook my head in mock exasperation, Clarice set in again. "But really— what did Chris want?"

"I don't know," I answered honestly. "He asked me to train with him after school."

"He wants to *train* with you?" Clarice asked, not bothering to hide her disbelief.

"That's what he said," I agreed as Andra walked up to join us,

"Did I just hear that Chris asked you to meet him after school?" Andra asked, eyebrows raised in appreciation as a knowing smile spread across her lips.

"It's not what it sounds like," I protested, but Andra nodded smugly.

"Right. So Max has a little competition," she winked, nudging Clarice.

"It's really not like that," I repeated, trying not to get worked up.

"So what *is* it like, then?" Clarice asked.

I stared at my friend, trying to read her expression. Clarice was very clearly unsettled—but I couldn't figure out what it was that upset her so much. The fact that unusual events were piling up in my life that I couldn't explain, or the fact that I was earning the attention of popular boys? Or was there something else?

Studying Clarice's face, I felt as though an anchor had been wrapped around my heart and dropped overboard. I couldn't trust Clarice. Now, when I needed a friend more than ever, I realized that I had lost my one and only confidante.

This was no small loss: Clarice had been my vault for over a decade, and I desperately wanted to believe that I could still confide in my dearest comrade. But just as I inexplicably knew that I would be chosen for the intergalactic mission, I subconsciously knew that I could not trust Clarice.

"I'm not sure," I muttered.

"But you *are* going to train with him, right?" Clarice asked pointedly.

"I am," I agreed. There was no use holding that information back—we'd planned to meet in a public setting where there would be many witnesses.

"Ooooh, I can't wait!" Andra squealed, totally ignorant of the subliminal messages being sent between me and Clarice. "Just wait until I tell Tessa and Madi!"

I mustered an uncomfortable smile for Andra's benefit, then exchanged a long, meaningful look with Clarice. No words were spoken; no words were needed.

"I guess we'll hear about it tomorrow," Clarice said flatly. Both of us knew there would not be any meaningful update.

"Sure," I lied.

"Don't forget *all* the details!" Andra gushed, still oblivious to the emotional climate. "I want to know what Chris wears, how he looks at you, and especially if he asks you to spend more time with him!!"

"We're going to be late for class," Clarice pointed out, mercifully bringing the conversation to a close as all three of us parted and walked to our respective classrooms.

"I hear you're training with Chris after school," Max mentioned casually halfway through fourth period.

"You, too?" I groaned, turning to look at Max in annoyance. "Good grief. We haven't even run a lap yet, and I feel as though I've suffered through a marathon," I whined.

Max didn't acknowledge her joke or let her off the hook. "What did he say to you?"

"Are we really going to do this?" I asked. "I've been through the grand inquisition already."

"Why does he want to train with you?" Max tried again, phrasing the question just a bit differently.

"I don't know," I sighed. "He didn't say."

Max was silent for a moment. Neither of us acknowledged the competition from the other day—not the fact that I had asked to compete against him, not the fact that we'd both performed well, not the fact that we'd helped one another in a moment of rivalry.

"We both know you're smarter than that, Alois. What's he playing at?" Max asked.

I measured Max's words before responding. Quietly I wondered if Max knew what lay behind Chris's request; the fact that Max was at a loss himself worried me and served as a reminder that I needed to be on high alert when I met with Chris.

"I really don't know," I answered quietly. "I've been trying to work that out myself."

We exchanged a meaningful glance; I looked away first.

Just because I'd lost Clarice didn't mean I could latch onto the next warm body that seemed to take interest in my well-being.

47

I was out at the track right at 4 PM. I didn't want to linger—I knew there would be a litany of eyes on us as it was…I didn't want to be scrutinized any more than would already be the case.

"You came." Chris's voice was relieved.

"I told you I would," I answered evenly, turning around to face Chris. He looked anxious and uncomfortable.

"Right. But I wasn't sure you'd actually show up."

I didn't say anything. Instead, I took the moment to silently assess the man before me. Awkward as I'd ever seen him, and…vulnerable? They weren't adjectives I'd ever associated with Chris before.

"Want to start running?" Chris asked a moment later.

I shrugged, caught off guard. "Sure," I agreed, following Chris's lead as he broke into a slow jog.

I'd promised myself that I'd come in without expectation, but I still found myself waiting for the moment where Chris explained why he'd asked me to meet him. There were dozens of pieces to the puzzle I hadn't yet placed, but I knew well enough that there was more to our rendezvous than mere cardio training.

"So many people watching," Chris muttered under his breath.

I almost missed the comment; I was working to match Chris's stride and fall into a consistent rhythm of breath. There did seem to be a greater number of people around the track than usual, but I wasn't usually on the track after school. And I wasn't usually tuned into who was watching.

"Why are we here?" I asked when we were one lap in.

"This seemed like the safest way to talk to you," Chris began.

Impatience bubbled inside of me as I waited for Chris to elaborate. "I wanted to talk to you about the intergalactic mission."

My heartbeat quickened. Without realizing it, I picked up the pace.

"Steady there, Selina," Chris chuckled. "Despite what some of our peers might think, I didn't invite you out here to compete. I'll leave that to Max."

"I wish you would just spit it out," I blurted, pulling back to regulate my pace. "Of course we're here to talk about the mission—why else would you ask to meet two days before the exam? But why meet with *me*?"

"They're sending eight," Chris blurted. He spoke so fast that I wasn't sure I'd heard him correctly. For one, he hadn't answered my question. And there was no context behind his words. Still, I didn't doubt his meaning.

"To each planet? Or total?" I asked, goosebumps decorating my arms like strings of popcorn on a Christmas tree.

"Total. Four to each."

I let the information settle in. We ran a full lap without conversation: the methodical slap of sneakers on the rubber track and the cadence of breath as the backdrop for my ruminations. *How did Chris know? When did he find out? Why was he telling me?*

"How do you know?" I finally asked. It seemed a good place to start, though I doubted Chris would answer honestly.

Chris remained silent, and I knew better than to ask twice…maybe I could figure out the answer on my own with a different point of entry.

"Why are you telling me?" I changed tactics.

"I thought you'd want to know," Chris answered coolly.

"Is that really all you're going to tell me?" I pressed, picking up the pace. This time, it was on purpose. Chris's selective silence was aggravating.

"I shouldn't have told you what I did," Chris snapped defensively.

"So why ask me to come here, if only to offer one sketchy, unverifiable piece of information to an acquaintance you have no allegiance to?" I asked. My voice rose an octave, but the nearest bystander was hundreds of feet away.

"It's not a sketchy piece of information," Chris countered. "You're going to have to trust me on that point. And I did it as a favor."

I heard the hesitation in this last comment and waited for the follow-up I was sure would come.

"Also…I wanted to ask you to please not pick me."

One Day Until Testing

My mind had reeled all evening. I couldn't figure what Chris had meant, and there was no one I could ask.

Please, don't pick me.

The words had been said in earnest—but Chris had not offered any further explanation. He'd made it clear that he was referring to the intergalactic mission, but I couldn't figure out what I might be asked to pick. I had no connection to the mission, and I certainly didn't carry any power or influence...that I knew of.

The events of the past week had me reevaluating all that I knew to be true: had I overlooked some major clue? It seemed as though everyone knew something that I didn't...

"Have either of you heard anything else about the mission?" I'd asked my parents at dinner.

I watched as they exchanged a look of concern before answering.

"We haven't," my dad confessed. "And we've been trying to learn more," he added, twirling his fork through leaves of arugula and spinach.

"I'm very disappointed in The Organization's decision to advertise the mission just days before the exam," my mother joined in. "A sentiment many share. We can't understand why Mr. Boothe would publish such scandalous material right before the most important test of your life."

I caught the pointed look my father sent to my mother and watched as my mother took a deep breath.

"It's almost as though the announcement is a part of the test," my dad spoke slowly.

I caught his line of thinking immediately and followed it with interest. It was an idea I hadn't yet entertained: that the mission was a complete fabrication, meant to test the mettle and reaction of the students in the junior class.

"Do you really think…" I trailed off, looking at my parents for help in unpacking the possibility.

"I wouldn't put it past them," my mother snapped. "But it's not very gracious."

Gracious? My mother must really be holding back. If it were all a ruse, The Organization was downright cruel.

"Have you been sleeping okay?" my dad wanted to know. "Any anxiety during the day?"

"I'm sleeping fine," I lied, without knowing why.

"And you're not feeling too anxious?" my mother prodded, eyes fixed on her one and only daughter.

"I'm a bit nervous, but that's to be expected, right?" I asked neutrally, trying not to let on just how distressed I really was.

I smiled at my parents before directing my focus to the food on my plate. There was no use in worrying my parents…they seemed as baffled by the past week's events as I was. If they knew about Mrs. Armand, my phys-ed challenge with Max, and the afternoon's run with Chris…

"I bought some melatonin, just in case," my mom offered, eyes still glued on me.
"I might try some tomorrow," I said, mostly to placate my mom. I had no intention of taking any medication—however natural it might be—but knew the gesture to be my mom's way of showing support and solidarity.

The rest of dinner passed in perfunctory and quiet fashion. I excused myself at the earliest reasonable time…presumably to read or study or unwind. In actuality, I brushed my teeth, changed into my pajamas, and fell asleep.

I was in a maze. Alone, with dark shadows rendering chilly temperatures that I wasn't properly dressed for. Jeans, a thin cotton t-shirt, and barefoot. Barefoot? I never went barefoot. I was running to keep warm. My hair was down, which was further proof that I hadn't prepared for the physical activity.

The walls of the maze were tall and cast long shadows that left me enveloped in darkness. The slate-gray cement was cold and austere and offered no clues as to the way out. I rounded one corner, then two corners, then three. Desperation began to sink in, the baby-fine hairs at the nape of my neck became slick with the dour-smelling sweat that accompanies fear.

"Look up, Selina!"

I wasn't sure who had called out to me: as far as I knew, I was the only one in the maze. But the voice was full of authority, and I implicitly trusted it. I stopped running, breath ragged as I turned my chin upwards. I was still cloaked in shadows, but I raised a hand to shield my eyes from the sun's bright light.

"The sun. Always look to the sun."

It was a new dream, but I knew it was connected to the others. It wasn't an empty dream—it carried weight and hidden meaning, also like the others. I couldn't pinpoint how I knew this to be true or what it meant, but there was a silent resolve in my belly that told me it was so.

I dressed impatiently. I seemed to be in a perpetual hurry these days—the unpredictability of my life had made me irritable and twitchy. I was afraid to stay in any one place too long—someone or something might crop up and demand something new of me. I was waterlogged with information as it was…I didn't think I could digest a single new piece of anything.

I'd barely made it through the front doors of the school when I was accosted by Andra, Tessa, Madi, and Clarice…all at once.

"Finally!" Madi exclaimed, running towards me. The other girls followed.

"Nothing," I told them crossly, holding my palms up and out to repel my friends. "Nothing happened."

"What are you talking about?" Tessa asked, looking at me in genuine confusion.

Now it was my turn to look confused. I'd assumed they were all waiting to hear about my time with Chris—if they weren't running after me for details, then what were they worked up about?

"Mr. Boothe is here," Madi told me breathlessly, cheeks pink with excitement. "Clarice saw him."

My wide eyes turned to Clarice. "Really?" I asked, searching her face for any unspoken clues or hints.

"He arrived thirty minutes ago and went into the main office immediately. No one knows why he's here," Clarice explained.

I nodded. At this point, nothing could surprise me.

"We're wondering if he's here to observe," Andra cut in, looking at me earnestly. It dawned on me that the girls were watching me closely; my opinion and perspective on the matter seemed to matter greatly.

"I have no idea what all of this is about," I told them, shaking my head in exasperation. "I feel like the world has been turned upside down," I added just to let them know that my frustration wasn't directed at them.

"This is miserable," Madi whined. "Why all the weirdness this year? Wasn't it enough to torture the junior class with a horrible exam responsible for determining their entire future? Why all of these new antics?"

"Perhaps they're hoping the entire junior class will die from heart attacks," Tessa quipped. "Their solution for earth's overpopulation."

"And their parents, too," Andra agreed. "I think my parents have aged five years overnight. You can tell they're trying so hard to maintain a calm demeanor for my benefit, but they're freaking out."

"You don't seem as surprised by all of this," Madi pointed out, her words directed towards me.

"Are you serious?!" I asked her. "I have absolutely no idea what all of this is about. I'm as baffled by all of this as you are."

"She's just responding differently than the rest of us," Clarice clarified, her voice carrying a note of authority that rubbed me the wrong way.

"Maybe that's it," Madi agreed. "I feel really distant from you this week."

There was a long silence. I wasn't sure how to respond: this accusation wasn't untrue. I *did* in fact feel distant from the girls, and they felt it, too. I couldn't explain what I was thinking or how I was feeling any more than I could divulge what Mrs. Armand or Chris had told me in secret.

"This is just a really weird time," I finally said, feeling pressure to respond.

"Yeah," the girls agreed quietly.

The conversation was over, but the girls stood awkwardly until the bell rang.

"I guess we'll find out soon enough what this is all about," I commented half-heartedly. I turned and walked to class without waiting to hear their response.

"Don't get comfortable. All the juniors have an assembly," my homeroom teacher announced as the students filed in.

As the rest of the class expressed their unease and surprise, I stood in place, quietly surveying our teacher. I could tell by her posture and tone of voice that she knew nothing about the assembly: not why it was called or who it would be run by or how long it would last. Ignoring the chatter, I waited for the class to line up and make their way to the auditorium. I preferred this time to stay in the back of the line, eyes peeled and senses alert. I didn't want to miss a thing.

Mr. Boothe was waiting center-stage this time. Feet hip-width distance apart, his expensive, nutmeg-brown leather shoes screamed privilege at the same time his clasped hands and square shoulders spoke to his authority and resolve.

The students were wise enough to receive these messages; silence hung over the auditorium as the junior class entered and quickly found seats. I slipped into a back-row seat in the hopes of looking inconspicuous.

Mr. Boothe was patient. He waited until every student was seated before stepping forward.

"Good morning, juniors."

I wasn't sure if he expected a reply—he waited a short moment but was met with abject silence. With a chuckle, Mr. Boothe looked down at his expensive shoes, nodded his head as though accepting the muted response, and looked up with resolve.

"It seems neither of us are in a mood to waste time, so I'll cut to the chase," Mr. Boothe told them. "I'm here today with a small contingent of officers from The Organization to administer the exam."

My spine went rigid. The exam? *Today?*

All around me, students went white and stiff as though in anaphylactic shock. As I worked to process this new information, I began to relax. It didn't matter, really. What difference would one day make? All it meant was one less day of vitamins and meditation exercises and brain-boosting superfoods.

Not all of my peers came to the same conclusion. A multitude of reactions broke out: tears, tremors, and total shock seemed to prevail in the auditorium. Strangely, these adverse reactions served to boost my confidence—this was my competition, if I could call it that. These individuals would be measured against me; no matter their intelligence, I knew I possessed more grit and tolerance for ambiguity. I was lost in this train of thought when I became aware of Mr. Boothe's gaze upon me.

"You don't look concerned, Selina," Mr. Boothe announced from the stage.

I reeled. I wondered if everyone in the room found Mr. Boothe's assessment odd. The fear that had been notably absent trickled in as I realized that nothing positive could come from Mr. Boothe knowing my name and personally addressing me from the stage.

Nervous as I was, I sensed that this was not the emotion to lean into. I wouldn't win whatever game Mr. Boothe was playing through an honest disclosure of my fears.

I waited a moment to answer, both to calm my heartbeat and make sure my words came out smooth. If I was going to deny fear, I needed my composure to be sound.

"I'm not," I answered evenly, voice carrying nicely from the back row to the stage.

"Why should I be?" I asked a moment later, a surge of confidence and conviction rushing through my veins. "We're all going to take the test. Twenty-four hours is peanuts compared to a lifetime of preparation."

Mr. Boothe didn't say anything at first. He was affronted by my words—he seemed to want to intimidate, and I'd robbed him of this satisfaction.

"Thank you for those words of wisdom," Mr. Boothe remarked, the condescension in his voice undeniable and yet oblique. "Some would argue in favor of a more precious interpretation of time. Twenty-four hours can mark the difference between life and death...mere seconds determine the successful reentry into Earth's atmosphere on a mission from, say, Venus or Heidel."

Mr. Boothe's reference to the intergalactic mission was so obvious in its attempt to intimidate that I laughed out loud. I didn't do it to mock Mr. Boothe, and it wasn't brash, but it was audible and noticed by all.

"Now you think the mission is a joke, Ms. Alois?" Mr. Boothe asked through gritted teeth.

"Not at all. But your twisted interpretation of time does not intimidate me," I shot back. Adrenaline coursed through my veins, and the axons and dendrites in my brain fired with alacrity. I was in my element, and I would not be cowed.

Mr. Boothe paused to consider how to proceed. He seemed to sense that I would not back down...I guessed he was worried my confidence might influence those around me.

"Are you volunteering to go first?" Mr. Boothe ended up asking.

"Sure," I replied without hesitation. "We're all going to be tested...I'm not sure what difference it makes."

"While the exam takes place in private, we typically ask one student to model the examination process for the rest of the students," Mr. Boothe intoned calmly. "It sounds like you are willing to volunteer yourself for this role."

I swallowed the spiteful laughter that rumbled upward in my throat. Mr. Boothe was grasping at straws, looking for anything he could to possibly intimidate me. Did I want my exam result to be shared publicly? No. Would my parents be appalled? Yes. But did it matter, in the scheme of things? No. My result was my result, and in time, everyone would know it.

"Why not?" I shrugged, determined to carry on with my charade of impenetrability. "Do you want me up there on stage?"

Mr. Boothe nodded in my direction, then crooked his finger to some unseen figure in the wings of the stage that soon materialized to carry equipment out onto the stage.

As though living out a scene from one of my mystifying dreams, I stood up and moved down to the stage. Every eye trailed me as I walked the aisle; the bride of fate, marching to marry my destiny.

A few faces stood out in the sea of astonished and wondrous gazes: Max's grim expression, Clarice's suspicious gaze, and Chris's anxious countenance. Personal reminders of just how much was at stake.

I waited patiently as the machinery was set up. I wasn't trying to insult or sabotage the exam, and I didn't want to misrepresent my feelings. When I was so directed to, I sat in the chair and counted my inhalations and exhalations. My temples were rubbed with cotton balls bathed in rubbing alcohol before electromagnetic patches were adhered just beside my ears, on my forehead, and on my chest.

One, two, three, four, five, six.

Six, five, four, three, two, one.

The measured breaths helped; I was grateful that no one could see my nerves. Although I'd never seen it done before, from what I understood, the exam only lasted a few minutes, and you didn't feel a thing.

I waited for Mr. Boothe to orate the various steps; he did so with little fanfare, explaining the procedure as though it were a routine dental cleaning. I heard his words but let them pass by without attachment. Then it got quiet.

"The actual test itself lasts mere minutes. It's best if you are totally silent and clear your mind, although the technology can look beyond a cluttered mind," Mr. Boothe pronounced to the crowd.

I knew I wouldn't get a more direct cue—I closed my eyes and tried to clear my mind. I didn't feel anything, and I wasn't sure if the exam had begun.

Mere minutes later, the patches were gently peeled from my skin. Blinking my eyes open, I looked expectantly at Mr. Boothe.

For a brief, intense moment our eyes locked. I couldn't glean any information from his clouded eyes before he looked away and addressed the audience.

"That's all there is to it," he ended, tone matter-of-fact.

"What about my result?" I asked, swinging my legs over the side of the recliner to rest on the ground. "You did administer the test, didn't you?"

"Results are private," Mr. Boothe told me, an edge to his voice. "We don't publicly announce outcomes."

"Right. And tests are administered in private, too. This was an exception, and I'm asking for my result," I protested.

Mr. Boothe hesitated. He didn't want to announce my result in front of the junior class—and I knew why. Smiling sardonically, I looked down at my feet for a pensive moment before looking up at Mr. Boothe. I spoke only loud enough for him to hear.

"It's okay, you don't have to announce my result to the crowd. I already know: I've been chosen for the mission, You can tell me later, in whatever way you want. I won't hold it against you," I told him before scooting out of the seat. I was halfway down the stage steps when Mr. Boothe spoke.

"Selina has been selected for the intergalactic mission," Mr. Boothe proclaimed, voice clear as a bell.

I froze in place. I'd known it to be true, guessed it to be true, predicted it to be true. And still...hearing the words spoken out loud brought a jolt of electricity rushing through my bones. It was *actually* true.

A man in official attire rushed on stage, and Mr. Boothe held up a hand to stop him.

"Selina, as the first one chosen for the mission, you have the opportunity to select your destination," Mr. Boothe announced. He didn't look too pleased to be extending the offer.

Venus's vitals are close enough. Mrs. Armand's words floated to the surface.

Always look to the sun. My most recent dream flashed before my eyes.

"Venus."

Mr. Boothe nodded evenly. "You won't be going alone. You'll be part of a team of four."

I nodded, remembering Chris's warning. Mr. Boothe's next words surprised me; it took me a moment to process the weight of his words.

"The exam will make final selections, but you have the ability now to select one comrade."

"I get to pick someone to come on the mission with me?" I asked, certain I must have heard incorrectly.

When Mr. Boothe nodded, the name slipped out of my mouth faster than a bar of soap in wet hands.

"Max."

Preparations

I hadn't planned to pick Max. I hadn't guessed that I would have the ability to choose an individual to take on the mission with me, so there was no way I could have prepared for Mr. Boothe's offer.

The moment I said Max's name, my heart seized with fear. I was anxious to look out in the crowd and find Max's face—I was worried to lock eyes. I couldn't even imagine what he might be thinking: was I *crazy*? We were mere acquaintances, and I'd just picked him as my partner in a life-or-death mission. An assignment that would require us to spend one-on-one time together, in a small space, for months—maybe even years—on end.

Basically, I'd just ruined his life. He hadn't needed the exam to determine his fate— a sassy, outspoken junior had just claimed that responsibility.

But when I made eye contact with Max, he didn't look upset. In fact, he didn't even seem surprised. When my gaze met his, he nodded his head in acceptance. In fact, his response was so calm that I wondered if the others suspected that we'd known the outcome in advance.

Suddenly feeling very small, I wasn't sure what to do next. My bravado expired the moment my fate was sealed. For all my expectation of being chosen, I hadn't actually thought about what might happen next.

I stood on the stage steps awkwardly, eyes traveling about the auditorium without resting on any specific faces. I was afraid of what I might find written on the countenances of my peers.

"So she's going to Venus," someone called out. "But will she be sterilized?"

I felt my cheeks blush cotton-candy pink. There was no precedent for sterilization for the assignment of intergalactic mission pioneer.

"No sterilization," Mr. Boothe announced through gritted teeth, clearly annoyed at the direction the exercise had taken. I felt sure he had meant to intimidate the junior class into adopting a healthy dose of fear and respect; instead, he was fielding obnoxious questions from nervous adolescents.

"There's no life on Venus," Mr. Boothe added curtly, an obvious dig directed at the brazen student who'd called out.

"No, but there's Max," the emboldened junior retorted, drawing guffaws from the crowd.

The rosy pink of my cheeks deepened to a blood-red. For all my earlier spunk and sass, I was suddenly desperate to be off the stage and alone. My nonchalance had evaporated: I was an insecure, fearful girl who'd been slotted for a terrifying task. And now I was being teased publicly.

"Do we get to request an earth artifact?" I blurted, eager to drive the conversation in a new direction. If Mr. Boothe couldn't silence the junior class, then I would take hold of the reins of the conversation.

"An earth artifact?" Mr. Boothe asked, eyebrows furrowed.

"Yes, like the moon explorers were able to take," I clarified, knowing full well that Mr. Boothe knew what I was referring to.

The first colonists had been entitled to a special artifact of their choosing—any physical item—that The Organization had procured on their behalf in a gesture of gratitude for participating in the dangerous mission. The thought behind the edict was that the space colonist might not survive the assignment and should therefore be allowed an item reminiscent of earth that would serve to comfort and ground the individual during stressful times.

It was hardly a precedent; intergalactic colonization had only taken place once before. At that time, the moon colonists had taken items such as MP3 players, stuffed animals, or even giant packages of gum.

Again, I hadn't thought through this element of the mission before that moment—but in my desperation to change the topic, I figured it was a valid question to ask. The bonus would be to get Mr. Boothe to agree to my request in front of a large group…that way, it would be harder for him to recant if my ask was extravagant.

Mr. Boothe seemed to recognize this point, too—he hesitated before responding.

"Surely you wouldn't deny us one earth artifact," Max spoke up, catching me off guard. "If we're going to risk our lives for the benefit of The Organization, it seems like a small concession to make."

Mr. Boothe, for all his show of infallibility, caved under the pressure. "Of course, each individual on assignment will be entitled to one earth artifact," he announced carefully.

"I'm glad to hear that," Max voiced. I felt his eyes on me and knew he was advocating on my behalf. Why, I wasn't sure. I'd just subjected him to a horrible fate—and he was doing me a favor?

"I think my comrade here has her earth artifact ready to request," Max added.

My heart raced. Max was trying to help—he also realized that if I announced my artifact now, Mr. Boothe would *have* to comply...it was my chance to request something elaborate. Clearly, he believed I had something already in mind...

My mind went into a rhythmic gymnastics routine: somersaults, cartwheels, and twirls of thoughts that I attempted to synergize into a single, coherent request.
I couldn't waste the demand: it needed to be a big ask; something I'd always wanted...but that was impossible to possess in my daily life on earth. Not something I could get on my own, or in time—something that was totally and utterly off-limits to individuals living on earth.

"Yes?" Mr. Boothe asked stiffly, the bitter edge of his words piercing through my contemplations.

The razor-sharp nature of his words offered the clarity I needed: suddenly, I knew exactly what I would request. Something I'd always wanted; something no one was permitted to enjoy in my lifetime.

A coy smile spread across my face, prompting the blood to drain from Mr. Boothe's. I hadn't voiced my request, but he knew from my expression that he wasn't going to like it. Also, that he was going to have to grant it to me.

"Thank you, Max," I began congenially before turning to address Mr. Boothe. "Yes, I do have a request for my earth artifact. We can go over specifics in private, but I would like a kitten."

Reality Hits

"A *kitten?*" Mr. Boothe spat, forgetting his composure in the wake of his outrage.

Max couldn't hold back a surprised chuckle himself, and I felt my cheeks turn a Benadryl-pink. My request was, in fact, ridiculous…but I had made it and I did in fact want it— that was enough to make me stand my ground.

"Yes, a kitten," I agreed. "People used to have pets, and they got along just fine. And since you've already sent a chimp on the intergalactic mission successfully, a kitten should survive."

In my head, I weighed out other arguments: I had a feeling Mr. Boothe wouldn't let it rest easily. It was a fact that up until a century ago, people had domesticated animals that were permitted to live with them—they were called, "pets." While a wide range of animals fell under this distinction, the most commonly adopted animals were dogs, cats, and small rodents or fish.

But then, the world started becoming too populated. Resources became scarce. Diseases became highly communicable and transferable through animals. And all of a sudden, pets were a luxury the world could no longer afford.

There were still domestic animals, but few—and those that were around were kept for scientific purposes or public entertainment. The era of private animal companionship and ownership was over.

"There are still kittens in existence," Max pointed out in the silence that stretched on from Mr. Boothe's lack of words.

"We'll talk about this later," Mr. Boothe blurted loudly, trying to regain control of the situation. "Your request has been noted," he added quickly before I (or anyone else) had the idea to protest.

I looked out at Max, then at Mr. Boothe. I shifted my weight uncomfortably from side to side, unsure of what I was expected to do next.

"Can I go back to my seat now?" I asked uncertainly.

"Yes, yes—you're dismissed," Mr. Boothe decided irritably, waving me away. "You're all dismissed. The exam will begin shortly—teachers, please escort your students back to homeroom."

I didn't try to make it back to my seat; instead, I waited for the crowd to dissipate. I didn't particularly relish the idea of standing up on stage with Mr. Boothe any longer than was necessary, but I *really* didn't like the thought of navigating the hallways with my peers staring me down and whispering about me.

The students, for their part, had been properly intimidated by the exercise. They walked back in silent, neat rows—I could hardly hear a footstep as they exited the auditorium.

Mr. Boothe watched their progression as well; we stood close to one another without exchanging a word. When the last juniors were filing out, I paused at the bottom of the stage steps.

"How did you know?" Mr. Boothe asked, stopping me short.

I could play dumb—there were a thousand things he could be referring to—but we both knew what he was asking. And I wasn't sure I had the answer. Even if I did have the answer, I wasn't sure I would tell Mr. Boothe.

"I didn't," I ended up answering. "I just had a feeling. I can't explain it," I told him, knowing my initial, vague response would not satisfy the leader.

"For how long?" Mr. Boothe wanted to know.

My head hurt. I wondered how much time I was going to have to spend with Mr. Boothe before the mission began—this felt like pure agony. I shrugged: not to blow Mr. Boothe off, but in a weary expression of my confusion.

Mr. Boothe pressed his lips tightly together: he was not pleased by my response, but he wouldn't hold it against me. At least, that's how I interpreted his expression.

"There will be plenty of time to discuss these matters later," Mr. Boothe acquiesced.

I took these words as permission to leave and didn't wait for a formal invitation. As I took quick steps up the aisleway and out the door, I was aware of Mr. Boothe's gaze following me, taking in my every movement.

I felt more uncertain and anxious entering homeroom than I had walking up on stage to take the exam. An hour ago, I'd been Selina Alois, student. Now, I was so much more. A mere sixty minutes had passed, and somehow I'd tacked so much more onto my identity. No longer was I merely a student in the junior class. I was Selina Alois, the chosen pioneer. Selina, destined for unparalleled distinction: either eternal glory or catastrophic demise. I'd suddenly become very interesting, and I knew I wouldn't be viewed the same way ever again.

Don't let it affect you, I told myself. This is going to be the new normal— start adjusting now.

Outside homeroom class, I took a deep breath and chewed on my lower lip. *It's going to be weird. It's going to be awkward and uncomfortable and awful. And that's okay.* The final pep talk complete, I walked into the classroom.

The class had been waiting for me.

The silence was so thick and pervasive, it felt like saran wrap had been pressed around the walls, suffocating noise through the air-tight seal. Thirty pairs of eyes studied me as though for the first time; thirty pairs of eyes bore holes through me as though I were swiss cheese. It was exactly what I'd expected, and that helped.

"Congratulations, Selina," my homeroom teacher announced, the congratulatory words incongruent with her uncertain, distant tone.

I got it. No one knew what to expect. Sure, being chosen was supposedly an honor—but it had also been made clear that death was a very real possibility. My teachers, kind and empathetic souls who were usually quick to offer words of wisdom, could not relate.

This experience would be played out in every class of the day: cool, polite responses from my peers and teachers that reflected a lack of understanding or relatability. Until the other juniors were selected, it was going to be a very lonely existence.

"Thank you." I smiled at my teacher before walking back to my seat and sitting down as I had hundreds of time before—as though nothing were the matter.

The teacher seemed to pick up on the fact that none of the students would be able to produce anything of value while so distracted, so she released the class to work independently. I was uncertain of how to spend my time; in the end, I pulled out my calculus work and revisited the Venus and Heidel calculations.

Mrs. Armand had been certain that the numbers for Heidel were incorrect…and she hadn't projected confidence in Venus's calculations, either. I wanted to study the figures myself to see if anything stood out.

"What did it feel like?"

The voice was quiet but firm, and it pulled me from my work, I looked up to find my classmate Michelle staring at me with insistent eyes and pursed lips. I glanced to either side: Michelle's question had been overheard by others who feigned preoccupation while eavesdropping to hear my response.

"It really didn't feel like anything," I answered honestly. "Mr. Boothe was honest about that part."

Michelle nodded but kept her gaze fixed on me. Clearly, she expected more. I coughed awkwardly and looked at my shoes. What else did she want from me?

"You knew," Michelle whispered, prodding me along. "How?"

This time, the surrounding students stilled their pencils and peeked over their shoulders in an obvious effort to focus on my every word.

"I just knew," I answered.

I wished I could give my peers something more meaningful to hold onto. I could imagine their anxiety and fear—they were looking for some kind of anchor or word of encouragement. I briefly considered adding the bit about my dreams, but something held me back. I wasn't sure whether that was natural or not, and it felt like something I was supposed to keep to myself.

My classmates looked away. Michelle continued to observe me—I felt the heat of her gaze. The pep talk's power faded, and I struggled not to squirm. I was jumping out of my skin, more uncomfortable than I'd ever been before in my life.

My classmates all wanted something from me...and I had nothing to offer. I could tell by their responses that they didn't believe that, and it made me feel terrible. I'd never been more aware of my "otherness"—there was no doubt that I stuck out like a sore thumb.

I spent the rest of homeroom fixated on the same calculus problem: the numbered scrawl came in and out of focus under my unyielding stare. I found that if I tilted my head forward, my hair hung like a partition, shielding me from curious eyes.

When the bell rang, I was the first out of the room. I'd moved past the point of trying to play it cool—I needed to find Max. Instead, I was sidelined by Clarice.

"They've started the exams," Clarice hissed, pulling me to the side of the hallway with a vise-like grip. "What did it feel like? Did you have any say in the decision? What were you thinking about during the test?" Clarice rifled the questions off with scarcely a breath in between.

"Clarice, I really don't know," I insisted, pulling my arm away. Clarice held firm, and I pulled harder.

"You don't have to believe me, but I'm telling the truth. I don't have anything else to tell you," I insisted, an edge of anger stitched into my response.

"You're holding something back," Clarice accused, her almond eyes narrowing to half-moon slits. "I know you better than anyone—you're hiding something. I just don't know what it is. And I don't know why you're keeping it from me, your best friend."

I was silent. I wasn't withholding any earth-shattering information, but it was true that I'd remained mute on a few factors. All things that my gut told me to keep private: the dreams, my inclinations, and the secrets shared with me in the last 48 hours. None of which seemed to directly affect Clarice; although Clarice seemed to think that any and all news was meant for her ears.

"You're not denying it," Clarice pointed out sharply.

"It's not information that affects you," I snapped back, asserting myself a bit more than usual. "I would tell you if it were."

"Would you?" Clarice challenged, her eyes never leaving my face.

"I would," I replied evenly.

Clarice's face did little to hide the fact that she didn't trust my response at all, but she kept her mouth shut. I tried hard to remind myself that my friend was extremely nervous and likely acting out of a place of pressure— I wanted to empathize with Clarice without succumbing to the pressure of divulging information I felt I should keep to myself.

"Do you think you're going to be chosen?" I asked suddenly. It hadn't occurred to me before that Clarice's behavior might be attributed to the fact that she worried she might be selected for the intergalactic mission.

Clarice's chin trembled for just a moment. "I don't think so," she answered with some hesitation. "But I don't know. If I knew a bit more about the selection process, it would help," she added in a thinly-veiled dig.

I worked to suppress my irritation and ignored the insult. "You'll know soon enough," was all I could think to say in the end.

Would Clarice be chosen? I had no way of knowing. It was interesting that Clarice hadn't questioned me about choosing Max—she hadn't asked why I'd chosen him or why I *hadn't* chosen her. Stress could do incredible things to the body and mind.

Aware that the precious few minutes of passing period were dwindling, I gave my friend a sympathetic smile before prying myself loose. I navigated the hallway like a fish swimming upstream in my quest to find Max, only this fish had the magical ability to split water: the students all parted like the Red Sea as I walked past. Remarkably, this did not help me to spot Max like I felt it should have.

"Selina!"

My heart sank as I recognized Chris's voice. *Not* who I was looking for! I pretended not to hear him…but soon he was beside me, fingers gently pressed against my shoulder in a gesture I couldn't ignore. I was sure the irritation in my eyes was recognizable as I turned to face him; Chris seemed slightly taken aback as he met my gaze. With raised eyebrows I waited for Chris to get to the point.

"Um—thanks for not choosing me," he mumbled.

"Yep," I responded brusquely. I stood on my tiptoes and looked over Chris's shoulder for any sign of Max.

Chris didn't leave like I wished he would. I sighed impatiently, no longer concerned that I might appear rude.

"Why did you choose Max?" Chris asked, lowering his voice just a bit.

"Do you know where he is?" I asked, ignoring Chris's question altogether. With every passing moment, the need to meet with Max felt more and more urgent.

Chris shook his head, and I gave him a false smile.

"I'm sure we'll have time to catch up later," I said dismissively. "Good luck on the exam."

Despair was beginning to wash over me like a bucket of cold water. I'd escaped the grips of Clarice and Chris, but for what purpose? There was still no sign of Max.

"Selina!"

I fought back the urge to burst into tears as I heard Max call my name. Not a second later, the bell rang.

"What class do you have right now?" Max asked.

Scanning the hallway, I noted that there were still quite a few students rushing to make it to their next period. It was an unusual day; there would be an extra measure of grace extended to tardy students, I was confident.

"Calculus. You?"

"Philosophical Theory, It can wait," Max added, catching the look on my face.

"I don't know what we should do," I admitted, aware that we couldn't stand talking in the hallway forever. "It's a little ridiculous to try to go through the day pretending like nothing's the matter. I need space and time to process. And I'm definitely not going to get it when I go home. What's going to happen to us?"

Max raised his eyebrows in exasperated agreement. He was kind enough not to point out that it was me who had secured his position in the tricky predicament. "You want to ditch?"

I chewed on the inside of my lip as I considered the option. I'd never before ditched a class…and while I wasn't against the idea in theory, I worried that this was a poor time to take liberties.

I couldn't know for sure, but I imagined that The Organization would be watching me closer than ever. And if my conversations with Mrs. Armand and Chris had told me anything, it was that there was a bounty of secrets I couldn't even begin to fathom.

"Do you think that's a good idea?" I worried aloud.

"Probably not," Max agreed. "But I don't know that we have any good ideas anymore. We're in uncharted territory, Alois."

"I know," I sighed. "Can we meet during lunch? We can go somewhere private…people might not even notice, they're so worked up about the exam."

"Done. Where should we meet?" Max asked.

"Do you have Mrs. Armand for Calculus? I think she'd let us use her room," I suggested.

Max nodded, then looked up at the now-vacant hallway. "So…go to fourth period, and meet up after?"

"Yeah," I sighed in relief, grateful there was some sort of plan in place. As Max turned to leave, I couldn't help myself. "Max!" He glanced back over his shoulder, "I'm glad you're coming with me."

Max nodded casually, as though I'd thanked him for holding open the door or picking up a dropped pencil.

Seconds later, the hallway was empty. I waited until Max had rounded the corner and was out of sight, then walked to Calculus.

Alliance

Mrs. Armand's response was admirably neutral when I walked in a full five minutes late. She was midway through a review of the homework—when I entered, Mrs. Armand nodded in acknowledgement of my arrival and carried on without missing a beat.

I felt eyes on me, but the attention was short-lived. Most of my peers were out-of-their-minds anxious about the exam: it seemed that every ten minutes or so, a member of The Organization came by to pull a student for the test.

I felt surprising gratitude towards Mr. Boothe that I'd been able to take my test straight-away: I could literally see the anticipation and anxiety eat away at those seated around me. Mrs. Armand seemed to recognize this; she was extremely patient in repeating answers, and she did not choose to introduce any new curriculum.

When the bell rang, most of the students bolted— I imagined they were eager to meet their friends and find out who had taken the exam and what the results were. Mrs. Armand shuffled papers at her desk, stalling for time as though she anticipated I would approach her.

"Thanks," I began, unsure of how much I should say. Was I being watched? Was Mrs. Armand being watched?

"You're welcome," Mrs. Armand replied evenly, looking up from her papers to fix me with a knowing look. "I'm glad you listened. I hope you know that we can't discuss anything further."

"I had a feeling," I answered.

Max appeared in the doorway, and Mrs. Armand's eyes followed my gaze. "Max and I were hoping you'd let us talk in here privately, just during lunch."

Mrs. Armand hesitated. "Sure," she finally decided. "Be careful," she muttered under her breath, collecting a stack of papers in her arms before sailing through the door.

I didn't give much care or concern to Mrs. Armand's warning: at this point, I figured I should probably be concerned and cautious about everything.

"So how many pairs of eyes are watching us right now?" Max quipped, sliding on top of the nearest stool.

"Too many," I snapped with a groan.

There was a stretch of silence. There was so much to say, but I wasn't sure where to begin. My thoughts were a conglomerate web without a central theme or linear path.

"So…we're going to Venus," Max began, offering me an open door.

"Right. And we have no idea when, or under what circumstances. Are we going to keep taking classes? Or are we going to get special training from The Organization for our mission? Is this an authentic mission, or is this just a PR stunt that's doomed to failure?" The words erupted from my mouth as though molten rock from a volcano.

"The mission is real," Max told her straight. "I believe that. If they're setting us up for doom, I don't know. But the need is real, and this is a legitimate method they've brainstormed to meet the increasing needs of the human population."

"Okay," I exhaled. Max's presence alone had a calming effect on me; his convictions carried heavy weight. "I heard that the mission to Heidel is doomed," I whispered a moment later.

"There's a lot of information out there," Max agreed hesitantly. "I'm trying to distinguish between fact and fiction right now."

"My source seemed pretty confident," I pushed.

"Fear is a powerful means of persuasion," Max countered. "There's a lot of fear in the air these days."

I couldn't argue with that. I was ready to launch into my next question when the intercom crackled to life.

"Selina Alois and Max Darnall, please report to the office. Selina Alois and Max Darnall, to the front office, please."

I looked at Max with wide eyes. Max laughed and raised his hands as he shrugged.

"We're in for an adventure, Alois. Did you expect anything less?"

I mirrored his smile with hesitation—I could not feign nonchalance like Max. With small footsteps, I made my way to the door; aware that any delay would only call more attention to our duo (and likely repeated announcements).

"We just stick together, okay?" I asked Max nervously. "Even when we meet the other two on our mission, I want it to stay the two of us." I looked at Max earnestly—I hadn't communicated my thoughts articulately, but I hoped he understood what I meant.

"Agreed," Max told me, eye contact direct. "We make a good team, Alois," he added. "We can trust our instincts."

I nodded and hoped Max was right. We walked in silence down the hallway, avoiding the hubbub of the lunchroom in our route to the office.

The large glass windows made it easy to see into the office, even from a distance. I noted the great number of members from The Organization huddled inside and swallowed hard. I'd been expecting that, but seeing it triggered something inside me.

Max stepped to the side to let me enter first; for once, I wished he were not such a gentleman. With jaw clenched, I walked into the office and into the lion's den.

"Selina, Max—glad we could track you down," one of the members of The Organization began. Her tone was friendly, her distinction evident through the gold-plated emblem pinned on the lapel of her navy-blue blazer.

I smiled uncertainly and willed my body to stay still (no fidgeting). I didn't want to give The Organization any reason to believe I was anything but cooperative and aligned with their core values: there was nothing to gain from a hostile relationship.

"There's a press release being sent out as we speak announcing the eight juniors selected for the intergalactic mission," another Organization member informed them. "Yes—that means that the other six members have been chosen," the man smiled, seeing the open curiosity on our faces.

I exercised great restraint and did not interrupt, though I badly wanted to know who the other six individuals were and where they were at the moment.

"The other six have already been briefed and are on their way home," the man continued as though reading my thoughts.

"All of the junior class has been dismissed," the woman added. "The exams have been completed and The Organization and school agreed that little academic value would come from keeping students for the rest of the day."

"Your parents will learn of your distinction at the same time as the rest of the world," the man carried on as though his female colleague had not interrupted. "I imagine they'll be anxious to see you and want to know as much information as possible."

He paused and looked to his colleagues. "Tonight will be your last night at home," another member spoke up, his voice low and gravelly. "There's no easy way to say it," he apologized.

"The mission ahead of you is very real, very dangerous, and very complex. To succeed, we'll need your total and complete devotion—and we'll need to start preparations immediately. Your education, as you've known it so far, is over.

"Tomorrow, you'll be transported to a training facility where you'll begin instruction geared towards your mission. Don't bother bringing any personal effects—you won't be able to keep them. We'll provide everything you need."

I had expected as much, but I still felt stunned into silence. Max didn't say a word, either.

"I know this is a lot to process. We're not really expecting you to sort through it all—it's best to just keep moving forward. The world's progress depends on you," the woman spoke up.

"Enjoy your time at home, but you'll do well not to create sentimental attachments or spend too much time reminiscing. Meet us here tomorrow morning at 8," the man finished.

The woman flitted to his side and whispered something in his ear. The man waved his hand impatiently.

"Just in case you want to see the press release," the woman chirped anxiously, "it's airing right now."

The flat screen flickered on. I stared as a very grave-looking reporter addressed the audience, her cardinal-red suit in direct contrast to her somber tone.

"This morning, The Organization surprised students and the community alike by dropping in to conduct the exams a day early," she began. "While The Organization has declined to comment on the reasoning behind this early testing, they have confirmed that all exams have been completed, and—" she paused here for dramatic effect, eyebrows arching in rainbow fashion—"I am here to introduce the eight brave souls who will voyage through The Milky Way to attempt colonization of Venus and Heidel.

"Please join me in congratulating Selina Alois, Max Darnall, Chris Levenson, Amanda Newall, Peyton Chen, Clarice Tran, Marcus Vivaldi, and Luke Niciu."

Photoshopped, glossy yearbook photos of my classmates and I graced the screen in tandem with the announcement. My heart dropped upon hearing Chris's and Clarice's names mentioned. I couldn't explain why, but I knew it was a mistake that they had been chosen. The reporter didn't distinguish who was going on which mission—and I was most anxious to learn that tidbit.

As the reporter cut to experts' analysis of the mission itself mixed with idle speculation and prattle on why The Organization had chosen to conduct the exams a day early (what was the point behind **one** day other than to terrorize the junior class and their parents?), the woman cut the programming.

"You're famous now," the woman said plainly, voice flat as matzo bread.

I bit back the sarcastic "yippee" that echoed in my mind. Famous for what, exactly? We hadn't done anything yet; we'd only been selected to make history. That was a lot of pressure to pile on the backs of sixteen-year-olds.

"The media is going to hound you for a bit," the man agreed. "We highly suggest you say little to nothing about your experience or thoughts on the mission. This is in your best interest, incidentally—we cannot protect you from the consequences that accompany personal indiscretion."

"What he means to say," the woman cut in reprovingly, "is that we're not going to try to control you. This is not some government program meant to hamstring you into submission and blind obedience. You wouldn't have been chosen for this program were that the case.

"You're believed to be unique, innovative individuals who can handle the spontaneity and surprise that space travel is certain to offer. With this individualism comes choice—choice that has the power to help or harm you."

"And your teammates," the man added. "Your actions affect your teammates, too."

"And who is part of our team?" Max asked. "We know who's been selected, but we haven't heard which two are traveling to Venus with us."

The members of The Organization glanced uneasily at one another before one man cleared his throat.

"It hasn't been determined yet," he began. "The Organization was meant to evaluate the eight individuals selected, and strategically assign each member to a team with a slated destination."

"They weren't supposed to let me pick," I surmised.

"No," the man told her baldly. "They weren't. And you picked not only a partner, but a destination, and an earth artifact...all in deviation from the plan," he continued irritably.

I chewed the inside of my lip and said nothing. The way the man spoke, it sounded like they were going to honor my decisions, although they certainly didn't seem pleased to do it. I wondered why Mr. Boothe had allowed me such liberties and realized my public selection probably had a lot to do with it.

"Sooo....they haven't decided yet?" I prodded.

The Organization members seemed reluctant to answer this question, but ultimately heads wagged from side to side.

"But we're going to get to stay together?" Max clarified, a note of earnest in his voice.

"Yes. It appears they plan to honor Selina's selection," the man agreed.

Max and I exchanged a look of relief. Realizing that we weren't going to get any further answers, I suddenly felt antsy to leave. I wanted to watch the full footage and commentary on the mission, salacious and flawed as it might be. And I could only imagine how my parents might respond to the news…I had a strange evening ahead of me.

"Is that all? Do you need anything else from us?" I asked, fidgeting slightly.

"Not at the moment," the woman answered, "Enjoy your last night at home."

Max was the first to leave. With a curt nod to the members of The Organization, he ducked through the door and down the hallway, pausing to wait for me when he was ten paces away.

"Well." Max stated. It wasn't a transition or a question; it was a simple, one-word sentence that somehow captured my sentiments perfectly.

I wanted to laugh out loud at the absurdity of our situation and Max's plain response.

"Well," I agreed. There was so much more to say, and yet there was no clear place to begin. It seemed more natural to stay silent than to try to verbalize the litany of thoughts that fell like Tetris puzzle pieces through the atmosphere of the mind.

We walked in silence through the desolate hallway of the school and to the front of the building. The usual pods had left long before; Max and I waited until one of the late-departure pods pulled up.

After programming our respective destinations, we sat in silence. I trusted Max implicitly, though I had no idea why.

My experience with Max had been, until very recently, extremely limited. And yet I knew I could trust him. I couldn't explain my thinking or pin it to anything objective, but that's the way it always was.

I'd learned from a young age to trust my subconscious at the same time society pushed hard the idea that the only real things, the only *truth* in the world was that which could be seen, heard, and touched. I'd always found that terribly ironic, considering that the most innovative, transformative research and "truth" came in the form of abstract math, microbiology, and inter-planetary discoveries that were imagined long before there was any quantifiable evidence.

There was power in my subconscious. I often wondered if all people possessed the ability to tap into their spirit and know the "unknowable," or if I was somehow special in this regard. It wasn't something I could discover through casual research, so it had gone unanswered.

"That's your stop, Alois," Max gently reminded me.

I looked up at the familiar building; my home for the past 16 years. My home for the last night. With a wry and bittersweet smile, I slid out of the pod.

"Good luck," I told Max softly, pausing momentarily in the gap of the pod. Our eyes met and held one another before I stepped outside. The *whoosh* of the pod's doors closing left me alone on the vacant sidewalk.

I'd been told there would be reporters. Curious speculators, nosy neighbors, and fearful community members—all poised to infringe my personal space. I didn't doubt The Organization's prediction...but it hadn't yet come to pass. For the moment, I could still pretend to be Selina Alois of the junior class. Student, daughter, friend, athlete...those were labels I'd grown up with and grown accustomed to. My world knew what to do with these labels and its conglomeration to provide me with an identity.

All of that was about to change.

The Divide

"We don't have much time."

The first words out of my mother's mouth were not what I had expected. I *had* expected to find both of my parents home from work early; I *had* expected them to want to talk to me; I *had* expected an endless stream of questions. But not this.

The urgency in my mother's tone told me this was more than a melancholic parental response to my impending and dramatic departure—this was somehow much more. Frowning with concern, I looked from my mother's knitted brow to my father's taut jawline. I stood frozen in place, hesitant even to close the door behind me.

"Come in," my mother rushed on impatiently. "I don't know how much time we have."

Obediently, robot-like, I took a segmented step forward. My father pulled me forward and deeper into the kitchen so that the door clicked shut behind me.

"You need to listen very carefully to what we're about to tell you," my mother told me sternly. "We won't have a chance to repeat what we're about to tell you, and it must never be repeated."

"If we are caught sharing this information with you, we'll likely all be executed," my father cut in, voice low and grave.

I stood stiff, arms at my sides like a mannequin doll. My parents were supposed to tell me how much they loved me, how shocked they were that I'd been picked, how honored they were, but how much they would miss me.

They were supposed to cook my favorite meal and share their favorite childhood memories with me and snuggle with me on the couch while we watched our favorite movies and wondered aloud what life in outer space would be like.

They were supposed to remind me to *be careful*, though they would of course have no idea in outer space what exactly I was supposed to be careful of. They were supposed to ask me one million questions and assure me that I was going to be successful and safe because I was special. I had no anticipatory set for the scene unfolding before me.

"Selina? Are you listening?" my father asked.

"Yes. Yes, I'm listening," I sputtered.

That I had no context for the narrative playing out did not excuse me from the responsibility of remembering it and committing it to memory.

"When you were a small child, there were words spoken over you," my mother began. Her voice became tinny and the last words were broken as my mother swallowed a sob. My heart beat like a jackhammer; my skin grew cold and clammy to the touch.

My father placed a firm palm on his wife's shoulder in a show of support. As she struggled to steady her breath, he spoke.

"When babies are born, there's the procedural testing," my father told me, searching my eyes for understanding. I nodded. I'd heard of these tests, given to infants to ensure that the mind and body were sound and worthy of life.

To my understanding, three tests took place over the span of six months—the records were private; sealed and locked away in the possession of The Organization. Not even parents were allowed access to these documents, as it was believed that they might be used to influence or sway the parents' management of the child.

"It's so much more than that," my father went on, each word falling on me like a ten-pound weight. "What you're not supposed to know—what no one is supposed to know—is that seers also assess each child."

My mind worked rapidly to try to find context for what I was being told—this latest admission was nothing I had ever heard about before, and I knew implicitly that this was where I needed to commit every detail to memory.

"You're not supposed to know about the seers," my mother cut in sharply. "There are only a few in existence—and their gifting is profound. They are able to see beyond and predict the traits, attributes, and strengths of a small child…and sometimes more."

Here, my mother looked to her husband uncertainly.

"We wouldn't have known all of this except that the seer who assessed you came and found us," my father explained, this time speaking slowly so that each word could take root.

"At great personal risk, he explained his job to us, then proceeded to tell us what an exceptional child you were—are. His feeling and intuition over your life were so strong, stronger than anything he had ever felt before, that he felt compelled to come and find us. To tell us, and also to warn us."

"You're very special, Selina," my mother told me, eyes brimming with tears as she reached out and cupped my hands in her own.

Rattled to the core, I looked down at the hands that had cooked countless "nutritionally-sound" meals, hands that had tucked me in at night and smoothed my hair into a ponytail years ago. Hands belonging to a woman who had always seemed impenetrable and austere; hands that now looked so small and fragile.

"I don't know quite how to explain this in a meaningful way," my father apologized. "We knew a day would come where we would need to share the seer's words with you, but I'm afraid I still feel unprepared."

"We don't understand what the words mean, but the seer spoke to us about you…he made it clear that these were words *for* you," my mother chimed in.

"Maybe they'll make more sense to you," my father said hopefully. "I don't think I'll have a chance to say it more than once."

"They're surely already on their way," my mother agreed. Her face was pale but resolute, a mask of determination. She nodded at her husband and held his hand tightly as he prepared to speak.

**"When the future looks uncertain, when life is filled with unrest—
Then the prophecy is ripening, she is ready for the test.
No exam of natural order, no trademark aspirations to aspire to—**

A calling greater than the world can comprehend, something new.

Embrace the unexpected, don't try to place what doesn't fit.
Trust your intuition, lean into your strengths, hold tight to your wit.
Close to the sun, all truth is revealed.
Impurities refined, past hurts healed.

Let go of expectations, launch forward into free fall.
Weightless and unfettered, answer the call.
You'll know in your spirit, what you're meant to do—
Don't cheapen the destiny you've been called to.

The danger is real, but so is your might.
Exhibit grace and flexibility, but be ready to fight.
Your enemy is fierce and will go to great lengths
To dishearten your spirits and eat away at your strength.

You've prepared for this moment, though you knew it not—
Your life one fluid lesson, and so much you've been taught.
Go forward and conquer, identity intact.
You were made to win this battle—that is a fact.

Relegated to earth, but this is not your home.
When you're the only person in a room, you are still not alone.
Hold fast to **truth**, not the subjectivity of what is *momentarily* true
Feelings don't matter; they'll often betray you.

Ask the right questions, and wait patiently to hear back
Conversations involve two parties; wise counsel will keep you on
track."

Finished, my father exhaled deeply. His body curled in like a sea anemone poked in the middle; when he looked up, I was dismayed to find that he looked as though he had aged ten years.

"We love you," he told me. He'd said the words thousands of times, but in that moment, they felt brand new. Fresh, fragrant, and weighty, I felt tears spring to my eyes.

"So much," my mother added, squeezing my hands tenderly, as though she were holding a wounded bird.

Not a second later, the doors to our home burst open and uniformed strangers I had never seen before poured in. I didn't make a sound as I pressed myself against the wall in shock.

"You were warned," one of the uniformed men snarled.

My saucer-like eyes looked from the strangers to my parents, who did not register the surprise I'd expected. My heart and stomach sank like a stone.

My parents said nothing as they were escorted out the door. I watched, utterly helpless. My parents didn't look back—they'd said what they'd needed to say to me. To risk further communication or affection would be painful at best, dangerous at worst.

"We'll be back for you," one of the women snapped at me before the doors closed in my face.

Dumbfounded and bewildered, I took the steps to the couch in a daze. I perched softly on the edge of the cushion, afraid the plush velvet might not support my weight; afraid the cushion might not exist at all. I was living in a dream, but I was awake and not dreaming at all. My actions seemed not to matter at all, and yet I knew the stakes to be higher than ever before.

I sat in total silence, weight carefully distributed and open palms resting on my knees. My gaze focused on the tiny spot of chocolate on the cream-colored rug at my feet. The blemish was my mistake, the result of a night of rebellious disobedience when I'd eaten chocolate ice cream outside of the kitchen. It was, unquestionably, my fault. Was this my fault, too?

"What did they tell you?"

I blinked and looked toward the door to see a small contingent of uniformed men and women standing in the entryway. Surprisingly cool and collected, I thought through how best to respond: clearly The Organization knew that I'd heard something I wasn't supposed to…my parents had alluded to that fact when they'd worried aloud how much time they had to deliver the message.

To lie outright would be to lose the trust of The Organization—I wasn't sure what price tag to attach to this intangible, but it seemed unwise to take aggressive action so early on. And yet, I needed time to determine the value and wisdom of the prophetic words spoken over my life—my parents had clearly believed the words to carry great importance.

"I heard about the other assessment—the personality disposition," I told them calmly, as though I were explaining what I'd eaten for lunch. "Then they started to tell me some poem that didn't make sense. They didn't get to finish." I shrugged and switched tactics. "So can someone explain to me what just happened? Are my parents being punished for my selection for the intergalactic mission?"

I figured that total ignorance would arouse suspicion—I'd been chosen for the mission in part because of my intelligence, so I couldn't play totally dumb—but if I could play it off like I was so consumed with the mission and somehow thought these events to be interrelated, then I might get away with pretending like I had dismissed my parents' words.

The members of The Organization exchanged looks and prepared to take their time responding. I didn't let them.
"I didn't tell them anything about my mission—I don't even know anything about it yet!" I added, introducing a hint of hysteria to my voice. "You shouldn't punish them for something I was chosen for!" If I was going to sell it, I was going to really sell it.

"We'll see about that," one of the men answered cagily. I saw his shoulders relax just a bit at the same time his jawline softened. He'd bought my lie— I'd convinced him that I believed my present circumstances were all due to the exam that had taken place that morning.

"Are you taking me now, then?" I asked defiantly, shoulders pushed back and eyebrows raised in challenge. It was easier to escape into this acting ruse than to honestly assess all that had happened. If I could pretend to be this naïve and sassy Selina, then maybe I could survive long enough to learn the truth.

"What instructions were you given?" the woman asked hesitantly. Her voice was not warm, but it was not unkind. I heard the uncertainty and it gave me confidence.

"They told me to report back tomorrow morning," I had my answer ready. "But I'm assuming that since you dragged my parents from me, you're also planning to take me."

"I think you can stay here the night," the man told me steadily.

"Why would I want to do that?" I snapped indignantly. "Is there some benefit to meditating on everything that has been taken from me? My future, my belongings, and now my parents? Your intent to strip me of all earthly connections has been made plain—I won't wallow in the pain of what will never be."

As the uniformed men and women waffled with indecision, I sealed the transaction. "Hey—I was selected for this mission. Meaning I possess some talent or quality that sets me apart from the others. I'm not an idiot, and I won't be played. I can see what's going on here, and I expect to be treated fairly."

My words did carry some truth: I did not care to spend a night alone in a home that I would never again visit, without the parents I had been raised by, surrounded by possessions I was not permitted to take with me. And yet the motive behind my words was to determine if the capture of my parents had been planned, and the answer was a definite "no."

In my confrontation, the members of The Organization did not know how to respond—they weren't prepared for my response and did not know what to do with me. The raid had been spontaneous.

"I'd grab my toothbrush, but I was told I didn't need any personal belongings," I announced with an air of authority not a moment later. "So I guess I'll just follow you." I flipped my hair over my shoulder and kept eye contact.

"Alright, let's go," the man conceded.

I absorbed my surprise and moved towards the door as though the interaction had gone exactly according to plan. My mind reeled—was I really going to walk out the front door of my own home without ever returning? Without one last walk-through, without taking anything with me?

Yes. Yes, I was. And I was going to pretend like it didn't hurt me.

I walked out the doorway and felt stinging pain as though I had been stuck with a push-pin. That was the best way to sum up my day: I was a life-size push-pin doll, every square inch of me pierced.

The Organization

When I walked through the doors to The Organization Headquarters, I was surprised by how simple it looked. I wasn't sure what I'd been expecting, but I was taken aback by how quiet and understated it was.

A small room, all pearl-white, with lockers covering every square inch of wall space. There was a single person sitting behind the spotless, lustrous counter: a woman in her forties who looked up with shuttered eyes. A quick appraisal of the situation, and the woman handed me a small card with a QR code. I wondered if I should explain who I was or what I was there for, but the woman didn't seem to care.

"You can head to your pod or the communal space," one of the women told me.

I watched as the woman pulled her own card from her pocket and walked toward the lockers. She held the card up to the locker; seconds later, the embedded scanner read the QR code and swung open. Kicking off her shoes, the woman lifted milk-white cotton slippers from the locker and placed her shoes inside.

Even though there was no shame in my inexperience—how was I to know what to do if I'd never been there before?— I did not want to humble myself by asking for instructions. Instead, I held my card up to a locker as I'd seen the woman do and felt relief when it opened without issue.

Besides the padded slippers I had seen the woman pull from the locker, there was a bathrobe, satin pajamas, a bath and wash towel, a toothbrush, hairbrush, and a bottle of water—all white. Without knowing where exactly I was going or what the rooms looked like, I didn't take any of the items with me—although I did change out of my shoes and into the standard-issue slippers.

In the minute it had taken for this simple transaction, the members of The Organization who had escorted me to the building had dispersed. I wasn't sure where they had gone (and I knew without a shadow of a doubt that I was still being watched) but I had also been left on my own.

How many surveillance cameras tracked my progress down the alabaster hallway? There was no way to know. My curiosity piqued when the hallway forked before two elevators: one emblazoned with a male figure painted in tangerine, the other adorned with a female figure painted in rose-pink.

With benign uncertainty I pushed the button for the female elevator; a moment later, the steel doors opened with the classic *ping* in F tone. For all the scientific advancements and state-of-the-art technology The Organization boasted, I was surprised by the antiquated and simple mode of transportation. It occurred to me that the heavy and oppressive metal design might serve a functional purpose; perhaps to conceal occupants and activity on the different levels from individuals not specifically assigned to surveillance.

The inside of the elevator put to bed any thoughts that The Organization's headquarters was not up to technological standards: the overwhelming number (and layout) of buttons caused me to stop and stare. Arranged in maze-like fashion, the buttons were all the same size, but were back-lit with a menagerie of pastel colors and coded with letter-and-number combinations that held no meaning for me.

"Dormitories or common room?" a voice disrupted the silence.

I jumped and looked around the four-foot square before realizing the voice had come through a speaker system.

Clearing my throat, "Common room."

I was curious to see the dormitories but figured it was early to go to bed…and I had a plan. Since it seemed my free time was limited, I planned to make the most of it. The Organization was famous for its oppressive tendencies: however closely I was being scrutinized at the moment, it would only escalate when I reported for "duty" in the morning. Since my arrival at headquarters was apparently unplanned, I needed to take advantage of this time.

I committed to memory the violet MF5 button that lit up as I was gently lifted up to the common room. Seconds later, the doors opened.

The expansive room that stood in front of me fell much more in line with how I had imagined The Organization's headquarters. The high ceilings and whimsical layout reminded me both of Gaudi's nature-inspired designs and Dr. Seuss' fanciful illustrations. Practical met indulgent in the expensive, snow-white tiles with golden veins that marched in meandering fashion through the heartbeat of the common room.

On either side were themed alcoves: lush, rainforest-like corners with giant hanging bird cages, modern spaces with alternating backdrops featuring major cosmopolitan cities, ocean-inspired landscapes with hammocks and giant fish tanks...even a child-like nook that featured rainbow-colored beanbags, oversized bunk beds, and a candy buffet bar.

People milled through this common room, which, I noted with irony, was anything but common. Men and women of variant ages roamed through the space; my arrival didn't spark any interest. Buffeted by the lack of intrigue, I looked around for a spot where I could carry out my planned research.

My eyes rested upon a room that I supposed was designed for research...although certainly nothing of a confidential nature. The square room had see-through plastic panels for walls and a baguette-like oak table with matching stools set up for a work space. Dry-erase markers and tablets lay atop; the precise tools I had been searching for. Better still, the room was empty.

Marching in, I didn't waste any time: I grabbed one of the tablets and began researching breeds of cat. It seemed like the most productive use of my time, and it would serve as a welcome, happy distraction from the madness of the past twenty-four hours.

Buoyed by the knowledge that The Organization planned to honor my request for a living earth artifact, I wanted to make my selection count. I could best do that by learning about the different breeds of cats—when I met with The Organization the next morning, I wanted to be prepared with a specific request.

In the back of my mind, the prophetic words niggled at me. They were there with perfect clarity: I knew I would never have to worry about forgetting what my parents had recited with great care. The emotions and drama attached to the memory were enough to sear them into my brain as though etched in stone.

I pushed any thoughts of what might happen to my parents or worries of what my mission might comprise from my brain entirely: there was no fruit in thinking about such things, And so, I dove head-first into research I was sure had never before been conducted in The Organization's headquarters. My notes, written in dry-erase marker, decorated the thick plastic walls.

Maine Coon: affectionate, BIG, curious.

Sphynx: intelligent, friendly, creepy-looking?

Bengal: adventurous, exotic, super active.

Ragdoll: sweet, docile, boring?

Devon Rex: playful, outgoing, inquisitive, loyal, quirky, loving, ADORABLE.

I knew even before I finished my comprehensive list what I was going to ask for. I made sure to look up every breed (so I could say I had done my due diligence), but the truth was that my heart was set on a Devon Rex the moment I saw a picture of the strange creature with elephantine ears, round eyes, and soft, curly fur. That they were rare (what cat *wasn't* these days?) and exhibited a rare and highly-desirable cocktail of characteristics only fanned the flames of my resolve.

Satisfied with my research and the warm glow in my middle that told me I had chosen correctly, I yawned and wondered how much time had elapsed. The soft artificial lighting in the common room made it impossible to guess what time it was. There were still a number of people wandering about, but I guessed that was always the case.

All of a sudden the emotional toll of the day's events hit. Weary and fatigued, I wiped down my multi-colored feline research from the plastic walls and stumbled back to the elevators. I was thankful to know my desired destination when I was queried once again by the speakers.

"Dormitories," I announced with confidence. I remembered too late the washcloth, pajamas, and toothbrush in my locker downstairs—but I also didn't care. All I wanted was a safe and private place to sleep. On some level, I was grateful that I had taken myself to a place of exhaustion—I would have no problem falling asleep. I hoped it would be dreamless.

The elevator doors parted with the pomp of curtains pulled back on opening night. I blinked.

The corridor before me had steel-gray marbled flooring that stood in stark contrast to the light and modern design of the rest of the building. Dim, yellow bubbles of light lined the aisleways like the emergency exit lighting strip on an airplane. A lengthy row of cylindrical cases was stacked one atop the next on either side of the aisle, all marked with neat stenciling and sharply-tipped arrows designating the identification number for each case. The pervasive silence made me immediately self-conscious: I assumed there were other people in this room, although I hadn't seen anyone yet. I worried about the time and the ding of the elevator and about where I should go.

The sound of a faucet captured my attention and redirected my focus to a side room I hadn't noticed. With careful steps, my slippered feet followed the sound of running water.

A simple but functional bathroom: faucets, counters, and even a side vanity. I noticed more lockers, bathrooms, and tiled cubes that I guessed to be showers. My gaze traveled next to the woman responsible for the noise: I watched surreptitiously as she toweled her face and threw the used linen in a hamper. For one uncomfortable moment, we made eye contact.

"Late night," the woman groused, her tone conspiratorial. "So ready to pass out," she sighed, shaking her head.

"Seriously," I agreed, taking careful note of the woman's card in hand. "Sleep well," I added as I made my way to the sink.

I waited a solid minute before reaching into my pocket for my own card. I was thankful to find it not much abused—and I was even more grateful when I saw a code printed in the upper left-hand corner that looked much like the character combinations I'd seen printed on the floor.

FM111.

I committed the sequence to memory as I made my way back to the corridor and down the hallway. Two-thirds of the way down, I found my space tucked on the left-hand side, halfway up the wall. My feet found the ladder steps built in and ascended the seven steps; I held the QR code before the small digital scanner.

Like the jaws of an alligator, the shuttered door to the cylinder opened wide to reveal a sleeping space eight feet long and three feet tall. A thick futon ran along the floor and a small shelf protruded just behind a modest pillow. A universal charger for electronics, a dimmer to control the lighting, and a dial to control the temperature of the cylinder completed the contents of the sleeping area.

I found relief in the simplicity of it all; I wasted no time in crawling inside. As the doors closed on me, I slipped under the blankets and made no adjustments to the lighting or temperature. And then, I slept.

I was on Venus. The copper-toned rocky surface made my footing unsteady, and even in my thick protective space suit, the scorching heat and humidity was oppressive. My breath fogged the inside of my helmet, my fingers badly wanted to wipe away the rivulet of sweat that trickled down the back of my neck. Max was beside me, and two other figures stood in the distance.

It's so hard to breathe here, I thought. *This helmet is making me claustrophobic.*

So take it off.

This thought was audible, and although it came from no physical being that I could see, it was not my own. Unsure of how to proceed, I spoke the next words out loud.

"The atmosphere is poisonous," I countered, repeating the words I'd heard thousands of times from my parents, teachers, and The Organization. It was a fact; an immutable truth. To take off my helmet? It was a certain death wish. Wasn't it?

I was disappointed when the voice didn't respond, then worried that the heat was addling my brain.

Meeee-ooowwww!

The high-pitched protest startled me. My gaze traveled to my right shoulder, where the Devon Rex kitty I'd aspired to adopt sat perched on my shoulder like a parrot. Outfitted in a space suit all his own, his gigantic ears stood at attention and his virid-green eyes were fixed on me. As I stood marveling over the fact that I had in fact gotten the kitten I'd asked for, the voice spoke again.

Just ask Felix.

Ask Felix? Who's Felix? I wondered, not without some attitude.

MOW!

This time, the meow was loud, aggressive, and undoubtedly a response to my question.

"You're Felix?" I asked, breath fogging up the inside of my helmet.

Meow. The taupe kitty with a striped tail seemed placated by this verbal admission and readjusted his weight on my shoulder. And then I woke up.

A New Life

It took me a moment to remember where I was and what had happened. It took another moment to orient myself from yet another bizarre and possibly meaningful dream.

Blinking into the soft amber glow of the dimmed light, I propped myself up onto my elbows and took a deep breath. The line between reality and the fantastical nature of my subconscious mind was becoming increasingly blurred.

Without knowing exactly what time it was, I figured the 8:00 hour was coming quickly (if it had not already passed). I wasn't sure if I was still expected to meet at the school now that I had settled at headquarters.

The beauty about having nothing was that there was nothing to collect as I left the pod and made my way back to the elevator. The first clock I set eyes on told me it was 9:15; the fact that no one had disturbed my sleep told me that either:
a. I was not expected to meet at the school or
b. I had just failed my first test as a chosen member of the intergalactic mission and would experience consequences for this transgression.

Instead of worrying over something that was out of my control, I pushed the button for the ground floor and ran my fingers through my hair in the hopes that I would appear marginally presentable.

"Hello, Selina," Mr. Boothe welcomed me, a hint of sarcasm in his voice as he stepped to the side to allow room for me to join the circle.
I gave a quick, false smile (no teeth showing) before sliding into place alongside Max.

"Did you want to explain your tardiness?" Mr. Boothe prodded.

Without knowing exactly what Mr. Boothe was playing at, I decided to respond in my now-characteristic straightforward and no-nonsense style.

"Sure, if you think it necessary," I snapped. "My parents were arrested last night moments after I made it home. The charges were unclear. I was brought here to headquarters—at my own request—and I spent the better part of the night researching what kind of cat I'd like to take with me on the mission as my earth artifact. Which, as it turns out, is a Devon Rex."

My words spilled out like the disclaimer at the end of an advertisement for a prescription drug. When I'd finished my diatribe, I looked at Mr. Boothe for a reaction; he gave none. Out of the corner of my eye I registered the surprised and frightened expressions on many of my peers' faces. I understood this to mean that none of them had experienced the jolting misfortune of parents stripped from their homes.

"I didn't have an alarm, and apparently I woke up late. I'm sorry if I've kept you waiting," I added when the silence stretched on.

"Apology accepted," Max proclaimed warmly, as though my confession were as scheduled as a recitation of the pledge of allegiance.

"Glad to hear it," I was quick to say. I had no interest in idle chatter or power struggles. "What did I miss?"

"Mr. Boothe was explaining to us the nature of the intergalactic mission," Clarice offered, her voice robotic. It could have been an olive branch, meant to smooth over the events of the past week—but it could have been a cool reminder of the space and distance that had been created in our once-warm friendship.

I nodded politely. I tried and failed to make eye contact with Clarice to get a sense of where she stood.

"I thanked everyone for agreeing to the mission, and I was beginning to explain the expectations and parameters," Mr. Boothe said, voice false.

Agreement? There was no choice. *Expectations?* More like r-u-l-e-s. I kept my thoughts to myself and waited for Mr. Boothe to continue.

"This is your home, moving forward. I understand you spent the night in the communal women's dormitory…you will henceforth sleep in a wing of the building designated for members of the intergalactic mission. It's important that all of you stay focused and disciplined during this time of preparation—the task before you is demanding, complex, and uncertain," Mr. Boothe explained.

"Do we all get to pick our earth artifacts, then?" Amanda asked, her golden blonde hair glittering in the artificial lighting as she leaned forward with expectation.

I bit my lower lip to keep from smiling as Mr. Boothe's smooth forehead wrinkled in irritation.

"There is no precedence for earth artifacts," he groused. "Selina's demand does not reflect past protocol."

"But you did agree to it," Chris pointed out, surprising me with this audacious claim. It seemed everyone was keen to have an earth artifact to take along with them.

Mr. Boothe's jaw clenched. His fingers curled into a fist as he shifted his weight from side to side. When he did speak, it was with resolve that surprised me.

"Yes, you can each take an earth artifact with you—as long as your item is within reason," he hurried to clarify. "Living persons and animals are *not* within reason," he warned, eyes glaring in my direction.

"One animal is more than enough," I agreed slyly.

I wasn't endearing myself to Mr. Boothe, that much was certain. I'm sure a wiser strategy would have had me winning the man's affections and earning myself favors and brownie points…but the past could not be undone, and I was not about to fold.

"Selina…the technology and expense to send life to Venus and Heidel is astronomical," Mr. Boothe began. I listened carefully to his words, but only to find my rebuttal. "It's a grievous misuse of taxpayer money and precious Organization resources to fund a cat's journey into space."

He'd obviously rehearsed the line. I'd known he would offer some resistance, and I was similarly prepared.

"Mr. Boothe, we both know that you've spent taxpayer money sending animals to these planets on exploratory missions…now, you'll be sending an animal for colonization purposes. The face of The Organization should be an individual of integrity—I can't imagine you'd be given much grace if you recanted your agreement now. If you're worried about the public response, I've thought through a few angles you can offer…" I trailed off. Both of us knew he wasn't concerned about how to spin the news to the public.

There was a stretch of silence that some might have felt was awkward. I have found victory time and time again in these moments, simply because I refuse to speak after I've said my piece.

"Who do we give our requests to?" Luke asked hesitantly into the expansive silence.

"Do you all have your artifact requests already?" Mr. Boothe asked irritably. "You should be concerned with what's to come, not what you're leaving behind," he muttered as we all nodded our heads in agreement.

It made perfect sense to me that we were all concerned with what we could take with us—if we were going to give everything over to The Organization, put it all on the line, then there should be some small concession and comfort object. After all, there was a very good chance that we'd never make it back to earth.
"Alright. Send me your request privately, and I'll get back to you on the feasibility of each request," Mr. Boothe agreed without enthusiasm. I cheered inwardly when I realized that he hadn't made any mention of my request. I was going to get my cat.

"Did I miss the mission assignments?" I asked, now focused on the next most important item.

"Not yet," Max broke in. "We asked the same question before you got here."

"The mission assignments have not been made yet," Mr. Boothe said crossly. His tone of voice made it clear that his threshold for new ideas and flexibility had been maxed.

I glanced at Max out of the corner of my eye; he met my gaze but said nothing. We were going to Venus. We'd been told that we were going to Venus. Mr. Boothe caught our gaze with a look so frosty that it cut short any ideas of protest. We'd challenged him and pushed him enough for one day…it was his pride and ego drawing the line. Another day, and he might respond differently. But Max and I were going to Venus, and that was that. I would save that fight for another day. Max seemed to have made the same decision, for he stayed quiet, too.

"But we were picked for the mission…" Clarice probed. "I thought our assignments were already chosen."

"You were selected for the mission, yes," Mr. Boothe agreed. "But there are a few diagnostic tests that must be administered before we can ascertain where you're headed."

"What kind of tests?" Luke wanted to know.

"You'll find out soon enough," Mr. Boothe told us. Then, in a rare display of empathy, he added, "I can imagine this is stressful—we're not trying to be mean. We want an honest read of your skills in different areas both to inform your designation and to gain understanding of what you'll need training in."

"How long will we be tested?" Chris asked.

"Are we being tested right now?" Marcus added.

"You are not being tested right now," Mr. Boothe answered. "Although your disposition, responses, and demeanor *are* being watched…along with your interactions with your peers."

"And how many tests will there be?" Peyton asked in earnest. It was a question they all wanted answered.

"The testing will be done in just a few days," Mr. Boothe assured them. "Try to relax—you have already been chosen. This is really the beginning of your preparations. We're partnering with you…we are not your adversary," he encouraged. His eyes lingered on me after this final proclamation. I kept eye contact—but not in a challenging way. I really wanted to believe that Mr. Boothe meant what he said.

"Mr. Boothe?" a perky young man armed with a tablet appeared and addressed the leader.

Mr. Boothe looked relieved at the man's arrival. "Yes, they're ready. You can show them to the west wing, and then take them to breakfast."

My stomach grumbled in response. *When had I last eaten?* I hadn't had a mind to eat last night after my parents had been taken…

My parents. My stomach flipped and curdled in a painful reminder of what had happened last night. I couldn't help myself, but I knew better than to take this issue public. As the rest of the "chosen ones" followed the chatty, over-caffeinated assistant down the corridor, I stepped closer to Mr. Boothe.

"Yes, Ms. Alois?" Mr. Boothe asked in a tone of voice that was both weary and suspicious.

"What happened to my parents?" I asked bluntly.

Mr. Boothe looked at me hard. He seemed to be measuring possible responses before he answered.
"The truth," I encouraged, purging my voice of all emotion.

"Your parents were executed this morning," Mr. Boothe said. There was no effort to wrap the news in comforting verbiage or consolation.

Despite myself, I choked on my astonishment. My mouth felt chalky, my fingers felt suddenly icy as a shiver of heat rushed up my spine. I'd asked for the truth, and I'd known the danger was real, and yet…executed?

"A matter I had no involvement in," Mr. Boothe added. "No matter what your opinion of me, you should know that I had no part in that decision. Unfortunately, the outcome was predetermined—the consequence for your parents' indiscretion was, and has always been, absolute."

I nodded and swallowed hard. In my astonishment, tears filled my eyes—I blinked rapidly and they rushed down my cheeks, eager to be free of their pendulous prison. I looked up at Mr. Boothe once—I wasn't keen for him to see me in such a vulnerable state, but I needed to search his eyes and know with certainty that he had told me the truth.

My parents were zealous in their conviction that life was for the living; they would not want me to dwell on their passing. If they had indeed been executed, I would need to find the strength to move forward. I could draw strength from their bravery, I could work to honor their memory, and I could fight against whatever had caused their unjust punishment…but I could not mope and give up.

I worried I might not possess this strength…it would have to be summoned from the certain, infallible, and irreparable sentence of death. This was why I looked Mr. Boothe in the eyes.

It was true. I could tell right away, but I held onto his gaze for a moment longer than I needed to just to be sure. I wouldn't punish myself with further specifics, although I was sure my mind would torture me with imagined details of their last minutes on earth later. This was my first test of resolve and discipline, one that had not been doled out by The Organization. I was determined to pass.

"Selina."

Mr. Boothe's words gave me pause and prompted me to look up into his eyes once more.

"I would be very careful of what you share regarding your parents' death," Mr. Boothe said carefully. The intensity behind his words hinted at a kindness I'd not yet experienced from him. He was trying to help me.

I nodded, then quickly wiped away my tears with the back of my hand. Jaw set and chin raised, I held myself with dignity as I thanked Mr. Boothe for his honesty and marched down the corridor to catch up with the rest of the group.

One more secret to keep. One more piece of information I had to bury deep inside myself. One more fact I had to pretend didn't exist. It was a lonely existence, and it was getting lonelier by the moment.

Your kitten.

The surprise debut of this thought startled and then warmed me. Fresh, hot tears blurred my vision, and I took quick swipes at my eyes to shove them aside.

Yes, my life was lonely. But there was hope. And there was still beauty to be seen and enjoyed. This was the truth I needed to cling to.

Embracing the Tension

By the time I caught up to the group, I'd pushed any thoughts of my parents from my mind. Someday, I was sure this would haunt me—I'd probably spend hours in a plush, oversized chair gushing tears like a running faucet while some PhD in neurological design and psychology counseled me through my adolescent trauma. It would cost a lot of money, take inordinate amounts of time, and flay my soul. But it still felt like the only thing to do, considering the circumstances.

I'd have enough other things to add into the mix, anyway. Who was I kidding? If I survived the mission ahead of me, I'd have a lot more to work through than just my parents' death. It was the price I had been told I must pay. To compartmentalize was to survive. And if I didn't survive, what honor was I showing to my parents? To adopt any weakness at this point was to cheapen their sacrifice.

"Everything okay?" Max mumbled to me as we made our way into the cafeteria. I noticed Clarice slow her steps surreptitiously; she was trying to eavesdrop without notice.

I nodded in Clarice's direction and made eye contact with Max. "Tell you later" I mouthed without making a sound. Max nodded and stayed at my side. The comfort this simple gesture offered was not to be overestimated; I found myself exceedingly grateful for his presence.

"What happened to your parents?" Clarice whispered to me. Her efforts to snoop thwarted, she had moved to plan b: the direct approach. Her words were loud enough for a few of the others to hear; I found myself with a small audience and felt my back stiffen in defense of the veiled attack.

"I don't want to talk about it," I said. My voice was short, and yet I worked to keep it from sounding mean. I didn't want to make any enemies.

"But were they really executed?" Clarice wanted to know.

Flames of anger surged in my belly; I felt my body temperature rise. A few aggressive and cutting remarks reeled through my brain—I swallowed these comebacks (some were really quite good) and told myself that the short-lived satisfaction of being nasty would not serve me in the long run.

"I don't want to talk about it," I repeated calmly. In truth, the words carried a weight that came across a little bit like a warning. Clarice didn't know how to respond, and the heavy topic intimidated the others from initiating conversation.

"Is everything okay?" the sprightly man asked in the way that people voice questions they already know the answers to.

"I think so," I said evenly. The rest of the group was quick to agree, much to the relief of the anxious assistant.

"Great," he chirped. "I wanted to bring you to the cafeteria first—after I take you to your dormitories, you can come back here for your breakfast. Food is available at all hours of the day, although the offerings change depending on the time. You'll find a wide range of options, and selections for even restricted diets." He paused here and chuckled. "Well, I guess that last part doesn't apply to your lot. If you had dietary restrictions, you wouldn't be here," he prattled on, more to himself than to the group.

"We can come here whenever we want?" Luke asked.

Selina rolled her eyes but felt some comfort in the predictability of the question. It was so like a male to wonder about the availability of food.

"Well…yes," the assistant affirmed. "But you will be busy much of the day. During your leisure time, you can come."

"Awesome," Luke announced, a genuine smile stretching across his face.

"You're asked to consume food only here," the assistant added. "No food in the dormitories." He paused here to make sure that the group understood. Heads nodded, and he went on. "Alright then, let's show you to your dormitories."

He led us down a quiet hallway to a single elevator that looked much like the one that I had used earlier. The difference was that this single elevator had mounted above it the words "West Wing." The nickel-plated lettering stood in stark contrast to the LED-light displays and marquee inscriptions that labeled most every other part of the headquarters. I wasn't sure if this carried any significance, but I noted it.

The elevator had only three levels listed: a simple 1, 2, 3 as compared to the elaborate array I had seen earlier. The assistant pushed "2."

I wondered at the significant time lapse between our departure and arrival at our destination. The labeled buttons implied only three levels, but I was sure that we traveled much further.

When the doors opened, I was intrigued to find a single bathroom, shower, and sink with mirror. Off this centrally-located space were three short corridors lined with lockers the size of those I'd seen before. The silence as we followed the assistant down one of the corridors was respectful and filled with unvoiced curiosity.

"There are three small wings here that share a single bathroom," the man explained. "The intention is to familiarize you with cramped quarters, shared living space, and also isolation. Your sleeping arrangements will likely change as The Organization experiments with mission groupings, so don't get too attached to your assigned pod."

I zoned out as he explained how the lockers and pods worked—to my understanding, it was the same as in the dormitory I'd slept in the night before. Instead, my gaze traveled to the fissured lines that crawled along the wall space of each dormitory wing: it hinted to me that a wall could be brought down.

I snapped back to attention in time to hear the initial sleeping arrangements. "In room one, we'll have the boys. In room two, the girls."

Some of the others reacted to this news; I was indifferent. I held everything loosely: my life was transient and fragile; anything could change at any moment. To hold conviction or attachment to any specific outcome was a sure set-up for disappointment or anxiety, and I wanted neither.

There was an awkward moment where we all stood surveying our new sleeping space—there were no belongings to drop off, and there was no possibility for making the space homey.

"Breakfast?" Chris offered after a moment of silence.

Murmurs of agreement led to our migration back downstairs to the cafeteria. The assistant left us as we grabbed trays and made our way to the buffet.

The heated serving dishes held all kinds of tasty dishes, all fresh and maintained at optimal serving temperature. My eyes widened in surprise as I surveyed the options: *bacon and eggs? Buttered cinnamon rolls?* The oatmeal was expected, as was the yogurt parfait and fruit platter. But some of the other selections? I'd never even had the option of trying bacon, and I wondered at its appearance on an assembly line of food prepared for individuals intended for a high-stakes intergalactic mission.

"Guess the days of strict eating and obsessive nutrition are over," Marcus practically sang. His eyes had doubled in size and he seemed to salivate in anticipation as he loaded his plate with the previously-forbidden foods.

"It does seem like a 180," Max agreed, tone suspicious.

I agreed. The Organization was investing a lot in us…it was possible that the freedom was a temporary perk, or potentially a nod to our likely-shortened life spans (who cared about cholesterol when there were only months left to live?), or…it was a test.

A test of self-control, my subconscious agreed.

I stayed quiet as some of the others piled plates high with carbohydrates and sugars, instead spooning a moderate amount of oatmeal in a bowl which I topped with blueberries and banana. Max, Chris, Clarice, and Peyton did the same.

"Are you serious?" Luke challenged. "You're going to miss out on the opportunity to try *bacon*?" he asked. "When are you ever going to get to eat this again?"

"We'll leave it to you to enjoy," Chris said congenially.

His simple rebuttal was met with incredulous scoffs and jeers from our less-nutritious counterparts, but no further pressure was applied. At no point did I envy them; even as their groans and gasps turned rapturous. There were going to be consequences for their indulgence; I knew it. It might not come immediately, and it might not be obvious. But I had no doubt that it would come.

"What do you think our first test will be?" Amanda asked in between bites.

"I think we've already had a few tests," Max mumbled in response.

Amanda stopped mid-bite. "What do you mean?" she asked, slowly swallowing her food and wiping the corners of her mouth with a napkin.

"They're always watching us," Max reminded her. "And I think they're making observations and analyzing our behavior and decisions even when we're not obviously being tested."

I'd assumed this was obvious, but the startled expressions on some of the others' faces suggested otherwise.

"On to lighter subjects," Clarice cut in. "What earth artifact are you all planning to ask for?"

I did my best to look breezy and nonchalant. "Everyone knows my request," I smiled.

"A Keurig," Peyton was the first to answer.

This drew laughter that immediately put Peyton on the defensive.

"Hey! I want good coffee," she explained. "And if we're caught in a bad situation, I want to access caffeine for that edge. You know you're hoping I'm assigned to your mission just so you can have coffee, too," she joked.

"X-Box," Marcus answered next. "For the downtime where there's nothing to do. It could get really boring."

"Heated sleeping pad," Amanda offered. "If I'm sent to Heidel, it'll be freezing. I don't want to count on the technology they're equipping us with…I want the comfort of my own bed."

"I want a printed copy of my favorite picture of my family," Chris answered, surprising me with his sentimentality. "In case we lose access to wireless content or technology, I want to see the people I love most."

"That's really sweet," Amanda offered, her tone suggesting guilt at her more superficial request.

"Mine's not sweet. I want to take mulberry silkworm Bombyx mori boxers…aka the most luxurious and breathable underwear of all time," Luke told us shamelessly.

We all burst into laughter, and Luke shrugged his shoulders. "Hey, who knows what discomfort space will bring? I want to wear silky underwear when it happens."

"I'm going to ask for a bag of sand," Max told them when the laughter had died. "Just as a reminder of home. A symbol of home to hold onto while we orbit through outer space."

I was a little bit surprised…both Max and Chris picked items of little value but full of emotional significance. The practical part of me wanted to challenge them to ask for something greater, but who was I to judge their ask?

"What about you, Clarice?" Peyton asked. "What are you going to ask for?"

"A sapphire necklace," she answered dreamily. "I have the piece picked out. Who knows if there are jewels where we're going? I want to take something beautiful with me…and if we do end up back at home, I can sell it and buy something useful."

"Ooooh, can we see a picture?" Peyton asked. "Oh my gosh—can you even imagine how glamorous you're going to look when we are interviewed by the press? We'll all be in The Organization's space suits, and Clarice will have a sapphire necklace around her neck. I love it."

I laughed aloud at the image, as did the others.

"Hey, hey—you're forgetting that I'll also be glamorous in my mulberry silk boxers," Luke challenged playfully.

This drew even greater laughs.

"Are you planning to let the press know?" Max teased.

"I'm planning to give them a fashion show!" Luke joked. "If the people want an inside scoop, they'll get one!"

"Ohhhhh….no thank you," Amanda laughed, her face twisting in mock disgust as she shook her head.

"This is all assuming we get our asks approved," Clarice pointed out, suddenly serious.

"Do you think they'd say no to any of our requests?" Marcus questioned.

"If they agreed to Selina's request to take a cat, I can't see how they can say no to the rest of us," Peyton said. "No offense, Selina."

"None taken," I assured her. "I agree. My ask is the biggest."

Clarice was poised to comment when the assistant returned, cheeks flushed as he hurried up to our table.

"Finish your breakfast, please." His words were polite but his tone was slightly tense. "It's time for your first test."

Living the Assessment

It was ironic, in so many ways. Being spared all the trivial assessments of adolescence only to face the most significant and trying tests of all. I was sure The Organization would put a different spin on it, but I saw it for what it was. I was also fairly confident that whatever lay ahead was *not* the first test…far from it.

I kept my thoughts to myself as we walked down the corridor. Idle chatter had come to an end: even Clarice and Peyton were quiet as we were led to our "first" trial. On a subconscious level, I think we all internalized and took our cues from the assistant—and his jitters and agitations did little to ease nerves.

They can't hurt you. This is meant to prepare you. Your fear is irrational.

The governor inside my head had become more active in its counsel—I wasn't sure if this was in response to the circumstances or if I was just more attuned to my subconscious. Every time the voice "spoke," it felt like a flashlight flicked on in my soul. The truth of the words was immutable, and the acceptance of the words felt like seeds planted in fertile soil. In a world of plan As and plan Bs and plan Cs, I had made the decision to put all of my eggs in one basket.

I walked into the room quietly, like all my peers, but without the fear I smelled on their tentative frames.

Mr. Boothe was waiting in the center of a domed amphitheater, legs hip-width distance and hands clasped below his belly button in a classic power stance. He was flanked by members of The Organization. But the real spotlight-stealer was the sea of monochromatic white light: from the domed ceiling to the tile flooring to the machinery stationed in the center of the room—all white.

"What is this place?" Amanda asked nervously under her breath.

"Welcome to the amphitheater," Mr. Boothe announced. The acoustics of the place amplified his voice. "I hope you found breakfast satisfactory."

The way he said it confirmed my earlier suspicion that the offerings had been intentionally selected to test our discipline.

"Are we about to throw it up?" Marcus asked, voice light but tinged with anxiety.

"I wouldn't have the slightest idea," Mr. Boothe laughed softly. "I hope not."

He paused for a moment and looked to his colleagues on either side. If I hadn't known better, I would have thought he was intentionally building in a pause to elevate the level of suspense.

"Your days leading to the mission launch will include some tests meant to ascertain your readiness and aptitude, which will help The Organization to determine your role in the mission. You will also be briefed on the conditions and suspected challenges for both Venus and Heidel. Your instructors are the brilliant men and women you see beside me," Mr. Boothe carried on. "You will get to know them intimately over time."

Apparently finished with his address, Mr. Boothe nodded to a woman in a stiff, starched lab coat. She stepped forward obediently and spoke deliberately to their group in what I supposed was a well-rehearsed speech.

"Your first test is a simulation."

My heart began to race, and I missed her next sentence as I opted instead to take a deep breath in and a deep breath out.

This is for your benefit. You are not in danger. This is meant to help you.

Properly recalibrated, I snapped back to attention in time to hear the woman continue.

"We'd like to assess your fortitude and aptitude in a recovery situation. The test itself is simple." She swiped her index finger across the tablet held in her left hand and a charcoal-black sky dotted with stars suddenly shone above us. In the center of the domed area was the moon: I recognized the pale-yellow glow and ash-gray crevices like the back of my hand. The space station stood proudly amidst a multitude of rectangular prisms I knew to be civilian housing.

"You should recognize the moon," the woman went on. She paused only long enough to survey the ripple of nods. "Most of the energy used on the moon comes from this generator." The woman tapped her finger once more on the tablet, and a chrome building lit up.

"In this simulation, an asteroid has punctured the generator. It must be sealed using this electron tarp. The current temperature on the moon is -200° F. Energy is leaking at the standard thin-oxide gate tunneling rate; leakage will increase by 10x for every 3 electrons without a shell. Which means," she surmised with a quick inhale, "that the entire population will be without power and life-sustaining energy in—"

"Three minutes," Chris interjected.

"Yes," the woman agreed, rewarding Chris with a curt nod.

Chris straightened a bit, and I guessed he felt more powerful and in control now that he'd been able to follow the simulation preliminaries. Some of the others looked intimidated: they hadn't been able to calculate the complex calculus equation in their head. I was in their company, but I didn't share in their angst.

"I want Chris on my team," Luke joked.
"There will not be teams," the woman said seriously. "This is a solo assessment. Your entry point into the atmosphere will be random, as will be the state of your protective clothing and equipment. The Organization's instructions are to preserve the generator at all costs."

"Now that you've heard the mission, who wants to go first?" Mr. Boothe asked matter-of-factly when the woman had finished speaking.

Without a word, my peers all turned and looked at me. My body tensed a bit but I said nothing. Luckily, I didn't have to.

"No, it won't be Selina leading the charge this time," Mr. Boothe said testily. "Who's going to step up?"

The silence stretched on. I glanced at the others, who had all mastered the art of eye-aversion in an attempt to buy time.

"Chris, you seemed confident in your mathematic analysis," Mr. Boothe pointed out. "Why don't you lead?"

All eyes turned to Chris, who had suddenly turned the color of buttered popcorn. He looked altogether unwell as he nodded in resignation and took a reluctant step forward.

"You haven't lost yet," Marcus joked. "Come on, Levenson—you've never been intimidated before. It's not as though you're battling a space dragon."

Chris cast a withering gaze at Marcus, but the comment seemed to lighten the mood. I'd wondered if Marcus' snide remark would put him on the spot instead, but Mr. Boothe seemed to observe the exchange without judgment.

"You will feel the effects of the elements in the simulation, although it will not be real or permanent," the woman explained as her fingers danced across the tablet at rapid speed to prepare the simulation.

"So...don't worry if we die in the simulation—we'll feel pain but won't actually die?" Max clarified with just a hint of sarcasm in his voice.

"Precisely," the woman agreed good-naturedly.

My heart thumped in my chest. I practiced the yoga breaths. This was meant to help me. I couldn't actually be hurt by the simulation. I had been picked for the mission because I was different; I had the skills to best situations that others might flounder in.

"Are you ready?" the woman asked.

Chris shrugged. "I guess?" He looked like a ghost and his knees shook like leaves in the fall breeze.

Not a second later, Chris was suspended in the atmosphere.

"Ohmygosh," Peyton couldn't help but gasp as her hand flew to cover her mouth.

Behind Chris, red digital numerals appeared. 3:00. And then immediately began counting down.

2:59.

2:58.

Chris looked behind him to the countdown clock and seemed to panic before hurrying into action.

The tarp was snagged on a metallic hinge that held together two corners of the space headquarters. It rippled in the wind like a flag waved by a picador before a raging bull. This also happened to be in the opposite direction of the leaking generator.

My gaze was transfixed on the gaping hole that spewed noxious gas; a trail of sparks and a dusty white cloud of debris poured out into the atmosphere where the asteroid had collided with the metal.

The silence was deafening. I wondered if the others held their breath like me. I watched Chris closely as he floundered in the atmosphere, legs kicking and arms flailing as he worked hard to push himself forward in zero gravity.

2:17.

2:16.

"He hasn't even made it to the tarp yet," Peyton said flaccidly.

No one answered.

After what seemed to take incredible effort, Chris made it to the tarp with 37 seconds to spare. Clearly exhausted, he held tightly to the edge of the tarp for a precious five seconds before yanking it free and continuing his desperate breaststroke to the generator. When time expired, he had not come close to accomplishing his objective.

Chris reappeared in our midst suddenly. Freed from the encumbering space gear, he doubled over with his hands on his knees, breathing deeply as drips of sweat fell from his cheeks and splashed onto the tile flooring below.

For a moment, there was stunned silence.

"It was that hard, huh?" Luke said dumbly.

Chris didn't even look at him—the struggle to regain even breathing seemed to be taking most of his energy.

"Who's next?" Mr. Boothe asked, discouraging discussion.

"I'll try," Marcus offered, perhaps emboldened by Chris's failure.

Again, the group watched with hawk-like focus as Marcus tried to push himself through space towards the tarp. His strategy seemed similar to Chris's, and his progress was nearly the same. Another fail.

One by one, each member of the group attempted the task—and each one fell short of task completion.

Peyton tried to somersault her way to the tarp but ended up propelling herself farther away from the headquarters—she didn't even make it to the tarp before the time expired.

Amanda hesitated too long—her attempt was the most painful to watch. She was so obviously uncertain of what to do that she defaulted to what she had seen Chris and Marcus do—but the fact that she was so much smaller and weaker meant she didn't come close to what they had been able to achieve.

Clarice seemed to take inspiration from Peyton's attempt: she corkscrewed her body in overhead tumbles that got her to the tarp in the quickest time…but then she was unable to move in the same way to the affected generator and quickly ran out of time.

No one spoke during or in between attempts. The timing in between was limited; I was certain this was intentional. We weren't learning much from the failures of our peers, that much was apparent.

Luke wasted too much time exploring the contents of his space suit—he seemed to believe the solution to the problem would be conveniently tucked inside the uniform that suddenly materialized when the simulation began. He was wrong, but his thinking ignited an idea.

My mind worked rapidly as I watched Max attempt the now-familiar task. At this point in the simulations, people were trying bizarre things…it was clear that extreme effort was not passing muster. Max adopted the somersault method of travel, but to the generator—not the tarp. I worked to try to guess at his logic for doing so but couldn't think of anything…and Max didn't seem to know what to do next, either—his time expired with him standing over the burnt-metal chasm. Defeated, just like the others.

"The generator is hot, but the gas isn't," Max muttered in a hurry under his breath. His words were for my ears only, and my pulse quickened as I tried to work out what he was telling me.

"You could channel the energy from that stream," was all Max was able to add before Mr. Boothe looked intentionally in my direction.

"Alright, Alois—here goes the last attempt."

Immediately, I was sailing in space. Without anything to anchor me in one place, I could feel myself drifting. I knew what I planned to do, and I didn't hesitate.

Breathe. You need to breathe.

I utilized a full ten seconds on breathing deeply. I didn't move anywhere; I didn't do a thing. I countered my racing heart with deep breaths that normalized my breathing. It wasn't a waste of time—it was the centerpiece of my strategy,

When I was confident in the amount of oxygen trapped inside my lungs, I did the unthinkable—I ripped my helmet off.

Immediately, the atmosphere struck me. My skin felt dry and parched and hot and I ignored it. With terrific effort, I threw my helmet away from my body as though I were an Olympic shot-putter.

Newton's Third Law: to every action, there is an equal and opposite reaction.

My body went flying in the opposite direction of the helmet—I made it to the tarp in record speed. I glanced at the clock. 2:02. I'd completed the first part in 58 seconds.

With the freed tarp in hand, I felt my way to the corner of the building and pinned either side of the roof with my space boots.

1:47.

At this point, I could definitely feel the effects of lack of oxygen. I was light-headed, nauseous, and the pressure bearing down on my brain was nearly unbearable. I'd expected that, but still felt unprepared for the strength of the effects.

Like a fisherman casting out a line, I pinched one corner of the massive tarp and launched the other end out and into the atmosphere. My boots groveled and groaned against the metal sides but held my body in place.

1:22.

My body felt weak and I wanted so badly to draw a deep and expansive breath…but to do so would have ushered in certain death. There was no oxygen in this atmosphere.

I don't know that I cared about my successful completion of the task, but I was aware when the tarp hit the stream current Max had referenced and I released my hold of the building.

The tarp was carried by the stream towards the generator, and my body went with it. When I was close to the generator, I took a dive—and successfully grabbed hold of the singed metal. It burned through my glove but gave me enough time to press the tarp down on top of the fissure.

0:14.

It was the last thing I saw before I was pulled from the simulation.

Welcome to the New Reality

"I can't believe you did it," Peyton gasped. Her words were startlingly clear; in space my senses had felt fuzzy towards the end.

"Nice job, Alois," Max whispered. There was pride in his voice that caught me by surprise...I would need to unpack that later.

For the moment, I tried to wrap my brain around what had just taken place.

"You accomplished the mission," Mr. Boothe offered his canned congratulations. I looked for signs of surprise but couldn't read him.

"And would have died in the next ten seconds," I laughed wryly.

"Your mission wasn't to survive," Mr. Boothe remarked baldly.

Peyton and Amanda gasped, but Mr. Boothe's words didn't faze me. He wasn't being cruel; he was being real.

I didn't know what to say, but everyone seemed to expect a response. Yes, I had completed the mission. Yes, I had survived—but only because I'd been pulled out of the mission. I was bold in ripping off my helmet because I knew—well, I'd guessed—that I could hold my breath for three minutes. There wasn't any permanent risk...to die would be to leave the simulation.

"Are we going to debrief, or what happens next?" Clarice asked, voice testy. She was annoyed that I'd mastered the simulation when she hadn't.

"We don't have to," Mr. Boothe answered carefully. "Would you like to?"

"Isn't that the point?" she snapped. "What is this, otherwise? Are we building morale in all these failed attempts? Or are we actually supposed to learn something from this?"

Mr. Boothe didn't answer this question. I was sure Clarice's response would be recorded and used to inform the ultimate mission assignments.

A man stepped up to Mr. Boothe's side. "Selina, maybe we should start with your response to the simulation. Do you want to explain your logic?" the man asked.

I hesitated. How much of my strategy did I know? How much did I want to give away? I was still trying to work out what would be wise to divulge and what I would be wise to keep to myself. Mr. Boothe read my hesitation and misappropriated it.

"This is Mr. Ague. He's a member of the Oversight Committee responsible for preparing you for the upcoming mission. He has a Ph.D. in Astrophysics and a Masters in Propulsion and Aerospace Structures," Mr. Boothe explained. The man's qualifications were the least of my concerns, but I nodded appreciatively and took the extra time to think through my response.

I could start with the easy part. "Newton's Third Law: to every action, there is an equal and opposite reaction. I knew that I needed a force more powerful than what I could create through kicking my arms and legs—if Chris couldn't make it happen, I certainly couldn't. Since the simulation was only three minutes long, I guessed I might be able to last without breathing…and I hoped that the helmet would not be too difficult to take off," I answered.

"It was an advantage of going last and having the opportunity to watch the rest of the group," I added modestly. The last thing I wanted to do was put a target on my back. I had already set myself apart in more than one way…I didn't want to widen the chasm.

"Very modest of you," Mr. Boothe was quick to reply. He couldn't help himself—he just had to insert his two cents. "And the manipulation of the jet stream?"

I faltered for just a moment. Mr. Boothe knew the answer but was waiting to see if I'd admit it to the group. To look at Max to try to discern his thoughts would be as good as giving things away, and yet I worried that my answer might implicate him as well. I was being forced to play my hand too early.

"Instinct," I lied evenly.

Mr. Boothe and Max knew my lie, but I doubted anyone else did. Mr. Boothe didn't say a word—his goal wasn't to expose me. He was just carefully gathering information like I'd suspected.

"Pretty strong instincts," Mr. Boothe praised me. His words were a veiled condemnation that I chose to ignore.

"Indeed," Mr. Ague agreed. "The jet propulsion stream was emitting noxious gas at a rate of..."

I zoned out as Mr. Ague explained the science behind my success. Was Clarice satisfied by the lengthy, highfalutin explanation? I had no idea. *I* wasn't—I knew that the chances of that information helping in a future intergalactic situation were slim to none. Instead, I wondered at Max's thoughts on the situation and at the notes that were taken down as a result of our actions.

"...and that's why Selina was successful," Mr. Ague finished in time for me to smile my acknowledgement.

"Are we going to try again?" Chris wanted to know. "To try and master the simulation?"

Mr. Ague shook his head and looked to Mr. Boothe for confirmation. "None of the tests will be repeated—the point is to try to generate excellent instincts as opposed to fluency and mastery of a single skill. The simulations are meant to be random."

"Will our order of performance be randomized in the future?" Peyton asked, and I watched Clarice nod her head in fervent agreement.

"Yes—there is a definite advantage to going last in the simulation. You get to take inventory of all the responses and improve your strategy," Clarice pointed out.

I was defensive even though I knew she was right. What did it matter? In theory, we were all a team. So why did our group already feel more fractured than a kaleidoscope?

"Every simulation will be different," Mr. Ague answered carefully, again glancing at Mr. Boothe to make sure he was not overstepping his bounds.

"That's the only test for the day," Mr. Boothe interrupted, ending any further dialogue. "Ms. Chang will be briefing you on breathing techniques at 2 PM. Please report to the cafeteria at that time—you'll be escorted to the appropriate classroom from there. In the meantime, please enjoy your new accommodations. Headquarters is yours to explore."

Our dismissal was implied, and we obediently marched out of the simulation room like third graders at a prep school. Outside of the room, everyone seemed to loosen up.

"Round two of snacks?" Luke joked.

"Luke, you're going to be obese by the time we finish training," Amanda criticized, the disdain in her voice evident.

"Might as well go out on top," he was quick to retort. "Even if we survive the mission, you know we're not going to be eating like this in space."

"Do we have any idea how long we'll be training before our mission?" Clarice asked. "They haven't said anything, have they?"

Heads shook silently; no one said a word. We didn't seem to know much of anything—I suspected this was less because The Organization wanted to keep us in the dark and more because they themselves were trying to work those details out.

"We're pretty much at their disposal," Marcus complained. "Whatever's most convenient for the Organization, goes."

"Did you expect it to be different?" Max wanted to know. "What did you think would happen?"

"I don't know—I guess I just thought it would be more straightforward. Like, we would know what training we would have and when we would be expected to do certain things," Marcus explained.

"Like class, but on steroids," Luke agreed. "With higher standards."

"We still don't even know why we were chosen," Amanda complained. "What did we have that set us apart from everyone else?"

"If you want to know, why don't you ask?" I finally spoke up. Eyes turned to stare at me. I hadn't even intended to, and I'd called attention to myself once again.

"Alright, Ms. Confident," Clarice began testily, "it's not always that easy. Some of us have reputations to protect."

"I have a reputation to protect," I couldn't help but snap. I knew I was being goaded into confrontation, and I knew it would be wisest to resist being drawn into any altercations, but I couldn't resist.

Clarice raised her eyebrows and cast a sideways smirk at Peyton and Amanda that I was intended to see. My jaw clenched and I felt the air in my lungs constrict as my muscles tightened in defense. And then, a hand on the small of my back.

Max.

"Selina and I are going to compose a formal proposal for our earth artifacts," Max announced evenly, gently nudging me forward and down the hallway. "We'll catch up with you this afternoon for the breathing exercises."

"What, are you guys like an official couple now?" Luke wanted to know.

"No," I snapped defensively at the same time my cheeks turned cran-apple red.

"Would it matter if we were?" Max asked coolly. I looked at him in surprise—what was he thinking?! And how on earth did he stay so calm all the time? I couldn't decide if I was irritated or impressed.

There was a brief stretch of silence.

"If it doesn't matter, then why are we talking about it? We have enough stress as it is," Max reasoned. He turned to walk away when Clarice spoke up.

"It does matter," she decided. "If you two are a couple, then that makes you an alliance. And that puts the rest of us at a disadvantage."

There were nods of agreement from the others.

"An *alliance*? Aren't we all on the same team? Since when are we plotting against each other?" I challenged.

"We don't know what to expect," Clarice clarified.

It probably wasn't intentional, but she took a confrontational step forward, closing the distance between us. Had we ever been best friends? Last week's truth felt like a dream of eons past.

"It just changes things if you two are helping each other, instead of everyone," Marcus added. "Are you looking out for all of us, or trying to help each other?"

"Of course we're trying to help everyone!" I gushed. I looked to Max to back me up, but he seemed content to stand back and take it all in.

"We're not even dating!" I added, my voice growing higher by the moment.

"So why sneak off just the two of you?" Clarice asked.

"We're not sneaking off," I growled.

"Can we come with you, then?" Marcus asked, sharing a glance with Clarice.

"Only if you're going to help *everyone*," I mocked. My body was trembling; I was more upset than I'd even realized.

"We're going to go," Max said evenly, taking gentle hold of my elbow and leading me away.

One thousand angry retorts and revengeful actions coursed through my mind, but I let Max lead me away. He didn't say anything to me until we were in the elevator traveling up to the third level.

"You really let them get to you," he observed. There wasn't judgment in his tone, and I felt my shoulders relax.

"I don't know what happened to Clarice," I began, the words rolling out of my mouth like oiled marbles. "We used to be friends. I thought I could trust her."

The elevator sang its now-familiar note indicating we'd arrived at the higher floor. I hadn't even looked to see where Max was leading us, so implicit was my trust in him. I lifted my head now to see the common area I'd found haven in the night before when I'd spent the better part of the night researching cat breeds.

"Wow," Max expressed his appreciation. "This is a really cool space."

"Yeah," I agreed half-heartedly, exhaling hot air.

"Which one is your favorite?" Max asked, turning to face me.

Caught off-guard, I surveyed the room once more. Last night, I'd been looking for a place to research...I hadn't considered which room was most appealing. Now, I found myself drawn to the forest-like enclosure outfitted with soft, kelly-green faux grass and wicker birdcages fitted with plush pillows. Max followed my gaze.

"I like that one, too," he agreed good-naturedly before taking steps in that direction.

The room was empty, and I wasted no time settling in on the cushion. Legs tucked up and to the side, my body seemed to melt into the curved back of the wooden cage like melted wax.

"Better?" Max asked. He didn't look directly at me, but I could tell he was taking it all in with an uncanny ability to process what I was feeling.

I nodded and laid my head to rest on the side of the cage. Somehow, sitting in the bird cage felt like protection from the outside world. The wicker branches were hardly a hardy barrier, but they were enough to bring my heart rate back to normal. That, and probably the fact that Max was sitting near me as sentry.

"What is happening?" I wondered aloud. I didn't expect an answer, and Max seemed to sense that. He remained quiet, his gaze on his feet.

"Too many changes, too fast," I mused a moment later. I was processing my thoughts in real-time, and Max's presence and supportive silence offered a platform for me to do that.

My thoughts jumped from images of my parents to taking the test on stage to the simulation had just taken place. My behavior was aberrant and I didn't know myself and I didn't know anything about my future and everything that I had known as an absolute truth had just been taken from me.

I was questioning the basic tenets of my LIFE and my brain was overwhelmed by all the decisions it was being asked to make. I wasn't allowed to assume anything anymore; one false move could end in disaster. I didn't have a blueprint for this new life.

"Thank you for coming with me," I spoke out after some time had passed. I wasn't sure how much; but my thoughts had run a few laps around my head and had warmed up enough to know that I was grateful for Max. So grateful.

"Of course," Max answered, as if his decision was, in fact, obvious. The truth was, it wasn't. He was gracious to come with me, and generous to put himself in a position to lose with very little to gain. It didn't make sense to me at all, but I was afraid to question it too much. I might not have been thinking too clearly, but I knew well enough not to point out to Max all the reasons why I should be abandoned.

"What time is it?" I asked suddenly. I didn't want to miss the breathing class—even though I wasn't exactly sure what I would be taught—and I didn't have any idea how long we'd been lounging.

"12:45."

"We have time," I breathed my relief.

"Plenty of time," Max agreed. "You're under a lot of pressure," he added a moment later. "It would be little bit incredible if you weren't feeling stressed. Give yourself some grace."

"You're under the same pressure!" I protested. "We're facing the same circumstances, Max—there's no reason for you to be so insanely at ease."

"I'm not relaxed," Max argued good-naturedly. "You just think I am."

"I'm not sure that's any better," I commented wryly. "That just makes me look like a hysterical teenager."

"You're NOT a hysterical teenager," Max affirmed me. "You're a high school junior who was singled out for a historic and risky mission that may well take your life, put on display for the entire student body to see, challenged and tested in front of a nation expecting a performance, isolated from peers…and who just witnessed the capture of her parents for execution." The last words were spoken gently, like a handler bringing fresh meat to an emaciated lion.

It felt better to protest and fight the truth than it did to agree with the chaotic summation of my present circumstances. I swallowed the bubble of grief that rose and fell in my throat and waited a full minute before responding.

"Why me?" I asked quietly.

There was no answer. Of course there was no answer. Was there *anyone* who had the answer? I didn't believe so.

"I'm here," Max told me softly. "I'll be here."

There was something in the unassuming fortitude of his words that felt like a crystal tower of strength, a spiral staircase circling up to freedom. I knew I could trust Max; I had tested his character and commitment a dozen times already without intending to. His words gave me strength to fight and push forward and soldier on at the same time they offered permission to be raw and vulnerable.

"I don't know why you're being so nice to me, but I don't care," I answered. My words were childish and immature—I was able to own that truth.

"You have enough questions to work through," Max laughed. "And me, too—despite what you might believe. You're good for me, Alois,"

I glanced up at him in surprise—that Max was a good influence on me was unquestionable….but *me*, a positive influence on *him*? It caught me off guard.

"It's true," Max confirmed, holding his right palm up as though making a solemn promise.

I gave him an expression that properly captured my doubt, then hugged my knees close into my chest. "We have enough time—I want to go find Mr. Boothe," I told Max with newfound determination.

Max didn't seem surprised; his eyes seemed to sparkle with laughter that never came.

"Can I ask what we're going to inquire about?" he asked.

"I have a lot of questions that need answers," I thought aloud. "And unlike the rest of the group, I intend to ask the difficult questions."

One supportive nod later, and I barreled down the hallway. I had no idea where Mr. Boothe's office would be…instead, I invited intuition to be my guide.

In the elevator, I was met with a menu of cryptic acronyms: CRF, LYH, MHA, and HQ* were the ones that initially caught my attention. Without much deliberation, I punched the HQ* button and waited for the denial I was sure would come—some automated voice assuring me that clearance to that level was far beyond my privileges.

It never came.

Instead, I felt the floor beneath me whisk upwards in obedient motion. I looked to Max with raised eyebrows, and he smirked.

"Didn't think that would happen?" he laughed. "Headquarters, but special?" he continued, guessing at my logic in selecting HQ*.

"Pretty much," I agreed. "But I'm not foolish enough to believe that it will take us straight to Mr. Boothe. We're going to have to find some secret path to him."

We were in the elevator longer than we'd ever been before, which told me that we escalated more than a few levels.

When the doors did part, it was to reveal more of the pearl-white marbled flooring and Corinthian columns meant solely for decoration and not function. I didn't see any offices at first, but soon became aware of small divots in the stone wall that I assumed led to these formal meeting places.

Max followed me without saying a word. I valued his companionship more than I knew how to express—his presence offered a solidarity and quiet confidence that I badly needed. He offered no suggestions; he imposed no judgment.

Where is he? My subconscious framed the question without my knowing exactly who I was hoping would answer the question. Then, a moment later, *Where do I go?* I supposed that was a better question to ask, assuming that I would receive a response. Maybe I wasn't meant to intercept Mr. Boothe right away—maybe there was some other, better divine appointment to be made.

There wasn't a revelatory firework that exploded in my brain, nor did James Earl Jones' voice direct my next steps. But I did feel a tug in a certain direction: my body veered right every time it was met with a divergent path.

"You following your instinct, or is this an intentional effort to make sure we can retrace our steps?" Max asked once.

"Instinct," I explained without any further elaboration. I was a bloodhound on the hunt; I could tell that I was closing in on something important if only by the increasing tempo of my heartbeat. Another five minutes, and we were stymied by a solid wall of marble and a bathroom off to the side.

But yet...I still had a hunch I was close to something. I scrutinized the marble for any fissures or skewed veins—anything that might indicate a passage to another room or corridor. Nothing.

My eyes traveled to the bathroom, marked with the universal white figure on blue background indicating it was a restroom for males only. *Even the rich and powerful cannot deny needs of the flesh*, I thought wryly. And then...

"Did you see any restrooms on the way in?" I asked Max, processing my thoughts aloud.

"None," Max verified.

I looked over at him; his gaze seemed to throw weight behind my present musings. It was a strange place to have a bathroom—there hadn't been any offices or pathways in the last stretch we'd traversed, and we were standing before what was meant to look like a dead end. Who exactly would use this restroom?

"Want me to go in first?" Max asked.

I nodded. "See if there's anyone in there."

Without any dramatic flair, Max nudged the door open with his right shoulder and stepped inside. My eyes searched the small window of space visible over Max's shoulder. I didn't doubt that Max would alert me right away if it was safe...I was just that impatient.

"No one that I can see," Max announced a moment later, popping his head out and then holding the door open for me to walk in. "And I didn't investigate anything yet," he assured me with a knowing smile.

Breezing past him, I was at first disappointed to take in what seemed to be a very kosher male restroom. The only unusual aspect was the fact that the urinals and stalls came first; the sinks were at the back end of the restroom.

"That's weird, right?" I asked Max. "To put the sinks far from the door?" I clarified in case my line of thinking was unclear.

"I haven't been in a bathroom like it before," Max agreed. "But then—the only bathroom I've been in since coming to headquarters is the unisex stall by the pods."

I didn't wait for Max to finish his thought…as he spoke, I inched closer to the nickel-plated fixtures and window-sized mirror. Two sinks, one mirror, and one stainless steel ledge protruding conspicuously from the wall in between the two sinks.

I looked at Max again—he was intuitive enough to nod his agreement without my needing to put words behind my line of thinking. He stepped up to the ledge and applied increasing pressure. Nothing happened, but I knew what he was getting at and I had the same hunch.

I walked up to the sinks and tried the handles on both faucets. Water gushed out with alarming strength, splashing the mirror and spilling over the sides of the sink to form puddles on the floor.

The sinks were operational, but obviously not used—there weren't any preexisting puddles or water marks on the mirror.

The mirror.

My eyes scoured the reflective rectangular prism before me with new vision. It was the entry-point to a hidden space; I knew it.

"The mirror. It's hiding something," I told Max, my excitement barring my ability to string together an articulate thought. "It's like a door or something," I tried again, waving my hands in gestures that did nothing to support my case.

"If it's a door, then knock," Max suggested squarely.

I stared at him, stunned by the simple brilliance of his suggestion. With fingers shaking, I stepped up to the mirror and rapped twice on the polished aluminum. Like a small child waiting on dessert, I snuck furtive glances in Max's direction…just to see what he thought.

His face was as unreadable as the marble wall we'd encountered earlier, but he caught my gaze and offered an encouraging smile. I caught my reflection in the mirror and noticed the high color in my cheeks, the dilation of my pupils that spoke to my present excitement. And then, the mirror fell.

Verdant Vault

I jumped back in fear as the mirror simply disappeared. As tangible as the mirror had been—my knuckles were rosy-red from tapping on the glass—it was suddenly gone. No shattered glass, no evident technological trick—just gone.

In its place, bright light shone through. Blinding white light that made it impossible to discern what lay on the other side. Without thinking, I held my hand out—Max's much-larger hand encapsulated my own and gave me a gentle squeeze.

"Do you want me to go first?" he asked.

"No," I whispered as I stepped up on the ledge. Still grasping Max's right hand, I lifted my left leg up and through the gulf.

Once inside, I was awed by the verdant beauty surrounding me; lush greenery and natural elements that were altogether otherworldly. Thick blades of grass long as the fingertips of a master pianist, ferns with velvet edges, dew-kissed spiderwebs spun like tea doilies perched between moist willow trees. A pond with water a celeste blue that sparkled with the luster of a thousand diamonds; prisms of white light dancing on the surface.

Max stepped through and stood by my side, presumably also awed into silence. There was something reverent about the room: I slipped out of my slippers and took a step forward barefoot. My body seemed to melt as muscles I didn't know were tense relaxed. The supple blades of grass tickled my toes and the soft soil sank gently under my weight. My eyes closed to bask in the warmth of the light that seemed to draw me in with a warm embrace.
The pleasure to be had in creation is really something divine; an experience I'd never truly had. In my technologically-oriented world protected from all unpredictability, nature did not have positive value. I knew the scene was artificially created even as I reveled in its stunning tranquility.

Without consciously determining to do so, I found myself on the edge of the pond. I peered down, and the utopian façade was shattered. The crystalline water should have reflected my own image back to me…but what I gazed down upon was a comprehensive network of surveillance footage of all corners of the headquarters.

The cafeteria. The common rooms. The dormitories. Offices I'd not yet seen. An exercise room. Classrooms. One classroom that had students trickling in.

"Max!" I suddenly gasped. I turned to find he was already standing at my side,

"What time is it?" I asked, knowing full well that neither of us had any way of tracking the time.

"We need to go," he agreed. "But let's make sure we know what we're coming back to," he added.

I nodded, grateful for the instinctual connection that Max and I shared. There was no question of whether or not we'd come back to this space…it was a matter of when we'd have the opportunity.

Together, we circled the room. In addition to the surveillance footage reflected from the pond, we found a command center of sorts: a touch-screen that covered a space six feet wide and four feet tall populated with dozens of programs that meant nothing to me.

"I'm not sure our luck will extend to allowing us access to these programs," Max surmised.

I agreed. I'd been shocked by the lack of barrier so far…I wasn't sure if I should be concerned that we were being set up.
And yet…we lived in a society trained how to think and behave by a demanding culture. A culture that had tricked its people into believing they operated out of free will, when really they were compliant minions too fearful to take a stand on anything. Fear was a powerful motivator and a belligerent taskmaster. It was hard to conceive of an individual who would dare to enter a space that he or she hadn't been previously authorized to visit.

"We're going to be late," I worried, thinking back to the footage I'd laid eyes on mere minutes before.

"Good thing the path out of here will be easy to follow," Max said with a wink.

The trip back always seems to take longer than the initial trek, and this experience was no different. I fought the urge to sprint down the hallways and instead focused on trying to keep up with Max's long-legged stride.

Left, left, left. Left. A painful wait for the elevator (I was sure someone would spot us in surveillance footage I knew was being shot in more spaces than the one we'd discovered). A slow descent.

When the elevator doors parted, we were greeted by a large digital clock hanging on the wall of the cafeteria.

1:59.

I didn't look at Max as we walked out of the elevator and into the cafeteria right as the digits announced the beginning of the 2 PM hour. My heart was beating out of my chest, but no one else knew that as we walked up to the group.

"Cutting it a little close, don't you think?" Clarice asked pointedly.

"We're here," Max answered peaceably, knowing I could not be trusted to do the same.

"We were waiting for you," Chris added, a subtle rebuke that stung. Chris was the type to avoid drama and confrontation—for him to say something meant that he was pretty worked up.

"I'm sorry you were waiting," I apologized honestly.

"We couldn't go to the classroom until you arrived," Chris explained.

"Punctuality is important," Clarice spoke up, unwilling to let the point go. "If this were an actual mission…"

"Luckily, it's not," a woman spoke out, bringing all conversation to a close.

Eyes turned to take in Ms. Chang, a slight Chinese woman with jet-black hair styled in a pixie cut. I was immediately captivated by her nutmeg brown eyes shaped like teardrops and silently thanked her for her kindness in ending the argument.

"My name is Ms. Chang." For her marginal stature, she had a powerful voice that rang clear as a bell. "You won't take many classes with me, but the few times we do meet I will review information that I believe you will find very worthwhile."

We all stood in respectful silence, waiting to hear how Ms. Chang wanted us to proceed. Now relieved of the fear of being late or being discovered, I was able to wonder what it was exactly that we would learn from Ms. Chang: breathing techniques was not a topic I'd ever given much thought.

"You're going to have to speak up at some point," Ms. Chang laughed. It was the mirth of a woman who knows she is intimidating and powerful and wields that authority with wisdom. "In the meantime, please follow me."

Ms. Chang set off down the corridor at a blistering pace that defied her short legs.

"She doesn't mess around," Marcus muttered to Luke under his breath as he struggled to keep up.

The classroom was apparently a long ways away, because we walked down hallway after hallway for the better part of ten minutes before Ms. Chang stopped. The boys were in line with Ms. Chang, the girls just behind. I noted that Max, Chris, Peyton and I were breathing normally, while the rest did their best to hide their ragged breaths. Ms. Chang noticed, too.

"Out of shape, out of shape, out of shape, out of shape," she accused, pointing an outstretched finger to Amanda, Clarice, Marcus and Luke. "Shallow breathing," she announced to Peyton, Max and I. "Too much lung breathing," she finished, glancing in Chris' direction. "But the best showing, all things considered."

"Out of shape? I work out every day!" Luke protested.

"Do you really work out?" Ms. Chang asked pointedly. "Or do you allow a machine to stimulate muscles in your body in exercises meant to replicate a physically strenuous activity?"

Luke blushed and fell silent.

"Right. Now that we've established the need and importance of proper breathing, let's go to the classroom," Ms. Chang suggested.

"Where have we been going?" Amanda wanted to know.

"Nowhere in particular," Ms. Chang answered honestly. "That was your pre-test."

I swallowed my smile as I saw annoyance and disbelief register on a few faces around me. Ms. Chang wasn't going to mess around, and I liked that. I wasn't intimidated or put off by the fact that she'd singled me out in my need for improvement…rather, I was excited to see what she could teach me.

Two minutes later, we were seated in a classroom with Ms. Chang stationed in front.

"Don't get too comfortable in those seats," she warned. "To properly teach you breathing techniques, we need practical application. I know you're accustomed to classes being taught in this format, and I'll deliver some instruction in this more traditional manner. But not much."

"I was under the impression that our mission shuttles wouldn't be that big," Marcus muttered, his voice muffled but audible enough for Ms. Chang to hear.

"And what is your point, Mr. Vivaldi?" Ms. Chang asked in a voice that suggested she knew exactly the point he was trying to make, and that it was stupid.

"We're not going to be doing all this walking," Marcus was happy to explain. "I don't understand why we're taking this breathing class."

Ms. Chang paused for only a moment. "Perhaps you would be willing to volunteer for a demonstration? Something that will show why this course is relevant?"

"This feels like a trick," Marcus said uncertainly, his unease clear as a freshly-washed window.

"There is no trick," Ms. Chang assured him. "I need a volunteer for this demonstration.

"You asked the question, man," Luke reminded Marcus as he waffled back and forth.

"Fine, whatever," Marcus agreed.

With cautious movements, he walked up to the front of the classroom to meet Ms. Chang. She gave him a knowing smile (an instant indication that he was about to regret his decision) and gestured for him to come up next to her.

"I'm going to fix these simple patches on Marcus so that we can monitor his breathing patterns," Ms. Chang explained as she took three square patches out of her pocket. With gentle, proficient motions she stuck a patch on both of Marcus' temples before motioning for him to lift up his shirt.

"You want me to take my shirt off?" Marcus asked. "Are you sure that's a good idea, Ms. Chang? I don't want to make the guys here jealous...and it'd probably be better not to torture the ladies with something they can't have."

"Oh, please!" Amanda moaned, rolling her eyes in disgust.

"She just said you're out of shape," Peyton joined in. "Our envy has already been curbed."

"I'm not asking you to take off your shirt," Ms. Chang answered evenly. "I just need to place this patch over your heart."

"He knew that," Chris couldn't help but say, and no one disagreed.

It *was* an interesting situation, though—we'd all grown up in the same digital world that isolated human encounter and disseminated educational content through a technological platform: that meant extreme privacy.

Doctor's visits were conducted behind screens that scanned the human bodies and highlighted areas and regions of potential concern. We learned about puberty and reproduction and disease through videos and interactive technological content...never by fixing eyes on actual bodies. There were no pool parties or locker rooms to change in—modesty was practiced even within the family unit. So to ask Marcus to lift his shirt was a little bit scandalous. Ms. Chang had to know that she was asking him to reveal a part of himself that no one (besides his parents, years ago) had ever seen.

I scanned the room for reactions. I knew right away that the guys would watch, if only to see how they compared to Marcus. But the girls? They'd be interested, surely—but also uncomfortable watching something like that take place given the norms that had been established through a conservative upbringing.

What was *I* going to do? I didn't know that, either—and I didn't have much time to think it through.

Marcus began to lift his shirt while my eyes were still fixed on him. I saw the pale, moon-colored skin of his midsection, flesh that was not flabby but still soft. And then I looked away.

"It's safe to look again, Alois," Max whispered. I heard the laughter in his voice but knew he wasn't making fun of me. Pink crept into my cheeks but I held my head high and said not a word as I looked back to the front.

"At this point, we can track Marcus' breathing patterns," Ms. Chang announced. With a push of her clicker, surround sound of Marcus' inhalations and exhalations filled the room. A digital timer not unlike the one from the simulation appeared in bold red lettering in the middle of the room.

"That tracks BPM, or beats per minute," Ms. Chang explained.

85.

84.

86.

"The rate is a bit high, but likely because he's nervous," Ms. Chang narrated. I wondered what it must feel like to be Marcus: treated like a lab rat and with public scrutiny to boot. And then I remembered: I had.

"We'll watch to see how Marcus' breathing and heart rate change in myriad of situations," Ms. Chang went on.

88.
"Ah, the anticipation of an unknown simulation brings a bit of anxiety," Ms. Chang noticed.

I had been focusing on the numbers displayed, but now turned my attention to the sounds. I strained to notice the difference between an 85 that came after an 83 and an 85 that came after an 86—they were different, but it wasn't obvious how.

My attention was secure in this manner when Ms. Chang walked into a back room that I'd failed to notice at first. Ten seconds later, she reappeared with a velvety-soft bunny that she held out to Marcus.

Marcus looked hesitant to accept the rabbit—I imagined that he worried there was more to the bunny than met the eye—and his BPM initially spiked to 97. But then, as he stroked the docile animal, his heart rate dipped to 64.

Ms. Chang said nothing. The change in sound was very obvious to pin now: the breathing was smooth and regular, the inhalations deeper than they had been before.

"AAHH!" Marcus cried out, startling us all.

123.

145.

157.

My eyes sought out a reason for Marcus' agony and found it in the hand of Ms. Chang, whose fingers were curled around a taser.

160.

The breathing was frenetic and variant. I'm sure my own heart rate accelerated just watching the scene before me play out.

"Please solve the equation before you," Ms. Chang instructed as though nothing unusual had taken place.

$2x + 3 = 9$.

Simple Algebra. Math we'd been taught to solve in the fourth grade. And I watched as Marcus struggled to answer the problem.

"Pet the bunny," Luke called out, seeing Marcus flounder and taking pity on him.

155.

Marcus pet the bunny, no longer with languid, caressing motions but with pressure and purpose.

154.

"Mr. Vivaldi, please solve the problem," Ms. Chang repeated.

156.

I wasn't sure how much time passed, but knew it was minutes. I felt embarrassed and uncomfortable that Marcus couldn't solve the problem. His selection for the mission meant he was fluent in high-level calculus and abstract math…this was not a reflection of his ability.

Ms. Chang held the taser up with her left hand. I stiffened, anticipating the shock that was to come. So did Marcus.

164.

"That's enough," Ms. Chang announced, surprising us all. "You may take your seat." She collected the bunny from Marcus and took it away. Marcus slumped to his seat in a daze.

"X equals three," Marcus spoke in a monotone voice when Ms. Chang reappeared.

"Indeed it does," Ms. Chang agreed neutrally.

130.
"Can I take this thing off?" Marcus wanted to know. His eyes studied the judgmental scarlet numerals projected before them all.

"Not yet," Ms. Chang responded. Turning to the group, "What did you observe?"

"Marcus had a hard time recovering from the shock of the taser," Chris observed matter-of-factly.

"You try getting tased!" Marcus erupted defensively.

"I'm just making an observation," Chris answered coolly, palms raised in a gesture of innocence.

"What else?" Ms. Chang prompted, ignoring the adversarial exchange.

"The breathing sounded labored after the first shock," Peyton offered. "Even when it started to dip back down, it sounded different."

"Correct," Ms. Chang praised. "What else?"

My heart thumped inside my chest. I knew what Ms. Chang wanted someone to point out, and I wondered why no one else was speaking up. It was so obvious…

"He couldn't perform the simplest of tasks when he started panicking," I spoke up. I felt release in my chest as the words escaped but knew there would be a social price to pay.

"And I bet you'll show us how it's done," Marcus said bitterly.

I chewed on the inside of my cheek to keep from saying something I would later regret. I was thankful when everyone else kept silent—I didn't need Max defending me, and I was relieved the others didn't gang up on me (although I knew this wasn't necessarily an indication of how they felt about me).

"I don't think that's the point," I replied neutrally. "I'm sure Ms. Chang chose you to demonstrate the practical truth we would all face in that situation."
"Very true, Ms. Alois," Ms. Chang agreed. "And you already bested Mr. Vivaldi, I'm afraid. Your neutral response just now, given the heated language and aggressive tone, demonstrated self-possession and restraint Marcus would do well to learn.

My cheeks flushed again—but this time, it wasn't only from embarrassment. I was beginning to wonder if the instructors—if *everyone* from The Organization—was singling me out on purpose. It felt like they were *trying* to isolate me and keep me from forming relationships with the rest of the group, and it frustrated me.

She's trying to upset you.

The thought suddenly occurred to me and I grabbed it with both fists. She was trying to get me worked up—she wanted to make me another example of what not to do. I could give in to the feeling of anger and normalize myself to the rest of the group I'd done such a good job of ostracizing, or I could knowingly push myself farther away by rising above the temptation of my flesh.

My eyes met Ms. Chang's for a moment, and my suspicions were confirmed: she was testing me. There was no such thing as a straight-forward test anymore (if there ever had been). Every test was a test within a test within a test alongside another test.

It would have been wise to make myself like all the others. I was becoming quite a target. But, my pride.

One, two, three, four, five, six, seven, eight, nine, I breathed in.

Nine, eight, seven, six, five, four, three, two, one, I breathed out.

My chest expanded and then contracted to accommodate the deep expanse of my breath. After a single round, I felt more relaxed. After two rounds, I felt more peaceful than I had when I'd first arrived in the classroom.

"Diaphragmatic breathing—very good," Ms. Chang announced. "By contracting the diaphragm in the thoracic cavity and abdominal cavity, Selina is stimulating her parasympathetic breathing system. This removes the need for 'fight or flight' and allows her to evenly distribute oxygen throughout the lungs."

I didn't look at any of the others.

One, two, three, four, five, six, seven.

Seven, six, five, four, three, two, one.

They hated me.

One, two, three, four, five, six, seven, eight.

Eight, seven, six, five, four, three, two, one.

"Selina, listen to this sequence of numbers: 8, 18, 11, 15, 5, 4, 14, 9, 19, 1, 7, 17, 6, 16. What are the next five numbers?" Ms. Chang asked.

They would hate me even more if I got this correct.

One, two, three, four, five.

Five, four, three, two, one.

Numbers, like the ones I was counting in my head. Eight. Eight. I left the number alone; let it float in the rafters of my brains as I focused my attention on my breathing.

One, two, three, four, five, six.

Six, five, four, three, two, one.

"Can anyone tell me the answer?" Ms. Chang asked.

I didn't know if she was trying to stress me out or not in opening the question up to the rest of the group—was I meant to feel anxious and pressured? It didn't matter. I ignored the signal flare for attention and ran through the numbers again.

Eight. Eighteen. Eleven. Fifteen. Five. Four. Fourteen. Nine. Nineteen.

My eyes flew open and I laughed out loud. I had it. I ran through the final numbers in the sequence to confirm my logic.

One, seven, seventeen, six, sixteen.

Satisfaction was mine—I had solved the riddle.

"Ten, thirteen, three, twelve, and two," I announced with the authority of a practiced reading of the Declaration of Independence.

"That's correct!" Ms. Chang exclaimed, her voice carrying the most emotion that we'd seen from her so far.

"I don't get it," Chris snapped, visibly disturbed that he hadn't procured the answer before me.

I released my breathing and looked to my peers. Their body language varied from annoyed to aggressive: Peyton with her weight slightly concentrated on her right hip; Clarice with her arms folded across her chest, Chris looked so intense I wondered if he might physically come after me.

"See the numbers in word form," I suggested, trying to convert some of the group's frustration into a productive outcome.

It was silent for a moment, and I hoped that they were working it through and not contemplating ways to murder me in my sleep. A moment later, I was surprised to hear Luke breathing deeply. Max was the second to practice the breaths, and the rest couldn't help but conform to the successful practice.

"They're listed alphabetically," Clarice answered two minutes later. She looked at me blankly before turning to Ms. Chang. "Starting with the 'e' in eight, the numbers go in alphabetical order until the 't' in two."

"Very good," Ms. Chang praised.

"I started breathing before she did," Luke pointed out. "And she got the answer faster,"

"A breathing technique doesn't create intelligence," Ms. Chang pointed out, her tone prickly. "It merely facilitates the deepest and most enlightened methods of cognition."

Luke's sour expression didn't change one iota.

"If Clarice is smarter than you, then Clarice is smarter than you," Marcus said pointedly, perhaps enjoying the opportunity to point out someone else's shortcoming. "Breathing can help, but it's not going to give you information you don't already have."

"You said this was a breathing class, which means there are many ways of breathing," I rushed in. My pride may have emboldened me to take the challenge, but it still felt uncomfortable to have such division amongst our group—I wanted it to dissipate.

"Indeed. And now I do believe I have your full attention to demonstrate those various techniques," Ms. Chang declared. "You may take a seat."

Uncharted Territory

I settled into my new life at The Organization Headquarters smoothly enough…my transition was definitely cleaner than it was for some of the others. I suspected some of my peers tried to carry fractions of their old lives with them into the present, and it didn't fit. They wanted to compare the two lives and fit every experience into a category of life that they had mapped out in their minds when the truth was, there was no blueprint for our current situation.

"No one is monitoring our diet," Amanda noted one afternoon as our group sat down to lunch.

"Of course they're not," Clarice replied indignantly. "We are adults, after all."

"We are not adults," Max disagreed. "We are sixteen. But that doesn't mean we're incapable of making those decisions for ourselves," he added.

"Clearly you haven't taken a peek at Marcus," Luke joked, elbowing his buddy in the mid-section. "I think all those burgers are starting to take their toll, man."

Marcus retaliated with a forceful shove that nearly sent Luke toppling over. "I don't know what you're talking about—I'm on the exercise machines every day, and my breathing techniques have never been better."

"The exercise machines can't save you from a fleshy middle," Peyton observed, raising one eyebrow in Marcus' direction. "You've completely abandoned eating any nutritious foods to stuff your face with junk food."

"What do you care?" Marcus asked, voice rising as color flooded his cheeks. I felt sorry for him at the same time that I agreed with the others. Marcus wasn't setting himself up for success…and his poor habits were starting to catch up with him.

"We care because you're going on a mission with us," Chris answered sharply. "And we need each other to be in tip-top shape. If we do find ourselves in a precarious situation, we need to be in peak condition to weather the trial."

Chris' rebuke hung in the air like the stench of day-old pizza.

"You need to take care of yourself," I added gently. "We *are* trying to make it back, no matter what the odds might be."

"Whatever," Marcus mumbled under his breath as he took a defiant bite of donut. A moment later, he threw the confection down onto his tray with disdain. "Thanks for ruining my meal," he grumbled.

"We're not saying you should totally cut out junk food," Max tried to reason with Marcus. "Just try to balance it out. Maybe eat some vegetables and limit the desserts, you know?"

Marcus said nothing. A moment later, he pushed away from the table and stalked out of the cafeteria.

"It needed to be said," Clarice offered her opinion without an ounce of remorse. "If we're going to be teammates, then we need to be able to be honest with one another."

"Agreed. So…you're kind of a terrible person," Luke spoke up. "You're mean and inflexible and super judgmental."

"I'm not sure this is the direction we want to go…" Max began, voice full of trepidation.

"Nope, I can take it," Clarice snapped. Her eyes bore through Luke's skull with laser-like focus and frightening intensity. "What else would you like to say?"

"I just think that you have this idea that you're better than everyone else," Luke went on. He did not meet Clarice's gaze head-on. "And you're not. I mean, we were all picked for this mission. Not just you. You're not better than us. We're all equal. Maybe Selina or Chris is better than the rest of us," he added after a moment of reflection.

I fought the physical urge to squirm and instead bit the inside of my cheek hard. I wished Luke had ended his commentary without mentioning me, but if everything was going to be put out in the open…

"Does anyone else feel this way?" Clarice challenged, chin jutted out and arms folded across her chest as her narrowed eyes swept across the room.

"You're pretty quick to jump on people," Amanda said softly.

"I think we need to remember the stress we're all under," Chris jumped in before further judgment could be passed. "I think we're all handling it remarkably well. I'm not bothered by you, Clarice."

"Thank you," Clarice said to Chris with exaggeration before returning frosty eyes on Luke and Amanda.

"Well of course Chris is going to say that," Amanda rolled her eyes. "You practically worship everything he does, Clarice. There's no reason for Chris to be offended by you."

"That's not true," Chris and Clarice protested in unison.

I snuck a glance over at Peyton and Max, who had wisely kept quiet. Both caught my gaze with some nervousness.

"This doesn't seem like a good idea," Peyton spoke up, echoing Max's earlier declaration.

"You'd rather us keep all this bottled up?" Luke asked.

"I'd rather we find a healthy way to work through these…issues," Peyton clarified.

"How are we going to know what "issues" we have to work through if we don't air them out now?" Clarice asked, and Peyton fell quiet.

"This is getting emotional," Max pointed out. "We learned from Ms. Chang how effective our cognitive practices are when we think while activated."

"You're right," Clarice conceded. "Why don't we all take some time this afternoon to compose a list of offenses and grievances to bring to dinner. That way we can practice bringing the topics up without emotion."

That was the last way I wanted to spend my afternoon, and I had little faith that a few hours conjuring a list of grievances would help separate the emotion from the offenses. But Clarice's arched eyebrows and jutted jawline were a force to reckon with; and this did not feel like my mountain to die on.

The hesitation of the group confirmed my hypothesis that no one was wild about the idea. Clarice interpreted the silence differently.

"Great," she said. "See you at dinner." With that, she flounced away from the table, silky hair swishing as she disappeared around the corner.

"Okay then," Chris sighed, pushing back and following Clarice's exit. "See you tonight."

"This is stupid," Luke muttered as he tossed his silverware on his plate with a metallic clatter.

"Who do you think will get the most heat?" Amanda asked when it was down to the last four.

Me. I would get the most hate thrown my direction—I had little doubt of that. I had a hard time imagining any of the others had earned as much malice.

"I don't know that this is going to help," Peyton worried aloud.

As Amanda prepared her defense of the idea, I found myself standing up. I didn't want to participate in this conversation; I didn't even want to hear it.

I waved goodbye without saying a word or making direct eye contact. I had already decided that I would not be creating any lists. I wouldn't waste my afternoon that way.

My fingers pushed buttons and my feet traveled down hallways without ever consciously making the decision of where to go.

Ten minutes later, I was standing back in the surveillance room. The hallways had been quiet; I hadn't run into anyone. There was a new freedom in walking straight into the room with confidence: knowing what the room was and what it held without the unspoken pressure that came with the presence of another. As comfortable as I was with Max, it felt liberating to be alone and totally responsible for my decisions.

I crept forward to the edge of the pond with reverent footsteps that acknowledged the importance of the site I had stumbled upon. During my first visit, I'd had the opportunity to notice what the room was without really exploring the depth and capacity that lay behind the monuments. Now, I targeted the surveillance equipment with purpose and curiosity.

The oversized, microscopically-pixelated flat screens showed with frightening alacrity scenes played out all over headquarters: dutiful workers tracking algorithms, employees resting in pods, Clarice typing out an aggressive list, and…my eyes stayed fixed on what appeared to be a meeting amongst some of the most important members of The Organization.

Of the hundreds of screens of footage, I had serious doubt I would be able to summon specific surveillance…especially without any training in the technology or clearance to access the high-tech tools.

You'll know in your spirit, what you're meant to do.

The prophetic words her parents had shared with her materialized quite unexpectedly.

"But I don't know what to do," I muttered grumpily under my breath.

Think. Use your brain.

I couldn't tell where the words came from, but they were not my own. I was either a genius or crazy.

"Use my mind? My mind?? Fine," I grumbled carelessly, waving my right hand in the air dramatically. This was ridiculous. "Screen, magnify!" I commanded, my right index finger pointed as if I were a wizard with a wand.

My mouth dropped open as the screen actually grew and settled into focus directly in front of me. I looked over both shoulders in disbelief…had *I* just done that?

I blinked once. Twice. The projection of the meeting stayed in focus, but I couldn't hear a thing.

"Audio up," I commanded, this time with a bit of authority.

As commanded, the sound grew until I raised an open palm to indicate that it had reached a satisfactory volume. Whatever was responsible for responding to my cues was capable of registering both auditory and visual input. I couldn't decide if I was disturbed or impressed. It was a decision I could make later. Drawing near to the display in anticipation, I was able to capture the exchange.

"We should launch in three weeks," one person proposed.

"Three weeks?" another questioned, making it clear through their tone of voice that they believed the proposition to be ludicrous. "Did you SEE the latest exchange in the cafeteria? And their performance on the last assessment? There's no way that they're ready."

"They're sixteen years old. Of course there's going to be drama," another vocalized.

"I thought we took efforts to select the most mature and intelligent juniors," another worried aloud. "Is this truly the best we have?"

"You're obviously forgetting what it's like to be sixteen," Mr. Boothe replied dryly.

"Boothe, this is the entire Organization on the line," one of the men retorted.

I wondered at the informality of the man's address and waited for Mr. Boothe's rebuke. None came. It was a table of equals, then. I wanted to know who each individual was…so many of our leaders were faceless. Their names carried weight, but anonymity was valuable and protected in our world.

"Not just The Organization," a woman chimed in emphatically. "This is the survival of the human race we're placing on the shoulders of a cohort of sixteen-year-olds."

"They're not doing that badly," one protested. "Look at Alois and Darnall, at Levenson."

The hairs on the back of my neck bristled and stood at attention at the mention of my last name. How many discussions like this had taken place? How extensively had this group speculated over our progress, strengths, and shortcomings?

"You can't count Alois," the woman protested. "We've been over this—we can't include her in our analysis of the group training. She's part of the mission, but she can never be considered more than a wild card."

My mind raced like the front-runner at the Daytona 500. What did they mean, I couldn't be included in discussions about the group? I was a *wild card*? What did that mean? My palms started sweating and I felt my heartbeat quicken and my body temperature rise. Deep breaths, I reminded myself. I needed to pay attention to what was said.

"Darnall, then. He's proven to be a fast learner, and quick to adapt. His EQ is high, too. I'm more impressed with him than with Levenson," another offered.

EQ. EQ... Ah! Emotional Quotient. They were referring to Max's superior emotional intelligence. The pace of the dialogue increased and I worked hard to keep up, no longer trying to pin words to faces and discern roles as I concentrated instead on processing what I heard.

"Levenson's been a disappointment."

"Not a disappointment! He's performed as expected, as the exam purposed he would."

"The exam doesn't measure everything."

"It measures the important things, the things we asked it to measure. And it hasn't been wrong."

"We should have put more emphasis on the EQ."

"We discussed the limitations of the EQ and determined to instead conduct thorough observations and assess interactions to judge for capability."

"Yes, but what of the kids already selected? We can judge them now, but we can't go back and undo what has been done."

"Of course we can. Nothing is final until they are launched into space—and even then, we could pull them back into orbit early."

"At exorbitant cost and with a heavy toll on credibility."

"Yes. But still possible."

There was a thoughtful, extended pause. It seemed they were uncertain of where the conversation should go next.

"I still think we should launch sooner rather than later."

"They're not ready!"

"They'll never be ready. And the situation is becoming more desperate. Think about what we got from Intel this morning. At what point do we take the plunge? We can't hope for favor forever…sooner or later they'll catch up with us."

"We can't make a decision based on fear or peer pressure from an opponent we've never even met."

"But we'd be foolish to ignore it, considering that the threat of obliterating the entire human race is on the line."

"What an outrageous claim! Hardly credible."

"It sounds incredible, and it may be incredible. But if it's not…"

"We're not ready to launch." It was Mr. Boothe who had the final word, even amongst the company of supposed equals. "I agree that expediency is a top priority, but they're not ready yet. They need to get tougher. They're still too soft."

"Tonight's discussion should ruffle some feathers and open some wounds."

There were murmurs of agreement.

"And the isolation scenario coming up, too. And it will be interesting to see the results of the emotional intelligence test. I'm really interested to see if Levenson's IQ and pragmatism will carry over to support him in this."

"That test is scheduled for this afternoon?"

"It is," Mr. Boothe agreed.

My heartbeat sped up again. We hadn't been informed of any tests in the afternoon...the element of surprise was apparently built into the assessment.

"Who's proctoring the exam?"

"Who wants to?" Mr. Boothe asked the panel of VIPs.

"I'll do it," an Indian man with creamy, butterscotch skin volunteered. I'll have satellite assistance and back up, correct?"

"Yes," Mr. Boothe agreed, looking to the others for confirmation.

A series of nods, and the meeting was apparently over.

"To the observation room, then," Mr. Boothe announced.

My legs felt frozen in place at the same time I knew I needed to high-tail it out of there. The group was coming up to this room...and I could not be standing in it. I wasn't supposed to be in there.

But then...what would they do to me? What *could* they do to me? What would they *dare* to do to me? I was the *wild card*, after all...whatever that meant. I was not expected to conform to expectations. Maybe they anticipated my presence in the room—it was possible that they had intentionally left the room unprotected knowing I would venture that way.

That was pretty much the extent of my thought process when Mr. Boothe and his comrades walked into the room. One look at their faces told me that they had definitely *not* anticipated my presence in the room.

"Hi," I announced into the startled silence. I had no plan but decided it would be wise to make the first move, to appear as though I were in control.

"Hello," Mr. Boothe responded suspiciously. The rest of the group remained silent.

"As the wild card, you may have guessed I'd make my way here," I went on, unsure of what angle to take.

Silence.

"So, we're not as ready as you'd like," I tried again. I only needed them to latch onto one statement…I prayed I'd find attractive bait quickly.

More silence. I counted to five slowly in my head and tried to measure my inhale to the same count. I couldn't get worked up now.

"Well, we don't want to be late to the EQ test," I concluded, clapping my hands together as I looked to the Indian man I'd seen in the projection. "Shall we?"

The closed expressions on the faces of the members of The Organization had me thinking that they had no protocol for how to respond. The contention I'd witnessed in their meeting had me thinking they wouldn't engage while in disunity (hence, the silence).

When I turned on my heel to leave, Mr. Boothe cleared his throat. "Ahem. Ms. Alois, what exactly are you doing in this room?"

He didn't ask why, and he didn't ask how long I'd been coming. He didn't even ask how. I decided to take his question at face value and answer honestly.

"Exploring. Looking for answers," I told him matter-of-factly. There was no need to elaborate when Mr. Boothe hadn't asked for it.

"And did you find what you were looking for?" Mr. Boothe asked carefully. Each word was stretched out like taffy, sticky and artificially sweet. He was buying time and trying to recover face.

"I did not. I have, however, come away with some new questions," I answered directly.

This response seemed to make the members of The Organization squirm, although there was no protest or request for further explanation.

"You've come away with new questions," Mr. Boothe parroted back.

"Yes," I agreed. "I'm interested to know what criteria were considered when conducting the exam that qualified us for this task, I'd like to know when we'll find out who will be on each mission, and I'd like to learn how many more assessments there will be, and what they'll be measuring." I paused. "And more than anything, I'd like to know when I'm going to receive my kitten."

A member of The Organization guffawed, presumably at my outrageously bold request. Mr. Boothe took a deep breath and looked at me with tired eyes.

"I think we may need to arrange for a private meeting, Selina," Mr. Boothe concluded, surprising me by using my first name. He'd taken effort to address me formally in previous encounters, and now he used my first name as though he were a childhood friend.

"Alright," I agreed. "And you'll bring the kitten?"

I was pushing the limit, and I knew it. I was tired of waiting and saw an opportunity to ensure delivery of a promise. Mr. Boothe exchanged glances with a couple of members before meeting my gaze once more.

"Yes, I'll bring a kitten," Mr. Boothe said, voice tinged with defeat.

"Not just *a* kitten," I corrected. "A Devon Rex."

"Right. A Devon Rex," Mr. Boothe repeated back.

"Okay," I said, containing the excitement that rattled inside of me like coins in a tin can. "When would you like to meet?"

"The sooner the better," Mr. Boothe was quick to retort, making it clear that he was not a fan of my expanded knowledge base. "This evening, after dinner."

"Here?" I asked. I wondered if Mr. Boothe would ask other Organization members to come along, or if it would just be the two of us.

"Here. When you finish eating, come on up," Mr. Boothe replied.

"You'll just be…" I trailed off, uncertain if the flexible timing would leave Mr. Boothe in limbo.

"I'll be watching," he snapped crankily. "I'm the one who is *supposed* to be watching this footage."

The rebuke hit but didn't sting too badly. I had upset Mr. Boothe and rattled members of The Organization, but I'd also achieved a victory in that I'd further set myself apart, I'd earned solo face-time with the leader of the mission, and I'd soon possess my kitten.

I nodded meekly. There was no use in a further show of confidence—I would earn nothing more further aggravating Mr. Boothe. We stood in statue-like formation until Mr. Boothe roused us with surly words.

"Well, get to the assessment," he groused.

The Indian man sprang to life, and I followed him as he took purposeful steps to the door. I looked over my shoulder as I left and found everyone unmoved, eyes exchanging layered messages I would never intercept. But I might yet get some answers…

EQ

The man's name was Mr. Prahalad, and he did not appreciate my company.

"Why don't you go on ahead?" he suggested with a prickly tone as I hurried to stay close to him.

"Are you asking me to run?" I asked with attitude all my own. We were already moving quickly—to pass him would mean jogging.

"I don't want to arrive together," Mr. Prahalad answered without ever addressing my question. "And you can't be late."

"Then you might want to stop by the restroom or something first," I suggested. "And where exactly am I supposed to go?"

"Wherever your friends are," he answered irritably, eager to be rid of me.

"As you mentioned in your earlier meeting, our group isn't exactly getting along. We agreed to split up and compile a list of offenses for each person," I explained. I wondered at Mr. Prahalad's apparent ignorance but made no comment.

"The cafeteria, then." He waved a dismissive hand in the air. "I'll get you when I'm ready."

I swallowed my frustration and kept my colorful thoughts to myself. I reminded myself that it must be aggravating to work with people who were of divergent mindsets and be undermined by an adolescent. I could be the bigger person in the situation.
As Mr. Prahalad wished, I arrived in the cafeteria a minute ahead of him. I noticed Peyton sitting at the table farthest from the entrance, but she appeared to be deep in thought—probably working on her list of transgressions. I made no attempt to wave or catch her attention; instead I slid into a seat on the opposite side of the room and waited for Mr. Prahalad to arrive.

When he did, it was with an impatient air of authority. Even though there were other people in the room, and there had been no announcement of this assessment, Mr. Prahalad looked put out that not every mission participant was seated and prepared to hang on his every word.

"Where is everyone?" he huffed, adjusting his belt and stuffing his stretched collared shirt over his pudgy belly.

Peyton looked up and noticed me for the first time; we exchanged a look and shrugged.

"Who are you looking for?" Peyton asked in a half-interested voice.

"Your group," Mr. Prahalad barked.

"No one said anything about meeting this afternoon," I announced, as though speaking to Mr. Prahalad for the first time.

He didn't even look over at me. "Well, I'm announcing it now. You're being tested."

This time, Peyton sat up straight and shifted her body to face Mr. Prahalad. "A test?" she asked, now at full attention.

"Get your friends," Mr. Prahalad snapped.

Peyton shot a look of indignation my direction before standing. "Selina, are you coming?"

"Sure."

In truth, I did not care to hunt down the rest of our group—but I knew well enough how Mr. Prahalad would feel about my continued companionship.

"He seems really warm and welcoming," Peyton intoned sarcastically as soon as the elevator doors closed us in.

I laughed. "Yeah, he's a teddy bear, all right," I agreed.

"I wonder what they're going to test us on," she added nervously. "Mr. Boothe didn't say anything about a test when he saw us earlier. I wonder if it's a physical test or a mental test. I shouldn't have eaten so much for lunch," she added as an afterthought. "If it's a physical test, I'll be in trouble."

"It's an emotional test," I told her. I didn't see much point in holding back the truth—she'd find out soon enough.

"How do you know?" Peyton asked, her head snapped in my direction.

"I heard a group of them talking about it. I don't know how they plan to test us, but it's a test meant to measure our emotional IQ," I answered.

Peyton eyed me curiously for a moment before saying anything. "You really are different," she finally said. "Are you *trying* to stand out so much?"

I appreciated her candor at the same time I realized I wasn't sure how to respond. Was I trying to stand out? No. But I was also making sure I didn't just "fit in."

"I'm not trying to stand out. But I'm not trying to hide, either," I explained.

"That's kind of what I thought. Some of the others think you're doing it on purpose," she told me.

I'd already figured that out, but it still bugged me to hear definitively that this was the case. There wasn't really anything to say in response.

"This whole thing is weird," Peyton offered a moment later. "I mean, who would have ever thought that we'd be chosen for a mission like this. It wasn't even a possibility we heard about."

"It is crazy," I agreed. I appreciated Peyton's attempt to establish common ground between us at the same time that I guarded against deep speculation. That seemed like the equivalent of navigating a field of land mines: not much to gain and everything to lose.

"I'm sorry about your parents," Peyton said quietly, seeming to read my thoughts. "I know you probably don't want to talk about it, but I'm sorry."

I'd packaged my feelings in a shoebox and safely tucked it in the back of the closet of my mind; Peyton's gentle acknowledgement of my loss nudged one edge of the cover open. My heart felt saturated with feeling, a sponge absorbing water too quickly. Tears flooded my eyes; a watery testament to the depth of my love for my parents.

"Sorry," Peyton rushed on. She saw my tears and looked away. I swiped underneath my eyes with my index fingers and tucked the stray hairs behind my ears.

"It's okay," I assured her. "And thanks."

We allowed for a moment of silence to clear emotions before Peyton changed the subject.

"Where do you think they all are?" she asked.

"Where would *you* choose to madly document all of the reasons why you hate the rest of the people you're going into outer space with?" I asked sardonically.

Peyton laughed. "It is kind of a terrible idea."

"The worst," I agreed. "We might find some of them in the common rooms, or in the pods?"

Our silent quest led us first through the extensive web of themed rooms, where we collected Chris, Amanda, Clarice, and Luke.

"We have a test," we explained matter-of-factly after summoning them over.

"You're kidding," Clarice protested, looking from Peyton to me for signs of a trick.

"I wish," Peyton told her. "There's a man waiting in the cafeteria—he asked us to go and get you."

"Where are Max and Marcus?" Chris wanted to know.

I shrugged. "We're looking for them, too. We just found you first."

"I think Marcus said something about sleeping," Luke offered. "Max might be in the pods, too. Want me to go and get them?"

"Sure," I answered indifferently. "Thanks."

As Luke took off in search of the last two, Clarice zeroed back in on the task at hand.

"You said we have a test: do we know what it's about?" she asked pointedly.

"He didn't say anything," Peyton answered coolly without looking in my direction. "He just told us to get you."

Clarice looked to me for confirmation. I wondered at Peyton's decision to keep the assessment a secret but didn't say anything.

"He didn't tell us anything about the assessment," I agreed.

Clarice rolled her eyes and shook her head in frustration. "And we're needed right now?"

"That's what he said," Peyton bristled. "We don't want to take a test either, Clarice," she pointed out.
Clarice didn't say anything. I imagined her list of offenses to be *very* long. I wondered how much space I took up.

"Well, let's go, then," Chris prompted.

The walk to the elevator was silent. When we were locked inside the metallic rectangular prism, Amanda spoke up.

"So, are we still planning to share our lists tonight?" she asked cautiously. Her question hung in the air without an immediate response.

"Let's just focus on the test for now," Chris advised. One look at his facial expression and body language, and you could see that he was already mentally preparing for the exam. Chris wasn't one to mess around.

Five minutes later, all eight of us stood in a semi-circle around Mr. Prahalad. The disgruntled member of The Organization looked just as annoyed as he had when Peyton and I had left him.

"Right. This is all of you?" Mr. Prahalad asked, eyes narrowed as he scanned our lot with suspicion.

"We're all here," Chris agreed.

Mr. Prahalad grunted, then waved a hand over his right shoulder. "Come with me."

We walked to a simple room with white-washed walls that seemed to make the room brighter. I squinted when I first walked in—the light seemed blinding. There wasn't any equipment or technology that I could see, but I knew from experience that didn't necessarily mean that the room was vacant.

"Take a seat," Mr. Prahalad instructed. There were exactly nine chairs in the room: eight lined up in a row at the front of the room, and one set at an angle in the corner.

I wondered if we would be evaluated on what seat we chose to take and how long we chose to find it as I situated myself front and center. Peyton settled to my right, and Chris to my left. The rest of the group found a spot and looked to Mr. Prahalad expectantly.

"You're about to take a test that will measure your emotional intelligence," Mr. Prahalad announced without an ounce of enthusiasm. He didn't even look up to gauge our expressions.

Out of the corner of my eye, I watched Chris sit up straighter; Clarice leaned forward with expectation. Luke leaned back in his seat, Peyton tucked her hair behind her right ear, and Amanda shifted in her chair. I couldn't see Marcus, but I noticed Max's posture and expression remained unchanged. A mystery, that's what Max was.

"Good, Selina," Mr. Prahalad praised, catching me off-guard. I looked up at him in surprise, eyebrows furrowed.

"I—I didn't do anything," I stuttered, reluctant to be singled out when I hadn't done anything out of the ordinary. Heat crept up my spine in spider-like, rose-red lace patterns that tessellated all the way up to my neck. I saw the resentful and irritated eyes of my peers boring holes through my profile…as if I weren't already despised!

"Don't be difficult," Mr. Prahalad cajoled, this time with a tone that hinted at the pleasure he received in pushing my buttons.

Anger was at my front doorstep, knocking louder with every moment. I thought of the breathing techniques Ms. Chang had taught us and resisted the urge to open the door and allow the headstrong emotion to carry me away.

"I'm not being difficult," I answered coolly. "I haven't done anything to merit your attention and distinction from my peers." My words were measured, my vocabulary on point. I was careful not to show evidence of the pride I felt in so carefully controlling my emotions.

"Why don't you share your take on your peers' responses to this assessment?" Mr. Prahalad suggested. "You won't deny that you took a quick read of the crowd, will you?"

I wasn't sure what Mr. Prahalad was getting at, and I hesitated to respond. His light tone assured me of the certain existence of a trap that I could not fully see. The lines were fuzzy and smudged…I appealed to my brain to ascertain the sharpie-fine boundary of entrapment that I could not make out.

"I did notice some minimal responses to your announcement," I agreed with hesitation.

"And what conclusion have you come to?" Mr. Prahalad pushed.

I knew what he wanted. He was looking for me to identify Chris and Clarice as highly competitive; Peyton and Amanda as anxious, Luke as indifferent. He wanted me to further isolate myself from the group in my accurate and unflattering read on each individual, and I would not do it. That was where the mirth came from…Mr. Prahalad knew my pride and mindset of high achievement superseded my need to belong.

A sudden idea niggled into my brain, catching me off-guard. Ms. Chang's breathing techniques had successfully allowed for inspiration. Buoyed by the reminder that a panel of top-Organization employees were watching this exchange, I stood ramrod-straight and looked Mr. Prahalad square in the eye.

"You'd like a read of the emotional and subconscious elements at play?" I asked in clarification without breaking eye contact,

"Yes," Mr. Prahalad confirmed; tone slightly less assured. He saw my confidence and it brought him unease.

"Very well," I began with an even expression and a nod of acquiescence. I gave myself a moment to gather my thoughts; in truth, I was allowing the elongation of my pause to build drama and anticipation.

"Mr. Prahalad, you are a marginalized and discontent employee of The Organization who imagines himself to be entitled to position and privilege far beyond your current role. Your daily goal is to do just enough to avoid scrutiny or reprimand—there is a complete lack of ambition or vision in your person. At one point, you did care—but you have been so distanced from those early aspirations that you have allowed your professional frustrations seep into your personal life.

"Your bitterness and resentment towards The Organization ensure that you depart from this building at the earliest possible moment when work ends, not because you have a loving wife and child to go home to but because you are determined not to offer even one additional ounce of effort to anyone or anything. You've allowed a series of disappointments to direct your life's path to abject misery, as evidenced by your cantankerous demeanor, focus on negative events, total unwillingness to help, and pudgy midsection that shows a lack of commitment to even use the convenient phys-ed equipment meant to keep our bodies operating healthfully.

"Your supposed indignation at executing such a 'menial' task as assessing emotional intelligence is a cheap cover meant to frost the truth: that you're desperate for an opportunity to feel important, valued, and respected. You don't get it from your wife at home, you don't get it from your colleagues or superiors at work— *you* don't even believe in your worth.

"So, you terrorize those you falsely believe you can control in an effort to try to gain position and power and prove to yourself that you are worthy at the same time your subconscious realizes the futility and impossibility of securing respect from the marginalization of others. You'll leave today feeling more depressed than you were when you began the day, only this time you'll finally have words and emotions to color the feelings and attitudes you carry around like hundred-pound weights each and every day.

"I'm sorry to be the one to make this report," I paused. I genuinely did feel empathy for miserable Mr. Prahalad, as I knew my analysis of his inner workings was spot on. I looked up to verify my accuracy in his twisted, pained expression.

"I also realize that this is not the emotional synopsis you were expecting me to make. I've twisted what was intended to be a further attempt to ostracize me from the group and made it into a personal attack on a leader of The Organization. Yes, I'm aware of my 'faux-paus.' I'm also aware that the most important individuals in The Organization are listening in, so my rather snide commentary is not meant to slight you alone."

I paused. There was more I could say, but I wasn't sure it needed to be said.

"I can continue, if you'd like," I offered. "I realize I haven't substantiated each claim that I made, although I can assure you that I have solid grounds for each inference and have no problem in spelling each item out if you think that would be valuable."

I didn't need to look at my peers to know that my response shocked them. I could imagine their stunned faces with no trouble...and I could imagine Max's pursed lips and laughing eyes. Maybe I had more emotional intelligence than I'd believed.

"Sit down, Selina," Mr. Boothe announced, bursting into the room with long strides and flushed cheeks that spoke to the speed with which he'd traveled from the observation room to the classroom.

Was it a good or bad thing that Mr. Boothe had swooped in and hijacked the class? I couldn't decide, although I knew it meant that I had surprised The Organization once again. This ability to behave outside the expected behavior had originally empowered me...as I thought about it more, I wondered at the competence of The Organization and worried that they might be inept and ill-equipped to the task of sending adolescents into outer space.

"Mr. Prahalad, thank you for your introduction to the emotional intelligence assessment," Mr. Boothe thanked the man with all sincerity. "You may report back to the third floor."

Mr. Prahalad seemed to be in a stupor: he didn't look at Mr. Boothe as he spoke. His eyes were glazed over in what I imagined was an inspired reflection on his life patterns and behavior.

"Mr. Prahalad," Mr. Boothe said again, tone soft as a freshly-plumped pillow.

Mr. Prahalad looked up at Mr. Boothe as if seeing him for the first time. He nodded once, locked eyes on me for an extended moment, and then shuffled out of the room.

My heart thudded in my chest, and the controlled breathing became more difficult. I worried that I'd done deeper damage than I'd realized: I'd intended to drive home a point, but I may have wounded an already-decrepit soul. The thought was full of condemnation and jarred me even as the silence stretched on.

"Impressive analysis, Selina," Mr. Boothe said drily. "You've made your point."

"Emotional ninja," Marcus exhaled in wonder, shaking his head in disbelief. "You roasted him!"

"I wasn't trying to," I said defensively, even as I knew it wasn't true. I had wanted to best Mr. Prahalad in his attempt to belittle me, and I had won. It didn't feel as rewarding as I'd imagined.

"The test today will measure your ability to read social situations and emotion," Mr. Boothe went on as though Marcus hadn't said a word. "Emotion that is not limited to humans, since your mission will likely bring you into contact with life outside our human race."

"Can we just call Selina the winner and go back to free time?" Marcus joked. "I'm tired just thinking about everything she said."

Mr. Boothe didn't even have a chance to turn him down before Chris jumped in.

"We don't know that Selina's the best," he was quick to state. The idea of capitulation without contest was too much for him to bear.

"Do we all have to compete?" Marcus asked. "What happens if we choose not to participate in an assessment?"

It was an interesting question—one I had not considered before. What *would* they do if we determined to bypass a test?

"You can go first, if you'd like," Mr. Boothe offered to Marcus, ignoring his question.

"Whatever," Marcus shrugged. "What do you want me to do?"

"We can start with your peers," Mr. Boothe began. "Would you like to select someone from the group to assess?"

Marcus looked at Mr. Boothe like he'd just asked if he wanted pink eye. "Are you serious? No one wants that."

"I'm not going to pick for you," Mr. Boothe said seriously. "The default would be to assess your family."

Marcus blanched. It was a low blow Mr. Boothe dealt...I couldn't imagine anyone wanting to see their family used as the centerpiece for this lesson. Marcus turned to face us and heads bobbed down in an effort to avoid eye contact.

"Come on, man," Marcus said softly, shaking his head.

There was a pregnant pause. I felt sorry for Marcus: his predicament was a tricky one and not his fault. I wondered at the others' reluctance...it wasn't like I was eager to have myself scrutinized, but how bad could it be? And, I had a sneaky suspicion we'd all have our turn under the microscope...

"I—" I began, fully intending to volunteer myself for the task and thus relieve Marcus from the pressure of choosing.

"We'll start with Chris," Mr. Boothe announced, cutting in and speaking loudly so that my voice was drowned out. The veins in his neck were taut and his jaw looked tight: I had further annoyed him with my gesture of goodwill. Glancing surreptitiously to the side, I caught Max looking in my direction. He raised his eyebrows in unspoken support before we both looked back at Mr. Boothe.

"I thought you—" Marcus began, but Mr. Boothe was, once again, swift to interrupt.

"We can start with Chris," he repeated.

All eyes traveled to Chris, who sat rigid and tense. His face carried no expression, but his tightly-clenched hands and planted feet told of his reluctance. Mr. Boothe's eyes also rested on Chris, and he offered a canned smile.

"Don't worry. We'll start with something simple. A picture of your childhood bedroom," Mr. Boothe assured.

Not a moment later, the image of Chris' bedroom appeared. Before scrutinizing the projection, I glanced over at Chris. His initial fear seemed to have ebbed: as he took in the benign scene of his bedroom, his body relaxed.

Chris' childhood bedroom. Introduced as though it were the sleeping place of a little boy when in fact it was the room Chris retreated to every day until a mere week ago.

Pristine condition. Bed perfectly made (navy-blue comforter), oak desk neat and tidy with a mantle of trophies and medals displayed above. The minimal décor included phys-ed equipment and a chart measuring progress on a list of goals: 3 academic, 1 physical, and 1 personal development. A single digital picture frame sat on the desk: I watched the photographs of Chris and his parents cycle through.

"What exactly do you want me to do?" Marcus asked uncertainly, glancing from Chris to Mr. Boothe.

"I want you to tell us what you can ascertain about Chris from evaluating his room," Mr. Boothe instructed simply. "Whenever you're ready."

I still felt sorry for Marcus (and also Chris), but I was also really curious to hear Marcus' take on Chris' room. What he found worthy of distinction and mention would tell me a great deal about Marcus and his own upbringing.

"He's clean, and neat. He works out," Marcus began uncertainly, looking for reassurance.

"How do you know?" Mr. Boothe asked. He tried to keep his voice neutral but I could tell that he was exasperated.

"Because it's clean? And he has phys-ed equipment?" Marcus asked. I couldn't tell if he was holding back or if that was really the best analysis he could give.

"You might as well say it all," Chris laughed drily. "If you don't, someone else will."

There was respectful silence as we waited for Marcus' response. He scratched the back of his neck in a sign of discomfort. "The fact that there isn't a single thing out of place shows that Chris is a perfectionist and that he likes order," he added. "The neutral colors of the walls and lack of decoration might also show that he doesn't have a lot of personality."

It was getting awkward. I didn't look over at Chris, but I could imagine his stoic expression—his armor when things were uncomfortable. Mr. Boothe didn't say anything, and the rest of us certainly didn't say anything. We were all apparently waiting for Mr. Boothe to indicate that the exercise was over, which didn't happen.

"Anything else?" Mr. Boothe prompted matter-of-factly.

"What exactly are you looking for?" Marcus asked, now visibly upset.

"I'm not looking for anything," Mr. Boothe replied neutrally. "Just want to make sure I give you the opportunity for a full analysis before I move to the next individual."

Marcus shook his head and looked at Chris and then his feet. He was wearing his heart on his sleeve, and it was clear he detested the work Mr. Boothe was asking him to do.

"I'll go next," Clarice volunteered.

I bit down on my lip to ensure nothing untoward came out of my mouth: the Clarice that had been revealed since her selection by The Organization was a stranger to me; far from the kind and well-intentioned girl I'd once called my best friend. This latest attempt to exploit the opportunity at the expense of Chris and Marcus added to these observations.

"Is there anything you'd like to add?" Mr. Boothe asked Marcus. Marcus just shook his head and raised open palms in defeat.

"Alright, Clarice—tell us about Marcus' response to the simulation," Mr. Boothe dictated, catching Clarice off-guard.

I hid the satisfied smile that threatened to spread across my lips as Clarice struggled to find words.

"You DO have a read on Marcus' response, don't you?" Mr. Boothe queried Clarice with a touch of mockery.

"Yes," Clarice answered, back-pedaling quickly. "Of course." She took a deep breath and straightened her spine before looking Mr. Boothe in the eye.

"Marcus is uncomfortable," Clarice began lamely. She knew it was a poor start and quickly added on. "He's more concerned with relationships than accomplishments, and this test is putting him in a position to risk the former. He'll fail the task rather than compromise his friendships."

Clarice glanced at Mr. Boothe to see if he had any commentary on her initial thoughts. He considered Clarice thoughtfully without saying a word.

"You're speculating," Amanda spoke up. All eyes turned to her.

"You're not basing your judgments off of Marcus' response right now, really...you're basing your thoughts on what you know to be true about Marcus in the past," Amanda explained.

The color rose in Clarice's cheeks and her nostrils flared in defiance of the dignified silence she maintained. I knew her well enough to guess that she was gnawing on the inside of her cheeks, too.

"Excellent point, Ms. Newall," Mr. Boothe praised. "Would you like to continue your assessment of Ms. Tran?"

Amanda blushed. "I wasn't trying to start something," she said while shaking her head gently from side to side. "I don't want to assess Clarice."

"I'm asking you to," Mr. Boothe clarified, voice firm.

The scene was becoming more tense by the moment...and I'd thought it had been uncomfortable that morning, when Clarice had insisted we create our list of transgressions! Those lists would quickly become irrelevant if Mr. Boothe continued playing this game.

"Okay," Amanda began. She glanced at Clarice. "This isn't personal," she explained. Whatever the intention, we all knew any declaration of impersonality signaled the initiation of some potentially very offensive musings.

"Do you want me to assess her immediate response, or include back history in my summation?" Amanda asked, suddenly hesitant.

"Why don't you begin with your interpretation of Ms. Tran's reaction to the task of judging Marcus, then provide context for her response and end with her feelings about your opinion," Mr. Boothe answered evenly.

He'd hardly finished speaking when Amanda jumped into her interpretation. I wondered how much of her musings had been bottled up, waiting for an opportunity to come out.

"Clarice is competitive and operates out of a limited-resource mindset," Amanda began. "Because her paradigm is based on the belief that there is a limited supply of resources that must be won through competition, she is ruthless in her pursuit of that which she believes has value and she could care less who is trampled along the way. This behavior was on display as Clarice volunteered to undermine and judge a compatriot rather than keep respectful silence or wait until she was called upon to compete—she sought out an opportunity to put herself ahead of another.

"She is used to relying on her wit and strong will to succeed and is not used to being held accountable for her actions; her effective intimidation is usually more than suitably able to jockey her into the position she desires. Her lame and obvious read of Marcus' response shows both unmerited confidence and foolhardy initiative; her embarrassment further proof of how rarely she is called out for this behavior. Because Clarice operates with such aggression, she'll be reviewing my words even now in an earnest attempt to undermine, disenfranchise, and destroy me. Not my case, mind you—*me*.

"This response will be rooted in fear that Clarice will never acknowledge. The part I'm uncertain of is whether Clarice herself actually comprehends what it is that has cultivated this ruthlessness or if she is mystified by its existence. The response will look the same in either case, although one holds the redemptive element of self-awareness with the potential for change." Amanda professed her evaluation as though lecturing on the distinctive differences between metaphase and anaphase.

Amanda had nailed Clarice—one aspect of Clarice, at least—she was far too complicated to be captured through a single lens. I was impressed…and interested to see Mr. Boothe's response. As Amanda had predicted, Clarice was stoic: depending on how familiar you were with Clarice, you might perceive her to be either regal and dignified or affronted and stiff. Both were true.

"Clarice? What do you make of Amanda's verdict?" Mr. Boothe asked, raising an eyebrow as he turned to face Clarice.

My body tensed instinctively…I knew Clarice well enough to know that he was poking the hornet's nest and challenging Clarice's pride at the innermost level. The fact that Mr. Boothe (a respected authority figure) had posed the question did not guarantee a benign response, and I braced for the potential vitriol that could spew forth.

Clarice's jaw could have been cut from marble; the lines of her face were hard and unyielding as she leveled her gaze with Mr. Boothe. She did not look over at Amanda, but we all knew there would be a harsh penalty exacted for her truth. Clarice was clever enough to wait…her fury would simmer beneath the surface until the opportune moment, at which point it would boil over and scald anyone and everyone in its path.

"A very thorough analysis, Mr. Boothe," Clarice answered levelly. "Clearly an interpretation that was well thought out…and also heavy on the speculation. But perhaps this detractor was overlooked in light of the depth to which Ms. Newall dove in her commentary—she was quite effective in driving her point home."

It was here that Clarice turned to face Amanda. Her eyes clouded with bitter rage, I could also see the respect settled in her gaze. If she'd doubted Amanda's selection to the mission before, she didn't now.

"Well done, Ms. Newall," Clarice acknowledged, addressing her peer formally, words evenly spaced out and spoken with warning laced through.

"Thank you," Amanda accepted the praise with a leveled gaze, but her lower lip trembled just enough to let me know that her moment of valor had passed and she now stood in realization of the situation she had created.

"Ah! It seems we're well on our way," Mr. Boothe praised, tone light and effervescent in stark contrast to the tension he had built amongst the adolescents around him.

His jubilant remark was met with silence. Would we each have to take a turn? Was Mr. Boothe keen to continue on this terrible path of merciless crucifixion of character?

"If you're looking for someone else to do *that*, you're out of luck," Marcus laughed bitterly. "I'm not sure what these tests are supposed to accomplish, but I'm not looking to build an army of enemies."

"Hardly the point," Mr. Boothe agreed. "Simply the direction the girls chose to take the exercise. Shall we return to the prior engagement?"

He didn't wait for a response. Instead, he snapped his fingers to bring back the projection of Chris' bedroom.

"I believe we've been primed for deeper analysis," Mr. Boothe said in a statement that simultaneously oversimplified and dismissed the irreparable relational trauma that had been created between the two girls. "Who would like to continue the analysis of Chris based on this image of his former bedroom?"

"Do we all have to do this?" Luke asked. "I mean, is it a matter of getting it over with? Or will there only be a few people who have to do this?"

"There will be an emotional intelligence quotient assigned to each of you at the end of the exercise, one way or another," Mr. Boothe replied neatly. He paused, then went on. "Scores have already been awarded to Selina, Amanda, Clarice, and Marcus."

I wondered how the scores were given out, and how the EQ's could possibly be fair given the very different responses each of us had offered. At best, the results would be highly subjective. And what of the EQ of the individuals rating us? A thought wormed its way into my head…one I welcomed with open arms.

"I'm assuming there are specific members of The Organization evaluating our responses," I began, voice clear and full of authority I didn't have.

Mr. Boothe didn't bother to hide his suspicion or irritation as he regarded me with sidelong glance.

"I worry about where you're taking this, Ms. Alois," Mr. Boothe warned.

"Oh, there's nothing to worry about," I chirped. "I'll take the lack of correction to assume that yes, we are being evaluated by members of The Organization. But, considering the highly subjective nature of the test, it bears questioning of the qualifications of those doing the judging. We don't receive our scores or the categories we're evaluated in, which seems to undermine any attempt to improve or grow from these exercises."

"Your point, Ms. Alois," Mr. Boothe barked.

"Who is evaluating us? And how are we to know that they are effective judges of emotional intelligence? What assessments or distinctions have they earned to qualify them for this role?" I asked.

In truth, I hardly cared. What were these tests? We'd already been selected for the mission…in my mind, these exercises were a formality to suffer through. But I knew not all of my peers shared this opinion, and morale was sinking lower by the moment. We'd singled one another out as obstacles to success or "victory," when in truth we should have been working together as a team. Our success in outer space would depend on it. And so, without too much finesse, I was attempting to reestablish a common opponent that we could unite against. Was my attempt feeble? Did Mr. Boothe suspect right away what I was up to? I didn't know. I wasn't sure it made any difference.

"A dignified panel of Organization employees make up the judging team," Mr. Boothe answered.

"What experience does this panel possess?" Max asked, linking eyes long enough to show that he understood my intent and would help as best he could.

"Years of surveillance," Mr. Boothe snapped. "I assure you, each individual is *over*qualified for this role."

"To assess any individual's reaction, or are they specialized in adolescent responses?" Max asked.

His question was a good one and it caught me off guard. The wheels in my brain worked to follow his line of thought. Mr. Boothe seemed similarly caught off-guard. His response was guarded.

"They can evaluate any behavior," he said slowly.

Max nodded in appreciation of the answer, then tilted his head to smile at me. Out of the corner of my eye, I saw Chris' head snap up. He figured it out before me, but my belly swelled with warmth and pride when he spoke out.

"I'll take my turn next," Chris spoke out. He gave a little nod to Max and made eye contact with me in the silence after his assertion.

"It's—it's your room," Mr. Boothe stumbled over his words, quickly covering his stutter. "You can't assess your own room."

"Are the members of The Organization watching right now?" Chris asked, ignoring Mr. Boothe's confusion.

"You can't assess your own room," Mr. Boothe repeated, this time with conviction.

"I'm asking you if the panel of judges are watching our interactions right now," Chris persisted, unruffled by Mr. Boothe's response.

"Yes. They've watched this entire exchange," Mr. Boothe groused. "But you can't evaluate your own room. That doesn't require the emotional intelligence we're measuring."

"No problem," Chris assured him. He turned on his heel to gaze up at each corner of the room. "I'm not sure where I should direct my words, but I'm guessing I can be seen and heard from where I am."

He paused just long enough to give Mr. Boothe a long, hard look.

"I'll begin," Chris went on. "I imagine the others will fall in line behind me. Mr. Boothe, your frustration and dismay are evident through the rush of blood to your capillaries, which lay quite close to the surface of your epidermis. This signals naturally fair skin. Were I to venture a guess, I'd imagine your ancestors are from Northern Europe."

Amanda laughed out loud; I did my best to stifle my own chuckles. Mr. Boothe looked stupefied and weary at the same time. He massaged his temples and exhaled deeply.

"Thanks for kicking it off, Chris," Luke cut in. "I'm sure you have more to say, but I'll take this opportunity to offer my two cents. That long exhale might have released stale breath in your lungs, but to truly refresh yourself and activate your parasympathetic nervous system, you need to engage in sama vritti breathing.

"As a leader in The Organization, I imagine you've learned the breathing techniques that Ms. Chang introduced us to, so you will have heard of this breathing strategy that measures equal count of breath in and breath out. The fact that you did not employ such therapeutic breathing signals either a disregard for best practices—very common amongst authority figures, I'm told—or stress that has short-circuited your ability to think clearly. Either way, your response signals discomfort and frustration that circumstances have evolved beyond your scope of influence and control."

My heart swelled with pride. It was working. My strategy was working! And Luke's analysis had been thoughtfully worded, to boot—the members of The Organization watching would very likely be impressed by his commentary. We were taking back control and drawing together at the same time.

"Excellent point, Mr. Niciu," Peyton agreed, her tone reminiscent of a newscaster in the throes of a well-planned exposé.

"If I might be allowed to add some speculative commentary…Mr. Boothe rushed into the room without warning in an effort to silence Ms. Alois. In his haste to try to take control of the unsavory situation, he did not have a clear exit strategy or plan for how to proceed after rescuing Mr, Prahalad. I would venture to guess that you are used to having the final word in any situation, Mr. Boothe, and your authority is only challenged on very rare occasions."

Peyton paused in a way that made it clear she had not finished her evaluation. Mr. Boothe was still working to process just how the tables had turned so quickly and could not muster a response in the moments before she carried on.

My heart was soaring to epic levels. Not just because of the feat we'd already managed to negotiate (on some level, I was sure, there would be a price to pay for our impudence), but because of the high level of skill and excellence each of my peers now exhibited.

Subconsciously, the effects of subjugation to The Organization's whims and procedures had eaten away at the confidence and ability of my peers…I had, at times, wondered why they had been identified by The Organization when their showing had thus far been so generic and poor.

Now, through a single act of defiance, we'd empowered the group and reawakened the aptitude and skill that lay inside each one. I was encouraged to see flair that spoke to the reasons why each had been marked as possessing extraordinary talent.

"I would also like to point out that The Organization seems to reward wit and the ability to think quickly," Peyton went on. "This characteristic is not unique to you alone, Mr. Boothe, but has been exhibited by many who have most recently been selected for special distinction within The Organization. This leads me to believe that it is a trait held by the individuals responsible for creating the diagnostic tools for earmarking "special" persons, who likely also possess a generous dose of pride."

"Impulsive behavior that does not always lead to wise decisions," Max agreed, voice soft. Max had a way of doing that—he had joined in the rebuke of Mr. Boothe but somehow his low, warm tone made it feel kind.

"Historically, rash action and quick thinking have kept mankind alive through some very dicey situations. It would be a mistake to allow history to dictate our behavior today—the circumstances might contain some parallels but are in no way the same situation. The Organization has demonstrated a concerning inclination to adhere to past protocol and patterns that have worked well in the past...patterns that would be well and good to follow if we were trying to succeed in the past.

"What worked in the past will not work today. That's the whole reason for our current situation," Max pointed out. "It's pure folly to forge ahead with an outdated game plan."

Max's final indictment hung in the air like pungent socks thrown on the ground. Their presence was evident and needed to be addressed, but no one wanted to be the one to pick them up off the floor.

"I believe you've gotten some words from each of us now," Chris pointed out, taking charge. "Has the assessment been carried out to your satisfaction?"

The words dripped with cynicism that wasn't carried in the tone. I wondered what the panel thought of the exchange: were they sitting up in the observation room horrified at what had taken place? Were they smug and pleased that someone had slighted Mr. Boothe, who had a tendency to behave in an arrogant manner? Were they concerned about our group's preparation for the mission?

In the end, Mr. Boothe couldn't have been more clear—although his body language and emotions were more difficult to discern after our damning assessment. Maybe he did consult with the panel before giving the next direction, but his next action appeared to be completely independent.

"The assessment is over," he announced conclusively. "Get out."

Promises Realized

I worried in the moments after Mr. Boothe sent us from the room. He was clearly upset, and I wasn't sure to what extent and depth we'd ruffled his feathers. Would he still want to meet with me that evening? And, more importantly...would I still get my kitten?

The good news was, of course, that our group had inched closer to operating as a team. No concrete walls had been bulldozed, but there were new cracks that the light shone through...there was the potential for unity that hadn't existed before.

"That was epic," Marcus announced as we left the room. "Mr. Boothe got roasted!"

"I hope the retaliation won't affect us *all*," Clarice said sourly. She couldn't just acknowledge the victory...she had to hold a grudge, and she would never show appreciation for a good idea that she hadn't birthed.

"It was a brilliant idea, Selina," Peyton praised, speaking over Clarice. "The first time we worked together as a team to pass a test," she added with a smile.

"I'm not taking any credit for this one," I was quick to speak up. I'd been singled out quite enough for my own good—the only thing that would detract from this win would be to pin the victory on a single person rather than the group effort. "Max is the one who really got things going, and Chris' opening remarks completely baffled Mr. Boothe!" I chuckled at the thought of Mr. Boothe's wide, clueless eyes.

"And then all of you followed up with total zingers," Luke laughed. "It was like each comment got better...Mr. Boothe barely had a chance to process one remark before we hit him with the next one. Max, your comment was pure brilliance."

Max smiled and accepted the fist-bump that Luke sent his way. It wasn't just me who felt grateful for the newfound team spirit...it was clear from the group's easy gait and light banter that everyone felt the release from a burden that had been carried around for too long, unnamed.

"If we weren't sold on the need to work together as a team before..." Chris spoke, letting the statement linger.

I was relieved that someone had made the observation most likely to propel us towards actual change... and I wasn't surprised that Chris was the one to make the assertion.

"So what you're saying is we should burn those lists we made earlier," Marcus joked.

"If you actually made a list, that would probably be a wise idea," Max said drily. "I can't see any benefit to sharing a list of accusations."

"It would clear the air," Clarice argued. She took great pains to keep her tone neutral. I had to marvel at Clarice's resolve: she was not one to let things go easily.

"We've started the work towards rebuilding relationships, but it really hasn't gone anywhere," she went on. "It seems like it would be best to put it all out there, and then move forward."

"It seems like we all have a pretty good read on each other," Peyton disagreed. "The last test proved our ability to make inferences and read emotions. We don't need to hear accusations read aloud."

"Are you worried about what might be written about you?" Clarice asked. Her tone was innocent, but I saw through her flagrant attempt to bully Peyton.

"No," Peyton countered quickly, nostrils flaring.

"*I* don't want to know what you have to say about Peyton," Marcus chimed in good-naturedly. "Or me," he added with just enough hesitation in between to make us laugh.

"Let's move forward," Chris agreed. "The past is the past, and there's no place for us there. The future is where we need to survive," he professed wisely.

He was right, and the fact that the group held him in unanimous high regard made his suggestion the final word on the matter. I wondered if he was trying to position himself as the "leader" of this newly-professed group…from what I knew about Chris, he would enjoy a place of elevated influence and position—anything that distinguished him from the pack.

In my mind, his desire for such a role was an immediate disqualifier (I worried about the purity of his motives), but I was also realistic enough to realize that the group was unlikely to accept Max as leader (the most trustworthy and natural leader, in my opinion). He didn't carry himself as an alpha, and he would probably politely discourage any attempt to elevate his status anyway.

I certainly didn't want to lead anything…I was under enough internal pressure trying to figure what my role as "wild card" meant at the same time I wrestled with the prophetic declaration over my life and the systematic execution of my parents. Among other things.

To think, a month ago, I'd worried about being made to eat too much avocado toast and if I'd be sterilized in the moments following the exam. The dramatic turn of events was so jarring it was almost comical…except that it was my life, and it was real. I couldn't think about it without being hit by emotion. This time, tears squirted from the corners of my eyes like an irrigation system with an overzealous sprinkler.

This was how grief caught me these days—in the simplest, most unexpected moments. Not when the pressure had built or when others' expectations threatened to suffocate me…not even when the danger rose to astronomical levels.

It was in the moments following any of these "highs": the nameless, faceless moments that should have carried nothing but the relief of survival that I instead felt the brunt of life's new gravity. The pattern had repeated itself enough times that I should have grown to expect it, but it continued to catch me off guard.

They all thought I was indestructible. I'm sure on some level they realized the impossibility of enduring trauma without any scars, but in their own spheres of confusion and protection of self, my hurt didn't register. It didn't even make their top twenty list of curiosities and unknowns.

I was quick to swipe my tears with the back of my hand, but the swollen silence assured me that my peers had seen my spontaneous episode of sorrow. We were presumably selected for our many talents and skills, however veiled and hidden they may have been. Mercifully, no one addressed my tears.

"So…how do we team-build?" Amanda asked, her compassionate tone further proof that my emotion had been noted.

"Team bonfire! Burn the lists!" Marcus suggested, nudging Clarice with his elbow. He was the only one who could get away with such a statement, and still Clarice rolled her eyes at him with mock disdain.

"Can you imagine? We'd set off every fire alarm in the building," Peyton mused, shaking her head.

"What better way to come together against The Organization?" Amanda joked. "Treat us better, or we'll burn down your building!"

"Throw in some graham crackers, marshmallows and chocolate, and we can make s'mores, too," Luke added.

"Luke, you're too focused on food," Amanda rebuked. "If we're going to survive this mission, you need to start taking better care of yourself."

Spoken lightly, there was weight to the words that wasn't lost on any of them. If they truly *were* going to operate as a team, they needed to start looking out for one another, taking care of themselves in order to take care of each other.

"Yeah, yeah," Luke dismissed with a wave of his hand. As silence settled like a wet blanket, he laughed nervously. "Okay!" he acquiesced with a shrug. "I'll pay more attention."

"We'll help you," Peyton assured him, and a few others chuckled.

"Yeah, I'm sure you will," Luke agreed sarcastically.

"We really do need to take care of each other," I couldn't keep from speaking up any longer. "I hate to sound cliché, but we're a unit now. Like a family."

"It's true," Chris agreed, throwing his authority behind my remark.

Even though his words were supportive, I felt the prickle of irritation at what I believed to be further confirmation of his posturing for position. He seemed to regard me as his competition…and the last thing I wanted was to battle for the role of monarch.

"I have an idea," I suggested shyly. I hesitated for just a moment—my idea was innocent and endearing in a way that might come across as idealistic or trite. Clarice half-rolled her eyes in my direction, but the others waited in earnest silence.

"What if we made new lists—lists that detail the *strengths* we each have?" I spoke cautiously, a ballerina tepidly fluttering to position in center-stage. "That seems like a way to restart in a positive way…you know, build a new foundation based on something good," I finished rather inarticulately, self-conscious that my idea would be laughed at.

"I love it," Peyton announced before anyone else had a chance to comment.

"Me too," Amanda agreed. "That's a list I'll actually look forward to hearing."

"In case anyone wondered who the more emotional gender is…" Marcus began, clearly amused. "I like the idea, too. But don't expect me to clap my hands or gush about it."

"It's a good idea," Chris nodded, and the others joined him in agreeing to the task. Even Clarice, who likely couldn't imagine a way to weasel out of the task without coming across as immature and further isolating herself.

"Our new afternoon task," Peyton sang happily.

"Should we share after dinner tonight?" Luke asked. "Will that give everyone enough time?"

There were nods and positive assertations, and my breath caught for just a moment. My meeting. The meeting with Mr. Boothe.

"It might need to be later," I began slowly, considering how to explain my situation. Eyes turned to face me, and I weighed my words carefully before continuing. To conceal the truth now, when we'd just taken a step forward in unity, would be foolish.

"Mr. Boothe asked to meet with me after dinner," I told the group simply. "I'm not sure what he wants to talk about, or how long it will take."

"Mr. Boothe wants to meet with *only* you?" Clarice asked, eyes narrowed in suspicion or curiosity (probably both).

"Yes." I fought the urge to qualify the statement. Those were the facts, and I shouldn't feel pressure to elaborate.

"Have you met with him privately before?" Amanda wanted to know.

"I have not," I answered simply.

"And he didn't tell you what the meeting would be about?" Chris asked, considering me carefully.

"Nope," I agreed.

"What is so different about you?" Chris wondered aloud. I blushed at the audible declaration of what we all wanted to know.

"Honestly, I wish I knew," I laughed. It wasn't funny, but it was ironic. I was trying to figure out the answer to that question, too. "Maybe I'll find out after the meeting tonight."

"Probably not," Max spoke up, winking at me,

"Probably not," I agreed. "But maybe I'll have a better idea of what's going on and what we're in for,"

"Did he—" Peyton began, but then cut herself off as she considered her question. "I have a lot of questions," she finally said, "but I doubt they're questions you can answer. Or if you can, you might not be allowed to."

"I don't want to keep secrets," I told the group, hoping to calm some nerves. The truth was, I was already carrying a slew of secrets...some that affected the group, others that only affected me.

"I believe you," Peyton professed, eyes meeting mine.

I wasn't sure exactly how, but we'd apparently built a bond of trust and deeper friendship in the past twenty-four hours. I was grateful for her allegiance at the same time that I wondered if this new dynamic would impact the larger group.

"We'll wait up for you," Luke said. "I don't think any of us will be able to sleep, anyway, knowing about that meeting."

The lists seemed to write themselves, and dinner came and went. I couldn't say what I ate or how it tasted. I tried to stay in the present moment, but the reality was that I was thinking ahead to my meeting with Mr. Boothe, wondering what he might ask me and what his intention was for meeting with me in the first place.

Before I knew it, I was clearing my tray. Mr. Boothe had assured me he would be watching dinner; that he would meet with me directly after.

The group said goodbye uncertainly as they made their way to the common area. I stood alone in front of the elevator, butterflies twirling in my stomach as I waited for my lift up.

The return trip to the observation room felt longer, my steps significant in what felt like a march towards destiny. I'd worried before that someone might see me as I navigated the restricted hallways, now, *knowing* that I was being watched (that my very presence was anticipated) made me stiff and awkward.

I went to and through the bathroom, and then I was standing in the observation room, grateful and also concerned when I found only Mr. Boothe waiting for me. It was just as he had said it would be.

"How was dinner?" Mr. Boothe asked simply, the topic light and frivolous considering the depth we were about to plunge to.

"Fine," I answered, shifting my weight from side to side. We were both nervous, and even if we tried to hide it, we were also both intuitive enough to pick up on the signs.

Mr. Boothe sighed and ran a hand through his hair. "We probably should have had this conversation earlier."

"Probably," I agreed, beginning to relax. I needed to be on guard, but I didn't get the impression I was under attack. It seemed as though Mr. Boothe wanted to have a candid conversation…could it be as simple as that?

Mr. Boothe seemed to consider me for a moment and come to the same conclusion himself.

"Why don't we sit down?" he suggested, gesturing to a pair of oversized armchairs nestled in the corner. "There isn't any hurry, and it might make things more comfortable."

As we settled into the space. I marveled at how deceiving the scene must appear to the unknowing spectator: had the circumstances been different, we could have been two friends getting cozy for a catch-up session with mugs of hot cocoa.

"How are you finding life at headquarters?" Mr. Boothe began. It wasn't the question he wanted to ask, and we both knew it. Was he being polite, or was he afraid or uncertain of how to initiate the conversation he *really* wanted to have?

"Why am I here, Mr. Boothe?" I asked, ignoring his question. "Why was I selected, why am I considered a wild card, why do I seem to respond differently than everyone else, and why are we having this conversation right now?" I went on, realizing my initial question could be interpreted any number of ways.

Mr. Boothe laughed. A wry, cynical chuckle that served as a warning: I was unlikely to come away with the answers I was looking for. "Selina, that is what we are all trying to figure out," he answered, shaking his head in open confusion.

"Well, you at least know why you picked me," I challenged. If hope was an inflated helium balloon, Mr. Boothe's uncertainty was the miniature pin from the pincushion that had subtly pricked the latex shell. It was a slow trickle, but air was leaving the balloon…and there was no sign of it stopping.

"The *exam* selected you," Mr. Boothe reminded me, eyebrows arched in the way of a reproachful elder.

"But you made the exam," I protested. "Or at least, you are part of the panel that created the exam—*understands* the exam…you must at least understand what the exam is measuring if you administer it," I thought aloud.

"I did not make the exam," Mr. Boothe began with caution. "But I do see the categories that the exam measures, and I know the results."

He paused, measuring his next words carefully. "There are a number of sub-categories, but the major evaluations are for physical fitness, morality, bodily health, textual intelligence, abstract reasoning, wisdom, interpersonal skill, resourcefulness, and self-awareness.

"These are all components that can be reduced to measurable outcomes and quantifiable responses. For example, physical fitness can be measured by speed, endurance, strength, and flexibility. Textual intelligence can be measured through academic performance. Interpersonal skill can be observed through verbal and bodily responses in any number of situations, as well as through an analysis of pre-frontal cortex activity during these encounters.

"There is one element to the exam that is not tangibly tied to something…it's not something anyone in The Organization can interpret or explain. You may have heard of the prophets…" he paused here to look at me.

My heart pumped faster, and I thought of my parents and the powerful words I had etched into my heart. I nodded to Mr. Boothe to continue.

"The prophets came up with the final measure. It was determined at that time, by everyone of importance, that this was an essential component to the exam that would measure the supernatural aptitude of the individual. I can't tell you much more than that, Selina," Mr. Boothe warned, probably because my eyes lit up and I couldn't help but lean forward in anticipation.

"The ten factors do not carry equal weight," Mr. Boothe went on. "Each one is awarded a score from 0-100, but it's not as simple as looking at the overall score after adding up each category. There's an algorithm that determines overall propensity for any given position…and it's based on a combination of factors as opposed to a single metric."

He paused, and my mind thrust into overdrive trying to fit all the pieces together. Already, this new information was helping me to make sense of what I had experienced. Synapses firing, I reflected on my frequent other-worldly dreams, the small guiding voices I carried with me in my head, and the fact that I seemed to know in my spirit an outcome long before I knew in my head.

"As you may have already guessed, your supernatural aptitude score was off the charts," Mr. Boothe explained. "Literally, the highest score we've seen in centuries. More pronounced, because the societal trend in this age of information and scientific discovery has led to the lowest average of all time."

"What was my score?" I couldn't help but ask.

"The average in supernatural aptitude for the past ten years has been a 13," Mr. Boothe began. "The highest score recorded in the past fifty years is a 41." He looked me straight in the eye. "And you scored an 89."

"Eighty-nine?" I asked faintly.

My voice sounded like an echo; hollow words that traveled through the air like vapor. As Mr. Boothe had unpacked the situation, I'd acknowledged my ability to comprehend things on a deeper level than most…I couldn't know for certain, seeing as I'd only ever been myself, but I was ready to accept it. But the astronomical gap between my skill and the rest of humanity? It was too much to accept. I might have been good, but I wasn't *that* good.

"I don't think that can be right," I told Mr. Boothe, shaking my head for measure. "I'm not trying to be modest—that really doesn't sound right," I was quick to add.

"Selina, we've considered the metric from every angle we can think of. And we've been following this for a lot longer than you. Not only does your score check out, but your response to these assessments seems to support the fact that you have extraordinary supernatural aptitude. And no one knows what to do with that," Mr. Boothe explained.

I stared at him, eyes wide and unblinking. Surprised? Horrified? Baffled? Check, check, check.

"Your peers are in awe of you, afraid of you, or jealous of you. And none of the rest of us know what to do with you. We train and teach for the other nine categories…we don't have a workshop for the supernatural. I know you picked up on our dissent—it's very real. There's never been a situation like this before," Mr. Boothe finished.

I didn't know what to say. How could I contest the fact that I was different when I'd never had the experience of being someone else? There was no logic I could employ to make the case I was quickly losing faith in.

"What do we do with that?" I asked uncertainly. He had asked to meet with me…I was hoping he had some sort of plan.

"What we're doing now," Mr. Boothe answered, making no attempt to sugar-coat the situation. "We put our heads together and see if we can come up with something."

"Are we really that far off?" I wanted to know. I was changing the subject, but it was a question I wanted answered. I wasn't in a place to directly unpack what Mr. Boothe had just shared: I knew I would continue to wrestle with the unsettling news no matter what we discussed.

"Your group, you mean?" Mr. Boothe asked. He didn't seem put out that I had redirected our conversation.

I nodded, gauging his response carefully. With a heavy sigh, he leaned back in his chair before fixing his eyes on me once again.

"It's hard to know. We've never sent students into the farthest realms of outer space," he reminded me. "The colonization of the moon is the closest attempt that's been made, but it's a far cry from Venus or Heidel."

"But your comments suggest that we're farther behind than the moon crew," I pointed out.

"That's not true," Mr. Boothe was quick to counter. "We didn't know as much about the moon crew. Also, they worked to colonize an object in outer space we knew a great deal about. We had tangible experience with humans visiting the moon…we were working to take the next step in establishing a permanent habitat there. We've never sent humans to Venus or Heidel…and our first attempt will also include the intentional formation of human civilization."

"So why not send exploratory crews?" I asked. "That seems like the logical first step. Why the pressure to suddenly send eight sixteen-year-olds to the ends of the universe?" When I put our reality into words, it did seem rather ridiculous.

Mr. Boothe hemmed, then hawed. I could imagine the chewed-up insides of his cheeks and the metallic taste of iron-rich blood that was probably settling in his mouth. He was holding something back.

"Just say it," I ordered. It was a bold, somewhat sassy demand, but I figured we'd passed formalities. Uncomfortable truths had already been unwrapped—we were no longer marveling at half-baked lies covered in pastel paper and thick ribbon. It was time to put it all on the table.

Mr. Boothe didn't correct me, he didn't reprimand me…he didn't even seem surprised by my mandate. "Don't judge me too harshly," he said without much emotion before clapping loudly.

An authoritative voice came from speakers I couldn't see. "Yes, Mr. Boothe? How may I assist you?"

I wondered if the voice belonged to a simple machine or sophisticated artificial intelligence. I also considered that the voice could be the party responsible for my ability to access the surveillance footage from earlier.

"Please pull up the data regarding Asteroid Atticus," Mr. Boothe announced solemnly. To me, he uttered a quick, "pay attention."

I didn't need the cue, but the way he said it suggested I would not have repeated opportunities to engage with whatever I was about to see. I sat up straight and waited expectantly.

Not a moment later, a holographic image appeared. The mountainous brown orb that I assumed was Asteroid Atticus looked like a crusted-over tangle of rubber bands: the sphere rose and fell in flaky crests the color of fiber-rich cereal. It began to move and spin, but it wasn't until it passed what I took to be Mars that I realized the size of the rock.

Mars appeared as a ping-pong ball next to the giant mass of metal and gas. Asteroid Atticus was a monster.

"Eighty percent iron, fifteen percent nickel, and five percent iridium, palladium, platinum, gold, and magnesium," Mr. Boothe announced, his tone detached in the way of well-versed tour guides. His eyes never moved from the projection of Asteroid Atticus as it hurtled past Mars and on towards Earth.

"Is it…" I began, unable to narrate the travesty I suspected I was about to witness.

"It is," Mr. Boothe confirmed.

Instinctively, I looked away. The asteroid was so…*big*, and Earth looked so puny in comparison. The clash would be terrible. I felt sick to my stomach—the utter and violent end of mankind was not something I cared to see.

"You asked. Watch," Mr. Boothe barked.

He had no real recourse with which to force me to comply, but I lifted my eyes and steeled my stomach and watched as Asteroid Atticus careered closer and closer and closer to Earth. I held my breath in the final stretches, every muscle in my body tense.

Mercifully, there was no sound. The visual of Earth—beautiful, majestic, vivacious Earth—exploding into a fiery ball of brilliant tangerine flame and charcoal rock upon contact with Asteroid Atticus was enough to frost my innards. The effects were far-reaching, the debris pluming from the point of impact like fireworks on the Fourth of July.

My mouth was dry. I swallowed hard, reminding my body to lubricate my throat as I searched for words.

"Five years from now," Mr. Boothe spoke into the silence, answering the question I couldn't vocalize.

"Five years?!" I rasped, incredulous. Five years, in space talk, might as well have been five minutes. The fastest recorded trip to Venus had taken just over three months…to colonize the planet would take significantly more time. A next-day departure might be too late.

"Perhaps our recent push makes more sense now," Mr. Boothe said drily.

"Why wait so long?" I asked, finding my voice again.

"It was never the intention," Mr. Boothe answered. "And not my idea," he added. "But it's the reality of where we are now…and we can only move forward."

My mind reeled. There was *way* more pressure on our mission than I'd realized…we weren't just colonizing new planets—we were the short-term solution for the survival of mankind. Our success would allow the human race to live on; our failure would preclude the end of life.

"How certain is this projection?" I asked quickly as goosebumps cropped up on my arms like kernels of popcorn.

"Definite," Mr. Boothe said resolutely, anticipating my question. "And we've already tried to deflect and target the asteroid to dismantle it. It's too big. At this point, further action invites the risk of the debris moving into a new orbit that would speed up the time of collision."

I could doubt Mr. Boothe's analysis, but I knew it wasn't Mr. Boothe's analysis. The doomsday theory was the conclusion of a conglomerate of highly-skilled researchers, scientists, physicists, mathematicians, and who-knows-who-else. And my doubt could grow larger than life, but it would do nothing to counter the effects that Mr. Boothe believed were inevitable.

The way I saw it, I could respond in fear, desperation, depression, or stubborn resolve and anxiety-induced action. The latter two seemed preferable, although I was not naïve to the heavy personal cost that this response would claim.

"I don't expect you to have much of a response," Mr. Boothe told me. "We can meet again, when you're ready. But I wanted you to see the stakes, to know what we're up against."

I nodded dumbly. I was glad to know—it was better to know the terrible truth than live in a cloud of fantastical illusion, wasn't it? I'd need to remind myself of this firm conviction when I struggled to fall asleep at night. Questions buzzed around in my mind like mosquitoes: too many, too close—I needed time to make sense of what the next steps should be.

"Can I see my result?" I asked in a moment of sudden inspiration.

"Your exam result?" Mr. Boothe clarified, his tone laced with caution.

"Yes. I want to see my other scores," I explained. I'd scored an incredible "89" in supernatural aptitude, but what of the other nine categories?

"I don't know if that's a good idea," Mr. Boothe spoke slowly.

"We're laying everything else out on the table!" I exclaimed. "I'm not sure what you're worried might happen…"

Still, Mr. Boothe hesitated. "You ask for a lot," he stated a moment later. "For someone selected for a program, you make quite a few demands."

"You're asking a lot of me," I countered, unwilling to be cowed into redacting my request. "And we should be *partnering* with you. If we're going to succeed, we're going to have to work together. That means I make requests as an equal, important counterpart."

"I really think it's better you not see," Mr. Boothe protested. "But I won't withhold the scores if you insist on seeing them."

I hesitated. I wanted to see my scores, and I wanted to see them even more now that Mr. Boothe questioned whether it was a good idea. My mind raced to try to figure out why he might not want me to.

"I want to see them," I announced stubbornly.

With a sigh, Mr. Boothe clapped once more. "Selina Alois' exam results, please."

Seconds later, my scores were projected in bold black lettering. My eyes raced over the numbers.

Physical Fitness—74
Morality—80
Bodily Health—68
Textual Intelligence—53
Abstract Reasoning—44
Wisdom—71
Interpersonal Skill—65
Resourcefulness—62
Self-awareness—33
Supernatural Aptitude—89

Disappointing scores, in my estimation. I looked to Mr. Boothe for interpretation.

"Pretty average," he agreed. "Morality is high, and physical fitness and wisdom are above average. But the rest of your skills are pretty in-line with your high-achieving peers. It's the supernatural aptitude that really tipped the scales."

"The others?" I wanted to know. "They had better scores?"

"I'm going to draw the line at pulling up the others' scores," Mr. Boothe told me directly. "But yes…holistically speaking, their scores are much higher."

This news frustrated me at the same time that it didn't really surprise me. I should have known as much—these were kids I'd been in school with for all of my life. We knew each other's strengths and weaknesses well by this point. The competitive part of me had secretly hoped I'd somehow outperformed them in all categories even as I knew it was better for our mission that I was grouped with individuals with talents that surpassed (and likely complemented) my own.

"And somehow I'm performing best in the assessments," I mused. It wasn't said with pride…I was truly interested in why that might be.

"Supernatural aptitude," Mr. Boothe reminded me. "Your instincts are uncanny."

The buzzing in my head grew louder. It wouldn't be wise to try to accrue any further resolution or understanding in that moment. Mr. Boothe read my expression and stood up.

"We can meet again. That's enough for tonight," he told me with more kindness than I remembered ever receiving from him.

I nodded and stood up, ready to retrace my steps back to the pods. I felt weary thinking about my peers waiting for a full report…the weight of the world had now fallen upon my supernaturally-strong but physically-fallible shoulders.

"Thanks," I remembered to offer before I left. For all my questions and suspicions and hesitations concerning Mr. Boothe, I had to also acknowledge his candor and resolve. I knew well enough to encourage every act of kindness and generosity, no matter how small.

"It's not all up to you, Selina," Mr. Boothe reminded me quietly.

I kept walking, lost in thought. But his next words sent vibrations of excitement barreling through my body. "You're not going to leave without your kitten, are you?"

Purrfection

I froze in place. Colors exploded in my brain at the same time I literally felt heat rush from my toes up my spine.

"My kitten." I repeated dumbly, looking up at Mr. Boothe with a heart full of hope and expectation.

Mr. Boothe chuckled. "For all your fussing, I'm shocked you almost left without him,"

"Him? It's a boy?" I asked. *Of course it's a boy, Selina. Remember your dream?*

"It is," Mr. Boothe agreed, unable to hold back a smile at my obvious wonder and excitement.

I looked around. I was still in a fog, but I hadn't recalled seeing any kitten in the observation vicinity.

A sharp clap from Mr. Boothe, then a simple proclamation: "Please bring in the kitten."

My mouth went dry; my fingers curled into fists. It was hard to blink. The room was temperature-controlled at a cool 65 degrees, and I was sweating with anticipation. I didn't want to miss a single moment with my kitten: I needed to be alert at the exact moment he arrived on the scene.

I'd asked for a kitten, I'd dreamt of the kitten, and I'd shamelessly pressed and pressed and pressed for the receipt of my furry bundle of joy. But now that the moment had come, I found that I was surprised.

On some level, I'd doubted I'd get him. I'd so badly wished for it to be true…I couldn't believe it was actually happening.

Could it possibly be so simple? I was used to battling for the things I got…and even then I often received a reduced version of what I'd hoped for. I marveled at this development at the same time I acknowledged the settled warmth in my belly that reminded me that I'd always known I would receive the kitten.

Supernatural aptitude, my subconscious reminded me. Now that I had a name for my intuition, I expected I would start attributing a lot more to this characteristic.

A petite woman of nondescript appearance walked into the room, My eyes immediately traveled to her crossed arms: a small nutmeg-brown ball of fur lay perched atop her forearms, resting like a sphinx. My heartbeat sped up.

"Meow." The shrill and confident cry didn't match the two-pound mass making its way towards me, and I laughed out loud.

"You two should make a fine pair," Mr. Boothe observed with some sarcasm. "Neither of you have much problem making yourself heard…you're both *quite* vocal."

Normally, I would have at least addressed the slight (or shot back with some sarcasm of my own), but I was so eager to collect my most precious earth artifact that I didn't say a word. For all my anticipation, I stayed rooted in place—to walk forward would be to break the spell. If this was in fact just a dream, I didn't want to pull myself out of it.

The woman drew near, and my eyes feasted on the kitty that was to be mine; on *Felix*. His bright green eyes regarded me with open curiosity, his oversized ears pointed in my direction. His fur was short, just like in the pictures I'd seen, and curled into slight ringlets just above his limbs. His striped tail spoke to his ferocity at the same time his slight body told of fragility.

"Hi Felix," I spoke quietly, testing the name and my kitty's response. It was the first time I'd said the name out loud and it rolled right off the tongue.

"Mowww," Felix replied.

Probably, it was in response to the greeting I very clearly directed at him, but on some level I wanted to believe my cat was a genius who already knew his name. It would only be fitting that Felix would share my supernatural aptitude, right?

I almost asked if I could hold him…then checked myself. He was *my* kitten. Of course I could.

A moment later, Felix was snuggled close to my middle, held tightly by arms that didn't want to ever let him go. I marveled at how soft he was and how quiet he was as he observed the exchange.

"The necessities have been put up in your pod: litter box, feeding and water bowls, and a few simple toys. You'll find food for Felix in the cafeteria when you take meals for yourself," Mr. Boothe explained.

I nodded without really absorbing what Mr. Boothe said. He could have told me that Felix would need a steady diet of hot-pink lizards and brass buttons, and I would have nodded my compliance. Felix was mine! He was here! And he was perfect. My eyes glazed over with tears much like a snow-globe, but none fell down my cheeks.

"You can leave. Thank you," I heard Mr. Boothe dismiss the woman.

I didn't take my eyes off Felix and he didn't take his eyes off of me. All joking aside, I knew right away that he was a special kitten.

"Where does he sleep? And where do I put him when I'm testing?" I asked suddenly. My window for asking the most pressing questions was closing, and I needed to get answers before I was truly on my own.

"I thought you'd want him to sleep with you," Mr. Boothe said slowly, seemingly surprised.

"I do," I snapped. I hadn't realized that was an option, but I latched onto it immediately. "He can stay with me all the time?"

"There's a large crate in your pod, in case you need to confine him," Mr. Boothe told me. "But I thought you'd want to train him to stay by your side. There's a leash in the basket of supplies that was taken up to you," he added.

I nodded my fervent agreement. Yes, Felix would be my constant companion. I stared down at my watchful kitty who was still silently taking it all in. I was going to have to do a *lot* more research—the responsibility required had never been more apparent than the present moment, when the furry ball was settled in the crook of my left arm.

"Thank you," I whispered to Mr. Boothe. Spoken softly, I'd never been more grateful. I looked up to Mr. Boothe and wondered at his gentle expression.

"Pets were a good thing," he said mildly. "I was sorry when we did away with them. I understand why it happened, but I miss the comfort and joy they brought. I suppose I should be grateful for your unorthodox request for an earth artifact...I can't imagine welcoming an animal into The Organization otherwise."

I nodded without looking up. I would stare at Felix all day and night...or as long as I could keep my eyes open.

"Your friends are waiting, right?" Mr. Boothe reminded me lightly.

"Oh! Right," I agreed, breaking free of my trance and finding movement once again. "Will you be watching?" I asked as I turned to leave—this time for real.

"As much as I can," Mr. Boothe answered honestly. "We're trying to figure you out as best we can, to help you as much as we can." He sounded weary as he spoke.

"Am I supposed to keep what I learned a secret?" I asked. My peers were expecting a report, and I needed to think through what I was allowed to divulge and consider what I *wanted* to share.

"I can't control your behavior," Mr. Boothe told me evenly. "I'll leave that to you and your supernatural aptitude to determine. Just remember the end goal and consider how best to set us up for success."

I nodded with quiet contemplation, smiled at Mr. Boothe, and then left.

I walked on clouds down the hallway and to the elevator and then to the pods. I wasn't aware of the distance I walked or how long it took...and I was grateful the path was even and easy, because my eyes were fixated on Felix and not the path that I walked.

I made it back to the pods too soon. I was exhausted and in no mood to talk or emotionally invest in anyone; if I did anything at all, I wanted it to be all focused on my new kitten. I was eager to see what supplies The Organization had dropped off for him and I fought down the mounting irritation that came when I thought about what was waiting for me.

I wished for the group to be asleep when I returned; I wished that they'd had the best of intentions for staying up to hear from me but that they'd been overcome with fatigue they turned in early. I knew the futility of my wish even as I spent energy imagining my ideal scenario.

"Selina's back!" I heard Amanda's voice call out when I took my first step into the room.

My body tensed and I forced myself to keep moving forward. I couldn't see anyone yet, but I heard the rustling of blankets and squeaking of metal as my peers presumably left their pods to come and greet me.

"You're still up," I said evenly when I rounded the corner and found all seven of them waiting for me.

"You sound disappointed," Clarice was quick to retort.

"I'm tired," I warned, my response an oblique attempt to dodge her question. I wouldn't withhold information and deprive them of the truth they needed to hear, but I wanted to manage expectations right off the bat. There was no way I was going to deliver news with passion.

"O-M-G," Peyton cut in. "Is that your kitten?!"

My arms instinctively wrapped tighter around Felix, who protested with a solid *meow*. I looked down into the face of my little feline and couldn't help but smile.

"This is Felix," I announced proudly, as though I was somehow responsible for his perfection.

"Ohmygoodness. He is soooo precious!" Amanda squealed.

Peyton stood with one hand over her open mouth. Her eyes were wide and she looked at me hopefully. "Please, can I hold him?"

"I'm supposed to hold him for the first twenty-four hours." The lie rolled easily off my tongue, a reproof to my high morality score. "They bond to their owner during that time. But you can pet him," I added, moving closer to Peyton.

Peyton's gaze of wonder never faded as she considered Felix's tiny frame. "Have any of the rest of you ever seen a pet?" she asked the others without taking her eyes off the kitten nestled in my arms.

The murmurs were united: no one had ever seen a pet in physical form; the stretch of silence that followed seemed to be in reverence for this new experience.

I watched like a hawk as Peyton extended a gentle hand out and stroked Felix's soft hind leg. She touched him softly, as though he was a porcelain doll or antique teacup from the Ming Dynasty. My body relaxed; I let down my guard and allowed my breath to fall into a regular rhythm as Peyton lovingly caressed Felix.

For the first time, I thought to look up at the others. There were tender expressions on every face…Felix elicited the delicate parts of each individual. Amanda even had tears in her eyes. Max was the only one who did not appear to be captivated by Felix: instead, his eyes seemed to regard *my* response.

I smiled tentatively, knowing Max's wisdom was such that he had probably already figured out my lie and source of hesitation. His ability to see beyond to the true nature of things had unnerved me in the beginning, but I was beginning to accept this truth without the accompanying feelings of judgment and anxiety. Max never used his insight to condemn.

"He is so precious," Peyton managed to choke out, throat constricted and words tight with emotion. She reluctantly backed away to allow Amanda a turn to pet Felix.

Felix, for his part, was quite content to be touched by each person. I'd forgotten to ask Mr. Boothe about his first months of life: had he been held by humans? Cared for by robots or some other form of artificial intelligence? What did he like to play with, and had he demonstrated any abnormalities or health scares? In my fog of emotion, I'd simply accepted my kitten. Now, I worried I was sorely underprepared.

"I wonder if we'll all get our earth artifacts soon, then," Luke thought aloud.

"It's possible," I said with a shrug. I felt a little bad that I hadn't thought to ask Mr. Boothe. "I think they're usually distributed close to the mission launch date…but in my case, we need to get used to each other first." This was my best guess, but Mr. Boothe had said nothing to confirm this logic.

"I wish I'd asked for a kitten," Amanda lamented.

"Me too," Peyton agreed.

"I should have asked for a dog. Like a Burmese Mountain dog," Marcus joked. "Imagine taking a beast like that into outer space!"

We laughed together at the sheer ridiculousness of Marcus' vision, knowing he was only kidding.

"None of us would have had our requests fulfilled," Clarice's negativity sliced through the air. "It's only because *Selina* made the request and she made it in public, in front of everyone, that she got her kitten. It was a strategic move," she ended with appreciation.

I swallowed the defensive response that pieced itself together in my mind. Clarice wasn't speaking for the entire group…she was speaking for herself and herself alone. And, if I were forced to be honest, I had to consider that there might be truth to her words. I didn't want to believe that I'd been treated differently, but it was very possibly true. My path to the present had been unorthodox, and I wasn't sure what rationale stood behind a good number of the decisions that had been made.

"That seems like as good a transition as any," Chris interjected. "I know we're all interested in knowing what Mr. Boothe had to say. And why he wanted to meet with you in the first place."

I nodded and took a deep breath.

"Should we move to the common room?" Amanda suggested. "We might as well get comfortable."

Ten minutes later, we were tucked in one of the private rooms. We sat in a circle with legs crossed like children ready to play a game of telephone. Max disappeared briefly on our way to the room; when he reappeared, it was with a steaming mug of coffee that he held out to me.

My heart leapt with gratitude as I accepted the mug and deeply inhaled the smell of the steaming hazelnut brew. "Thank you," I exhaled, voice full of appreciation. Max's ability to intuit my needs—needs that I wasn't even able to identify myself—was uncanny. I worried that maybe he knew me better than I knew myself.

"And the Boyfriend of the Year award goes to Max Darnall," Marcus teased, his voice full of mirth.

"He's not my boyfriend," I forced myself to say in defense of Max. My reluctance caught me off guard: another thing I would need to consider. Was it my fatigue and gratitude speaking, or did I hold a deep affection for Max that crossed the boundary of friendship? I didn't know. If I ever had the opportunity for self-reflection, I would be busy for years unpacking all the layers of my inner self.

"But he wants to be," Luke muttered under his breath.

My cheeks reddened and my heart swelled with hope that I couldn't latch onto. My eyes flitted up to Max just long enough to see that he wasn't flustered at all by the banter. I was, and I looked down at the ground and tucked my hair behind my ear nervously before attempting to move past the teasing.

"Let's let her speak without interrupting," Peyton scolded, nodding her encouragement to me.

I didn't know where to begin: how far back did I want to go, and how much did I want to divulge? I almost wished Mr. Boothe had given me firm parameters regarding what I was and was not allowed to share…the ambiguity of my present situation meant I needed to tread very carefully. No matter what I said, I would be judged. No matter what I said, things would change. Those were certainties.

"How did you know you were going to be picked?" Clarice asked. Her words were direct, but not mean. I suspected it was a question that had nagged her for weeks.

"I just knew," I answered honestly, knowing as I spoke that she would be annoyed and dissatisfied with my response. I would need to add more to keep them from feeling dismissed. "The exam is split into ten categories," I went on carefully.

"One of those categories is supernatural aptitude. When I just met with Mr. Boothe, I learned that my score in this area was highest. My intuition and ability to tap into things not of this world is my greatest strength. So I'm being honest when I say that I don't know. I know what I know without knowing why or how."

I had rapt attention, and I considered how to go on. Felix yawned in my lap and curled into a doughnut. A pitter-pat in my heart, and I took the opportunity to snuggle him closer to me.

"This is apparently an unusual category to score highly in," I explained slowly. "And it's not a strength they've seen in a long time. I get the impression they're not really sure what to do with me." I let go of the breath I had been holding in, satisfied that I had shared an important truth without compromising any secret data.

"You saw your scores?" Chris asked. I'd known this fact would irk him—he itched to learn his own scores immediately upon hearing that I'd gotten mine.

"I did. I'm not sure Mr. Boothe was wild about sharing them with me," I answered honestly. "I pressed a little bit. Not all of it was super flattering, and I didn't see any of your scores," I added, anticipating what questions I might get next.

"What do you mean, they weren't super flattering?" Amanda wanted to know.

"I mean, I wish I'd scored higher in certain categories," I laughed. Even if they pressed me, I wouldn't share my marks in each category. I didn't see anything positive that could come from it.

"You don't plan to share your individual scores, do you?" Clarice asked. It was a judgment that I let roll of my shoulders.

"No," I answered directly. I fought the urge to justify my actions…to do so would suggest I was defensive and speaking from a place of obligation that I did not in fact accept.

"Sooo….he wanted to speak to you to tell you about this strength?" Marcus asked. "What was the point of meeting?"

"I don't know exactly why he wanted to meet," I answered truthfully. "He never said. Honestly, the tension between us has been building ever since the week of the exam—and I think he saw a lot of my behavior as defiant. I think he wanted to try to understand where I was coming from…and in the process, I got some answers."

"Did you talk about your parents?" Peyton asked quietly.

"We did not." My answer was cursory and matter-of-fact. Some grief gurgled from the depths of my belly that I worked to submerge. No, I was not going to entertain thoughts of my parents right now. I had enough emotional wreckage to sort through without also trying to unpack the circumstances of their death.

"Did you get what you needed from the meeting?" Max asked.

I knew what he was getting at, but I chose to answer lightly. I lifted Felix up and smiled. "I got my kitten."

This made everyone smile, even Clarice.

"I wish we could all find out our scores," Chris said wistfully. "Do you think we'll find out at some point?"

"Does it make a difference?" Amanda asked him. "I'm sure we're all curious, but it doesn't really change the outcome—we were all chosen, and we're all here now. I don't know that it would be helpful to find out."

"If we know our strengths and weaknesses, then we can assign leadership roles most appropriately," Chris was quick to respond. He'd clearly already worked through his rationale.

"That might not be the wisest way to allocate roles," Max disagreed. "A score doesn't tell the whole story."

"Right," I agreed. "That's exactly what Mr. Boothe said."

I didn't mention that my scores alone would likely not have earned me a spot on the mission. We were just beginning to build trust in our group—we were far from a place where I felt comfortable confiding that fact. I could anticipate already who would file that information away to pull out and use against me in the future.

"Do we even know what the categories are?" Peyton asked.

My heart lifted—this was something I could share without recompense. "Yes! Let's see if I remember them all." I looked up and counted off on my fingers as I recalled the ten categories. "Physical fitness, textual intelligence, bodily health, interpersonal skill, morality, self-awareness, abstract reasoning..." I struggled to remember the last couple. "Resourcefulness...wisdom, and supernatural aptitude."

I watched as each person considered these categories and quietly speculated as to his or her scores in each area.

"It seems like knowing our scores would help," Chris persisted a moment later. "It would help us to know who to take seriously and who to look to in certain situations."

"We should already know that based on our interactions," I disagreed. "Besides, looking at individual scores doesn't take into consideration the different combinations of scores."

"Your scores must have been really poor," Clarice commented drily.

I reddened and bit my tongue. *Don't say anything, Selina. Not a word. Don't stoop to her level.*

"Come on, Clarice," Marcus chided.

"Well, it's true!" Clarice exclaimed. "Why else would she be working so hard to keep the scores a secret?"

"You can try to learn your scores," I told Clarice, shrugging to emphasize my indifference. "I just don't think it will be helpful. If you want to ask, knock yourself out."

"Moving on..." Amanda cut in, trying to lead us back to more diplomatic discussion. "I think the second reason we were staying up late was to share our lists with each other."

I hadn't brought any list but knew well enough what I could say about each person in the group. It was tempting to allow for the transition to this lighter topic, but my conscience instructed me to reveal just a little more.

"Before we do that..." I began, taking a deep breath. "There's something else you should know."

I hesitated, not for dramatic effect, but as I considered how to break such depressing news. As if reading my thoughts, Luke interrupted.

"Just say it," he blurted.

"There's an asteroid coming for Earth. Asteroid Atticus. It's huge, and there's no chance it will be diverted. It will crash into Earth in five years' time," I announced.

"Five years?!" Peyton squawked.

"Five years," I repeated grimly.

"Why did they wait so long to form the mission groups?" Clarice snapped.

"I asked the same thing," I told Clarice, shrugging my shoulders to show that I had no part in the matter. "Mr. Boothe didn't have an answer. He just said that it was never the intention."

"Well, I'd hope not," Luke snorted. "They've set us up for disaster. If I'm understanding your news correctly, this means that we have a total of five years to explore the new planets, return to Earth, colonize the planet, and evacuate all of mankind."

"IF the planets turn out to be hospitable to human life," Clarice interjected.

"Please tell me this is a joke…or at least that The Organization has a plan," Peyton pleaded, her features twisted into a mask of panic.

I pursed my lips and looked down before shaking my head silently. To say the words out loud was to risk breaking the fragile morale that hung over our group.

There were a few choice expletives, some incredulous chuckles, and hands to the forehead. I was still processing the news myself…I didn't imagine any of us would sleep fitfully that night.

"Did you just find out, too?" Max wanted to know.

I nodded solemnly, eyebrows raised in shared concern.

"Wow," Chris exhaled. "I'm guessing that means we launch soon. Do you have any idea of when?"

I shook my head, wondering if I should reveal more. I caught Max's gaze and he nodded in encouragement, urging me to share more.

"I heard them arguing over when to send us," I added. "The Organization can't agree on whether or not we are ready. They're concerned about our performance on the assessments and our lack of unity."

The words fell heavy with condemnation, which had not been my intention. If I were honest, there probably wasn't any way to deliver that news without also bringing down the hammer of judgment.

"How many assessments are left?" Chris asked.

"How many trainings do we have left?" Amanda asked not a half-second later.

"I don't know." I felt defensive even as I knew that The Organization's decisions and actions bore no reflection on my own thoughts and behavior.

I stifled a yawn. My flesh seemed to sag on my bones; gravity pulled me down in invitation to collapse into a puddle on the floor. It was an offer that was hard to pass up.

"I'm not in the mood to share my list anymore," Amanda spoke up.

"Me, neither," Marcus agreed.

I stayed silent to wait for the group consensus, inwardly hoping that everyone would agree. I wasn't in the mood, and I didn't have the energy.

"I don't think any of us have the heart to do a good job exhorting one another right now," Max said wisely.

"We should still keep the lists," Peyton cut in, and everyone nodded their agreement.

"I don't think we're abandoning the idea…just recognizing that this isn't the best time," Max clarified. "It's been an emotional night, and we have a lot to process already."

There was no dispute. That we'd been emotionally wrung out was undeniable.

"We'll reconvene in the morning, then," Chris asserted.

"Sounds good. Sleep well, everyone," Marcus offered before walking to his pod.

"Goodnight," I mumbled before stumbling to my own pod.

As I climbed the ladder steps to my sleeping place, I noted the cardboard box of cat items resting on the floor. I looked at Felix, snuggled into the crook of my arm, fast asleep. Tomorrow, I would need to sort it out—but for now, sleep beckoned...and I could no longer resist her cry.

I should have known that I would not sleep fitfully. There was far too much for my subconscious to work through. I'd wished for heavy, deep slumber that would lead to complete refreshment in the morning—this was not to be the case.

I couldn't tell you what I dreamt about the first part of the night, but I knew that I woke up in a cold sweat, heart racing. My skin felt like it was crawling and every square inch of my body wanted to jump up and flee from an unknown assailant. I relaxed a bit when I remembered Felix and saw him curled against my tummy. He seemed to understand my distress: his bright green eyes penetrated the darkness to consider my expression.

Is my kitty supernatural? Can he read my mind?

In my paranoid state, I worried that nothing was as it seemed. But then, Felix yawned, his snow-white whiskers fanning as his bubblegum-pink tongue stretched out. It was a harmless and adorable action that restored my calm. No, Felix was not supernatural—he was a cat. The scent of stale tuna wafted to my nostrils and I smiled. My kitty might be quirky, but he was still very much a cat.

I worked to regulate my breathing as I considered the rush of thoughts and panic that had suddenly flooded my brain. Now armed with vocabulary to describe my proclivity for dreams and intuition, I worried that every dream was a prophetic warning—and my dreams were mostly bad, and I had no idea what they meant.

Breathe, Selina. One task at a time.

I considered what to do. There wasn't a guru or guide to turn to—Mr. Boothe had been clear in stating that my talent for the supernatural was beyond what he'd seen before.

Ask, Selina. You can't get what you don't ask for.

I was uncertain where the voice came from but had learned by now that these thoughts often served to guide me to the next right thing.

"Okay," I mumbled into the darkness, nuzzling Felix's fuzzy head. "I'm at a loss. What do I do next? Help me to understand."

After whispering my plea, I closed my eyes and cleared my mind of distractions. I wanted a clean palette; a blank slate. If I did get something, I wanted it to be obvious.

Faith, Selina. You still doubt too much.

The voice sounded a lot like my own, which made it easy to ignore or overlook at times. But the wording was different than what I would have constructed, and it often came packaged with a feeling of peace and epiphany that I knew was not my own doing.

Obediently, I squeezed my eyes tighter and rephrased my narrative.

***When** I get something, I want it to be obvious,* I corrected.

The slate-grey of my mind swirled with mustard-yellow. I maintained my deep breaths and waited. Then, an answer.

A lego structure, of all things. A castle of yellow, red, and blue blocks that stretched up to the ceiling. Hundreds of legos fixed one on top of the other in the three primary colors. There was no rhyme or reason to the color pattern, but it seemed to me that there was an equal number of each hue.

In the front, a small window: a space with the width of a single lego block. Easy to miss, if you weren't looking for it. A charcoal shade in contrast to the brighter colors.

I had no idea what it was or why my gaze seemed drawn to certain aspects of the structure.

This castle is you, Selina.

Anticipation mounted and I waited eagerly for the continued explanation.

*The castle is **you**, and the blocks represent the different parts of you. There are three primary components to your life, represented by the three primary colors. Yellow, your physical body. Blue, your soul. And red, your spirit. The three are intertwined and cannot be separated: together, they build you.*

You've lived thus far believing that you are made up of the same lego bricks...your solution to every issue has been to treat it as though it is the same. Few can make the distinction between the different building blocks of their being, as indicated through the small door. This understanding brings the key to enlightenment and true health and wholeness in body, spirit, and soul.

The words should have discouraged me. After all, it was basically a statement that I didn't know myself and had taken poor care of my being. But the words carried with them surprising peace...even as I acknowledged that I didn't have a clue how to identify the different fibers of my being.

Please—show me that key. I believe you.

The heartfelt plea expressed, I fell into deep sleep.

The Key

I woke in a fog, wondering what was real and what I'd imagined. The lines had blurred irreparably. Rubbing the sleep from my eyes, I sat up to stretch.

"Meeeoooooww!"

My yawn ended abruptly as I looked down in surprise to see Felix arch his back and leap from his cozy spot curled beside me. Not everything was a dream, then. I suspected I would need continuous reminders of the new reality that I was a pet owner.

I watched in wonder as the small frame pressed his two front paws on my chest and stretched forward to protest once more.

"Meeoowwwwww," came the second, mournful cry.

"Shhh!" I whispered to Felix, hurrying to scoop him up in my arms. I didn't know if anyone else was sleeping, but worried that even a deep sleeper might be roused by Felix's high-pitched cry.

The kitty squirmed and wiggled in my arms in an attempt to get free and I held him closer at the same time I worked to negotiate my way down the ladder steps and to the box. Felix's meows grew louder as we approached: he seemed to sense that I was working to attend to his needs (and urged me to hurry).

Thankfully, the contents of the box were not hard to intuit: a single litter box and bag of litter sat inside, two different bags of treats, a bag of kibble, a few toys, and some grooming accessories that came with printed instructions (items I would investigate later).

Opening the bag of kibble, I poured a generous portion into the small glass bowl and watched as Felix fought for his freedom from my arms like a toddler escaping a nap. I didn't have any idea how much food a kitten needed to eat—that was something I would need to research. In the meantime, I figured the little squirt could probably use any and all sustenance.

His voracious appetite quelled, Felix made short work of the litter box (amazing how there was literally no training involved) before wandering back to my feet. He looked up at me with open curiosity, intermittently licking his paws to capture every last morsel of breakfast.

"Do you want me to pick you up?" I asked Felix, uncertain of feline protocol. I was sure Felix would let me know if I offended him. Instead, he sat expectantly and made no protest when I lifted him up and into my arms.

"Let's go see where everyone else is," I explained to Felix. I knew he didn't understand what I was saying, but he watched me attentively and seemed earnest to pick up on my cues.

Fifteen minutes later, I found myself sitting with my cohorts in the cafeteria. I'd managed to dress and brush my teeth with a single arm (Felix perpetually cradled in the other), and now I worked to eat with an interested and hungry kitten in my lap.

"Did you feed him?" Marcus asked, looking sidelong at my cat who tracked every morsel of food with laser-like focus.

"You'd never guess it, but I did," I assured Marcus. "I think I fed him enough…like a whole cup's worth of kibble. He's so tiny…how much can he eat?"

"Want some egg, little guy?" Luke asked, holding out some scrambled egg in his open palm.

Felix seemed to know Luke was talking to him—he launched up and out of my arms and after the egg with vengeance before I had a chance to respond.

"Ow!" Luke yelped as crimson-red blood trickled from his index finger. "He bit me," he added in disbelief.

"He didn't mean to," I snapped, snatching Felix back into my arms. "Besides, what were you thinking? You can't just feed him anything. For all you know, eggs are poisonous to cats."

"Yeah man—you should know better than to come between a mom and her young," Marcus ribbed. "Felix may be a cat, but Selina's a proud mom."

I bristled, unsure if Marcus was making fun of me. But then, I relaxed. Mocking or not, he was probably right. I *was* protective of Felix,

"*Are* eggs poisonous?" Luke asked, suddenly contrite.

"No," I responded sharply. "But there *are* foods that are poisonous to him that we eat. I don't have the list with me, but I'm going to get it. Don't feed him without asking me."

"Moving on from the cat," Clarice cut in, her irritation clear. "Did we hear about any assessments or classes today?"

A chorus of heads shook from side to side.

"It could be a good time to go through our lists," Amanda suggested tentatively.

"As good a time as any," Chris agreed with a shrug.

"I left mine up in the pods," Peyton told us.

"I did, too," Luke agreed.

I didn't even have a list. But I knew what I would say for each individual. I'd spent my entire life growing alongside them: it would be easier to describe their strengths and weaknesses than it would be to try and explain my own.

"Are we all in agreement?" Max asked. "Should we go and get our lists?"

There were no protests, so Peyton, Luke, Max, and Amanda stood up to retrieve their lists from the pods. Even without a list to collect, I took in the two groups and determined to travel back up to the pods. Our group was quiet until the elevator button had been pushed.

"Did everyone sleep well last night?" Max asked to make polite conversation. He was typically quiet and reserved, so his initiation of talk caught me off guard.

"Like a rock," Luke answered first. "I was exhausted."

"I don't know how you can sleep like that after hearing such upsetting news," Peyton griped good-naturedly. "I was tossing and turning all night."

"Me too," Amanda agreed. "I think my subconscious was working through everything we heard."

"How did you sleep, Max?" I asked. I wondered if his motive for asking the question was something that he wanted to share.

"Well enough," he answered agreeably. He hesitated. "I just got the feeling that someone had something significant happen in the night," he added carefully. He tried to mention this last piece matter-of-factly, but I knew better. Goosebumps prickled my arms and legs as Max looked meaningfully at me.

I may have had supernatural aptitude, but Max did, too. It looked different, maybe, but Max's intuition was uncanny and left me feeling exposed.

"I had a weird dream," I admitted casually.

No one said anything as all eyes regarded me with interest. I wasn't sure I wanted to share my dream but figured the group before me was trustworthy.

"I don't know if it's important," I cautioned, well aware that I'd been labeled as some intuitive genius. I half-hoped one of the group would jump in and change the subject or let me off the hook by agreeing that my dream was probably just that…a dream. When no one said a word, I reluctantly continued.

"I saw this tall, complicated lego structure made out of red, yellow, and blue lego blocks. It had a small door leading to the inside. It seemed significant somehow, and then it came to me that the lego building was a symbol for me. I got this feeling that I needed the key to unlock the door and make it inside, and that was it," I finished without looking up. I didn't want to know if they thought I was crazy, dumb, or self-important.

"When you get these...*feelings*, how do they come?" Peyton asked. There was no judgment in her tone, just open curiosity.

"It's hard to explain. It's not anything I can measure or even describe. I just know, like it's something that's been buried in me since forever but that just bubbled up to the surface for me to discover," I told her.

"Did you wake up at the end?" Max asked gently.

"This happened after I had already woken up from the dream," I clarified. "So I guess it wasn't really a dream. I did dream, but I don't remember what happened."

"So you had a vision," Max distinguished.

I was uncomfortable with the terminology and wondered if I was digging a hole for myself, but I nodded. If I had to put my experience into words, it could best be described as a vision.

"That's so crazy," Amanda said softly in an appreciative tone. "It must be so cool to have supernatural aptitude."

I didn't know if it was *cool*—I found it more confusing than anything else. But I smiled at Amanda anyway.

"What happened after the vision?" Max persisted.

He'd suspected my nocturnal activity, and he had an instinct about it that he was chasing down. I was nervous to know the significance of my vision but felt relief in being able to share my experience with the others. It made it feel like *our* burden instead of something I needed to carry on my own.

"I made a request, and then I went back to sleep."

The follow-up question was painfully obvious, but I still waited for someone to ask it.

"What did you ask for?" Luke said, taking the bait.

"I asked for the key," I answered, reducing my emotional, layered ask to a simple request.

"You just asked out loud?" Amanda wanted to know.

"I just asked the question out loud," I agreed.

"What are you hoping will happen?" Peyton asked. They were all in agreement with Max now—they were just as interested in the outcome.

"I don't know what I'm hoping for," I laughed dismissively. The attention was unnerving, and I hated being under the microscope. I wished Max had asked the question privately. "I think sometimes I hope I'll just be normal. But if the past cycle repeats itself, I'll probably get another vision or inclination of what the key or next step is."

"You'll tell us when that happens?" Luke asked with a sidelong glance.

"Sure," I forced myself to agree. I swallowed the frustration and resentment that surfaced with this request. I didn't want to be responsible to anyone else...I was having a difficult enough time trying to work everything out on my own.

There wasn't time for further conversation—we henceforth found ourselves back in the cafeteria, rejoining the group. We'd scarcely made our way to the table when Chris spoke up.

"Selina, Mr. Boothe was looking for you," he reported.

My heart sank. *Already?* I'd been hoping for at least *one* day of normalcy. My expression must have said it all, because he didn't stop there.

"Don't worry—he said it wouldn't take long," he assured me.

"Did he say what it was about?" I asked in resignation.

"All he said was that he had a key for you," Chris answered.

My heart stopped, and I avoided eye contact with everyone but Chris. No. It couldn't be. It was ridiculous to even think it could be true.

"Excuse me— what did he say?" I asked steadily, working to keep my voice from shaking. Chris' answer rang loud and clear.

"He said he had a key for you. Well actually, he said he had *the* key for you. I assume it's for a locker for Felix's things or something," Chris clarified.

The roar in my brain was like the ocean's waves mid-storm in February. I felt at least four pairs of eyes on me, the intensity boring holes in my skull.

"Shut the front door," Amanda proclaimed, laughing out loud in disbelief.

"Dang, girl—you are seriously supernatural," Luke apprised, eyebrows raised in appreciation.

"What are we missing?" Clarice snapped, eyes on us like a hawk.

"Selina had a vision, and it already came true," Amanda told her gleefully. "I bet you didn't think it would happen just like that," she added, looking at me with mirth in her eyes.

I shook my head and offered a weak smile that had no weight behind it. To everyone else, this was entertaining—fascinating—encouraging, even. To live it out—to be the one experiencing the supernatural—well, that was another matter entirely. I wasn't as thrilled.

"What was the vision?" Chris was quick to ask.

Every eye was trained on me, each person respectfully quiet to allow me space to share my vision. It was uncertain how much wind I had in my sails to begin with, but I definitely flagged now. I opened my mouth, then closed it. If I had a fixed amount of energy, I needed to expend it in the right places.

"Did Mr. Boothe say where he was?" I asked Chris.

"If you're so supernatural, don't you already know?" Clarice mocked.

I ignored her and watched as Chris shook his head no. Even without a destination or direction, I knew I couldn't stay.

"Sorry," I apologized. "I don't know how long this will take…I'll be back when I can."

"Of course," Clarice intoned sarcastically. "Please, leave again. In fact, why don't you go to Venus all by yourself, too. That's what you'd prefer, isn't it?"

"Clarice…" Amanda began, but I surprised both of us when I cut her off.

"It's okay," I assured her. "I get it. I'm not even sure I would think differently, to be honest. But Clarice—" I paused here and looked her in the eye. "You've known me longer than anyone here. I'd be really sorry and disappointed if that's really what you believe is true."

"I don't feel like I know anything about you," Clarice snapped back. She was still sharp and prickly, but I caught the soft underbelly of her tone. She wasn't completely lost to me.

"Do you want someone to go with you?" Max asked.

I hadn't considered taking anyone with me…and I knew Mr. Boothe would prefer I come alone. Truth be told, I was nervous. What key was I going to get, and what would it mean?

"I think I probably need to go alone," I said, even as I wished for a different truth. "I'll be back," I added for a second time.

"Good luck," Peyton offered.

"Do you have any supernatural inclinations about what is going to happen?" Luke wanted to know before I left.

I shook my head, trying to figure how to explain the visions I received. It wasn't on command, and it wasn't always clear. I dreaded my gift more than I appreciated it because of the fear and uncertainty that it brought into my life. There was no way I could wrap the emotion and inkling into words, so I decided it was as good a time as any to walk away.

Walking out of the cafeteria, I considered where I might find Mr. Boothe. When no immediate ideas came to mind, I decided to go spend some time alone. Mr. Boothe would track me down—I was certain of it.

I found myself punching every elevator button that coincided with a level of headquarters I hadn't yet explored. I still didn't have a destination, but I had a direction. I was going somewhere I'd never gone before, and my soul was leading the way.

The elevator doors opened twice without me taking a single step out. I knew as soon as the doors parted that it was not my floor. The third time the doors parted, I knew I was supposed to exit. There weren't any bright lights or fireworks or explosions of heat—Luke would be disappointed—but there was a pull deep in my belly like a fire that'd just been fed with fresh kindling.

"It's our floor," I announced to Felix before stepping out. "I don't know where we're going, but we're going."

There was some comfort in saying the words out loud and in carrying a companion…even if it was a cat.

The floor had thick velvet carpeting that made me feel as though I was walking on clouds. The color palette of the floor and walls and ceiling was chrome-gray and burgundy-red and rusted-gold: it was regal, but dark. At the end of the hallway, a tiered chandelier demanded attention, the clouded metal in desperate need of a good cleaning.

It didn't fit with the sterile and bright décor that outfitted the rest of headquarters. As far as I could tell, it appeared to be another abandoned floor: there was scant evidence of life. Somehow, this fueled my movement forward.

My eyes have always been drawn to the details, the things that others miss. I noted that the carpet was fraying along the edges, that the old-fashioned lamps protruding from the walls had a layer of dust covering them, that bits of splintered baseboard flecked the carpet.

In short, I was quickly able to determine why the floor was empty: in every direction was a health hazard that society had been trained to fear and avoid at all cost. My generation, my parents' generation—they were nothing if not obedient, frightened rule-followers. Maybe that's why the floor was so appealing to me.

The hallway ended in a hexagonal rotunda. Long, rectangular windows traveled the vertical expanse of each side of the room. Each was dressed up in obtrusive cabernet curtains tied with braided gold cord. Still following instinct, I made my way to the curtain and first caressed the velvet with my fingertips. In a culture of texture-minimalization (too many germs), the simple touch of fabric could prove to be a sensual experience.

Felix didn't make any sound, but I felt the weight in my arms shift as he craned his little body forward to investigate alongside me. The oppressively thick fabric seemed to be a shield; a metaphor for The Organization's dogmatic effort to protect and shield mankind from the uncertain danger that lay lurking at every corner.

We'd been trained not to look, that it was safer to just *let things be*, to trust that *things were being taken care of*. We'd learned to accept the truths that were told to us and to stay in line…to stay in a place of safety.

So ingrained was this philosophy that it sparked heat in my heart that went racing down my arm as I pulled the curtain back.

It was a slate-gray day: the sidewalk, buildings, street, and low-hanging clouds seemed to profess melancholy through their united monochromatism. I stood that way for a long moment, fingers gingerly pinching the velvet as my eyes searched the landscape for something, *anything* inspiring.

Every few minutes, a pod obediently whirred down the street and collected a stoic individual, always a man or woman standing erect (a positive byproduct of the exercise-stimulation machines issued to each household) and dressed in shoes made of recycled rubber and harvested algae that provided the recommended level of cushioning to protect the lumbar spine. It was a practical, efficient, and health-oriented world we lived in. And yet, as I searched the faces of each man and woman, I didn't see evidence of joy.

"It's the great irony of life, isn't it?" a rough voice crackled.

I jumped in alarm, prompting Felix to meow in fright as I dropped my grip of the curtain and bumped into the window ledge. My fingers gripped the wood like talons around fresh prey as I took in the man standing behind me.

Even before laying eyes on him, I knew he would defy custom. His voice alone was unlike anything I'd ever heard before: if a neutral tone of voice was a college-ruled 8.5 x 11 lined piece of paper, this man's voice was uneven papyrus with singed edges that curled upwards.

His appearance was no different. Such a deviation from the societal norm should have been alarming; instead, his clear scorn for conformity angered me. It wasn't an attempt to be original and unique—it was a bold, incendiary statement intended to undermine and scoff at the world I'd grown up in.

I was no defender of the vanilla culture I'd been raised in, but I found his approach and extremism off-putting. I was grateful to hold this mindset: irritation readily consumes fear, and I was not intimidated by the stranger who had surprised me.

The man before me was about six feet tall. His natural stature caused him to tilt forward just slightly so that he always carried the appearance of leaning in to deliver a secret. His limbs were wiry, his middle soft. He wore his salt-and-pepper hair long: it fell straight to the space just below his shoulders, where it curled gently. Bushy eyebrows, piercing blue eyes shadowed with glaucoma, and a hawk-like nose that curved over thin lips were clear indicators of advanced age.

He wore faded blue jeans held up by a thin brown belt—jeans that had not been strategically bleached for effect but rather that spoke to the contours of the old man's body and the places in which he required more of the durable denim. A thin, satin-like cream shirt was haphazardly tucked in just in the front and was hidden beneath an oversized flannel button-up in green and gold plaid.

The man's craggy face showed no sign of discomfort as we stood staring at one another. Affronted, I straightened up and turned my body so that I was squarely facing the man. I stayed silent, but my body language very clearly spoke to my chagrin.

The old man chuckled, his thick eyebrows arched in good-natured surprise. "I knew you would be different than the others—you *had* to be different than the others—but I'm still amused by you," he told me.

"I'm not sure how you knew I would come here, or who you are," I protested, voice haughty. The solitude of the floor had lulled me into a false sense of security that this man's presence now violated. A snarky tone of voice somehow felt like a repossession of the dignity lost in my startled jump.

"I'm John," the man offered. He clasped his hands together just below his belt and made no movement to extend his hand. Maybe he knew better. But his eyes smiled at me, his eyebrows seemed to mock me, and his lips curled and rattled as though he were holding back a second chuckle.

"Selina." What was it about the omission of auxiliary words that made language so pointy and aggressive? In any event, John was not deterred by my frosty demeanor.

"It's nice to meet you, Selina. I've hoped for a long time that we would meet," John spoke cordially.

"Who are you?" I asked suspiciously, eyes narrowed as I worked feverishly to discern who this man might be and why he seemed so familiar and comfortable with me.

"John," he repeated with a light-hearted wink.

I rolled my eyes and tilted my head to the side. "Why are you here, John?" I tried a different approach.

"I actually live here," John was delighted to answer. His eyes sparkled and this time his lips cracked to reveal his top row of teeth. I wasn't trying to, but I was playing right into John's agenda, whatever that was.

"You live here?" I wasn't able to hide the surprise in my voice—my tone changed as I realized I was the one in violation.

"Just over there," John agreed, pointing a finger to a heavy wooden door covered in peeling, wine-red paint.

My feet felt antsy and I fought the urge to take off running. My intuition had led me to this floor…why? I wanted out.

"It's okay that you're here," John assured me. "I didn't know how long it would take you to make it here. You even beat Mr. Boothe."

"Mr. Boothe?" I asked with furrowed brows.

"He didn't intercept you before you made it here, did he?" John asked. "You don't have the key in your possession, do you?"

The key. My heart pounded like an African drum. John knew about the key? I knew at once it went way deeper than that—John didn't just *know* about the key, he was somehow connected to the key.

"I don't have the key," I said quietly.

It was funny how quickly I'd reached this level of humility: I'd gone from feeling upset to feeling small in a matter of mere minutes.

"I didn't think so," John said. "It's just as well…perhaps even better that I caught you before Mr. Boothe. He may have felt the need to *prepare* you for our introduction—I much prefer this organic crossing of paths."

I smiled uncertainly, unsure of how to respond.

"We can stand out here, if you'd prefer, but I think we'd both be more comfortable seated in my study," John continued. He watched closely for my response.

I'd been raised to fear anyone out of compliance with the norm—any individual who lived as an outlier in society was not to be trusted. John embodied everything I'd been taught to flee from, and yet I knew he possessed the same *supernatural aptitude* that I hadn't learned how to harness. We looked different, but we were cut from the same cloth. I could only advance to the next level by following him.

"You're the key, aren't you?" I asked, the edges of the puzzle falling into place.

John laughed in delight and wagged his finger in my direction. "You *are* a clever one. They told me you were. There's an actual key for you, but if I may be so bold, I would agree with you that I'm a better key than the cut brass you'll receive later."

I nodded in agreement. The fleeting anxiety had been replaced with an overwhelming need for answers that I knew John could offer me. Questions rose inside of me like bubbles in a soapy tub; it took massive self-control to hold back and wait until we were safely housed inside the study.

I waited and watched as John took deliberate steps to the door he'd identified as his own. He walked with a lilt that suggested he had a bad right hip: his weight was unevenly distributed, his progress a bit painful to watch…yet still possessive of a cadence of grace.

I wondered at the oversized, intricately-molded key that he pulled from his pocket and inserted into the door lock—of course, I had heard of locks…but I'd never before seen one used. Such inefficiency had long ago been digitized with retinal scanners, QR codes, and automatic doors.

Even with his back to me, I knew that John noticed my interest—the way he fiddled with the key in the lock and angled his body to the side to allow me to view his progress told me he greatly enjoyed the novelty of his ways to my sheltered upbringing.

And the key was only the beginning. When John opened the door with a satisfying *click* of the lock and *squeak* of the door hinge, he padded forward into a perfectly disorganized, overwhelming, and magical land of chaos.

Here, my pride nearly forgot itself: I had to consciously swallow the gasp that warbled low in my larynx and glue my jaw shut in place. Never had I seen so many artifacts of the past in real, three-dimensional form. *Pictures* of the treasures? Yes. *Written accounts* about the functionality and purpose of each? Certainly. But to enter into John's room was to set foot in a living history museum.

In a true departure from The Organization's prized theme of simplicity, cleanliness, and functionality, John's room was an eclectic collection of rich colors, mixed textures, and furniture covered with superfluous knick-knacks. The bottom two inches of my shoes sank in the thick and fringed burgundy carpeting; the walls were papered in a motif of green and white daisies.

An espresso-colored coffee table stood low to the ground with spindly legs that bore chips (it looked rather like an apple that has had been bitten into, revealing the pearly-white flesh of fruit), a black leather couch wrinkled and sagged just beside it. A cheap white mug with coffee stains sat atop the violated table amidst water rings that spoke to poor care.

An end table with a camel-colored lampshade fringed with amber beads hung low over sticks of incense that released their mystical fragrance in intoxicating patterns into the air above. Piles of smoky ash collected in the white dish beneath; just as much lay in a small molehill atop the end table.

The wall behind was outfitted with rectangular prism blocks that housed books—real, physical books with peeling hard covers and cheap, made-for-the-masses paperbacks that had been stacked spine in and spine out, up and down and also horizontally.

There was no rhyme or reason to any element of the room, and my eyes couldn't decide where to focus their attention. Everywhere I looked, a safety hazard. Everything I saw, a violation of the clean and pristine lifestyle mandated by The Organization.

"That response never gets old," John chuckled, glancing in my direction only surreptitiously before shuffling to the couch. He plopped down onto the cushion and I noted little resistance. The couch looked to be as old (if not older) than John, and it did not look too inviting. John grunted as he adjusted his weight and then swept breadcrumbs from the table.

"Are you going to sit down?" John asked, beckoning me forward with a sweep of his hand.

"They let you live like this?" I couldn't help but ask. I knew it was a rude question (exactly the type you were not supposed to ask), but I couldn't help myself.

"They leave me alone as long as I stay out of their way and supply them with the information they need," John answered. I noted the measure of pride that poked out of his words like thorns on a rose bush: overlooked visually but felt with alacrity.

He knew my next question—I'd been trying to figure out who he was and what his role was since we'd first met—but I also knew he wouldn't give the answer easily.

Alright, John—I'll play your game.

"I'd like to take a look around first, if you don't mind," I responded casually, taking neat, quiet steps from the doorway to the opposite side of the room. Olive-green drapes were pulled back from a window that I gravitated towards—was it my imagination, or did it look out onto a deck?

John wasn't the least bit miffed by my interest. "Be my guest," he extended a blanket invitation with an outstretched hand and reached for the mug on the table. I noted with some revulsion that the remaining liquid seemed to have congealed a bit on top…and it had to have lost all warmth. John only took one sip before grimacing. The mug was replaced on the table with resolve—it would not be revisited.

I felt the pull towards the layers of dust-covered books, piled one atop another like thick layers of frosting on a cake…a few even carried the distinction of housing sticky layers of spider webbing. I was attracted to the hard-back volumes with shiny, golden pages that glowed rich in the lamp light. There was no fluorescent lighting in *this* room.

I wasn't sure how much time I had before Mr. Boothe might make an appearance, so I pushed myself to keep moving towards the supposed patio. Sure enough, the window looked out upon a sizeable deck littered with myriad of colorful pots filled with ferns, bushes, and succulents. I leaned in for a closer look when a flash of black fur darted from the periphery of my gaze and towards me.

"Whatwasthat?!" I squealed at the same time I jumped back. One hand covered my heart in what I was certain was a very lame response. I scanned the room for the creature and, seeing no evidence of a small mammal, I turned to John for explanation.

"That was Midnight, my cat," John answered with a scarcely-suppressed smile. "There are a few cats and a dog mulling around," he added.

A *few* cats? A *dog*? I'd been led to believe The Organization had forbidden all pets.

"They let you—" I cut my own question short as I realized the better question to ask. Clearly, they *did* allow John free reign of this wing of The Organization headquarters. "How do you get everything you need for your…pets?"

The last word felt strange coming out of my mouth. For all the words I'd said aloud in context of conversation and academic instruction, it had never been required. I hugged Felix closer to my chest a bit protectively, uncertain how he might respond to the beasts roaming around this untamed savanna also known as John's living space.

"The Organization has access to far more than you might realize," John answered me. He retained the sparkle in his eye, but his words carried a new weight that I observed. He wanted to make sure I was not only hearing his words, but listening, too.

"And it's not as securely fortified and protected as they lead people to believe," I mused in a veiled acknowledgement of John's hinting.

John's shoulders relaxed a bit, and he nodded his approval. "Yes, The Organization can be surprisingly lax in some areas," he agreed. "But shockingly stringent and perfunctory in others. I expect those are the areas you're most familiar with, seeing as you grew up as part of the society."

I nodded, wondering if John had grown up with the same observations and realities as I had. His comment suggested an element of rogue operation that intrigued me.

It was only natural, I knew, to base your world and truths and reality based on your personal experience. And yet it was becoming startlingly clear that I'd been misled in my way of thinking. I was a guppy that had suddenly found its way into the Pacific Ocean…and if I thought The Organization was overwhelming, what would I find when I left Earth, and then the Milky Way Galaxy?

"It's a lot," John observed, reading my thought progression as he reached for a contemplative sip of his defunct beverage. His cup was only partially lifted when he remembered its violated contents and set it down with a measure of disappointment.
I could feel the emotions gurgling inside of me. Panic, at the realization that I was in fact very, very, *very* small and insignificant. Anxiety, from the comprehension that I was quite clueless and ill-suited for the task for which I'd been chosen. Shame, in recognizing that I had behaved in a manner that displayed pride and competence when the truth had now been unmasked.

But also energy—this was harder to name. There was a shy heartbeat of adrenaline that seemed to quicken in my chest. The roof had been blown off of my expectations and perception of life once again, but it didn't have to limit me. What if there was more? What if, in the expansion of my world, there was more space for me to grow and learn and become something even greater? What if this was the beginning of something incredible?

I was standing at the crossroads of two divergent paths of thought and it was all I could do to remember how to breathe correctly.

"Try to visualize it," John spoke slowly, watching me with unmasked interest.

I turned to him and really looked at him—not with heavy eyelids or with a sidelong glance, but with wide, open eyes that allowed John to see inside of me the way I could tell he was straining to. It was a vulnerable move, but I knew it was right.

"See the emotions you can name," John clarified, adding description to his first vague instruction. "And see what picture comes to your mind. It's okay if it doesn't make sense."

I closed my eyes and squeezed tight.

"You don't have to close your eyes," John couldn't help but interrupt. "If it helps you in the beginning, go ahead and try it. But there's nothing magical about closing your eyes."

I kept my eyes closed and took deep breaths. At first, colors swirled through my brain in kaleidoscopic patterns and no shortage of psychedelic hues.

But then, the warm burnt-amber I knew to represent peace settled in my mind's eye. A cobalt-blue flash of light twinkled, and the visual materialized.

I was standing on a dusty road. I was looking down at my shoes, which I knew had once been white but which were now covered in insolent red and brown dirt. I'd been walking a long time; my legs felt heavy.

*Focus on what you can **see**,* I reminded myself.

The road forked, and a rudimentary wooden sign bore two arrows pointing in opposing directions and with labels above. Even without reading the labels, I could guess at what each path represented. But since this was a visual exercise, I trudged closer.

Both the path to the left and the path to the right began narrowly…and they seemed to skirt the original trail. But as my gaze traveled farther down each path, I saw the marked differences. The path to the left snaked downwards before disappearing out of sight; the path to the right led to the base of a rather significant mountain where protruding boulders hinted at the path to the apex. Then, the scrawl above the arrows:

Left: Panic, Anxiety, Shame. Easy trail, little resistance. Limited growth potential, no view.

Right: Courage, Hope, Faith. Challenging trail, strenuous hike. Great growth potential, stunning view.

I choose right.

I opened my eyes and looked to John. "I chose right," I told him, assuming he knew what I'd seen.

"You were able to visualize it," John said with a smile. "What did you see?" he asked, to my marginal disappointment. I'd secretly hoped he was a wizard with unlimited wisdom at my disposal.

"There were two paths," I began. "I stood before a sign that pointed in each direction with a description of where the trail led. One path looked easy to walk, and it was associated with negative emotions. The other path looked difficult but promised a rewarding view."

"And you chose the more difficult path," John stated, looking at me for approval.

"I did," I agreed. "When I read the signs, it was easy to choose. Even though it looked hard, it would have been stupid to pick the path linked with panic and anxiety and shame." I was processing aloud, with John as witness to my thoughts.

"You summoned the visual quickly," John pointed out. "Have you done that before?"

I paused. I wasn't sure what he meant. Had I purposefully put images to my feelings before? Not that I knew of. But John was right—it wasn't difficult to do.

"I haven't tried that before," I answered, choosing my words carefully. "But I've had visions in my dreams."

"How often?" John wanted to know. He leaned forward, elbows folded atop bent knees.

"I'm not sure. I haven't kept track. There've been a lot more recently. Maybe once or twice a week?" I ventured to guess.

"And how are the visions different than the dreams?" John asked. I got the impression that he wasn't asking because he didn't already know but rather because he was trying to clarify a theory he had in mind.

"They feel different. They're fictional, but there's an element of truth in them. I—I just kind of know that there's significance to them," I struggled to explain.

John sat quietly, waiting for me to go on. I wasn't sure what else to say— how *did* I know a vision from a dream?

"There's a color—this yellowish glow—that comes before a vision. And a quick flicker of blue light. And I carry this feeling deep within me, like some compass of truth. It's hard to describe," I finished, aware of how cheesy and lame my words sounded.

Still, John waited. I began to feel a bit self-conscious…what was he looking for? I wasn't going to be able to capture the phenomenon in words, because I wasn't even sure of what took place. John seemed to sense my hesitation, for he jumped in with words of encouragement.

"What does it feel like?"

"It's warm. Comfortable. It's like a pebble that's been thrown into water and finds its way to the bottom of the pond. It's nestled in its proper place and knows it's where it's supposed to be. It's an idea that's landed." It was easier to speak in similes than to try to explain in concrete terms what it felt like.

John wasn't put off by my abstract description—if anything, his smile of mysterious origins stretched wider. He leaned back in his chair, causing the legs to squeak. He looked me up and down before declaring, "you're prophetic."

I don't know what I expected him to say, but it wasn't that. My eyebrows shot up, my head snapped back and my eyebrows furrowed.

Prophetic? Nope, not me. I was still trying to digest the fact that I had supernatural aptitude that surpassed that of my peers. I was thinking through my respectful rebuke of this distinction when Mr. Boothe walked into the room.

"You two have found each other," he began, a note of displeasure in his voice. If my judgment was correct, he also appeared nervous.

"I heard you wanted to see me," I explained.

"And you came here?" Mr. Boothe asked doubtfully, skepticism written all over his face.

"I didn't know where you would be." I tried to justify my actions at the same time I realized that I didn't owe Mr. Boothe an explanation. I'd picked up on his judgmental vibe, but he hadn't specifically required I explain my behavior.

Mr. Boothe's eyes narrowed not as an act of intimidation but in suspicious contemplation of what I had just told him. My pulse quickened and I imagined the narrative running through Mr. Boothe's mind.

"Is this your first time up here?" Mr. Boothe asked with some reservation.

"Yes."

"Did anyone tell you to come up here?" Mr. Boothe asked next. He threw a quick glance in John's direction—I followed his gaze and noted the satisfied smirk that sat on John's face. I was playing into his agenda in some way, though I had no idea how.

"No."

I was offering simple, one-word answers. Until I knew what these two men were up to, I was going to play it as safe as possible.

"And you were looking for me...here?" Mr. Boothe asked doubtfully, looking around the room with some measure of disdain.

I blushed. Surely, this was not a place Mr. Boothe would frequent.

"I didn't know where you would be. I didn't put much thought into where I was going, and I ended up here." It was the truth, but it sounded weak. I heard the words and felt how brittle they were.

Mr. Boothe looked once more at John. His expression was mixed: there was fear and frustration and disbelief—these were the emotions that were easy to read. There was more wrapped up in his stern countenance, but I didn't have the time to unpack it further. John had won some victory over Mr. Boothe, though I had no idea what any of it was about.

"I was told you had a key for me," I spoke gently, hoping to redirect our conversation. I wasn't one to shy away from confrontation, but the undertones in the room had me walking on eggshells.

"I do," Mr. Boothe snapped irritably.

"I don't really understand what's going on," I found myself saying. My discomfort had grown beyond what I could swallow—I didn't want to take on anyone else's negative energy.

"It's not your issue," John assured me, rising up out of his seat. He seemed suddenly restless. My unease grew as he walked over towards the deck and looked out the window. I looked to Mr. Boothe for explanation.

"Do you know who he is?" Mr. Boothe asked me.

"John," I answered, knowing that wasn't what Mr. Boothe meant. I knew his name, but I still didn't know who this man in front of me *was*.

"What have you told her?" Mr. Boothe asked John's backside. John didn't move an inch.

"What has he told you?" Mr. Boothe tried again, this time looking at me.

My mind worked quickly to try to piece together all that had been nonverbally conveyed in the past minutes. John was exceptionally powerful...I'd gathered that much. What I didn't yet understand was how he'd climbed to a place of such authority and power within The Organization; how he'd come to position himself above the rules and the implicit expectations of societal life. Even Mr. Boothe seemed to hold him in high regard—he didn't push him to answer but instead accepted his silence.

"He hasn't really told me anything," I spoke carefully. "He's mostly asked *me* questions."

Mr. Boothe sighed in what sounded like a mixture of relief and irritation. "Are you planning to tell her, or would you like me to?" he asked.

John took his time in turning around. It was a clear power move, meant to show Mr. Boothe that he was not in charge nor did he carry any kind of weight or influence with which to rush John. He considered Mr. Boothe with a look of measured indifference before speaking.

"I'd rather like to hear how you explain it," he answered smoothly. "I do wonder whether you consider me a prodigy or delinquent—now's my chance to hear exactly how you describe me."

My body was tense; my throat caught. I felt trapped in the middle of a game of pickle—no matter which way I turned, I found myself in trouble. More than anything, I wished to know the reasoning behind the very clear tension between the two men. I worried about how things might progress…why couldn't I just get my key and leave?

"John is a prophet," Mr. Boothe snapped.

My heartbeat quickened and I fought to quiet the thunderous sound pounding in my ears. A *prophet?* I'd never met a prophet before. I hadn't known prophets were real until weeks ago, when my parents had explained to me the prophecy spoken over my life.

"Not just any prophet," John cut in. "Is that all you're going to say?" he asked Mr. Boothe, voice thick with accusation.

"You wanted to hear what I would say, and you're not letting me finish," Mr. Boothe barked.

"That was a rather long pause," John pointed out.

"I'm giving her a chance to process what I said," Mr. Boothe said defensively. "It's a loaded title, don't forget."

"Oh, for goodness' sake. She's a prophet herself—she'll understand," John groused.

The din in my mind grew louder. *John was a prophet, and not just any prophet. He was a special prophet.*

My mind buzzed with this news—my subconscious fought to summon forth concrete understanding that my conscious wasn't yet able to grasp. *And...I was a prophet. I was a prophet. Was I a prophet?*

John said it matter-of-factly, as though he were commenting on the weather outside. He hadn't spoken with any degree of uncertainty; he seemed to know more about my identity than I had ever considered.

Mr. Boothe looked livid. He glared at John with fiery eyes at the same time that he glanced over in my direction to take in my reaction. I wasn't sure how I should respond to this news—was it better to play it cool, and act as though I already knew I was a prophet? Or should I respond with honesty and reveal how dumbfounded I was by this knowledge.

"She's never been told she's a prophet," Mr. Boothe hissed at John under his breath.

John rolled his eyes. "Seriously, Boothe? She has regular visions. She's been told she's off the chart in her supernatural aptitude. It's obvious."

It was at this point that Shame walked over to the side of the house and opened the window to slide in. I watched—just as John had instructed me—as Shame lifted one leg and then the other to climb in. I was a prophet, and it was obvious. Everyone around me knew it; knew it like they knew that two plus two equals four. And somehow this very obvious fact had escaped my own understanding.

"Selina, did you know that you are a prophet?" Mr. Boothe asked me, considering my countenance carefully.

"I just recently learned about prophets," I answered honestly. "And it never occurred to me that I might be one."

John's disappointment was impossible to miss, and I felt the sting of his judgment. I'd just started my journey as a prophet, and I was already failing. Mr. Boothe looked triumphantly at John, eyes full of scorn.

"I told you to tread carefully, and this is what I meant. You're going to put too much on her, too early," Mr. Boothe criticized.

"You can't guard her from the truth of who she is or the reality of our present situation," John spoke back. "Those things aren't going to change, and there's no benefit to hiding them from her. She needs to know who she is and what she's up against if we have any hope at all of pulling this mission off."

"I'm not disagreeing with you—but you run the risk of crushing her spirit and destroying the entire operation if you approach it all like a bull entering a china shop," Mr. Boothe accused.

They were talking about me like I was an object instead of a human being. They were talking about me as though I wasn't standing right before them.

"It's okay," I began uncertainly. "I can handle it. Is there anything else I should know?" In the back of my mind, I wondered how this could possibly be connected to the key I had been promised.

"There's a lot you should know," John snapped, looking pointedly at Mr. Boothe with eyebrows raised.

Mr. Boothe sighed heavily. His lower jaw hyperextended and he gnashed his teeth while working to restrain himself from saying something he might regret.

"Selina—John is the most credible prophet of our age…one of very few prophets on earth. His prophecies have consistently come to fruition, and he is considered a master," Mr. Boothe began. His words carried great respect in spite of his obvious aggravation at John's behavior. He paused after this introduction, considering his next words carefully.

"He also identified your supernatural aptitude before we were able to measure it," Mr. Boothe went on.

"I prophesied over you," John interrupted, unable to hold back any longer. I looked at John blankly, making sure I understood what he was saying. *He* was the prophet who had spoken over my life. The prophet my parents had heard from. He knew who I was and what I was capable of before I knew it myself.

"You're the—" I began, lifting a shaky finger to point in his direction.

"Yes," John agreed, meeting my gaze and staring directly into my eyes as he nodded his head up and down. "I am."

"John believes you have great potential," Mr. Boothe added. "He's asked to work with you to fine-tune your supernatural aptitude and hone your prophetic skill."

"We *know* you have great potential," John corrected. "Your score for supernatural aptitude is the highest we've seen in decades. Higher than mine," John said this last bit with a snort of laughter.

"But I didn't even know I was a prophet," I said shyly, suddenly insecure and uncertain about my level of skill.

"You're so obviously a prophet," John assured me. "You didn't have context for it, but you'll take off as soon as you're taught how to tap into your potential. Just look at how you were able to visualize your feelings moments ago."

Mr. Boothe looked at me curiously. He didn't know anything about the exercise John had walked me through moments before. I had no way to measure my supernatural aptitude or prophetic potential...I had to rely on what they believed I could do. I didn't know what to say, so I said nothing.

"The key is to another room in this wing," Mr. Boothe told me, drawing the conversation back to the original reason for the meeting. "John would like to work with you."

Prepare to Launch

Adults are funny when they ask questions that aren't *really* questions. You know, the kind where they wait for you to give your answer but they will only actually accept one predetermined, "correct" response.

This was the situation I found myself in: Mr. Boothe and John looked at me expectantly, waiting for my response to John's desire to work with me. Obviously, I was supposed to say yes. And I actually did want to work with John, if only because I knew he was the only way I might get my questions answered.

Still, I didn't answer straight away. The back-and-forth conversation that had just taken place had left me unsettled and overwhelmingly conscious of the limited information and power of my situation. I struggled to win back some of my confidence by making the two men wait.

"There's a lot I can teach you," John explained a moment later.

It was enough. "I'd appreciate that," I told John, taking care not to speak too earnestly.

I glanced at Mr. Boothe to gauge his reaction. Was he truly only brokering the deal, or did he have something invested in our partnership? There was an underlying dynamic I was still working to piece together, and I searched his expression for clues.

"We can start right away," John added, pulling my attention away from my fruitless analysis of Mr. Boothe.

"She's quite detached from the rest of her cohort," Mr. Boothe said mildly. "This will increase the barrier."

"The barrier isn't coming down anytime soon regardless," John snapped defensively. "They've already determined that she's different from them."

"This won't help," John warned, eyebrow raised in an unspoken challenge.

They were discussing my future as though I weren't in the room again. Was it better to stay silent and scrutinize what was said in an attempt to learn more about my situation or speak up and establish my personhood?

"It's not going to cause any further trauma, either," John argued, his voice a bit whiny.

"I'm not telling you no," Mr. Boothe pointed out. "I'm the one who invited Selina to set this up. I just think it's important to recognize the situation for what it is.

"We're going to launch soon, correct?" I spoke up.

Both men glanced over at me as though surprised to find I could speak.

"Yes," John answered directly.

"We have no choice," Mr. Boothe sighed heavily.

"Then it seems to me that I need to do everything in my power to prepare," I said, confidence growing as I spoke. "Anything less would be negligence."

John nodded his head in agreement at the same time Mr. Boothe shook his head.

"This isn't just about preparation, Selina. I have no doubt that John can teach you some very valuable skills...but the relationships between you and your peers is very fragile at the moment. When you're in space, you're going to need to trust each other implicitly—and you're going to need to work together seamlessly."

He paused, hesitant to proceed. My brain worked feverishly to ascertain what he might be holding back; in the end, I was grateful that he chose a direct approach.

"There aren't second chances on this mission—for you, or for humanity. You've already learned the unfortunate reality that all of our eggs are in this one basket.

"The last group had synergy like you wouldn't believe—the group that colonized the moon, that is. They were friends, but the bonds ran far deeper than just affinity. There was a deep mutual respect, unbounded trust, and loyalty like I've never seen before or since. They knew each other well, could anticipate the response and action of each member before it was taken, and had faith in the individual strengths of each member," Mr. Boothe explained.

"It's the reason they were successful," John spoke up with a prickly tone.

"The Organization credits the tight-knit community for contributing to the successful colonization of the moon, but it also identified some areas of weakness that nearly led to ruin," Mr. Boothe told me.

"*Nearly* led to ruin," John pointed out. "It was the quality of the relationships that kept the mission from disaster."

"The Organization took great pains to identify the areas of weakness in the former mission and worked to select individuals exhibiting strengths in these areas," Mr. Boothe went on. "The group that has been chosen carries strengths in every category deemed important for the mission's success."

"Without taking into account any of the relationships that saved the first mission," John accused. "So you have a group of catty individuals who are somehow supposed to bond and birth a nearly-impossible dream of intergalactic colonization that far surpasses the scope and sequence of the first feat." His pupils dilated as he dropped into the weathered cushions of the couch in frustration.

"That's not correct," Mr. Boothe kept his tone neutral, but I could hear the frustration laced in his words. "Selina's selection did not comply with The Organization's algorithm—"

"A small concession, all things considered," John scoffed, cutting Mr. Boothe off.

"We're on the same team," Mr. Boothe reminded John quietly.

The wind in John's sails seemed to deflate, his body seemed to uncoil and relax into the compliant cushions beneath him.

"As we already discussed, your selection for this mission was not based on the scientific algorithm and scoring system developed by The Organization," Mr. Boothe explained, taking care to fill me in. "And your choice to bring Max was another concession."

This news alarmed me—I'd worried before that I'd mistakenly roped Max into a doomed mission…now I felt the weight of that decision more than ever before. I glanced anxiously at John to gauge his reaction.

"Darnall is prophetic, too—just not as much as you. He's intuitive, emotionally intelligent, and prioritizes relationships over information. He was a brilliant choice, and would have certainly been chosen given the original qualifications for mission selection," John assured me.

"I agree," Mr. Boothe told me.

Placated for the moment, I worked not to engage with the other thoughts vying for my attention. Thoughts of my underqualification, of the danger associated with the mission, and the odds that were stacked against our success.

"You have a mixed group—academic geniuses with relational and supernatural geniuses," John summed it up. "Hardly the ideal mixture, considering that the two groups operate off of completely divergent mindsets and haven't established any sort of bond."

"There hasn't been time," Mr. Boothe stated.

"There *won't* be time," John corrected.

Mr. Boothe sighed but didn't disagree. "I'll leave you two to it, then," he said. "I'd be happy to pass along a message to the others, if you'd like," Mr. Boothe added, looking in my direction.

I hesitated—put on the spot, I wasn't sure what to say.

"What will they be doing while I'm here?" I asked Mr. Boothe.

"Team-building exercises," Mr. Boothe said flatly, shooting daggers in John's direction. John raised his eyebrows in a gesture that obviously showed he had much to say on the topic—but he kept his mouth shut.

"Will you tell them that I'm trying to learn as much as I can, so I can be the best teammate possible?" I asked. It sounded a bit lame, but it was true. I couldn't control how they might interpret my words, but at least I could offer them.

Mr. Boothe nodded his head longer than was necessary. Before leaving, he tucked his hand in his pocket and looked up at me.

"The key," he offered, extending a single brass key toward me.

Shifting Felix in my arms, I accepted with some reverence—it was my first time ever holding a physical key. Where was I supposed to put it? I couldn't think of a place that seemed safe enough.

"Your pocket will do for now," John offered, guessing at my thoughts. "We'll get you a chain so you can wear it around your neck."

I nodded, grateful that a decision had been made for me. There was thoughtful silence as Mr. Boothe left the room. I don't know that either of us knew how to proceed from the rather awkward conversation that had taken place. My eyes traveled expectantly to John, waiting for him to take the reins.

"I'm glad you agreed," John began simply enough.

I nodded. "It sounds like you have a lot to teach me. It sounds like you already know a lot about me," I added.

"I've been watching you for a long time. I've gotten information about you for even longer than that," John told me. "I'm sure you have some questions for me—I'd like to answer those first, to build trust. But know that our time together will be limited, and I'd like to spend more of it proactively planning for the future than reflecting on the past."

I nodded again, grateful that I would have the opportunity to release some of the questions that gurgled and churned in my belly like magma and volcanic ash ready to erupt. The question I really wanted answered was too weighty to lead with—I needed to ease into the questioning for both of our sakes.

"Has The Organization tried to launch another mission between the colonization of the moon and this mission?" I asked curiously. It seemed like a safe place to start—a question with no emotional pull.

"There have been talks about launching another mission, but it never amounted to more than mere speculation and idle chatter," John told me directly. "It's solidly their fault that we're in this conundrum now. They can go to great lengths denying it, but it's the truth."

"What exactly is your role here?" I asked tentatively, unsure if it was too soon to transition into more intense questions. "And what is your relationship with The Organization?"

"We get along better than you might imagine after that latest interaction," John assured me. "I'm not much of a pushover—my communication style is very direct. As I'm sure you're well aware, that's not the way of the world these days…there's a lot of emphasis placed on behaving in a way that is 'politically correct.' I make a lot of people uncomfortable in the way that I clearly articulate my thoughts and opinions. But I actually like Mr. Boothe, for the record."

John paused here—he seemed to have forgotten his train of thought.

"What is your role?" I asked again, gently pushing him back to my original question.

"That's hard to explain," John sighed deeply. "You've already heard me described as a prophet—and that's true. I don't know that The Organization has ever given me further distinction, although my accuracy in foretelling future events has distinguished me from my peers. It's the reason I have an entire wing on site, while the others live in shoebox apartments and report to day jobs."

He still hadn't answered my question, but he was slowly pirouetting his way there.

"The Organization relies on my advice…sometimes," John grumbled. "My prophetic talent is valuable enough to them that they keep me here, close by so that they can come to me at a moment's notice to get my input. But that doesn't always mean that they heed my advice."

"Like the tardiness of initiating this mission…" I prompted, looking at John for approval. I wondered what other suggestions he had given to The Organization that had been ignored.

"Like the tardiness of this mission," John agreed. "And a number of other things," he added pointedly. "They're not worth mentioning, but you should know that The Organization is generally quite risk-averse, even when circumstances call for courage and decisive action. It's my biggest pet peeve with The Organization—they can be slow to move, and they bring too many people into the decision-making process."

"How did you know you were a prophet?" I asked next. I wondered about John's journey to his current role in The Organization and if it carried any parallels to my own.

"I always carried a different perspective on life, like you," John began, looking me straight in the eye.

There was some indication of doubt on my face, because John leaned forward and smiled.

"Yes, you have always seen the world a bit differently," John told me, voice weighed down with certainty. "Remember, I've been watching you a long time."

The babbling brook of questions grew louder, but I forced myself to stay quiet. John hadn't yet answered my question, and I wanted resolution on the matter before we moved to another topic.

"It took me a long time to realize I was a prophet," John opened up. "No one initially recognized my skill, and I hardly knew that I was different or that I possessed any special talent. That's the trouble of it all—since we don't see how others think, we assume everyone thinks like we do. And they don't. At all."

I studied John with interest, imagining how he must have come to this conclusion.

"The first hint came when I realized that I could trust my gut," John explained. "I thought everyone carried this otherworldly sense that gave away secret wisdom and directed me towards the truth…it was quite a shock to learn that this was a unique gift that only I possessed."

"How did you find out?" I wanted to know.

"Gradually, I began to get the impression that others did not have access to this multi-dimensional thinking," John explained. "I began to ask careful questions—not enough to place a target on my back for my unusual talent, but to better understand how other people made decisions. No one knew what I was talking about when I explained my own experience…all put forward as a hypothetical scenario, of course.

"I was quiet about my skill at first—I was curious to learn more about it and I was uncertain of how to harness its full potential. Through trial and error, I learned how to tap into this *knowing* and discern its prompting from my own inclinations. From there, I started tracking my 'prophecies' and recorded my accuracy rates. It was a surprisingly scientific process," John confided. "Eventually I got quite good."

"You must have made some really important prophecy," I guessed.

"I did." John winked at me and a small smile spread across his face in memory of the event. "It was a prophecy about climate change, about forty years ago."

I couldn't help it—I gasped aloud. "The decade of severe weather," I whispered in excitement.

John nodded with forlorn pride—it was a great and terrible thing to have foretold.

"Like you, it started with dreams," John began. "I saw the storms and droughts and tornadoes and typhoons in my dreams; dreams that kept coming, and with increasing intensity and frequency. I knew right away that there was something to it, but I didn't know what. I started paying attention and looking for clues, and before long I started getting symbols."

My heart raced a bit faster hearing John explain the phenomenon that I had come to know so well; the aberrant thinking and feelings that made me feel closed off from the rest of the world.

Here before me was someone who not only understood, but who shared these experiences and who could help me to harness my own potential. It was an overwhelming realization—tears congregated in the corners of my eyes like moths drawn to warm light. What a relief to learn that there was someone else who thought like me. I was not alone.

"I wasn't sure what the symbols meant—I thought so hard about it and searched for signs everywhere. I gave myself headaches from thinking so much and with such intensity…and I didn't get anywhere. The understanding seemed to come in *spite* of my effort—a breakthrough or epiphany came on the heels of a dream or random, detached thought.

"It always just appeared, like a garment plucked from the back of a stuffed closet. It had always been there, but it hadn't been noticed. And then suddenly I found myself holding the hanger and admiring the piece, seeing it in a new light."

"That's exactly how it is!" I cried, overcome with emotion at John's precise description of my supernatural inclinations. "That's it exactly," I whispered again, burying John's words into the depths of my being.

John did not appear surprised by my spontaneous outburst. He continued his narrative without pause.

"I figured out that the storms in my dream were a quite literal foretelling of the weather to come, and the symbols spoke to the number of years that the storm would last and the regions that would be hit. It got as specific as the crops that would fail, the cities that would be destroyed, and the companies that possessed the potential to help the world recover from the aftershock," John told me.

"I wasn't sure who to tell—who would believe me, and who could be trusted with such information?" John asked the questions with the innocence of youth he must have felt so many years ago.

"The Organization," I murmured.

"No," John disagreed, catching me off guard. A wan smile crossed his face. "I knew better. The government is slow, cautious, and reactive. If my prophecy was correct, like I believed it was, I needed it to fall upon receptive ears—ears that would take my information to heart and do something about it."

"Who did you go to?" I couldn't help but ask. I was putty in John's hands, and I didn't care. I was invested in the story; my emotions were wrapped up in the outcome and the commonalities between John's experience and my own.

"Wall Street," John smiled.

I laughed out loud, then clapped a hand over my open mouth. "Did you really?" I asked, thoroughly entertained.

"I did," John confirmed. "I went to a few enterprising trading companies known for their affinity for risk and I explained my situation. I wasn't even granted an audience when I walked through the door of the first two companies, but I persisted. It wasn't too long before I found a firm willing to bet on my prophetic insight."

"And?" I urged, leaning forward.

"As you know, the capricious weather patterns I prophesied came to pass, exactly as I had foretold. The firm's stunning success garnered international attention during a time of overall economic depression—the traders were integrous enough to credit my prediction for their success, and I was heralded as a financial wizard. Laughable," John acknowledged, shaking his head good-naturedly.

"But it was the attention I needed. While I obviously carried not a lick of interest in the realm of financial markets—and turned down a myriad of offers not just for work but also for speaking opportunities and management roles—I was also contacted by The Organization. Money *does* speak—it garners attention that might not otherwise be awarded.

"As you can imagine, The Organization was interested in my financial shrewdness and wanted more intel behind my insight. Once I was sure that I had the proper audience—authority figures who carried clout and power to make decisions—I explained that it was not financial acumen that I possessed but prophetic insight.

"I'd been careful to document all of my prophesies, and I shared the next two events I'd recorded. Events tied to the weather; things I could not be accused of meddling in. And then I waited.

John's face seemed to relax at the memory of what came next—his jowls slackened and his eyebrows settled in muted pleasure.

"The first event came to pass, and a junior-level staffer from The Organization reached out to gather my thoughts. I ignored the inquiry—I knew that if anything were going to come of my skill, I would need to learn to wield the power of negotiation along with it.

"When the second event took place, it was the head of The Organization who personally showed up on my doorstep. He asked to see my full list of prophecies, and I asked what he had to offer me in exchange. He offered me a permanent position as advisor and prophet to The Organization on the spot," John remembered.

"Had they ever had someone in that position before?" I asked.

"Never," John said. "Right from the start, it was obvious that they weren't sure what to do with me. I didn't fit in with the other members of The Organization, and worse—I seemed to run interference with their stated objective.

"They wanted me there—they made that very clear—but they didn't know where to place me. And that turned into this," John smiled, waving his arms around him to indicate his expansive and secluded living space.

"And they just let you do what you want?" I asked, searching for the caveat.

"More or less," John confirmed. "My prophesies have all come true, which makes me an indispensable resource. They don't understand the nature of the prophetic—there are still some individuals that want to walk away with immediate answers on a very particular topic—and they aren't always pleased by the words of knowledge that I happen upon."

"Can you control the content of what you see?" I asked curiously. I could no less channel a particular vision than I could summon rain clouds on a dry July afternoon.

"I can enhance my vision, and I can sometimes increase the scope to include aspects that did not manifest at first," John explained. "But I cannot direct my prophetic nature to prophesy on something that has not been inspired."

This knowledge relieved me and assured me that I was in fact in possession of supernatural aptitude. John seemed to guess at my thoughts, because he winked conspiratorially in my direction.

"That's why they were so perturbed," he told me. "On any given day, I might prophesy about the weather, the political candidate to be elected into office, or the specialty latte that would be first to sell out that season. Some prophecies, hugely useful. Others, quite inconsequential."

"And you prophesied about me," I remembered, taking hold of an opportunity to address one of my questions.

"I did," John answered quite gravely.

I waited for him to elaborate, but he did not.

"I only learned about your prophecy recently," I prodded, watching John's face carefully for any nonverbal clues that might materialize.

"I was very sorry to hear about the circumstances," John said solemnly, voice dropping an octave.

I swallowed hard in an attempt to not only cast down superfluous saliva but also to submerge the emotions that swam to the surface. I blinked in rapid succession and straightened my spine to ramrod straight.

"Thanks," I acknowledged sharply. My tone was curt and impersonal—a far cry from how I felt. I was the one who had asked the question, after all—I wouldn't allow myself to bury my head in the sand now.

John was watching me carefully—I could feel his gaze trained on my face as I worked to keep my expression in check.

"Your prophetic gifting will increase if you allow yourself to feel," John remarked casually.

My head snapped up, my eyes searched his for the deeper meaning locked in his words.

"It's the way of The Organization to lock up emotions and keep in control at all times," John clarified. "You can't reason and use logic to work out the mysteries of the world. Your efforts to keep your every thought and emotion in check will always limit your supernatural aptitude. It's one of the reasons why your visions have so far only come to you in dreams, when your mind is quieted."

The arrow of truth hit its mark, and inwardly, I reeled. There was no doubting the wisdom and correctness of John's statement—the moment the words were spoken, the spirit of conviction pressed into my flesh like the branding of livestock. I spent an inordinate amount of time suppressing emotions—I couldn't even fathom what it might look like to embrace the feelings I worked so hard to hide from.

"It's a lot, I know," John acknowledged empathetically. "For better or worse, this is how the prophetic path to promotion will look. It won't be linear, it won't be chronological, and it won't be pretty. It will look messy, complicated, and erratic. You have to be willing to embrace the chaos to make progress."

I nodded, unsure of what to say. There was a moment of silence before John spoke again.

"Why don't you ruminate on that thought for the time being," John suggested. "I think we need to grow your comfort in the idea of venturing into the unknown before we can take the step into practical application."

"It's not that I'm uncomfortable with the unknown," I argued, feeling slightly defensive at John's indictment.

"Oh, I know you can handle challenges," John acknowledged quickly. "You're about to launch into outer space, for Pete's sake. Tangible risk is acceptable…you're afraid of yourself."

I opened my mouth to respond, then closed it. I was afraid of myself?

"You work hard to balance the ecosystem of your inner thought life so that you are in a position to take on external challenges," John wisely pronounced.

I nodded again as I worked to digest the far-reaching effects of this truth. John stood and rested a weathered hand on my shoulder.

"Explore your feelings," he encouraged me. Turning behind him, he pulled a leather-back journal and fountain pen from the clutter stacked on his end-table. "I know we live in a digital world, but it always helped me to scratch out my thoughts."

I accepted the cinnamon-brown journal with gratitude and held the smooth, creamy leather close to Felix's small frame.

"Come back when you have some thoughts to share," John advised. "This is a safe place to air your deepest feelings, fears, and dreams."

"Thanks," I muttered, shuffling towards the front door.

"Self-awareness and understanding are crucial to the honest demonstration of empathy towards others," John asserted before I padded out the door. It was implicit encouragement to explore my feelings before returning to my friends, and it was a suggestion I planned to take.

Journey to Nowhere

Thirty minutes later, I found myself sitting on the roof. Amanda had readily agreed to watch Felix while I took care of my "homework," as I'd cryptically captured it. I hadn't bothered to ask what team-building activities the group had participated in—I had a singular desire and inexplicable newfound sense of urgency to unpack the feelings I'd so aptly suppressed for the past decade and a half.

My feet had marched up one, two, and then three flights of stairs. I couldn't be bothered to wait for the elevator. I found the stairwells empty and I relished the thrumming of my heart against the walls of my chest as I pounded up the stairs. What I really craved was a run, but such an activity was incongruent with the task of journaling.

Instead, I marched up the four, fifth, and sixth flights of stairs until I came to a heavy metal door at the very top of the building. There wasn't any signage indicating that I had trespassed or overstepped my limits. I doubted that any such warnings would have deterred me, anyway.

Pressing down on the germ-ridden metallic handle, I noted the tinny squeak of resistance that told of very few visitors. Emboldened by a sense of voyeurism, I pressed my shoulder against the door and pushed.

At once, I was struck by the wind that seemed to roar with a vengeance. My hair whipped about in a chaotic frenzy of activity and I pulled my arms close across my chest to protect against the cold. It was an expanse of slate-gray concrete, uninspiring in its singular expression of one-dimensional, spackled cement.

Pulling my hair back, I twisted it into a knot that I tucked into the hood of my sweater at the same time I forced loose hairs into submission behind my ears. A quick sweep of the roof showed little variance in view; I settled indiscriminately in a spot close to the ledge and overlooking the city below.

I didn't pull out my journal right away. It was enough knowing that it was tucked just beneath my sweater, close to my chest and therefore the feelings that I was to draw out. I was so used to having an agenda, a goal—something to work towards, something I was working to achieve—that it was a new concept to sit with myself without any expectation.

The view from the roof inspired this perspective—looking down upon the dynamic world below gave me the impression that I was far removed from the busyness and hubbub that seemed to rule in the lower altitudes. The people looked small, the pods and streetlights inconsequential and even a bit cartoonish. The nippy air seemed to warble its agreement, the rushing wind drowned out any temptation to entertain the worries or demands of the flesh. It was other-worldly, and it was freeing.

I sat cross-legged, looking down upon the world that had shaped my reality and understanding of the human experience. A world of safety, of rules, of boundaries. A world that promised certain outcomes on the basis of prescribed inputs and behaviors that I had been diligent in following. A manual for life on earth that the public accepted without contest that had recently been proven to be an absolute farce.

It was a shock to realize that I'd built my life upon a false reality; even more shocking to come to the realization that the entire world *continued* to operate under the guise of this counterfeit paradigm without the slightest suspicion that their faith might be misplaced.

I watched the monotony of life unfold in scenes below: men and women dutifully reporting to work, presumably completing the tasks set before them during their working hours, and then returning "home" to refuel and recharge before waking up to do more of the same the next day.

The work was of little consequence—and the discretionary free time spent primarily engaged in activities meant to support and enhance the time spent at work. The ultimate goal: promotion.

And what of this promotion? An entire life could be spent in pursuit of this false idol, this idealized panacea that, once achieved, offered the cheap tribute of short-lived recognition and chintzy reward before dangling the carrot of the next, *better* promotion.

It was a miserable existence. And it was the reality of the world. The ones who had caught on to the ways of the world were the ones who self-medicated, either through substance abuse (the range of options was quite expansive) or the absolute submersion into activity meant to numb and distract.

Then there were those who had not yet wised up to the cruel, meager promises the world had to offer—these were the individuals who lived out their days with some degree of tension. The truth embedded deep in their souls, they continued to march forward to the daily rhythm and cadence of life as outlined by society. Like a child determined to believe in Santa Clause, the truth lay thinly obscured behind sheer curtains that were intentionally never pulled back.

Finally, there were the blind fools that I envied most—the group that I had, until recently, been a part of. These individuals believed in the economic model of worldly living that taught that the right actions led to the prized outcomes of success, happiness, and progress. They worked in idealistic fashion, believing their inventions and investments would provide a cure for deadly diseases and inefficiency.

This group heralded scientific progress and the creation of advanced machinery without recognizing that the increased longevity of life created the new problem of limited resources and overpopulation; that the progressive technology had eliminated jobs and therefore the livelihood for a percentage of the population they had hoped to help.

It was simultaneously laughable and pitiful: entire lifetimes were spent working to find lasting solutions to problems that, once accomplished, only introduced a new set of issues.

What was human existence? I considered the question lightly, aware that a complete analysis would undoubtedly spend me spiraling into a depression. The answer didn't matter; it was only the response that carried any meaning. I couldn't change humanity or rewrite the purpose of human life—but I could adapt my worldview and work to make a positive influence in the area that mattered most.

I couldn't decide if it was fortunate or pitiful to live in the shadow of the hopelessness of the human condition; this seemed to preclude any next steps I might take.

I wasn't sure how long I sat with these questions, allowing them to float like fluffy cumulus clouds through the stratosphere of my mind. I didn't come to a conclusion, but I hadn't expected to. Instead, the questions seemed to settle—this seemed to be my invitation to begin writing.

There wasn't anything about my time on the roof that felt rushed. I'd spent so much of my life in a feeding frenzy, anxiously chasing down accomplishment after accomplishment without pausing to consider what it all meant. Time was a commodity I never seemed to accumulate enough of, and I'd been taught not to waste a single moment.

But the soulful element of my current assignment gave me pause and seemed to demand space to move and breathe and grow. This was no cheap one-night-stand with myself—I knew better. This was to be a soulful courtship of the heart like nothing I'd ever experienced.

So it was with a light, butterfly-like touch that I reached underneath my sweater and retrieved the journal. I allowed myself to consider the smoky, musty scent of the leather that enveloped thick, cotton-woven pages of lined paper. My fingers grazed the textured pages with reverence; I imagined what it must have been like to live in a time where most dictation took place in just such a fashion.

I'd known a very different reality: one that utilized technology, one that couldn't be inconvenienced by the waste and inefficiency cultivated through words written by hand.

We'd all learned proper penmanship in school, of course—it was considered an art form and a "cultural skill" demonstrative of class and choice upbringing, much like the minuet during 18th century England. A single year of instruction was hardly sufficient to create lasting impact, and my scrawl had deteriorated over the years. It wasn't chicken scratch, but it didn't hold a candle to the languid scrawl I'd admired with fascination on the Declaration of Independence, for example.

I led the pen in somersaults before twisting off the cap. There was some anticipation in making the first mark: I was loath to mar the page with a misshapen letter or dull word (one that I would later regret). There was a commitment to writing with pen—pressure in knowing that I couldn't tap a button twice on a keyboard and undo any memory of a mistaken mark.

My perfectionism, coming out to play. Or perhaps the high value and romanticism I attached to artifacts of the past. No matter the reason, I had to consciously push myself to make the first scratches on the page—and then it was an uncertain rendition of my first and last name written out in the top corner.

You're lame, Selina. It's just paper, and no one is going to read what you write. Just start.

Without knowing what I might write or where it was going, my pen made contact with the paper. And then it didn't stop.

The stream of consciousness of my thoughts poured onto the pages first like maple syrup, then like lemonade—my initial shyness gave way to a torrential downpour of words. There was no rhyme or reason or even straight line with which to guide my thoughts…they stretched across the page and squeezed into the margins and bled into the rich paper with a satisfying ombre effect.

I wasn't aware of the passage of time; I was in time but not held by it, on earth but not grounded. I wrote until I felt emptied of things to say, and then noted that I'd filled both sides of seven pages with the contents of my addled brain. I didn't feel the need to look over what I'd written—it was enough that I'd freed the thoughts from the cage of my mind to be released into the atmosphere.

Closing the journal, I set it by my side and hugged my knees close to my chest. Once more, I looked out on the people navigating the streets below. I took a deep breath in, a deep breath out, and then I pushed myself up off the unforgiving concrete and down into the belly of The Organization headquarters once more.

I found myself walking back to the common rooms, where I hoped I might find my peers. I'd been gone for too long; John hadn't had to put much work into convincing me that community and relationships were of incredible value when trying to accomplish something difficult. I worried about the group's fragmentation and I looked forward to sharing the list of positive qualities I saw in each of my comrades.

Each had shortcomings, to be sure—but it wasn't hard to pick out the reasons why each had been picked for this mission. Every individual had undeniable strengths—qualities I admired, appreciated, and even envied. Even Clarice, with her newfound competitive edge and synergy-sabotaging behavior.

Clarice is not herself.

The thought popped into my mind like a ferret poking up and out of its hole in the ground—it wasn't a particularly clever or insightful comment, and I would have disregarded it had it not been for the color the thought carried with it.

The electrifying cobalt-blue flashed brilliantly against the backdrop of my mind, capturing my attention. I was a novice in navigating the prophetic, but I *had* recognized the pattern of this hue and a supernatural inkling to follow. The trouble was, there wasn't anything obviously inspired about the thought about Clarice.

That Clarice had been a self-centered brat and divisive member of our cohort was obvious; even janitorial staff working at the headquarters could attest to her irascibility.

But maybe—maybe I'd emptied the closet of my mind enough to notice the garment that had been stuffed in the bowels between the domineering winter coats.

Okay, I allowed myself to entertain the thought. *Why is Clarice not herself? What am I missing?*

I closed my eyes—no matter what John might say, it helped me to connect with my gifting more quickly.

For a moment, nothing. Then…

Then, an understanding came over my body. My blood ran cold and my spine stiffened. I didn't want it to be true at the same time that I held no doubt that it was.

Clarice was not herself. Literally, she was not herself. Someone—
some*thing*—had taken over her being. I'd ascribed her erratic behavior and
mean-spirited tendencies to jealousy and the unpredictable, stressful nature
of our new reality. I saw now that this was a massive oversight on my
part—Clarice was not enabling the worst parts of herself…her identity had
been hijacked!

The natural next question was…by who? What had possessed Clarice to
change her so completely?

Urgency crept into my bones once more; I entertained these thoughts
during my rapid descent back to John's wing of the building. My fingers
shook as I rattled the key into the lock without knocking. I pushed the door
open with nervous energy and looked around for John.

"John?" I called out, voice crackling with nerves.

There was no immediate reply; cold dread wrapped around me like a wet
blanket. My mind raced with imagined tragedies and I could not
differentiate between the wild, unfounded thoughts and the inspired
judgments.

"Selina?"

The familiar scratchy voice brought relief that made me want to melt into
the floor. This rollercoaster of emotion must have been transparent through
my facial expressions because John studied me with surprise and
unvarnished concern.

"You look like you've seen a ghost," he commented, eyebrows furrowed.
"What is it?"

"It's Clarice. She's been taken over," I announced breathlessly. I had no
expectation that John would follow my capricious train of thought but
searched his face for any indication of understanding.

He was quiet and contemplative; his expression gave nothing away. I
waited impatiently for a reaction—John *had* to know about this
catastrophe—he was prophetic too, after all.

"What do you mean?" John asked carefully. He was taking me seriously,
but I couldn't tell if he knew more than he let on.

"I got something—you know, like a supernatural inkling. It happened after I finished journaling my thoughts. There's something the matter with Clarice," I explained. My heart rate had skyrocketed and my words came out in a rush.

"What else?" John asked, eyes narrowed.

"What do you mean, what else?" I asked. "There isn't anything else. That's all that I got. Isn't that enough? What do we do?"

"What *can* we do, given that information?" John pointed out. "That isn't much to go off of."

"But that's all I got," I repeated stubbornly. It wasn't as though I had cut the declaration short—it was all I had received.

John picked up on my frustration and eased his tone. "Until you get more, there isn't anything we can do."

"How do I get more?" I lamented, voice laced with discouragement.

"You'll get more," John assured me without explaining how or why.

"How do you know?" I asked, suspicious of the confidence in his voice.

"It's on your radar now," John explained. "You didn't see it before, so any clues or indicators went unnoticed. Now that you know there's something amiss, you'll pick up on all the discrepancies."

I worried that John might be wrong, but his logic seemed correct. It was true that I now possessed heightened awareness regarding Clarice that would make it difficult to overlook future signs. But what if the clues didn't come quickly enough?

"Talk it out," John encouraged me. He waited patiently for the vocalization of my thoughts with a neutral countenance that I knew masked a deep and vested interest.

"I'm just thinking through different scenarios…wondering if I'll be able to act natural, and if it matters that I behave naturally. I have no idea what has taken over Clarice or if it's dangerous. I'm thinking about the signs to look for and what a given sign might mean. It's a lot," I confessed.

"It is," John agreed. "But I don't think it's necessary for you to know the answers to all of those questions. I would just sit with it—and try to act natural."

It was that last bit that concerned me most—the acting natural bit.

"Your behavior has run the gamut already," John assured me. "Clarice will hardly attribute any odd reaction to your receipt of new information. You've been standoffish and trite with her already."

This was true, and it helped me to relax.

"You don't have any idea what has taken over Clarice?" I asked John again. I was certain of my revelation, and I guessed that John harbored some guesses at what might be at play.

"Nothing more than idle speculation," John answered lightly in a way that suggested he wanted to breeze past the subject.

"I'd like to know your thoughts," I said pointedly.

"It's not a good idea," John answered, just as direct. "It's better not to color your line of thinking. As it is now, you'll go into the situation with a clean palette."

Objectively, John was probably right. There were so many possibilities with regards to how things could play out and what could be the matter that it was probably irresponsible to try to come to conclusions prematurely. At the same time, I was desperate to know what was happening to Clarice…and I worried that I would have no context for the reality. I was already feeling out of bounds and in deep water…I didn't carry any confidence in my ability to place the truth, even if it struck me right between the eyes.

I stood before John, thinking through the possibilities and resisting the urge to demand possible explanations. John didn't rush me or indicate any frustration; he waited placidly for me to come full circle.

"Okay," I finally conceded. "I'll just sit with it."

"You'll figure it out," John assured me with annoying confidence.

"You hope," I muttered sarcastically. Everyone around me seemed to hold a level of confidence in my ability to perform that I did *not* share. It frustrated me, knowing there was an expectation and flippant disregard for the very real possibility that it might **not** work out.

"You're forgetting who I am," John remarked, keeping his voice light as he winked conspiratorially at me.

A few choice thoughts came to mind, none of which were kind or flattering. *If you're such a great prophet, why didn't you foresee this situation with Clarice?* Or: *If you know what's going to happen next, why don't you just tell me?* I didn't see any value or point to the intentional withholding of information.

"I'm holding my tongue," I told John with some attitude.

"I know you are," he was quick to reply.

"I guess I'll go now," I offered. It was an anticlimactic exit, but it seemed the only recourse.

John nodded, and once again I found myself walking away. This time, my gait was not open and whimsical but determined: I went directly back to the common area and searched for my peers.

I suppose I might have felt some dread or apprehension walking into such a loaded situation, but I was instead stuffed with irritation that eclipsed all other emotions.

I had supernatural aptitude, but only in select situations. It wasn't a gifting I seemed to have any control over, and I seemed to possess just enough intel to know when something was wrong without knowing how to fix it. My guidance was scant, and the problems I needed addressed were left to me to solve.

Everyone seemed to trust in talent I hadn't learned how to harness…skill that seemed incomplete and undeveloped, at best. This truth earned no favors in the circumstances of time prescience and impending doom—my failure to deliver would not translate to some small error. It would, quite literally, mean the end of the world. And no one, besides me, found this very concerning.

"You're back!" Amanda exclaimed as I walked into the room.

It was hard to stay cross as I took in Amanda's very genuine smile and Felix's loud "meeee-ow" as I walked closer. I smiled and held my arms open to hug Felix close at the same time I looked around for the others.

"They're all here," Amanda told me, reading my thoughts. "Everyone dispersed to do their own thing, but no one left. We still want to go over our lists."

I smiled and nodded, relieved that I had not missed a crucial team-building activity and also that I would have an activity to participate in that would not require me to stand as the center of attention.

"Selina's back!" I heard Peyton call out as she walked into the room.

Moments later, the group shuffled through the door with varied expressions. Some looked genuinely pleased to see me; others appeared annoyed and put out by the announcement.

"And the court pays homage to her Majesty," Clarice quipped.

If she'd spoken even hours before, her snippy tone would have gotten underneath my skin. But now that I knew Clarice had somehow been compromised, I was on an entirely different mission…one that mandated my good behavior and excellent detective skills. I couldn't afford to be offended by behavior that I was meant to study.

"Is that how you feel?" I asked Clarice pointedly. It wasn't meant to be confrontational, but it came across that way.

Clarice looked up at me with interest, and a slow smile spread across her face. "It is," she agreed without breaking eye contact. "I'm surprised that you've suddenly taken interest in how I feel—how very kind of you to humble yourself to the level of your subjects."

I didn't respond right away. For one, I didn't trust my knee-jerk reaction to be graceful or even fair…I was blessed with wit that I could wield like a weapon (and often later regretted). For another thing, I wanted to give my subconscious the opportunity to send me any pertinent information before I opened my mouth.

My hesitation empowered Clarice with false confidence: she incorrectly surmised that I was at a loss for what to say, and there was no doubting her pleasure in gaining what she believed to be the upper hand.

"Oh, don't tell me that you suddenly care what the rest of us think," Clarice went on, laughing meanly. "Did they really just instill the value of fairness in you, or are you worried about what we wrote about you on our lists?"

"I'm not worried, just interested," I answered honestly as I considered the approach I wanted to take. "And I'm really only interested right now in what *you* think. You seem to be the one offended by me."

Clarice's grandeur faltered here; she was caught off-guard by my direct tactic. "Of course I'm offended by you, Selina," Clarice practically growled.

"We grew up together; performed equally well in nearly all regards. I thought we were best friends who didn't keep secrets from each other. And then all of a sudden you're mysterious and distant. Next, you're singled out as the godsend of our generation—praised for abilities that apparently none of us the rest of us possess. Talents *I've* never seen or heard about. At what point did you exclude me from your life? How long have you been living this charade?"

"Charade?" I pushed the words out, each thickly coated with disbelief. "Clarice, I was never faking anything."

I was trying to wrap my brain around her accusation and understand why she might feel the way she did. My words were an irritant; a stick plunged into the depths of a hornet's nest.

"You realize that every denial just ruins your credibility, don't you?" Clarice asked, lip curled in disgust.

She really believed that I had tricked her, that much was abundantly clear. I couldn't imagine what she thought my motivation would be for such a sneaky maneuver, especially considering how much I had lost in the past month.

You're giving her too much time.

The thought bubbled up like an orb of mozzarella on an oven-baked pizza. I didn't have time to figure all that the prompting hinted at; instead I dove headfirst into a line of questioning that I hoped would point me in the right direction.

"You're just jealous," I accused. If I was to speed things up, the fastest way I knew how was to play at an emotional level.

"Jealous?" Clarice squawked. She opened her mouth to release a torrent of accusations, but I cut her short.

"*So* jealous," I emphasized, throwing dry logs on a raging fire. "I'm sorry it's been painful to watch me outshine you. I'm sorry you were never that special to begin with. And I'm especially sorry we ever wasted time as friends if this is how you really feel about me."

It was weird to say the words without actually feeling them—kind of creepy, actually, to say nasty things in a such a smooth and calculated way. I was also catching the wind of inspiration with regards to what the thought might have been getting at, and I was determined to see Clarice crack.

"Jealous? *JEALOUS?*" Clarice's voice rose to operatic levels. She looked ready to foam at the mouth in unbridled fury.

"You've always been jealous," I said evenly. "It's obvious in the way that you just stated that we've been equals. We've never been on the same level—but you wanted to believe so."

"Girls…" It was Luke, watching the escalation of our interaction with growing unease. Neither of us acknowledged him—we were both aware that we had an audience, and neither of us cared.

"Pretty big words from someone who only shows skill in supernatural aptitude. You wouldn't even qualify for this mission in any of the other categories," Clarice spat. Her words cracked and her face was a blotchy mixture of pepperoni-red and Pepto-Bismol pink.

"I did great on the test," I lied. "I was outstanding in supernatural aptitude, but I still outperformed you in every other category."

"You did not," Clarice snapped. "Your self-awareness sucks."

She was right, and I didn't flinch. I'd been hoping she would slip up and reveal that she knew more than she was letting on.

"It's better than yours," I adjusted tactic slightly.

"You don't know my score," Clarice spat.

Bingo. I forced myself to play the part and look upset.

"No way did you score higher than 73," I shot back.

"You didn't score a 73! You got a measly 33!" Clarice wailed.

"Whatever," I said dismissively, scanning the faces of the rest of the group for the first time.

I'd just discovered that Clarice knew more than she was supposed to—and I knew the group was smart enough to pick up on this right away. I hoped they would hold back comment...Clarice didn't seem to catch her error, and I wanted to keep it that way. I tried to make meaningful eye contact with as many as possible.

"Should we share our lists now?" I asked cheerfully, changing topics abruptly.

"Now?!" Marcus asked incredulously. "I don't think I want to share anything while the two of you are in the same room," Marcus exclaimed emphatically.

"It's as good a time as any," Max countered neutrally. I knew he'd picked up on my vibe, and I also knew he could be counted on to handle the whole situation discreetly.

"I don't really feel like sharing," Luke hesitated.

"Maybe it will help," Amanda offered, shooting me an encouraging smile. I couldn't tell if she had also picked up on my leading or if she was just trying to be a supportive friend—either way, I appreciated her efforts.

"I don't care when we share," Peyton chimed in, tone dismissive. "I also don't care to argue with anyone. So if you have anything terrible or nasty to say about me, keep it to yourself. I don't have skin that thick," she admitted candidly, looking from Clarice to me.

"That's not what the lists are supposed to be about," Chris asserted in his typical authoritative way. I guessed that he'd sensed the energy but didn't know what to make of it. He was smart and quick-witted…he would certainly figure out that Clarice had slipped, and I hoped he would not question her on the fact until I'd had the opportunity to plan out my next move.

"My lists aren't negative," I agreed. "I have nice things to say, even about Clarice."

Clarice snorted. "I should hope there's at least one nice thing you can think of to say about me after that litany of complaints."

There was more. I could just feel it—I had flustered Clarice to the point that she could slip up more and I didn't want to lose the opportunity. Once again, I began to form a plan while I spoke.

"I think we should add a twist to this exercise," I suggested, earning the immediate suspicion of the group.

"I think we should keep things the way we planned it," Chris responded with some unease.

"We've already ruffled feathers…" Marcus agreed.

"Right. What's a few more?" Clarice snapped bitterly, glaring at me. "What's your great idea, Alois?"

"I think we should be able to ask some questions, too. It's great to share compliments and air concerns or complaints, but isn't the goal to come together as a single unit in the end? I have some questions I need answered for that to happen," I explained.

"If you're going to ask hard questions, you better be prepared for hard answers," Clarice threatened with a gaze of steel.

"I *want* the hard answers," I challenged, raising one eyebrow in defiance.

"You might not like them," Clarice snarled.

"You're right. I'll probably love them," I wrinkled my nose and smiled at her in condescension that elicited scarcely-suppressed ire.

"Go," Clarice growled.

Once again, the rest of the group was forgotten—and not one of them seemed eager to join the fray. There was abject silence as Clarice and I entered the ring once more. The song and dance around the boxing arena had already taken place—any punches pulled or thrown here on out would be knockout shots intended to clinch the match.

"What planet do you want to go to?"

"Mars."

"That's not an option," I protested.

"You didn't specify any parameters," Clarice pointed out.

"How long did you prepare for the assessment?"

"Twelve years."

"Who do you trust most of all?"

"I don't trust anyone."

"Why do you hate everyone?"

"I only hate you."

"What's your favorite subject?"

"Math."

The speed was increasing with each question asked; this was an intentional effort on my part. I purposely varied the questions to include some that would activate her and require multiple words in response and others than could be summarily answered with a single word. A few more, and I suspected I would get the only answer I really cared to learn.

"How often did your parents make you train?"

"Every night."

"How old are you?"

"Sixteen."

"Why are you such a terrible person?"

"Shut up."

"What planet are you from?"

"Heidel. I mean—Earth. I'm *going* to Heidel…or, it *seems* like I'll be going to Heidel."

There it was. There it *was!!* "Clarice" had recovered quickly, but not before I'd gotten my suspicions confirmed. I quelled my excitement and attempted to eke out one more answer. I wanted to end with a few benign questions that gave Clarice the impression that she'd dodged suspicion.

"Who's your calculus teacher?"

"Ms. Armand."

"And how long have you tried to sabotage this mission?"

"I'm **not** trying to sabotage the mission," Clarice was quick to snap." I don't know what you're talking about."

I fell quiet and nodded my head.

Clarice was *not* in fact Clarice. I hadn't figured how it was possible or how it had happened, but something had taken over Clarice, and it was apparently from Heidel.

"What's really happening right now?" Max's warm breath tickled the back of my ear as he leaned forward to whisper in my ear.

He couldn't have expected me to answer; what could I possibly say with everyone standing right there in front of us? Any and every action would be extensively scrutinized at this point…I didn't want to give the group any reason to doubt my allegiance or motive (beyond what had already transpired…that was out of my control).

"Okay, you're right—the questions part of the exercise is stupid," I conceded. If I moved quickly between topics, no one would have the chance to truly process what had just taken place. I saw that as an advantage, knowing that my participation in the list-sharing would be cursory and perfunctory at best…in reality, I would be working like a fiend to translate the feelings and suspicions nested in my inner being into a language my brain could understand.

"I'm glad *that's* settled," Max exhaled in exaggerated relief, taking my cue as he worked to move things along. Gratitude emanated my entire being; I couldn't undersell the value of an ally in my present circumstances.

"*Is* it settled?" Peyton asked uncertainly.

"It's obvious Selina and Clarice have some issues to work through," Max acknowledged. "But that doesn't affect the rest of us. I think we should move forward to share our lists—maybe that will even help."

"Okay," Amanda agreed, glancing at me quickly out of the corner of her eye. A second ally.

"I'd like to share my list before I change my mind about everything positive I wrote down," Marcus joked, his tone of voice revealing the fragility of his jest. He really did seem worried that he might hate everyone in the group before too long.

"Right. I'll start," Chris cut in, resuming his self-appointed role as leader and initiator of the group.

I zoned out as Chris shared a rather bland and uninspired list of strengths he had noted in each member of the group. There was nothing insulting in his list—no underhanded slight or obvious dig—but there was also nothing insightful. His observations read like a resumé of job experience and education history: it was limited to facts and the obvious.

Next was Peyton. Her list was slightly more discerning, but there was a definite pattern of safety and security embedded in the lists—no one seemed willing to venture deeper than surface level to share their observations of one another. Either that, or they truly didn't have anything. I found that less likely, but it was possible.

As my peers rifled through notes as personal as grocery lists, I tried to piece together what I had just learned about Clarice. Or rather, what had *happened* to Clarice. It wasn't perhaps fair to pin all the oblique, low-level behaviors on someone who wasn't in her right mind. Or who possibly didn't even have control over her actions.

It was important to consider the facts objectively; not only to come to an accurate conclusion, but because I was thoroughly unnerved thinking about what had happened to the girl I'd known my entire life. I needed to keep my wits about me if I were going to be of any help. And so, I resorted to my own grocery list of facts:

1. Clarice was compromised.
2. Clarice *had* been compromised, for an unknown amount of time.
3. Something from Heidel had infiltrated Earth.
4. There was life on Heidel, because it had come to Earth.
5. The being from Heidel did not appear to be on a positive or peaceful mission.
6. The Heidel being was capable of feeling emotion (as evidenced through the manifestation of anger through Clarice)—was it also constrained by other human frailties?
7. Clarice didn't seem to be able to protect or guard aspects of her mind from the being.
8. There was no noticeable physical change in Clarice—besides a personality shift, it was unclear what other indicators of foul play might exist.

I ruminated over the list with a concerted effort to stay calm. As I took the opportunity to distance myself from what had already taken place, I felt warmth permeate my body. It seemed to start in my middle—the epicenter—and travel out like a homing device to my extremities. There was no obvious source of this new, increasing heat—but it seemed to be connected to Clarice. I had no idea how.

"Dude, Selina—she didn't even say anything bad," Marcus called out, his voice far resounding in the back of my brain as I worked to pull myself back.

"What?" I asked, confused by his rather random comment.

"You look like you're getting a root canal," Luke agreed. "What's wrong with you?"

"Nothing," I snapped defensively. "I'm thinking through what I'm going to say." It was crazy how easily the lies came to me once I committed to them.

"Geeze, save me for last," Marcus chortled drily. "If that expression says anything about what you're going to say, I don't know that I want to hear."

I rolled my eyes and avoided looking at Clarice. I was sure I had drawn attention to myself, and I didn't want to further suspicion. My time was limited as it was. The temperature of my body continued to rise, creating a sense of urgency I could not deny. I guessed that my cheeks were visibly changing color and wondered what the others would make of it.

"Is it my turn?" I asked, trying to change the subject as I kept my tone upbeat.

"Do you *want* to go next?" Luke asked pointedly.

"Sure. I'm ready," I answered breezily, trying to disguise the fact that I'd been thousands of miles away until moments ago. I smiled in an effort to disarm those who looked quite uptight, then opened my mouth to begin my commentary on my peers (which was far more perceptive and discerning than anything that had been shared up to that point).

I don't think I ever said a word. I say "think" because I don't actually know what I did or what anyone saw.

No sooner had I made the decision to speak than an explosion of warmth detonated like a bomb, sending super-heated shrapnel throughout my entire body. With this overpowering physical action came the blinding cobalt-blue flash of light that I'd learned to associate with the supernatural…but demonstrated in a far greater capacity than I'd ever seen before. Something like a balloon popped inside of me, and everything went black.

Danger

It's hard to separate the fact from fiction in the events that followed. If I were to explain my experience without the limitations of what we know to be real and true about life on Earth, this is what I would say happened:

I left my body and floated up into the atmosphere, something like a balloon when it's untethered and soars up into the sky. Peaceful but intentional— there was no denying the quick progression through the variant levels of the troposphere, and there was also no mechanism with which to control direction or destination. I was beholden to nature and the expression of the wind.

As I floated, my body began to cool down. I got the impression this was a result of the distance put between my body and Earth as opposed to a change in the actual temperature in the sky. I watched, fascinated and oddly detached, as I soared higher and higher away from Earth's surface. I found that I could breathe in outer space and I had the sense that someone or something was controlling my movement.

As quickly as I'd clipped through the atmosphere, I came to a screeching halt. Earth was now a small orb in the distance, no larger than a bouncy ball. I knew to keep my gaze fixed on my home planet and watched with interest (and increasing heart rate) as golden pods descended to Earth with increasing speed. It was difficult to determine just how many there were.

I followed the path of the butterscotch orbs as they arched through the heavens and down towards Earth. When they entered Earth's atmosphere, the pods opened like flowers to send dandelion-colored parachutes down onto land.

Completely unrecognized by Earth's tracking devices.

The answer to my unspoken question materialized without delay. My eyes focused on the parachutes as they slipped closer and closer to land. Intuitively I knew that this—whatever "this" was—was from Heidel. And somehow explained Clarice's bizarre behavior. Like an earnest yet inept student of advanced trigonometry, I endeavored to connect the dots between what I'd seen through Clarice, what I'd intuited through supernatural aptitude, and what I was watching unfold before my own two eyes.

My thoughts muddied and my vision clouded. The myriad of colors that swathed the landscape of my inner thoughts weren't in rainbow formation; rather, the colors overlapped in chaotic puddles reminiscent of amateur finger-painting. I got the impression that I was not going to figure out the inner workings of what was taking place with the immediacy that I was craving, so I switched tactics.

Without knowing precisely what was happening, I could work out that Heidel had orchestrated a hostile invasion of Earth, and that the infiltration had already begun. How and why this act of aggression had been taken were of course crucial details, but also pressing was the accumulation of statistics such as the number of humans who had been affected, where the Heidel perpetrators were currently residing, and if there was any way to stop or impede progress of the invasion that was already underway.

An invasion. An *invasion*. The reality was horrifying, and yet I was able to conjure the words without any emotional or physiological response.

They're targeting The Organization.

I couldn't summon or otherwise control the intuitions that came to me, so I felt thankful that I was the recipient of helpful bits of knowledge.

I watched as the parachutes descended in the vicinity of The Organization headquarters. Upon landing, they went dark—I couldn't track their movement any further.

I hovered in space for some moments before I was pressed back towards Earth. I was pushed back into the atmosphere with startling speed that took my breath away; first because of the torque behind my movement, then because I drew close enough to watch a Heidel being insidiously slide inside a home and then a human.

It wasn't gruesome, distorted, or markedly unnatural—and that was precisely why it was so disturbing. I saw the tangible wisp of what appeared to be vapor waft into the room and then close to the human—in this case, a middle-aged man.

When the man took a breath, the vapor slipped inside and disappeared. There was no noticeable change in the man apart from stiffening of bones that had moments before appeared relaxed. No resistance, either—I suspected the man had no idea anything had changed.

In my altered state, I was able to keep my gaze fixed on the scene before me without even blinking my eyes. The man stood in place for a prolonged moment, then resumed his activities as though nothing had ever happened.

And then, as abruptly as the experience had started, it ended.

When I came to, I was lying flat on my back, cool and unforgiving travertine tiles pressed against my spine. Gone was the blissful attachment I'd enjoyed during my vision: my head throbbed and nausea thrust her fist inside my stomach in an authoritative demand; my innards responded at once with woeful obedience.

The act of vomiting catapulted my body up; the projectile of that morning's breakfast narrowly missing my legs and landing in a heap in front of me. I felt dizzy, I felt sick, and my head hurt as though someone were hammering my skull with a Dalluge 7180. I wanted to die.

Eyes tightly closed and head bent between my knees, I focused on my breathing and prayed I would not vomit a second time. Then I prayed that I *would* vomit a second time and rid my body of the violence that had induced such anarchy. I'm not sure either happened, but in time the otherworldly aching ebbed and I was able to register voices.

"Selina? Selina?"

The urgent and repetitive calling of my name suggested that I'd been unresponsive for some time. A cold washcloth was pressed against my forehead, and I groaned.

"Selina? Are you okay?" I could make out Peyton's voice this time. I wasn't sure what might happen should I try to respond—would I be able to answer, or would I throw up again? I worked instead to squint one eye and then the other open.

The room looked soft and fuzzy, almost like an Instagram filter had been applied. There was a crowd of faces bent over me, all with wide eyes and drawn expressions. Most seemed to be searching my face for an answer I wasn't sure I possessed.

"Selina? Are you okay?" Peyton tried again.

I turned my head just a bit and felt stiffness in my spine but no nausea. The foul aftertaste of bile caked my mouth and I fought not to gag.

"Water," I croaked, closing my eyes once again. If I threw up again, it would be the result of my disgust and not a mandate of my body.

Someone guided my fingers to wrap around a glass of water and then pushed the cool cup to my lips and kept me propped up as I took conservative sips of water.

Like magic, the water seemed to inspire life back into my body. I felt like the tin man from *Wizard of Oz* as I opened my eyes with ease and pushed back and away from the vomit.

The first person I made eye contact with was Max; there was no surprise that he was the one who had supported me as I drank water.

His expressive eyes didn't stray from mine: there were dozens of questions that lay in suspension in those pigmented orbs of his, but he didn't voice a single one.

"Are you okay?" he asked pointedly, regarding me carefully.

"I think so," I laughed hoarsely in an effort to downplay the absurdity of what had just transpired.

"What happened to you?" Marcus wanted to know. "You just dropped to the ground. It was wild."

My eyes darted around the circle to take in the startled (and troubled) expressions of my peers. My gaze stopped when I took in Clarice.

To her credit, she looked as disturbed as the rest of the group (possibly for different reasons), but what caught my eye was the turmeric-colored splotch on her forehead. It looked as though someone had drenched a brush in the orange-colored paint and then cast a wide stroke across her forehead.

She caught my gaze and narrowed her eyes.

"What?" she asked, not necessarily in accusation but with a definite edge.

"My head really hurts," I groaned, putting my head back in my hands. I was still working to put the pieces together and I couldn't trust myself to answer the group's questions.

"Do we need to get Mr. Boothe?" I heard Amanda whisper to the group. "She fell hard and totally out of the blue. What if there's long-lasting damage? We don't know what happened to her."

"I agree," Chris announced, not bothering to whisper. "She might not be fit for the mission."

"I didn't say that," Amanda chirped in reprove. "I just worry that she needs help that we can't give her."

"You may not have said it, but I'm thinking it," Chris took on an unusually bold stance. "Her *episode* was without warning, and we don't know what happened. If something like that were to happen in outer space, while on a mission…"

"We'd work to help her however we could," Peyton's response was full of judgment.

"We're trying to colonize a new planet and save Earth," Chris reminded her. "We don't know what extemporaneous challenges will arise during our mission—the last thing we need is for one of us to go down with a seizure."

"We don't know it was a seizure," Amanda said coldly.

"It wasn't a seizure," I heard myself say. I hadn't planned on offering any explanation until I'd had the opportunity to work through on my own just what it was that *had* happened, but I couldn't stand watching them discuss it all as though I weren't right there.

All eyes shifted to me.

"What did happen?" Amanda asked. It was an honest inquiry, devoid of judgment.

"I'm still trying to work that part out," I confessed, back-pedaling a bit as I thought about how much I wanted to divulge to the group. "I didn't have any warning that it was about to happen, either."

I saw Max's jaw tighten out of the corner of my eyes, and Peyton bit her lower lip uncertainly. I'd answered incorrectly; I'd added to the argument against me without intending to.

"It wasn't a seizure, because it wasn't medical—it's not like my mind went blank or something," I hastened to correct my error.

"It looked like a seizure," Marcus explained carefully, his voice neutral as he stuck to empirical facts. "Your eyes rolled back into your head, and then you fell like a tree. You convulsed a bit before we were able to prop you up, and you didn't respond when we called your name and tried to shake you awake."

There was a moment of silence from the group that explained to me just how scary my episode must have looked.

"I'm sorry," I managed, unsure of what to say. "That's not how it felt—it was more peaceful for me, except for the waking back up part."

"Chris still makes a valid point," Clarice cut in, disregarding my account. "It doesn't really matter what it felt like to Selina or what happened if it means that she can't be trusted to stand beside us at full strength."

"Of *course* you would say that," Peyton shook her head in disgust. "Can you put your feelings about Selina aside for just one moment to consider what this means for the entire group?"

"I *am*," Clarice answered, indignant. "That's exactly why I think it's dangerous to have her with us. I believe Selina when she says that it didn't feel scary for her...but it was scary for us. And it doesn't change the fact that we weren't able to communicate with her while she had her 'experience.'"

"You said it wasn't scary—what happened?" Marcus wanted to know.

"I don't know exactly what happened," I began honestly. "Nothing like that has ever happened to me before. But it was kind of like I was dreaming." I fought the urge to explain the vision I'd received—it might explain my behavior and assure the group that I was healthy, but it would raise an entirely new set of questions that I wasn't prepared to answer.

"I still think you need to see a physician," Max cut in. His words felt like a betrayal even as I knew that he would never act in opposition to me.

Slowly, everyone in the group seemed to come to the consensus that this was the next thing to do.

"I'll tell Mr. Boothe where she is, just in case we're asked to train or take another assessment," Luke volunteered.

As much as I did not want to see a physician, I knew this would buy me time to think through what *my* next step needed to be. It might also allow for some privacy.

"I'll watch Felix," Peyton was quick to volunteer.

I nodded even as I disliked the idea of being separated from my kitten. It made more sense for him to stay with someone who could look after him and ensure his safety, and I trusted Peyton—but I wished to keep Felix by my side.

"I'll go with you," Max assured me.

"Want to carry her there, too?" Clarice couldn't help herself. "Might be safer," she quipped with a mean wink.

"I imagine she can walk there, but I'll happily lend a hand if it's needed," Max managed to answer levelly.

The mark. Remember the mark, Selina. Clarice is not herself—you can't attribute this foul behavior to her.

But it was so hard not to. I bit the inside of my cheek hard to keep from saying something that I would either regret or have to explain as Max gently took my arm and guided me to my feet.

"Okay?" he asked with genuine concern when I stood up.

I waited a moment before responding, allowing time to orient myself and to chase the yellow spots from the periphery of my vision.

"I'm okay," I answered quietly, thankful for the guidance of his tender but firm grip.

Together we made our way down the hall and towards the physician's quarters.

"Clarice is possessed by something from Heidel," I announced when we were out of earshot.

I felt Max's muscles tighten but otherwise didn't get a response.

"I had a vision," I explained, eager to unload the truth of what had happened to someone I trusted. I had the feeling that sharing my experience out loud would help me to process what had happened, too.

"I saw the beings from Heidel on their way to Earth, and I saw them begin to infiltrate. They are targeting The Organization," I hurried on. "And I saw that Clarice was affected. And then when I woke up, I could see this big yellow mark on her forehead."

Here I paused and looked at Max for confirmation. "There's not actually a yellow mark on her forehead, is there?"

Max shook his head slowly. He seemed to be thinking through everything I had just told him.

"That's what I thought. So now I can see who has been compromised," I explained. "I don't know that I understand what happened. And I obviously have a lot of questions. But I know that what I saw is true."

Max nodded with contemplation before responding. "You don't know how to defend against the beings?" he asked, looking me in the eye seriously.

"No," I answered, voice thick with regret. That was obviously the important key that I was missing. "They were coming with increasing speed," I mused as an afterthought.

We walked the rest of the way in silence. It felt foolish to make small talk; I knew we were both seriously considering what a reasonable plan of action might be.

When we arrived at the physician's quarters, I looked to Max once again. He didn't hesitate at all.

"Selina just had what appeared to be a fainting episode, except that she was unconscious for a couple of minutes," Max explained to the woman who hurried to assist us. "We're part of the group selected for the colonization mission," he added in afterthought.

"We'll be sure to notify Mr. Boothe right away," the woman assured us, her expression showing significant concern. "Please, follow me."

I felt like a small child as Max escorted me after the woman down a hallway bathed in sky blue and sea-foam green. The woman stopped in front of an examination room and looked to Max.

"I'm afraid this is as far as you can go," she explained.

"I'll be sitting right here," Max told me, pointing to the wall just opposite of the door I was to go through. "I'll be sure to stay out of the way of the physicians and medical attendants coming through," he assured the woman before she had a chance to protest.

It was rare for Max to speak with such authority, and I knew he was standing beside me in a show of support. If there was any trouble at all, I needed only to raise my voice, and I knew Max would come to my aid. I nodded to Max to show I understood, then took a step forward towards the door the woman was working to open.

It was only after walking into the examination room that I began to panic. I hadn't really considered what the visit to the physician might look like— all medical examinations growing up had been house or school visits conducted by trained professionals who carried with them the necessary diagnostic tools and equipment.

Every examination had been done within the confines of a safe, known space…and had included the watchful eyes of people I trusted. I'd never needed treatment or a procedure that necessitated my presence in a hospital…and now that I found myself in just such a space, I struggled to remain calm.

The room was a small white cube; brightly-lit but with little variation, which made the space feel tight and confined. Hostile, steel-plated instruments sat like trophies on the industrial shelving—I couldn't begin to fathom what function each might hold. I knew well enough not to expend any mental energy on the subject if I wanted to keep my composure.

Moments later, a woman walked into the room. She smiled in obligatory fashion before looking down at the tablet in her hand. "Selina Alois?"

I nodded.

"You fell?"

I nodded again and swallowed hard, hoping my nerves would be washed away with my stale saliva.

"I'm just going to take your vitals before Dr. Medera sees you," the nurse explained.

I nodded, thankful when I noted the familiar tools that would be used to check my system. I felt my body further calm as I heard the nurse read out familiar metrics—perhaps there was nothing to worry about.

"Alright, Selina—your numbers look good," the nurse confirmed what I had already deduced. "Dr. Medera will be with you in a moment."

The nurse was halfway out the door when she turned to look back at me—the second time total in our entire interaction. "Make yourself comfortable," she encouraged in an affected falsetto before slipping out of view.

I'd long since determined that I would not find comfort in the pearly prison I found myself in: how any patient might find peace and calm with such mechanical bedside manner was another matter entirely. To try to empty my mind of all thoughts was not only futile but dangerous, as was any intentional effort to think deeply on a topic: anxiety was a familiar companion who knew her way around the house too well.

I counted multiples of 7 all the way up to 427 before there was a perfunctory knock on the door.

"Come in," I warbled, my voice devoid of the self-assurance I'd hoped to convey.

The door opened, and another female—this one swathed in a pressed white coat decorated with badges—walked through the door. Her practical, androgynous black shoes and plain appearance somehow added to her credibility as a doctor: the message seemed to be that she placed an emphasis on her work and not her looks.

Similar to the nurse before her, Dr. Medera had her head bent over her tablet. I focused on the inch-thick line of gray hair that traced the midsection of her hairline, betraying the otherwise rich, cinnamon-brown locks that had been pulled into a neat ponytail. Her part, dead center. Unflattering.

"I'm sorry to hear about your fall, Selina," Dr. Medera began, her tone sincere even as her face remained focused on the screen below.

"Thanks," I replied, only because it felt rude to remain silent. What else was I supposed to say?

"Any prior episodes of fainting that have somehow been overlooked in your records?" Dr. Medera continued. Her fingers flew across the screen with the intensity of raindrops on a windowpane, then stopped just as suddenly. I wondered what she was looking through and wondered why she hadn't introduced herself and wondered why all the medical attendants in the facility seemed to interact with me like I was some kind of robot. But for all my wondering, I said not a word.

"No."

"I understand you're part of the mission," Dr. Medera continued.

Finally, she was making an effort to get to know me…to establish context surrounding her patient and the circumstances that had led me to my current place in the hospital.

"That's correct," I answered, unable to keep pride from my voice.

"How's that going?" Dr. Medera prodded.

I opened my mouth to answer, then closed it. I couldn't explain where the feeling originated, but I got the sense that I needed to be careful. Something didn't feel right.

"It's going well," I replied neutrally, flustered by my sudden discontent.

"You must be getting ready to launch soon," Dr. Medera continued. Her persistence on the topic struck me as off, considering the first impression I'd received of her. "Do you know yet where you'll be traveling, or who might be accompanying you?"

"It's going well," I repeated dumbly. I couldn't think of how to dodge the question without arousing suspicion, and I worried I might be regarded as defiant or incorrigible if I refused to answer.

This repetition elicited a physical response from Dr. Medera: she stopped tapping on the tablet and looked up to regard me with open curiosity. I fought to stay still and resisted the urge to squirm as she studied me with interest that went beyond a study for medical prognosis.

Look up.

The voice was more insistent than usual, and I guessed that my downcast eyes communicated fear and uncertainty that would later work against me. But then I looked up.

It would be impossible to capture the visceral reaction that awakened in every cell of my body as I looked into Dr. Medera's eyes. There was nothing notable about her eyes; my gaze didn't linger there for more than a second. Rather, they traveled immediately to the wide yellow brushstroke smeared across her forehead.

I couldn't control it: my skin went cold and clammy, then burned as though I had yellow fever. I shook with fear that I couldn't control.

It was the first time I really doubted that I would be okay. I'd stubbornly held onto the belief that I could—that I *would*—get through whatever was thrown my way, but now I wasn't sure. Now, looking at the implicating mark on Dr. Medera's face, I worried that I was in way over my head. Correction: I'd *been* in way over my head for a long time. But now I was beginning to understand just how much was stacked up against me.

Clarice had been compromised, this doctor had been compromised…who else had fallen prey to Heidel's infiltration? I'd battled nerves regarding the mission prior to this new development—I couldn't decide if this discernment was a curse or a gift. I'd held some level of confidence whilst in ignorance; now that I had the ability to see the extent of the damage, I felt that I was in entirely new territory. And I wanted out.

Max. I suddenly remembered Max was sitting outside, and he had assured me that he would come to my aid for any reason. And looking at Dr. Medera gave me more than just a hint of a reason: her entire being seemed to emanate malevolence. My feelings couldn't be trusted, but this was the barometer I had intact: and it was on panic mode at full-throttle.

"Selina?" Dr. Medera asked again, studying me closely.

My throat constricted to the point that it felt hard to breathe. My vision grew blurry and the room seemed to grow smaller. I *felt* more than I saw or sensed the harm that Dr. Medera wanted to inflict.

I looked up at her without speaking, still working to find my voice, to call out to Max, who would come to my aid.

"Can you describe how your body feels, Selina?" Dr. Medera asked, pulling her attention away from the tablet to focus on me.

My skin crawled as though covered with beetles; the room smelled like sulfur. The lights seemed to rise and fall in melody with the sinister cadence of my thoughts. My skin burned with growing intensity, and I had no words for Dr. Medera.

Lean in.

The thought was not my own, and I made no move to accept it. *Lean in?* What was that supposed to mean? Was I really being encouraged to move *closer* to a woman I knew to be evil? I was disgusted by the mere thought—there was no way I would make an effort to embrace what was certain to destroy me.

And yet…there was an insistence behind the thought, and a sense of urgency. As much as I wanted to push the idea from my brain, I forced myself to recall that I had supernatural aptitude that I could trust; and that by its very definition the supernatural would defy what might seem to be common sense, or *natural*.

I stayed put, considering my options and playing out scenarios in my mind. I could not imagine what might happen if I "leaned in," but I felt growing certainty that it was the thing I needed to do.

"I'm experiencing some heat, and some cold," I answered matter-of-factly, working to buy myself time. That was how the supernatural seemed to speak to me—it wasn't with the big picture all at once, but rather it seemed to come gradually, with just enough information for me to take the next step or position myself for the next piece.

"Did you experience that same feeling before, during, or after your fainting episode?" Dr. Medera asked. It was the familiar song-and-dance of a doctor and patient narrative, but in this case it also masked the underlying examinations we were both carrying out.

"No," I answered directly. "I didn't experience any change of temperature before now."

Dr. Medera nodded wisely without taking her eyes off me.

Touch her.

I nearly choked on the thought; instead, a loud cough came out.

"Another new symptom?" Dr. Medera asked.

I shook my head, grateful for the coughs that hid my loss for words. I was supposed to *touch* her? My mind suddenly understood this to be the way I was supposed to "lean in." I was to press in and get closer to Dr. Medera by quite literally making physical contact with her. I was supposed to make physical connection even when every inch of the woman repulsed me.

It would be easier to call for Max. Also: I hadn't made it as far as I had by doing what was easy.

"This is what it feels like,"

Leaning forward, I pressed my palms against Dr. Medera's forearms, wrapping my fingers around her limbs in a vise-like grip. I hadn't planned the maneuver, and there wasn't any aggression in my grasp. But I didn't let go.

The moment we touched, I felt electricity course through my body. I wasn't sure where it originated: was it Dr. Medera's body that trembled? Was it my own? The current was strong, and my veins seemed to crackle with live energy. The hairs on my arms stood on end, and still I didn't let go.

My action seemed to have caught Dr. Medera completely off guard: I noted a similar physical response in her body, but with the added element of distorted facial features. Her wide eyes regarded me with shock at the same time mine considered what all of this meant.

And then, the smell. I was pulled from my thoughts as I inhaled the undeniable, revolting stench of burning flesh. Fear was masked by surprise as I watched steam rise from Dr. Medera's arms like smoke from a George Foreman grill. Her body shook with increasing intensity and sweat ran in rivers down the sides of her face. I looked into the doctor's eyes and noted the reptilian yellow-green of her irises and the swollen red veins that crisscrossed her corneas.

I still didn't let go.

I wasn't sure why I held on, but I did. If anything, my grip tightened. And then, just moments later, the vision hit.

I call it a vision because it's the closest word that comes to mind to describe the experience I had. But it was not like the visions I'd had before, with shapes and colors that held meaning. Everything went black, like the utter and complete darkness of a movie theater before the feature film flickers to life. Then, words and impressions were pressed into my mind like the branding of livestock.

The messages were clear, deep, and bold—they seemed to permeate my flesh and bones and wrap around my sinews. As profound as my previous supernatural inclinations had felt, this one trumped them all with its voracity.

Destroy from within.

Infiltrate without arousing suspicion, and plant the seeds of doubt, bitterness, animosity, and hopelessness.

Start slow, then grow.

Target the five sectors of influence: business, education, government, the arts & entertainment, and the family unit.

Find influential individuals to possess, then wait for the effects to trickle down to all subsets of culture and society.

Patience.

Work with, and not against, the individual. Don't give them reason to question your presence or recognize the violence being done to and through them.

Subtlety is key.

I released Dr. Medera when the variant impressions had synergized to form a cohesive and disturbing picture in my mind. There was no longer any doubt regarding what Heidel was trying to accomplish on Earth, and I had the added benefit of now recognizing just how they intended to accomplish their goal.

"Did you feel how hot my flesh is?" I asked Dr. Medera innocently, hoping she had not had a supernatural experience similar to mine.

Dr. Medera, frazzled, wet, and overheated, looked at me with dismay. Her expression suggested that she had absolutely no idea what had just taken place, and I decided to base my next move off this assumption.

"I agree with you that this could be the fever going around," I sighed. "Do you think I can just sleep it off, or do I need an antibiotic?"

Dr. Medera's mouth lay slightly suspended. She moved to close it as she regained her composure and looked down at her tablet, swallowing hard. "Yes, the fever. Let me just consult with my colleagues for a moment regarding medication. I'll be back in a moment."

Dr. Medera scuttled out of the room in a hurry, and my hands flew to my head. *What was going on?! What had I just done? Was I safe, sitting in that room? Was Dr. Medera really going to speak with her colleagues, or was she gathering reinforcements?* My mind went wild, but my bottom stayed rooted in place on the examination table.

Not two minutes later, Dr. Medera came back into the room. She limited her eye contact and seemed eager to be rid of me as quickly as possible— she thrust some medicine that I would never take into my hand and advised me to come back in 48 hours to check on the fever. And then, she was gone.

I sat for a prolonged moment, one hand wrapped around a pill bottle, one hand resting on my thigh. My bottom protested against the unforgiving metallic seat, and I wiggled from side to side in an effort to win comfort. In the end, I found my voice.

"Max."

The throaty whisper was not vociferous, but it summoned Max as I'd hoped it would. My heart felt relief when Max's head poked through the door, eyes anxiously surveying the scene.

"You're okay," he muttered in relief.

"I'm okay," I agreed, scooting off the edge of the examination table.

"That doctor left your room looking like hell," Max cut to the chase, speaking with more gravity than I was used to.

A half-hearted chuckle escaped my lips and Max looked me over with concern.

"What happened in there?" he wanted to know. "And did she figure out what was wrong with you?"

"She has the mark," I told him.

Max's eyes doubled in size. "Dr. Medera?" he asked in surprise.

"Dr. Medera," I nodded my agreement.

"Whoa. How many others are there?" Max wondered aloud. It wasn't a question he meant for me to answer; he worried, like me, about the scope and damage of the infiltration.

"I know. I'm worried, too," I agreed.

"Sooo…did she examine you?"

"I guess you could say that. She seemed to have ulterior motives in her questioning, and I followed my gut and turned the examination tables on her," I explained. "I touched her, and her flesh seemed to burn. And then I got this impression of what she's doing here."

I went on to describe to Max the bizarre sensations and understanding I'd gotten from making physical contact with Dr. Medera. Max listened intently with furrowed brow. When I finished my narration, he inhaled deeply and let the extra air collect in puffed cheeks. He held the air there for an extended moment before blowing it all out.

"This is serious," he said, stating what we both knew to be obvious.

"I know. I'm worried how many others I'll see that are affected, now that I can suddenly tell who has been compromised," I told Max.

He nodded, a grimace fixed upon his face.

"They're going for the most influential people," I worried aloud. "What if we find that Mr. Boothe or John or someone like that is affected?"

Max met my gaze and shrugged. "I don't know. We'll have to figure that out."

I appreciated the fact that neither of us worked to sugar-coat the terrible truth we faced. It was one thing to approach a situation with optimism, and another to naively and stupidly gallivant into danger without a care or concern.

"I want to get out of here," I blurted, suddenly anxious to leave. I was filled with nervous energy and felt the urge to move.

Without a word, Max pushed the door ajar and held it that way for me to slip through. We barreled down the hallways and out the exit like toy soldiers before pausing to create a plan in the confines of the empty corridor.

"What do you want to do?" Max asked me.

"I want to figure out who I can trust," I thought aloud. "And come up with a strategy with the others who have not been compromised. I'm worried about how far-reaching Heidel's influence might already be."

Max nodded seriously. "To the common room? To John? Mr. Boothe?" he asked, gauging my expression for clues of where to go.

"John."

Exposed

I don't remember walking to John's wing, but I did. I don't remember what I explained to Max on the walk over, but I said enough to put him on high alert and to paint a broad picture of what the situation was. Either that, or he used his uncanny ability to intuit the state of affairs.

All I know is that when I knocked on John's door (I had the key, but declined to use it—the information I was about to download into his schema would be obtrusive enough), Max stood beside me with solidarity stronger than that which is cultivated through mere friendship. There was confidence in his upright spine and even a bit of hutzpah in his stance, as evidenced by his legs spread farther apart than usual.

John answered on the third knock, and I wondered if he had expected me. It was certainly possible, knowing his gift of all things prophetic. His eyes read the panic splashed across my face at the same time my eyes sought out his forehead for the terrible mark of treachery. Seeing nothing suspicious, I leaned closer and squinted, even going so far as to brazenly push the few hairs covering his forehead to one side to *really* get a good look.

Pale pink flesh stared back at me: a blank canvas of aged skin dotted with sunspots. I whimpered in exaggerated relief as my body melted like putty into the plush carpeting below.

"What happened?" John asked sharply, grabbing one of my elbows. With Max's help, the two pulled me through the threshold of John's abode and closed the door definitively.

Max hesitated only for a moment, and I got the impression he was not weighing his words and considering what was safe to tell John but rather that he was thinking through just how to chronicle the events of the past hours.

"I heard she fainted," John stated, offering Max a reference point he readily took.

"It looked like she fainted," Max agreed. "She had a vision."

I felt John's eyes scrutinizing me, working furiously to piece together what I had learned that had undone me so completely. If I'd had the wherewithal to explain what had happened myself, I would have done so. But I didn't. I lay in a puddle at their feet, limbs askew and cheek pressed against the carpeting with force that I knew would leave red splotches.

"Who knows that you came here?" John snapped, looking over one shoulder and then the other in paranoid fashion I'd only seen in spy-thriller films.

"I—I don't know," Max stumbled, catching me off guard. John's questioning and behavior were rattling Max, too. "We came straight from the hospital, and it didn't look like anyone followed us. We didn't tell anyone we were coming here," he managed to tell John.

"We don't have much time," John urged Max to go on. "We could be interrupted at any moment. What happened?"

"It looked like she was having a seizure," Max spat, words tumbling out like the Running of the Bulls in Pamplona. "She fell to the ground and her limbs started shaking, and she didn't respond to any of us—not when we called her name or touched her or waved our hands in front of her face." He paused for the briefest moment to take in John's response before catapulting himself back into the narration.

"She was out for a few minutes. And then when she came to, she was disoriented. She knew she'd had a vision—and she told us that she'd had a vision—but she either had trouble explaining what she had seen, or she knew better than to give too many details. The group was worried, and I was concerned that she might divulge too much information, so I suggested we take her to the hospital. The group approved of the idea and we went straight there," Max rambled.

"The mark," I heard myself whisper, loud enough that I won the attention of both men.

"What mark?" John barked, bending down close to me. I would receive no sympathy for what I had undergone; time was of the essence, and John's demeanor suggested great danger.

"I see the marks now," I croaked, pushing up to a seat as I used my eyes to plead with John to understand. *Please, please understand, John. Please know what I am talking about. Please don't be surprised or caught off guard by this revelation. Please know.*

"Where is the mark?" John asked, revealing nothing of his background knowledge on the matter (or lack thereof).

"The forehead." With great tenderness, I pressed the tips of my fingers to my forehead in indication of just where the mark had made its diabolical debut. "It's yellow. Like a brush stroke," I added as an afterthought.

"And you've seen multiple people with it?" John questioned, by now crouched low. We were at eye level, and he looked at me without blinking.

"Clarice," I began, and John nodded as though unsurprised. "And Dr. Medera," I carried on.

"The doctor she went to see," Max cut in.

John nodded and kept his eyes on me, to see if I would offer more.

"We're being infiltrated by Heidel," I said bluntly. I hoped and willed that John had somehow prophetically come to this truth on his own, for I had no idea how I would be able to explain it.

"Yes." John's response was brief but emphatic. While it was confirmation of the worst possible reality, it was also comforting to know that my assessment was correct…and to know that I had a teammate with which to fight the awful truth.

"Have you told anyone?" Max asked John, looking at the prophet in surprise. "Do you see the marks, too?"

"I don't see yellow marks, no," John answered. "I perceive the supernatural differently. I smell it."

"The sulfur," I murmured under my breath.

John's head swiveled in my direction so fast it was like it had been yanked by a chain. "You perceive the supernatural through multiple thresholds?" he asked, voice excited and breathless.

"I—I don't know what you mean," I confessed uncertainly, worried I'd somehow overstepped my boundaries.

"You've *seen* the supernatural," John explained impatiently, hands gesturing in a way that did nothing to promote understanding but certainly spoke to his frenetic energy and sense of urgency. "But you can *smell* it, too?"

I saw what he was getting at, and I wasn't sure of my answer. My encounter with Dr. Medera was the first time I'd had knowledge in an alternative sense, and I wasn't sure if the experience was indicative of my new abilities or an outlier in the realm of my supernatural aptitude.

"I don't know," I answered honestly, feeling John's impatience as though it were my own. "That was the first time I smelled anything."

"What else did you notice?" John wanted to know. The intensity of his questioning was such that I doubted he'd glance over if a polar bear did cartwheels through the room or the sofa started talking.

"My skin—it felt like it had insects crawling on it, and then it felt hot— really hot. And the lights seemed to dim and then go bright," I recalled, thinking hard if there was something else I'd failed to recollect.

"You sense in multiple modalities," John sat back, voice full of awe as he regarded me with new eyes. "I've never seen it."

"What do you mean? What does that mean?" I asked nervously, voice high-pitched and desperate. John had never seen anything like it? That did nothing for nerves that had already seen far too much variation for their liking. I wanted familiar, comfortable, known.

"It means you can perceive the supernatural through more than just your vision," John explained, still in a state of disbelief. "I thought you had a powerful sense of vision—but it's so much more than that."

"I don't know what that means," I protested, trying not to become hysterical. "And I don't know how to control it."

"You don't control it. You can't control any of the gifts," John assured me.

"Then how exactly are they *gifts*?" I whined. "I don't want them! I don't like them! I don't know what's happening to my body, and I want to go back to how things were."

"I'm going to ignore that comment," John chided me.

I knew my comment was immature and impossible, but by this point I was exhausted, overwhelmed, and frightened. What was true? What was inevitable? What was in my control? I didn't know the answers to any of these questions.

For all my supposed talent, I felt quite empty. A ship tossed in the waves of a restless sea. And my navigator? He seemed to have gone below deck, only to resurface arbitrarily to offer a short-sighted directive that did nothing to position me for long-term success…or to ease my nerves with a plan or outline of what to expect next.

I was known for my strength, my resilience, and my grit. My fortitude was counted on, as were my nerves of steel. I'd felt discouraged, downtrodden, and anxious, but I'd never reached a breaking point. And I suspected I'd just reached it.

"Did you smell anything on Clarice?" Max wanted to know. He was changing the subject, guiding me back to still waters I felt comfortable navigating.

"I didn't smell anything on Clarice," I responded, an element of surprise in my tone. "And I was pretty close to her," I mused.

"Do you think that means anything?" Max asked John, who stroked his beard thoughtfully in contemplation.

"Probably that the doctor was more deeply affected than Clarice," John guessed.

"What does that mean?" Max asked, and I leaned forward to hear the answer. As overwhelmed as I felt, I still wanted to know.

John opened his mouth to answer, then shook his head. "You've been gone too long," he realized suddenly. "They haven't come for us yet, which means that they don't know what you know. We need to keep it that way—you need to leave,"

"Leave?!" I squealed in alarm. "You want me to go back to where those Heidel aliens are? We don't even know if we're safe, mingling with them. What if they overtake us in the night?"

"I think you got enough through your inklings to know that won't happen," John dismissed my fears. "At the very least, that's not their strategy. They don't want to attract attention—their entire operation and success rests on their ability to fly under the radar. Let's not give them a reason to react violently and show us their physical strength."

I shuddered and fell silent. I knew John was right, and I hated it.

"You don't think we're at risk, rubbing shoulders with them?" Max asked.

"Short term, no," John answered. "You'll be okay within the pods."

"Why didn't you tell us?" I asked, suddenly picking up on the element of betrayal lingering in John's withholding of this information.

"Who's to say I didn't plan on telling you?" John asked. "We only just met hours ago. Things have escalated quickly. Things *are* escalating quickly," he corrected. "We really don't have much time."

"That's what everyone keeps saying," I grumbled under my breath.

"No—you *really* don't have much time," John repeated, doubling down on the "really" to make sure I got his point.

"How much time are you thinking?" Max asked, folding his arms across his chest protectively.

"Given what I've perceived, and what Selina saw today—you have days. The Heidel beings are picking up their pace, and your mission isn't just to navigate to a new planet…it's to preserve humanity. But that's an objective created on the assumption that there's a human race to save…and Heidel is moving quickly to try to expunge humanity," John counseled seriously.

I swallowed hard. I wanted nothing more than to revert back to the days of infancy: of being held, fed, and rocked to sleep. I would also accept an extended hibernation in a remote cave outfitted with thermal sleeping bags and a winter's supply of protein bars, water bottles, and goldfish.

Instead, I pulled myself up and off of the floor. I smoothed my wrinkled clothes, tucked stray hairs behind my ears, and took a long, deep breath with eyes closed.

I was stronger than this. Everything in me wanted to give up, but I would not.

"Clearly, you have a lot to share," I spoke to John with authority and composure that made a late arrival to bump defeat and capitulation. "When is it safe to meet again?"

"Later tonight," John answered, surprising me.

"I thought you said—"

"You can't be gone for long now, right after your episode and the inheritance of additional gifting. But the urgency of our situation can't be denied. There is much you need to know. Both of you," John explained.

"Where should we say we're going?" Max asked.

"Be creative," John shrugged. "People think you like each other, right? Use that to your advantage," he suggested with a sly grin.

I scoffed but stopped when John caught my eye.

"Desperate times call for desperate measures, and it seems to me this is a rather small concession to make," John pointed out.

I swallowed my protest and turned to leave.

"Oh—and bring Felix."

John's pronouncements echoed in my mind as we walked back to the pods.

"What do you want to tell the others?" Max asked as soon as we left. "I have a couple of suggestions," he hurried on to say as he caught my look of desperation.

"I'd love to hear your ideas." I was quick to take Max up on his offer; my brain was so saturated with thoughts, emotions, and questions that I didn't have the bandwidth to concoct any clever ruse. Merely entertaining Max's ideas and picking out a superlative option would be work enough.

"I think we should be honest about seeing the doctor," Max began slowly, watching close for my reaction. To my knowledge, I didn't react—I waited patiently to hear all that he had in mind.

"And we won't have to lie when we tell them that the doctor wasn't able to figure out what happened to you, and that you were instructed to rest and come back in a couple of days." Max paused here and waited for a response.

"There's nothing controversial about that," I agreed. I was in complete agreement that it would be to our advantage to lie as little as possible…in our aggravated state it would be easy to slip up and mention something that didn't coincide with our "story." The fewer details we shared and the fewer falsehoods we told, the better.

"As far as what happened to you…you can say that the doctor thinks the episodes might be the result of stress?" Max offered.

I liked his line of thinking but remembered what I had already said about the experience. "I already said I had a vision," I reminded Max with a sigh.

"Okay, then let's stick with that. But with as few details as possible," Max suggested.

"That's the hard part," I lamented. "What do I say that doesn't sound suspicious?" My head hurt.

"Selina!" Max chided kindly. "You're making it complicated. Keep it simple. What did you have a vision about?"

"About how the beings from Heidel are evil and taking over earth," I answered sarcastically, knowing full well I was being unfairly difficult and uncooperative.

To his credit, Max ignored my grumblings and cut straight to the solution. "So, you had a *dream* about what might happen to earth if we don't take on the mission we're training for. It revealed the importance of the work we are doing and the need for us to succeed without giving much detail."

I considered Max's take and withheld comment as I worked to find the holes in his narration. I was pleasantly surprised as I came to the conclusion that his suggested story was safe.

"I wouldn't use the word *vision*," Max explained his earlier choice of words. "They already know you had some kind of supernatural, otherworldly experience—I would try to keep it as neutral as possible."

"You don't think Clarice will figure it out?" I asked nervously. That was one of my greatest concerns—that Clarice would know right away that I'd seen her mark and knew her secret.

Max hesitated and chose his words carefully. "I think Clarice has had that mark for a while...I don't think it's new. I think she'll know something is up if you act funny around her...but I don't think she'll know otherwise. Your ability to see the mark of the Heidel beings is new, but no one knows that but you. It's not like *you* have a mark," Max pointed out. "If you act like nothing has changed, I think she'll operate the same way."

I nodded, trying to play out in my mind what it would look like to interact with Clarice as though nothing had happened.

"You can do it," Max assured me, reading my thoughts.

"I don't know..." I worried.

"The two of you are already strained and awkward—I can't see how you could make things worse," Max explained, more direct than usual.

"You're right," I determined. There was no reason why I couldn't act in this way...and if our situation was as urgent as John had suggested, I wouldn't need to act for much longer.

We were nearing the pods; when we stepped into the elevator, there was comfortable silence. I knew what we both were thinking: there was no way we could guess at what the next 24 to 48 hours might hold...we'd already been surprised and caught off guard by what the past *three* hours had brought.

"And tonight?" I suddenly panicked. We may have strategized for the interrogation to come, but we hadn't planned for our later rendezvous.

"What about it?" Max asked, nonplussed.

"How are we going to sneak away? How will we know when we're supposed to meet John?" I worried.

"Selina...you will most certainly know when we're supposed to leave to meet John. You're ridiculously prophetic, remember? Just pay attention to how you're feeling," Max assured me. "As for the group—leave that to me."

He smiled at me in a way that suggested I didn't want to know what he had planned…and I wasn't about to ask. The elevator doors opened, and my spine straightened. Battle face set, I took authoritative steps forward that gave little credence to the trepidation I felt simmering just beneath my skin.

The first thing I did was collect Felix. With my kitten tucked in the crook of my elbow and pressed close to my bosom, I was reminded of the reasons why I was fighting. I was invigorated thinking about the good I had in my life.

Without any summons, the group migrated into the main area and circled around Max and I as though we were the watering hole in the middle of the African plains.

"Are you okay?" Amanda asked first, her face one of genuine concern.

I nodded and smiled slowly, fighting back panic at the thought of finding another yellow mark atop a forehead. I forced myself to make eye contact with everyone in the group and felt immense relief when I didn't see any new forehead stains. Still, my heart sank as I looked at Clarice and regarded her Heidel mark with depressed spirits.

"I think so," I answered. "The doctor wants me to come back in a couple of days to check in, but I feel better."

"What happened?" Luke asked.

"I still don't really know," I answered honestly. "And the doctor isn't really sure, either. I'm sure stress had something to do with it."

"A stress-induced fainting spell?" Amanda suggested.

She was offering me an easy way out—more grace than I deserved—and I knew the others wouldn't accept such a flimsy excuse.

"Not quite," I rebuffed. "There was definitely an element of the supernatural mixed in—the dream I had was really powerful."

I had everyone's attention, and if I played it right, got the sense that my response would satiate the group's growing appetite for answers and explanations.

"I had a dream—that's the best way to describe it—where we went on our mission. At first it seemed normal, but then it turned into a nightmare because everything went wrong," I told them, using vague terms that were close to the truth.

"What happened in the dream?" Marcus asked, chewing on his fingernail nervously.

"My dreams—they're not like the dreams you know," I did my best to explain. "It's not like there are pictures or scenes like in a movie. It's like a dream because you're unconscious, and you see ideas and get impressions, but not through images like you're thinking of. So I don't know what to worry about, I just know to worry."

This was not entirely true, but I believed the group would accept this response and it would not alert Clarice to the depth of my understanding. I wasn't sure what about my episode would be communicated or to whom…and I knew it was in my best interest that everyone believe my response was an overreaction to a fairly benign vision.

"So,,,what did you get?" Marcus asked, determined not to give up on the topic.

I looked at him and shrugged apologetically.

"That's it?" he raised his eyebrows in disappointment and disbelief. "Seriously?"

"I wish I had more to tell you," I emphasized, my face pleading with him to understand. "I'm hoping I'll get more later—sometimes that happens."

"Sounds like a terrible gift," Clarice muttered under her breath. I didn't disagree.

"She's still learning how to harness the gift," Max spoke predictably on my behalf.

"Who's coaching her?" Chris wanted to know. Max and I stayed silent—it would not be wise to bring John into the mix.

"No one has had supernatural aptitude like Selina, remember?" Peyton reminded Chris. "There probably *isn't* anyone who can teach her."

"I'm trying," I offered, glossing over this last point. "If you think it's frustrating to hear, imagine how it feels to live with it."

"Where do we go from here?" Clarice sighed dramatically, hugging her knees close to her chest and cocking her head to one side expectantly.

"We just keep going forward as though it never happened," Chris determined.

"And hope that Selina doesn't have another debilitating episode? At least, not while we're on our mission?" Luke asked, tone a bit snide.

"Or hope that she *does* have another episode, so that we better understand the dangers waiting for us in outer space," Amanda countered.

I smiled without much credibility and looked down at my feet in false modesty. I felt confident that they'd bought my story, and I was safe...for the moment.

"I'm sorry, Selina," Peyton offered, genuinely displaying concern. "How are you feeling now?"

"Better," I smiled at her. "Just tired. And a bit overwhelmed." All of these things were very, very true.

There was a moment of stunned silence—no one seemed to be in the mood to revisit the lists we'd been sharing earlier, nor did anyone seem keen to talk through supposed outcomes and dangers of the upcoming mission.

"Sometimes I just wish things could go back to the way they were," Peyton sighed, lower lip protruding in childlike fashion. "I know it's supposed to be this great honor that we were selected for the mission, but there's so much pressure. And I thought I was stressed when I was eating hemp seeds and studying for the exam!"

Marcus laughed aloud. "I hear you. Besides the food upgrade, this deal is the worst. I'd even go back to Calculus," he joked.

"Things felt simpler, but you know we could never go back," Chris pointed out, ever-focused on the empirical. "We know the stakes earth is up against, and the others don't—at least not to the extent that we do—but that doesn't change the facts. Earth won't survive much longer, and it's up to us to determine and colonize a suitable second home."

"Yes, we know," Luke looked at Chris with disdain. "How could we forget? It's what we're reminded of every waking moment here in The Organization."

Chris looked genuinely taken aback, and I wondered just how naïve he believed us to be.

Reminisce.

The one-word impression came to me as so many supernatural inklings did, and I checked out of the conversation taking place long enough to masticate on the term.

Reminisce. Reminisce. Reminisce!

My face must have lit up with understanding, because I won the immediate attention of Amanda, Max, and Clarice.

"What is it?" Amanda wanted to know.

I forced myself to slow my thoughts and pitch my idea neutrally. "I was just thinking that it might be nice to reminisce about the past," I eased into the suggestion. "It might boost our spirits to remember the best of the best—you know, as a reminder of why we are doing what we are."

Clarice made a face, and no one responded right away. I looked at Amanda and Peyton imploringly, hoping to enlist some support.

"It can't hurt," Amanda said. Far from the endorsement I was hoping for, but it was a start.

"We don't have anything better to do," Peyton agreed with a shrug.

"Are you sure we won't be pulled for a surprise assessment or impromptu training?" Marcus asked sarcastically.

"If we are, we'll stop," I answered matter-of-factly, eager to begin the exercise. The way I saw it, this was an opportunity to learn more about the Heidel beings and their level of access to the humans they chose to take over.

When no one disagreed, I seized the opportunity.

"Clarice, do you remember playing make-believe as little girls?" I asked good-naturedly, smiling at my former close friend.

Clarice blinked once and looked at me with a blank expression.

"I used to play make-believe!" Peyton jumped in, her joy apparent. "What did you like to pretend? I always loved to imagine that I was shopping, like in the old days. I'd push a cart and look at all the items on the shelves and the racks and carefully read the product descriptions before sticking something into my cart."

Her rapturous description brought a smile to my face—it was always the smallest and silliest things that seemed to entrance children. I peeked over at Clarice to see how she would respond to this nostalgic memory. Nothing—her face was still a blank canvas.

"Clarice, what did you like to play?" I asked pointedly, willing Peyton and the others to stay quiet long enough for Clarice to feel the pressure to respond.

"I didn't like to play pretend," Clarice answered somewhat stiffly.

"Not ever?" I prompted, knowing this was not the case.

"I was always studying for the exam," Clarice said directly.

"Uggghhh, the exam!" Marcus was more than eager to join in the complaint session. "My parents were ALWAYS on my back about that. I could never catch a break—and look what good it did for me! Thanks Mom and Dad, I did great on the exam…and now I'm being sent on a doomed mission into outer space, most likely to die a violent death. It was all worth it!"

Max and Amanda looked appalled, but Luke and Clarice laughed readily. It was crass, but it was also the morbid reality that we found ourselves in.

I took a back seat and listened as the conversation wove in and out of discussion surrounding the exam or favorite childhood programming or the wonder embedded in that first opportunity to meet another child (a special occasion that was possible only after a series of vaccinations and assessments had been given, usually around age 6). I'd gotten what I'd needed from the conversation—I knew now that the Heidel beings didn't have unfettered access to our human emotions and memories.

I wasn't sure how helpful this information would be, but I claimed victory in uncovering an instrumental factor that had not been revealed to me through the supernatural. The Heidel being seemed to be very well-versed in human life on Earth: common traditions, stressors, and rites of passage…but it did not know the intimate details of the human's life that it inhabited.

There was comfort in knowing this. However small the victory, it reassured me that humanity was not wholly lost. Clarice still maintained ownership over her private life and childhood memories. It occurred to me that this could be an aspect of the mind that succumbed to alien inhabitation over time…I would need to be on guard for that. For now…I claimed the triumph.

"That was a good idea, Selina," Amanda leaned over to whisper in my ear. "We needed a reminder of the good things in life."

Our murmurs caught the attention of Marcus, who wasted no time pulling us back into the conversation.

"Hey, Miss Selina," Marcus called out. "You started this conversation, and you haven't even told us what you used to like to pretend."

That was an easy question to answer…what *hadn't* I liked to act out?

"Baking," I began. "Did you ever watch those old shows that showed people how to cook? You know, with the bowls and tools and with knives and all?"

The "ooohs" and groans were all I needed to encourage my account.

"I used to love to pretend to mix the ingredients together and slice the fruits and vegetables up and sauté them on the stove or stick them inside the oven. I'd even wrap a shirt around my waist like an apron and put my hair in a bun, like the ladies on the shows," I smiled as I recounted my childhood innocence.

"I did that, too!" Amanda and Peyton laughed. "Which show did you like best?"

What had begun as an experiment descended into a genuinely pleasurable way to pass the time. There were giggles and groans and moments of commiseration as we all remembered the "innocence" of our childhood…all except for Clarice, that is. She didn't disengage from the conversation, but she stayed noticeably on the fringes, laughing when it was expected and plastering the right expression on her face without ever contributing.

The afternoon stretched into the evening, which brought protests of hunger from the males in the group. The easy banter continued through dinner—for once, we were not elite, set-apart teenagers chosen for a high-pressure, high-stress mission…we were just kids sitting around a table talking about life. It was refreshing, cathartic, and *so* needed.

Four hours later, and it felt like we were better friends—without trying to, we'd built rapport and established trust through the uncovering of common ground. I lay in my bunk with a smile on my face, Felix snuggled up against my side.

Not for long.

I woke with surprise, realizing that I'd fallen asleep at some point. It wasn't surprising, really, when you considered the fact that I was curled up in a ball in a bed, tucked beneath a mountain of blankets with a warm kitten against my middle. But it wasn't something I'd planned on doing, and so I felt out of sorts as I worked to orient myself.

It was dark in the room, and quiet. The heavy kind of quiet, when it's clear that everyone is in deep REM sleep and no one is tossing or turning or breathing incongruously. I blinked into the blackness, knowing that something had stirred me from slumber…but I had no idea what.

Within minutes my eyes were able to make out shapes. My heart thudded in my chest and I did my best not to move a muscle—I got the feeling that I was being watched, and I hoped my rousing had somehow gone unnoticed until I was better aware of the situation.

I counted bodies in beds—those that I could see—and didn't get the impression that anything was amiss. I was trusting my instincts more: I knew that I couldn't necessarily trust my eyes, and that I needed to rely more on my gut. The worry, of course, was that a Heidel hijacking would take place under my very nose.

But then, I caught the figure standing in the corner. There was nothing aggressive or intimidating about his posture, but the casual way he leaned against the door jamb almost disturbed me more. How long had he been there, watching? My heart caught in my throat.

John.

I exhaled the breath I didn't know I'd sucked in as I recognized the familiar stance and garments. My espionage-related aspirations were summarily shot down as I watched John beckon for me to come out of my pod and to him. So much for my attempt to go unnoticed.

As quietly and gingerly as possible, I lifted the covers and wiggled my body to the edge of the pod. I felt Felix protest and grimaced, anticipating a brash meow of outrage. His whiskers flexed as he yawned in protest, stretching his paws so that they pushed against my cheek—clear communication of his disdain for my disruptive behavior. But he didn't make a sound.

I was careful to scoop Felix into my jacket and zip it up before he had the chance to reconsider his graceful silence. With light movements, I descended the couple of steps to the floor and didn't bother putting on shoes. I tiptoed in stockinged feet across the tile floor to where John stood.

John still didn't say anything; he didn't make any move to leave, either. I stood, perplexed, until I followed his gaze to where Max was climbing down from his own pod.

I was relieved to see that Max would join us—whatever serious discussion was about to take place, I would not need to make any decisions on my own—at the same time I felt slightly miffed by Max's ability to also sense John's presence.

Wasn't I the one with the uncanny, superior ability to gauge the supernatural? How had Max picked up on John's arrival? Was I losing my edge so quickly? Was Max growing exponentially in his own ability?

I glanced back to ensure no one had noticed our departure, then followed John out into the hallway and to the elevator. It wasn't until the lift doors had closed behind us that he spoke.

"The presence with Clarice is strong," he announced, catching me off guard and pulling me from my thoughts.

"You can sense it, too?" Max asked. "I can't tell at all."

"Do you see it, hear it, smell it…?" I trailed off, curious to learn how John's supernatural perception worked.

"I actually didn't pick up anything that way," John answered honestly. "It's more a feeling. There's a darkness in the pods. I don't know what it felt like before, but there's definitely a cloud of negativity that surrounds Clarice and extends beyond her to the people around her."

"Wow," Max breathed with noticeable alarm. "I didn't know that was possible."

"Oh, yes—it's very possible. The Heidel beings—any alien inhabitant, I imagine—have the power to change the atmosphere. It's why you're so paranoid around her, Selina," John explained, singling me out.

I recoiled in surprise, then irritation. I was about to protest when I realized that he was right…the negative thoughts and anxiety I seemed to consistently battle peaked when I was within range of Clarice.

"How do I stop it?" I asked, annoyed with myself for missing the connection and frustrated in general that Clarice could have that effect on me.

"Your awareness of the situation is a solid start," John encouraged me. "You have to agree with the thought and accept it as your own for it to have any power or influence. If you dismiss the thought and acknowledge the positive, it will leave."

Anger simmered beneath the surface of my being—anger that I was thankfully now able to direct at Heidel and their unconscionable behavior instead of at the humans claimed as puppets.

"How much do you know?" I couldn't help but burst out. I knew we were walking back to his refuge to talk, but I couldn't walk in silence any longer knowing that dark and dastardly things had been taking place for an unspecified amount of time without my knowledge…and while I stood by in complete ignorance.

"I know pieces," John indulged my impatience with a measured response. "I've put a lot more together in the last twenty-four hours, after you shared what you figured out. It mystifyied me for a long time, but I think I'm finally figuring it out."

"What's the bottom line?" Max wanted to know.

"Maybe that's the best place to start," John agreed. "You two are leaving for Heidel—not Venus—and you'll need to leave within the next two days."

I blanched; I stared at John with eyes wide as frisbees.

"Heidel? Two days?" I was reduced to the narration of an idiot parrot or broken doll…all I could do was repeat what John had clearly said.

"You must have a lot to tell us," Max surmised before falling silent.

I followed suit, knowing I would have nothing of importance to add until I understood just what John proposed take place.

"You already know that Heidel has ramped up their invasion," John began, slipping his key into the lock to his room and twisting left.

I waited for the sequel thought that hung on the edge of his initial assertion, but it never came. A pregnant pause, and John's hand froze for just a second too long. With a pointed look at Max and I, he twisted the knob and pushed the door open.

Fear crept up my spine like ivy on a neglected Victorian brick mansion, and I braced myself for whatever it was that had set John off. John's back sagged for just a moment—a sure sign of defeat—and then he straightened up and stepped forward with resolve.

Mr. Boothe stood in the center of the room. He was dressed quite professionally, considering it was the middle of the night: his polished shoes sunk an inch into John's eccentric carpet and his hands were neatly tucked inside his pockets as though he were a man of leisure waiting on a dock for his yacht to pull into harbor.

His countenance, quite difficult to read. He didn't look upset, but he didn't crack a smile, either. His straight eyebrows suggested he was there to discuss something serious, and his very presence in John's home—not expected by John—was a violation of personal space that filled in any gaps in understanding. This was not a friendly visit. But then, I'd already determined that with a single look at Mr. Boothe and his golden forehead.

Change of Plans

I knew Max wouldn't be able to see the mark. I also hoped that his emotional intelligence was great enough that he would pick up on John's reservation and my fear, which I was relatively certain emanated from every pore of my body.

"Mr. Boothe," John said flatly, almost like a child identifying colors in a primary book.

"John," Mr. Boothe responded, no less informally.

For a moment, neither moved. Then, John walked inside to turn on the lamps and clear the clutter that seemed to always festoon the tops of the end tables.

"To what do I owe the pleasure?" John asked without looking at Mr. Boothe.

My eyes darted back and forth from one man to the other, desperate for some intuition or supernatural inkling that might help in my present situation.

"Sit down, John," Mr. Boothe commanded, perturbed by John's lack of attention.

Max and I stood awkwardly, unsure of where we fit into the mess. John either didn't hear Mr. Boothe's instruction, or he intentionally disregarded it as he continued to shuffle through papers and straighten things up.

"Sit down, John," Mr. Boothe repeated, this time with a warning laced into his tone.

The hairs on my arms stood at attention and my nerves began warming up, running laps around the track of panic as John didn't so much as acknowledge Mr. Boothe's assertion.

There was a clear power struggle playing out, and it seemed to me that Mr. Boothe had the upper hand. I knew I couldn't underestimate John's prophetic ability…and I also didn't see how it would help him in our current predicament. The warm-up was over: the starting gun had been fired and my nerves took off in an all-out sprint.

"Don't make me use force, John," Mr. Boothe's final warning was nearly whispered, the tone calling to mind quiet, gravelly threats dispelled by cut-throat men of the mafia.

With a sigh, John pulled his attention away from his frenzied organization efforts to face Mr. Boothe. He had in his hand a stack of crumpled papers tessellated with rings of coffee stains and smudges of indecipherable food glommed onto the pages. The stack stood suspended for a moment longer than was necessary; John's gaze traveled to meet my own before he set the papers down, threw a book on top, and turned to face the provoked Mr. Boothe.

My eyes lingered on the papers and I exercised great restraint as I kept myself from grabbing the stack straight-away. I hoped—and suspected— that Mr. Boothe had not caught John's subtle hint. I didn't dare look at Max as John lumbered over to the couch and plopped down.

"Alright, Boothe—what is it?" John asked.

I never admired him more. He had to have been terrified—I'd seen the way his hand stalled in the lock, and I'd seen Mr. Boothe's callous and unfeeling work with my own eyes. And yet, the way John addressed Mr. Boothe showed none of that.

Watching John, you might have come to the conclusion that Mr. Boothe was his colleague, annoying childhood friend, or tolerable brother-in-law. I stood in awe of his nerve and called upon my own strength.

"You know why I'm here, John," Mr. Boothe said simply.

"Do I?" John asked, eyeing Mr. Boothe closely.

I couldn't tell if this song-and-dance was a continuation of the power struggle or a ruse to force Mr. Boothe to state the facts (perhaps for my benefit). Mr. Boothe sighed, apparently weary of the conversation.

"It's been a long night, John," Mr. Boothe began.

"I agree. Why don't we meet back up again in the morning, when we've had the chance to process the day's events and come to the table with a fresh perspective." John was happy to agree.

It was an option that would never be considered—we all knew it. I couldn't figure out exactly what was happening, but I knew it was important. I hung on to every word and willed my sleep-deprived body to attend to every detail. I might not have had the perspective to differentiate between the core and fringe particulars in my present state, but the rolodex of facts would prove useful in the future, I was sure.

Mr. Boothe sighed, and I caught the puffy, lined skin that seemed crumpled like tissue paper beneath his dull eyes. Mr. Boothe's body may have been usurped by a Heidel being, but he was not exempt from the limitations of humanity. He looked tired, irritable, and even a little sickly.

"John, there's no advantage to this. I would rather we cut to the chase. But, if you insist, we can lay it all out. It won't make any difference for Selina or Max," Mr. Boothe acknowledged our presence in the room for the first time, but still without so much as a glance in our direction.

John stayed quiet.

"As you wish," Mr. Boothe continued. "Selina and Max, you may as well sit down," he added, this time with an indifferent glance in our direction.

There was something about his demeanor that suggested I was no more relevant than last week's newspaper. My interactions up to this point might have felt overwhelming or stressful, but they'd always suggested I carried importance and influence. I couldn't fathom what had changed. *Had* anything changed, or had the past events been part of a carefully-scripted charade?

"John, you've been on dangerous ground for a long time," Mr. Boothe began simply.

"For as long as you've known me, really," John agreed.

Mr. Boothe ignored the comment and carried on. "Your blatant disregard for the rules is at best reckless, at worst, treacherous. We've overlooked your most-egregious transgressions in the past simply because you carried with you an undeniable gift for the prophetic…something we didn't know how to replicate, and that proved to be very useful to The Organization."

I didn't like where this was going. My stomach filled with cold dread as I began to anticipate how things would end.

"And it's no longer useful," John finished for Mr. Boothe.

"Correct. Not only has your talent been eclipsed," Mr. Boothe paused here to glance in my direction, "but we've come up with synthetic avenues to replicate the gift you possess that once seemed so elusive. You're not needed anymore, and your repugnant behavior doesn't need to be tolerated any longer."

A shiver crept up my spine: the indifferent tone would have been appropriate for selecting lunch meat for a sandwich…it was wholly unpalatable when applied to a conversation deposing a living, breathing human being.

"What do you plan to do with me?" John asked, looking Mr. Boothe straight in the eye.

"You know the punishment for traitors," Mr. Boothe answered evenly.

"So I am to be considered a traitor," John clarified.

The cold in my stomach began to rise: my torso and then my chest felt the chill of trepidation. First, my parents. Now, I worried that I would be made to watch as John was also knocked off.

A switch went off in my brain, and I began to distance myself from the events unfolding before my eyes. I was witnessing the exchange without being present within it; I removed myself from any emotional engagement. My soul couldn't absorb the shock and trauma of another personal blow.

"You *are* a traitor," Mr. Boothe corrected, rocking the weight of his body from his heels to his shiny, glossy-tipped shoes and then back again. "This communication with Selina and Max is just the latest betrayal."

"You meant to introduce us," Max cut in, rising to John's defense even amidst futile circumstances.

Mr. Boothe made it very clear that he was put out by the need for explanation, but he did answer.

"You were introduced for a very specific purpose: to be trained and encouraged in your supernatural giftings; objective instruction that abstained from personal beliefs. These exercises were to take place under the surveillance and supervision of The Organization—if not video monitored, then reported on summarily with total transparency. This was the simple requirement mandated for John's quite extensive freedom and privilege," Mr. Boothe explained.

"Instead, you have violated our generous arrangement by training these two in secret, and in opposition to The Organization's founding principles," Mr. Boothe formally condemned John.

"He hasn't trained us in secret," Max protested. "This is the first time we've met with him like this—and it wasn't even his idea!"

All of the words floated through the atmosphere, and I didn't grab onto a single one. It wasn't an attempt to be Switzerland; it was an endeavor to save my soul. I could not afford to invest in this argument—I couldn't even risk engaging in it. My limbs had relaxed—already I had created quite a bit of mental space and distance between the situation before me and my heart.

Deep inside, there was a piece of me that pitied Max and his feeble attempt to save John. At one time, I would have commended his earnest effort to extricate John from his indictment…now, my experience had jaded my utopian and enterprising spirit to scorn his naïve entreaty.

"He was very clearly counseled in how his interactions with you two were to look, and he has very clearly disregarded those instructions," Mr. Boothe rebuffed simply.

"He knows I was bringing you here to warn you about The Organization," John conceded. His quick capitulation indicated that he wanted to keep his real objective hidden.

"As he should," Max agreed, "if this is how they treat their valuable assets!"

I was partially surprised by the vigor with which Max was protesting—he was normally so passive and laid-back—but I figured he was making an effort to make up for my silence.

"You don't even know why he brought us here," Max blurted out a moment later, when his first refutation was met with silence.

"He just said why he brought you here—to warn you about The Organization," Mr. Boothe replied without much emotion.

"But you didn't know that," Max argued. "He just said it—you suspected it, maybe…but why did you really come here?"

"You might imagine your efforts to be admirable, young man, but you are actually embarrassing yourself," Mr. Boothe told Max, an edge of anger creeping into his voice.

"It's okay, Max," John told him. "I knew this might come—I just didn't expect it to happen so soon."

"Why do you insist on working against The Organization?" Mr. Boothe asked, re-engaging in the conversation.

He doesn't suspect that we know about Heidel.

In the scenario playing out before us, it was a small and seemingly-insignificant fact. But worth noting.

"I've never insisted on working against anyone or anything," John disagreed. "But I have always believed in championing the truth and empowering the individual over the herd."

"And by explaining the dysfunctions of The Organization's leadership, you'd somehow empower these two?" Mr. Boothe challenged, voice full of disdain.

"They should know what they're working with," John agreed, reducing the true motives for our collaboration to mere peanuts.

"Another misguided crusader," Mr. Boothe groaned. "I'm sorry it came to this."

It was clear things were wrapping up—while I wasn't sure what that would look like, I knew it wouldn't be pretty. John was apparently thinking the same thing: he gave me a pointed look before again glancing at the pile of papers he'd strategically positioned on the end table.

I'd marooned my powers of emotional engagement on a distant island, but now I worked to pull them back. John was sending yet another message…perhaps his last.

"What exactly do you intend to do with me?" John asked in an effort to buy time.

I fought the urge to disengage and instead focused on how to get the papers. I didn't want to hear what John's fate would be—didn't want to be reminded of what my parents' fate had been—didn't want to consider what *my* fate might be,

"Nonviolent execution," Mr. Boothe answered with the passion of a meteorologist announcing the day's weather.

"A paradox if I ever heard one," John joked, making light of his death sentence. "Do I get to choose the means of execution?"

"What's going to happen to us?" I interrupted, catching all three men off guard. I wasn't going to sit around and listen to terms of execution…and I also had the beginnings of a plan.

"You'll be sent on your mission, as planned," Mr. Boothe assured me. "But without the benefit of supernatural training, and we'll need to push the timeline up. We'll also have to wipe your memory of these latest events…we don't want you spreading a negative message about The Organization to your peers."

"A memory wipe?" Max asked, face pale.

"Don't worry—your intellect and personality will be kept wholly intact. It's the emotional region of the brain that we target through the wipe. It's in our best interest to keep you fortified with all the empirical data you currently possess, but without the emotional charge," Mr. Boothe explained.

"You want to make us like Chris!" I blurted out in horror. Chris' mechanical tendencies suddenly made sense.

"Chris did require the memory wipe some years ago," Mr. Boothe agreed, sending a wave of shock through my body.

I hadn't known that Chris' memory had been wiped…I'd just made the connection between his bizarre affect and the characteristics of a memory wipe on the spot. That Chris had actually had his memory wiped was horrifying.

"When is all this happening?" Max asked, exerting great effort to keep his voice steady.

"First things first," Mr. Boothe chuckled, his earlier fatigue abandoned for twisted mirth. "We'll need to take care of John before we address the memory wipe. I'm not one to prolong suspense—we can take care of the execution straight away…but memory wipes work best after a good night's rest. That, at least, can wait until morning."

No one said a word, but our expressions must have said it all—Mr. Boothe laughed aloud. "We're launching the missions within the week. We don't have time to waste. Selina and Max—you'll be under heightened surveillance, with the idea that any misbehavior will result in immediate condemnation and execution. Don't think you're too valuable to avoid this kind of fate—hopefully the example of John will set things straight."

"I don't want to wait," I protested with authority, winning the surprise of Mr. Boothe.

"Our memory wipe teams are not on call right now," Mr. Boothe countered. "And it works best in the morning. Soon enough. In the meantime, I need your key. This room is to be razed immediately following our departure, so your key will be useless, anyway."

My mind raced. I needed to get to the papers, and I needed time away from Mr. Boothe.

"Time to go," Mr. Boothe announced gruffly, motioning for John to stand. "I'd like to get at least a few hours of sleep before the memory wipe."

John stood up, but not before we made eye contact once more.

"This is all your fault!" I exclaimed, rushing over to confront John.

I spliced my emotions from my logic as I pushed him roughly back down on the sofa. He winced and looked at me just long enough for me to glance meaningfully at the stack of papers.

"This is not helpful!" Mr. Boothe raised his voice as John summoned a look of outrage that I knew was not meant for me.

With steely determination, he struck my cheek and pushed me to the side. My cheek smarted and stung, and my first response was to engage muscles to keep me upright—but I allowed myself to fall to the side and onto the end table. I would have bruises on my shins and hip bones and possibly my elbows...but it was a small price to pay as I knocked the table over and sent the items resting on top flying forward.

On all fours, with my back to Mr. Boothe, I pretended to find my footing. Mr. Boothe was yelling out in agitation—I didn't make any attempt to listen to his protest. Instead, my eyes raked over the books and papers and tchotchkes that had been dumped over. When my eyes rested on the papers I was looking for, I extended an arm and in one smartly-timed swipe pulled them close to my middle as though clutching my stomach in pain. I tucked the papers under the belt-line of my pants then let my shirt fall loosely over the contraband.

I stood up slowly, arms folded over my stomach and shoulders hunched as though I were in pain.

"This is totally unnecessary, and frankly, immature," Mr. Boothe scolded, visibly angry. "John, you will do well to remember your place. As of right now, you have the opportunity to die with your dignity intact. Don't forfeit that right."

Turning to me, "Selina—you are not indispensable."

Apparently that was threat enough, because the speech ended with the single-word warning.

I looked to Max in a plea for physical support at the same time that Mr. Boothe's arm clutched John's possessively. Our visit was over.

"Don't go anywhere that will get you in trouble," Mr. Boothe warned Max as he led John from the room. "We'll collect you at dawn for the memory wipe—you will do well to let it happen without a fight."

I kept my head bowed low to continue the charade of pain in my stomach and to hide the tears. John may have transgressed in the past, but it was his support and effort to assist *us* that was now leading him to his death.

A braver person would have communicated thanks through a meaningful glance at the very least—but I could not bring myself to do this. With the exception of the internal bruising I expected to come, the shell of my body was spotless, a complete contradiction to the scars and gashes that lacerated my soul.

The defining moments of one's life can be so anticlimactic. I wondered if it felt different—somehow profound—to John as Mr. Boothe led him quietly from the room. A simple moment, unmarred by distinct noise or smell or even feeling.

"Let's go," Mr. Boothe motioned for us to follow him out the door, where he checked to make sure the door locked before leading John away down the hall.

"Get some sleep," he called over his shoulder before turning the corner.

What's a natural next step after you watch an evil man lead an ally to his death? I wanted to vomit, and I also wanted to eat and sleep and pretend it had never happened. Such is the human condition, I suppose.

"We're going to let him go," Max began hesitantly, his tone intentionally devoid of judgment at the same time that it questioned where I was mentally and emotionally.

"I don't think there's anything we can do," I answered honestly. "I don't even know what John was going to tell us. I don't know that he would *want* us to come after him—he might even have a trick up his sleeve. This could be part of his plan." I said this last bit hopefully, perhaps in an effort to ease my conscience. I wanted to believe that John had a plan—and maybe he did. But I could not disregard his first, defeated response to Mr. Boothe's presence.

"I'm not getting a memory wipe," Max asserted, pulling me from my spiral of depression with his determination.

"I'm not, either," I agreed. "We need to get away from surveillance," I added under my breath. I wasn't sure where we needed to go to escape watch—and I was aware that this was in direct opposition to Mr. Boothe's directive—but our success depended upon it.

"Roof?" Max suggested, and I nodded in quick agreement.

I wasn't sure if Max had seen me pluck the papers from the pile, or if he suspected my real ploy in tackling John, but I could explain everything soon enough. More than anything, I wanted John's death to mean something—and I worried it would be an effort made in vain if I did not have the time to look over and assess the papers that he'd taken such pains to highlight to me.

We hustled to the roof. Without discussing it, I think we both came to the conclusion that surveillance would likely be focused on Mr. Boothe and John before they received instructions to also keep a close eye on us—if we could slip off the radar before the execution, we might buy ourselves some additional time.

The roof was not the idyllic haven I'd remembered. I'd suspected as much; I knew that circumstances have a way of coloring and influencing our memory in ways we can't fathom and can rarely anticipate.

I still felt a twinge of disappointment as the warm night air seemed to extract my remaining energy with callous determination, a dragon belching stale, putrid air on the last vestiges of my grit and optimism. The roof was a safe, secure location—to my knowledge, free from surveillance—and it would suit our needs just fine.

I felt irritation and then hopelessness mount in my chest as I searched for the *right* place to work. I walked the perimeter of the roof and then made bunny trails through the insides, waiting for the moment or space that resonated with my soul. This turned out to be a fruitless hunt: my feet never traversed ground that felt sanctified or otherwise singled out.

This was the blessing and curse that came with supernatural aptitude, that by-product of my gifting that I'd grown into without ever realizing its atypicality. It was only in this latest enlightening chapter of life that I'd come to realize that not everyone *felt* what condiments they were supposed to put on their sandwich or which path to take to the bathroom or who to go out of their way to say hello to. The multitude of daily decisions too inconsequential to note—these were opportunities to connect with the supernatural that, surprisingly, had directives for these daily nuances of life.

To assume that these cues were consistent would be to make a great and mighty blunder. Some days, I felt the presence and direction like the saber of a Jedi knight…other days, I felt like a Midwestern farmer scouring the horizon for a single gray cloud promising rain. It was incredibly aggravating and deflating to experience such radical, otherworldly power and then…nothing at all.

Most days, I would mitigate the humps of my supernatural inclination by living as normally as possible (and avoiding situations that called for decisions with long-lasting impact). But even with this plan in place, I spent an inordinate amount of time hemming and hawing over the simplest of decisions.

I found myself in just such a situation now. I needed my supernatural gifting more than ever—not just because I *wanted* it, but because my circumstances necessitated it if I was to survive and save humanity. My morale plummeted when I detected not a wisp of inspiration.

"Selina?" Max asked hesitantly.

I turned around to find my friend genuinely concerned—he'd been faithfully following me in circles around the roof as I negotiated my way through a psychotic meltdown. Now he looked at me with open worry.

Tears marched like disturbed fire ants to my eyes. I looked up and willed them to retreat before meeting Max's eyes.

"Mhhmmm?" I asked. I didn't trust myself to speak, but I could muster a couple of basic communicative syllables.

Max's eyes housed an arsenal of empathetic messages that awakened my soul from its self-induced slumber. The fire ants would not be held back any longer: the tears began to slide down my cheeks in a vainglorious dribble.

Max searched my countenance for unspoken truths, then swallowed hard in a gesture I understood to be sympathy withheld: Max was far too wise and kind to gush or insist on a hug or other ritual of comfort that would surely send me plummeting into the abyss of my emotions. The swallow was a sure sign of the restraint he would exercise.

"What do you need from me?" he asked evenly, neatly skirting any discussion of our feelings or the situation or even our odds for success.

It was Max's even-keeled temperament that anchored my soul in that moment—the absence of the supernatural had left me temporarily despondent, but his consistency reignited my resilience and fortitude.

"Did you see Max hide the papers?" I asked, swiping away the tears that neither of us acknowledged.

"I noticed him spend an absurd amount of time cleaning when it was clear Mr. Boothe was there for a different reason," Max answered. "But I didn't have a view of what he was doing. I have to confess I was more focused on Mr. Boothe."

"John was cleaning because he was searching for papers he wanted us to see," I went on. I was fine as long as we discussed events like scientists focused solely on the objective and empirical data points. "I saw him rummage through the pile and then strategically place the papers on the table under a book."

"Is that what that whole bizarre fight was about?" Max asked, eyes lit with new understanding.

"Yes. I wasn't sure how else to get them," I verified.

"Annnnd…" Max was apprehensive to ask the question outright.

"I got them," I told him, a small spark of success shooting up in my heart. There was, at least, *one* thing that had gone right.

Max said nothing, but his expression was full of excitement. Without hesitation, I pulled the papers out from underneath their hiding spot and glanced around once more for a place to look them over. My earlier anxiety over finding the right spot had melted away—now I was primarily concerned with finding a place that would allow for us to pore over the papers without them blowing away.

"Over here," Max suggested, reading my thoughts. He crouched low at the perimeter where the wall provided a barrier to the breeze.

I made short work of flattening the papers on the ground, angled so that both Max and I could read them.

My eyes scoured the pages and I felt steely resolve corkscrew up and around my core. Occasionally, a word or mark was obscured by a coffee stain, but never so that the meaning of the line was uncertain. It was ironic that the decision of where to look over the papers had put me in a tizzy when the actual contents didn't inspire the slightest uptick in heart rate.

"Are you seeing what I'm seeing?" Max asked, voice heavy with understanding and obligation.

"It looks like we're going to Heidel," I announced without emotion.

"Yeah, looks like it. And fast," Max added.

Both our eyes slaked over the pages of text that included lists of materials and notes of observation logged informally in diagonal script. I understood what John meant when he'd said that he was working to put the pieces together—most of his compiled data was anecdotal and fragmented, contributing only supporting evidence to the greater truth that we were all working to uncover.

"It's like Noah's Ark," I mused aloud, pointing to the extensive and comprehensive list John had put together detailing what to bring to Heidel.

"I think it is," Max said seriously, combing over the list himself. "I don't get the impression that John envisioned a return trip to Earth." He raised his eyebrows suggestively and rifled through the pages to pull the more technical blueprints to the top.

My eyes glazed over a bit: I'd never taken to engineering principles...I could follow calculus and physics well enough, but I carried no interest or natural inclination for either. The blueprints in hand looked like artifacts from a museum—not just for their faded hue and curled edges, but because diagrams and coinciding formulas had been sketched out in thick graphite.

"I don't understand any of it," I confessed immediately, noting the highly-specific and complex nature of what had been written down.

"I can only follow some of it," Max agreed. "We'll need to enlist the help of someone who does understand this."

"I didn't know John was so technical," I thought aloud, frowning as I flipped through more and more pages of formulaic text and precise algorithms and models.

"I don't think this was John," Max said uncertainly.

Immediately, I knew he was right. Of course it wasn't John—that wasn't his gifting. But his status and privilege may have led him to connect with someone who shared his vision and who did possess this scientific talent.

"But John probably had the access to these old-school materials," Max pointed out. Until an hour before, John had enjoyed unfettered access to any materials he wanted.

"And these are clearly blueprints intended to be kept secret. Hence the pains taken to draw them by hand, when it would be far easier to model with technology," Max went on.

"So there's no possibility of its contents being recorded," I realized, following Max's logic. "This is very, *very* top secret."

"And not to fall in the wrong hands, considering John's final effort to ensure that it landed in your possession and not with The Organization," Max agreed.

"Or even destroyed. John wanted us to see this," I pointed out, thinking of how John's home was being destroyed that very moment.

"We need to find someone who can read this—these look like the specs to reach Heidel," Max stated.

"And we need to start collecting the items John wrote down," I added. "Do you think we need all of it?"

Max hesitated, and I took the opportunity to skim over the list.

50 crates of protein bars
100 hydration gel capsules
Toothbrush/toothpaste
25 bars of soap
15 gallons of shampoo
1 cycle ergometer

"I think those items are packed on every spacecraft," Max interrupted, pointing to the portion of the list I'd been studying. "But we might need to check quantities. I think it's the starred items that we need to focus on."

My gaze traveled down the page to find the spot Max referred to. These items seemed slightly out of place—unexpected items that didn't quite seem to fit in with everything else on the docket.

Sunflower seeds, fresh from greenhouse
1 Austrian crystal
3 oz. Frankincense essential oil
3 pairs (each) combed cotton underwear
20 See's lollipops

"Do you think it's a joke?" I asked Max, puzzling over the random and nonsensical items.

"With everything that's transpired these past few weeks, I'm taking very little as a joke," Max answered seriously. "It doesn't make sense right now, but I don't want to take any chances. Can we get these things? If so, they're coming."

My mind spun and I shifted through the other papers in the pile again. Besides the list of materials and engineering models, there was a set of coordinates and John's observation log, which ended with the words "Feel," "Trust," and "Hope" scribbled in all capital letters and underlined three times in undeniable emphasis.

"What do we do with this?" I asked Max, wondering if he was working towards the same conclusion I was.

"John was clearly preparing for a trip to Heidel—and these metrics mean something. I'm not sure how different they are from what's already been planned for the missions…I wish I had a baseline for where things stand now," Max answered honestly.

"Do we know anyone in our group who's really good at that?" I asked, chewing on my fingernail nervously. I was trying not to panic, but it was clear that we didn't have much time.

"Surprisingly, Marcus was brilliant in astrophysics and abstract mathematics—he doesn't act like it, but the guy's a genius," Max told me.

"Really?" I asked hopefully, eager to latch on to some favorable news. Then, "do you think we can trust him?"

Max hesitated just long enough to organize his thoughts. "I don't know Marcus too well, but I haven't seen anything that gives me reservation. And he doesn't have the yellow mark, right?"

I nodded, now chewing the inside of my cheek instead of my fingernails. We were making big decisions now—life-changing decisions, in fact—and it was all happening faster than I would have liked.

"The spacecraft and missions were designed for us to bring four people. Do we want to bring anyone else?" Max asked me.

We were moving forward quickly, assuming the best-possible outcome in every situation.

"Amanda or Peyton," I blurted, my gut reaction finding voice. "I trust them," I explained without qualification.

Max nodded, his trust in my instincts absolute. "I feel good about both of them. Who do you want to bring along?"

This posed a new problem—I couldn't figure a reason one would be superior to the other. Anxiety began to stroll down the street, turning the corner to saunter my way.

Nope. No, you do not have time to entertain these thoughts. Go away. I was surprised when my willpower did indeed swallow uncertainty and offered a new and better idea in its place.

"We can involve them both," I told Max confidently. "And see which one of them wants to come. We'll need help down here, too—someone to check in with."

"Assuming that there is an earth to come back to," Max reminded me soberly.

"Assuming we survive the trip into space to come back at all," I quickly countered.

There was silence as we both allowed the grim reality to shape our mindset once again. There were no "good" options—only better options.

"We need to move quickly, then," Max spoke up. "I'm not sure how long it will take for Mr. Boothe and his team to recognize that we went missing."

"Agreed. But I also get the impression that they don't care where we go as long as we stay inside headquarters," I thought aloud. "Boothe seems to think that memory wipe will take care of everything...or else he's got some other tricks up his sleeve."

"Let's not find out," Max said humorlessly.

"Right," I agreed. "And we're going to wake the three and talk to them secretly...here?"

"I don't think it will escape notice that we spoke with the other three," Max said plainly. "I think the moment we wake them, we'll be damning them to a memory wipe, too—if we're around to receive it in the morning. There's no way to move forward without incriminating other people and making a mess of things. So, I think we need to operate with the understanding that we are leaving Earth before dawn."

My stomach seized and my blood chilled. It made perfect sense, and as soon as Max explained his plan, I knew it was a good one. And still, I was shocked by the urgency we now operated with. The stress of every little thing that would need to be taken care of was too much—we had the big picture agenda, and now I needed to focus on the next right thing. I couldn't become entrenched in details at the same time I couldn't ignore fringe factors that might influence our chances of survival.

"I know it sounds sudden," Max acknowledged, raking his hand through his hair in what I knew to be an unusual indicator of his stress levels.

"You're right," I cut in, saving him the effort of explanation. "Let's go. We can wake the three and then go to one of the common rooms."

Max nodded and without further discussion we rose to our feet. Stuffing the papers back underneath my shirt, I wasted no time leaving the roof. The countdown had begun.

Wake Up, and Come to Space

I didn't have much of a chance to think about how we might wake the others up. The list of people we were trying to avoid and sneak past was growing longer by the minute, and with it, our odds of success. I tried not to let that color my perspective or summoned courage as we whispered outside the pod entrance.

"I'll get Marcus, and you'll get Amanda and Peyton," Max clarified, looking to me for confirmation.

I nodded, wondering how I would manage to rouse both girls without also winning the unwanted attention of Clarice. I'd given Max the cue he'd been waiting for: he waited a split second longer before making his way inside.

I hesitated for a moment longer, knowing that it was hardly the time for deliberation. The decision had been made; we were moving forward with the best viable option. The *only* viable option, it started to seem.

Looking down at Felix, I lifted a finger to my lips in a plea of silence—a futile, vain attempt considering the fact that he was a cat inclined to behave exactly as he pleased. I'm sure it didn't make any difference, but I held my breath as I tiptoed across the room and over to where I knew the girls were sleeping.

Finding Amanda in the bottom pod, I moved to wake her first. While the wake-up would be surprising no matter how it was conducted, my goal was to rouse her with certainty and also in a manner that would keep her from making any sound. I bit my lower lip, knelt down, and pushed firmly against her right shoulder.

It did the trick.

With groggy, confused motions, Amanda rolled over in bed and squinted her eyes open. Instinctively I moved closer and put my open palm over her mouth at the same time I gestured for silence with my other.

When I was certain she wouldn't speak, I pulled my hand back and motioned for her to follow me, still with my finger lifted to indicate silence. Amanda's compliance was quick: after rubbing the sleep from her eyes and pushing her hair from out of her face, she slipped out of the pod bunk.

Out of the corner of my eye, I saw movement: Max had successfully woken Marcus. I pointed Amanda to the two males; when I was sure she understood my intention, I looked to Peyton's bunk.

Amanda had been easy enough to wake, because she slept in the pod just below me. Peyton's sleeping arrangements presented more of a challenge—she slept just above Clarice. To wake Peyton without also waking Clarice would be no small feat.

Time was ticking. If I'd had more time, I would have thought through multiple scenarios and considered which was most likely to yield success. I didn't have that time.

With lizard-like agility, I crawled up into my own pod before poking my head out and around to peer in at Peyton. Her feet were closest to my bunk, and I grabbed her ankles while praying she would not make a sound.

It has been said that fortune favors the bold, and I felt the blessing of this adage as Peyton shot up in bed without a word. Her frantic gaze traveled the perimeter to find the culprit; when her eyes made their way to me, I was fixed and ready with my cue for silence. This time, I added in a direct finger point to Clarice's bunk below along with emphatic gesturing that she was not to be disturbed.

Like Amanda, Peyton observed complete quiet as she delicately made her way down. She was quick to guess at our intention—she didn't require any additional prompting to make her way towards the group huddled by the pod entrance.

I didn't look back to see if we'd managed to slip out unnoticed; it didn't seem relevant. If we were caught, we were caught—but until something stopped us, I planned to move forward as though everything were right on track.

When the elevator doors closed behind us, I felt marginal relief. The first obstacle had been hurdled successfully.

"We're headed to one of the common rooms," I announced at my first opportunity. "What we're about to do is top secret and could lead to our death—just so we're clear what's at stake right now. If we don't take action, our death is certain—so there's not much incentive to stay passive," I added.

To their credit, none of the three sported shocked or alarmed expressions, even as I knew they were surprised by my announcement. With battle-hardened faces, they awaited further information with commendable patience.

"We picked you three because we believe we can trust you, and we need your loyalty and skill set to pull this off. Also, if we're successful, four of us will be leaving for Heidel before sunrise," I elaborated just enough to outline what was about to take place without giving away the details we needed to hammer out in the common room.

Still, the group observed silence—although I noticed that the grim expressions had become further set.

I'd taken the lead on explaining the situation, but Max took control in finding us a spot to strategize. There was an authoritative element to his gait as he traversed the hallway with purpose until stumbling upon the ideal meeting spot—an empty enclave tucked away from the main hallway. Under surveillance, almost certainly, but removed from prying eyes.

No one wasted any time sitting down; it had already been made clear that time was of the essence.

"Heidel has invaded Earth," I began, getting straight to the point. "More specifically, they've targeted specific humans that they've taken over in an attempt to destroy Earth from within. Many of these targets are within The Organization, as you might imagine. Two names that will carry special significance include Mr. Boothe or Clarice," I explained.

"Selina can see who has been affected. That was part of the after-effect of her 'fainting episode' that was really a disturbing vision of how Heidel has been working to infiltrate Earth. Since that incident, she's been able to literally see who is infested with a Heidel being—the individuals have a yellow mark on their forehead," Max cut in.

Eyes grew wide, but silence was still observed. I was grateful—there was so much we needed to explain, and I didn't want to engage with questions before we'd had the opportunity to lay everything on the table.

"I'd just begun meeting with a prophet named John—some of you may have heard of him," I went on. "Before me, he had the highest known levels of supernatural aptitude, and I was scheduled to train with him.

"Following my vision, I went to him to try to understand what had happened—he contributed some additional pieces to the puzzle before he was confronted by Mr. Boothe hours ago. Max and I watched as Boothe took John away for immediate execution under the pretenses of helping me in ways that had not been authorized. Max and I are going to have our memories wiped of the experience first thing in the morning," I summarized.

"And so now we're going to Heidel?" Marcus asked, altogether uncertain of how we had come to such a surprising conclusion.

"Heidel is meaning to destroy Earth, and they very well might succeed," Max fielded the question with ease. "We're hoping that we'll leave Earth in time to provide a solution—or at the very least, to escape our own destruction."

"We need to learn more about what's happening, and we have to go directly to the source to answer those questions," I added. "I'm partially relying on my supernatural aptitude in determining this, but I've also seen enough to know it's the right thing to do."

"Before John was taken away, he recovered some documents that he managed to slip to us without Boothe seeing. There are notes, technical blueprints, and a list of items to take with us into space. This is where you come in," Max began, bridging the gap between what we had explained and the role the three would play in carrying it out.

"Marcus, we're hoping you can help us assess and make sense of the blueprints," he stated, glancing over in my direction before settling eyes on Marcus.

I wasted no time in pulling the blueprints out from their hiding place and over to Marcus. I watched with anxious anticipation as Marcus looked them over. If he couldn't read the blueprints, our plan was finished before it had even started.

"This looks like algorithm code," Marcus thought aloud, finger tracing the series of numbers scrawled atop the sketches. "There's some directional code, but this looks like the launch code to get to Heidel. It's in the ballpark of what we learned, but it varies significantly."

"You can read it, then," I exhaled in relief.

"It's not too complicated," Marcus confirmed, thumbing through the pages and scanning the codes and numbers. "Yeah—I get it."

"Well enough to take us to Heidel?" Max asked directly.

It was an aggressive question, but it was also one that needed an affirmative answer if we were to move to the next step. Marcus paused to think through potential snags, then looked up with confidence.

"I can get us there," he declared. "Assuming that I'm given a fully-functioning, state-of-the-art spacecraft," he hedged. "This is complicated code that requires the latest technology. I can input all of it and track the integrity of our progress, but I can't fly it manually."

"No one would expect you to do that," I assured him.

"Have you ever flown manually?" Max wanted to know.

I was surprised by Max's deep digging—in my eyes, Marcus had already far and above exceeded my hopes and expectations for flight to Heidel. But I bit my tongue and stayed silent.

"I've flown using some of the older simulations," Marcus explained, "but I haven't flown using any of the newer models. They're moving away from manual flight instruments altogether—everything is done technically. I don't even know what instruments exist in the newest spacecraft."

"But you can fly the older models?" Max pressed.

"Yes," Marcus agreed. "It's been a while, but I used to be pretty good."

"Okay, good," Max finally relented. "We're not planning on needing that skill set, of course, but I want to know what we have at our disposal. Technology is great until it's not—and we're not just taking a simple trip to the moon. This is Heidel we're talking about."

"I get it," Marcus agreed, palms up to show he took no offense. "This is serious, man."

"Amanda, Peyton—only one of you needs to come with us on the mission. We're hoping the other will stay here and serve as our main contact during the flight...we're going to need to know what is happening on Earth," I explained, taking inventory of their expressions to read their initial thoughts on the matter.

"I mean...I don't think any of us want to stay on Earth now that we know it's likely to explode or become overrun with aliens in the next few months," Amanda pointed out.

"We're hoping that won't happen," I countered, at the same time I realized the magnitude of our ask. It was no small thing, to be sure.

"I wouldn't mind staying here," Peyton offered, surprising us all.

"Are you serious?" Amanda asked, looking at her friend with raised brows. "I wasn't trying to force you to stay. I was just explaining my point of view."

"I really don't mind," Peyton repeated. "I think it's smart to have someone here who can keep you in the loop, and I don't think anyone will suspect me. Most here underestimate my abilities. And *all* the positions we're talking about are risky," she added. "Leaving Earth, staying on Earth...we're all just trying to survive."

"That's true," I couldn't help but agree. "We'll need to wipe the security cameras of our time spent here and leaving the pods, so no one knows you are in cahoots with us."

"On it," Marcus cut in, winning everyone's attention. "That's not hard to do—it's easy code. You show me where the control panel is, and I'll wipe it."

"Max, you can show him..." I trailed off hopefully.

"You've got it," Max agreed. "What's our plan?"

"Okay, so Peyton will stay here—we need to figure out our line of communication. Marcus has quite a lot to do—he's going to wipe the memory drive of the surveillance footage, and he also needs to look into the particulars of the spacecraft we'll take to Heidel. You're going to need to become very familiar with it before we take off in mere hours," I pointed out, looking at Marcus seriously.

Marcus nodded, nonplussed by these weighty responsibilities.

"And Amanda—there's a long list of items we're supposed to take with us. I'm guessing that some of them are already loaded onto the spacecraft—but there are some peculiar things listed that we'll need to look for. I'm hoping you can help me track those things down and load them onto the craft," I finished.

"I can do that," Amanda agreed.

I looked to Max, wondering if I was forgetting something.

"Probably," Max answered my unspoken question. "But we can't worry about that. I think our plan is a good one."

"I'm hoping we'll get more details later on how exactly these Heidel beings attack humans and why we're going *to* the home planet of this source of evil," Marcus quipped.

My laugh was ragged as I shook my head in solidarity with Marcus and his innocent question. "You and I both, Marcus," I exclaimed. "I don't think any of us know exactly what's going on, but we know that we're in danger…and this seems to be the best thing to do."

"Thanks for including us," Peyton said sincerely. "You can trust that I'll never breathe a word of any of this—I swear on pain of death."

"The thing we're all working really hard to avoid," Amanda said snidely, rising to her feet. "We'd better get started, then. We don't have much time."

It wasn't a vision, but it felt like one—the flurry of activity was surreal, especially when I stopped to consider what we were actually trying to pull off. It was nutty.

As Max and Marcus left to investigate the spacecraft and Amanda left to stockpile the items on the list, I was left with Peyton.

"Are you sure you don't mind staying behind on Earth?" I asked. It was a bit silly to ask, since there wasn't an alternative, but it felt strange to leave her behind while the rest of us made a break for it.

"I'd rather stay behind, honestly," Peyton assured me. "Space travel frightens me…I'd rather stick to the places I know. We're all taking risks, Selina," she reminded me.

I nodded my agreement and lapsed into silence as I thought through our plan. If there were obvious holes or factors we'd overlooked, I wanted to find them. Peyton seemed to guess at my logic and fell into comfortable silence herself.

"I can't think of what we might be missing," I lamented aloud, looking over at Peyton. "It's not like we're just taking a trip to the moon—this is Heidel we're talking about. If we forget something, it had better be something small. Or something we can live without."

"I think you should take some time to tap into your supernatural," Peyton suggested gently without addressing my concerns. "Max just came back— I'm going to check with him about the memory wipe and who might know about our present rendezvous."

With grace, Peyton stood and walked over to Max. I watched their initial interaction and felt a surge of gratitude that I was flanked by a crew that was so capable—not only in talent but also in understanding emotional needs.

For all the things I was worried about, it never crossed my mind that any of the four might fail in the tasks they'd said they could carry out. Somehow, in our handful of interactions together since being selected, we'd come together as a unit.

Peyton's suggestion was a good one—although I had to admit that I didn't carry much confidence in my ability to summon supernatural understanding on command. I was far past the point of denying my connection to the paranormal—too many powerful and inexplicable events had taken place—but I seemed to be no closer to harnessing the talent.

I was like a puppet on strings, I thought with some frustration. I very clearly received messages, but the communication seemed to be one-sided. There was not yet any evidence that my thoughts and pleas had made any waves in the realm of the supernatural, and this was very discouraging.

Don't give up so easily, I coached myself. So many things had happened in mere weeks; it would be folly to jump to the conclusion that the upgrades in gifting had peaked already.

Nestled in the corner, I worked to clear my head of the worries and distractions that dotted the landscape of my mind. This was no small feat, considering the circumstances.

But I was stubborn. I determined to regard each troubling thought like a weed in a garden: I visualized myself plucking each defunct plant out of the soil, roots and all, and very intentionally dumping it in the compost bin. I felt clever for thinking of this mental exercise and methodically worked my way through a myriad of troubles.

I wasn't acutely aware of how much time had passed, but I'd worked my way through dozens of thoughts and found that some resurfaced (disobediently making their way out of the refuse pile) at the same time that the queue of original worries never seemed to ebb. Frustration burned in my bones; I took a deep breath to push it out.

I would just need to try harder, I thought with resolve—fists clenched and jaw set. I would not rest until I'd buried every last antagonistic thought. I *would* clear my mind.

You're trying too hard.

This thought did not have its origins in my psyche; this was an otherworldly thought that came to rest in the outer annex of my brain.

I don't really have much of a choice, I thought back angrily.

I had no idea if my feelings were transferred back, and I certainly didn't know the most effective mode of communication (if it was, indeed, possible).

You can't control the supernatural.

"I KNOW!" I blurted out loud in frustration, completely glossing over the fact that my thought had made its way into the otherworld.

"I know," I fumed a second time, this time with less volume. "It's very aggravating."

Was I talking to myself? Did I have an audience? I couldn't be sure…and I didn't care. I exhaled loudly and slumped against the wall, knees pulled close to my chest as I hung my head low. Liquid frustration amassed in my eyes and I didn't resist as it began to leak out and down my cheeks.

I didn't know how to *not* try, and I didn't imagine that would be helpful to our mission in any way, shape, or form. And yet, it was clear that my earnest attempts to make things happen were not working.

"I don't know what to do," I confessed quietly, mumbling into the now-slippery crook of my elbow. "No one trained me or taught me what to do. I'm trying and it's not working."

I'd been dogmatic and unyielding in my fight for so long that I didn't stop myself from descending into the pity party that my subconscious had been planning for quite some time. It wasn't fair—none of it was fair. It didn't make sense, either.

I didn't ask for this, I emphasized in my head. *I didn't ask for supernatural aptitude, I didn't ask to be singled out by The Organization, I didn't ask to be sent on this mission.* I was building quite the case. *The only thing I asked for was Felix. Everything else was thrust on me.*

My wallowing was well underway before I finished my argument for why the circumstances were so grossly unfair. As expected, I was met with silence. It figured—I'd already known that I didn't get consistent responses, and now that I was complaining…well, I doubted anyone would choose to engage with me in my current state.

Snot dribbled onto my knees and my vision blurred with tears. I hugged my legs in closer and took the deepest breath yet—one that seemed to ransack all the air from the atmosphere before expelling it in a wheezy exhale. My forehead came to rest in between my knees, a private sanctuary that seemed to shield me from the world.

As my breathing slowed to neutral and my trembling relented, I felt my limbs sink with weight I hadn't realized they'd been carrying. My body seemed to fold in on itself like chocolate melting on a summer day…and the cacophony in my mind stopped.

My body heaved with every breath, and the wet expanse of flesh on my legs was somehow soothing against my cheek.

You're going to be okay.

It was another trespassing thought—one I did not immediately address. Part of me wanted to launch into an argument: to call the voice a liar and remind it of all the obstacles that lay in my path. But that required energy that I no longer possessed. Also…I wanted to believe the voice. I wanted to believe that I would be okay.

I was also offended; hurt that this entity—whatever the supernatural voice could be attributed to—assumed that it could just thrust information upon me at a whim, order me around with absolute authority, and then abandon me when I asked for help or clarification. I didn't like our relationship. My head stayed put and my heart stayed putty-like. I wasn't ready to re-engage.

We're not leaving you.

The voice was easier to discern now—the impressions deeply imprinted and without any competing thoughts. Still, I stayed put.

We haven't left you—you just don't always recognize our presence. We're always with you…we have been for a long time. You're understanding more now—that's the only difference.

I didn't understand, but part of me felt soothed by this empathetic communication—at least the entity understood that my feelings had been hurt.

I'm going to need more, I thought with conviction. *If you want to partner with me, you need to show me that I can count on you. This is wild and scary and totally out of my comfort zone…I don't like it at all.*

I was pushing for a major concession when I had nothing to offer. I was up against a wall—I needed the supernatural if I had any hope of survival, and it…didn't need me at all. But my stubborn nature was more than ready to implode or give up if I didn't get some sign of encouragement. I was warring hard for survival—but what use did I have for life if it was to be so grim? At the moment, it seemed a lame prize to win.

Silence descended upon my thoughts once more, this time with a thickness that hadn't existed before. I could *feel* the quiet and the peace it wrapped around me like a warm blanket. I knew that I was not alone in my space, but I was left to revel in the stillness.

The familiar blue light sparkled in the periphery of my mind's eye as I thought through the proposed plan without stumbling upon any roadblocks. I ran through the plan two, three, and then four times—trying to imagine the steps and scenarios from a variety of angles and points of view. With each smooth run-through, my confidence grew.

It was wild—a long shot, to be sure—but maybe we could pull it off. The blue light of the supernatural seemed to inspire assurance inside of me that it could be done.

After the fifth run-through, I was so relaxed that I worried I might fall asleep—there was no time for that. I hadn't dreamt up any pitfalls, and our departure was mere hours away. It was time to reengage with reality and assist with any preparations that still needed to take place.

Begrudgingly, I had to acknowledge that the supernatural had in fact helped me—not only in hinting at the most effective way to receive inspiration, but also in calming me down. I was no closer to understanding how our relationship worked, and I hadn't forgotten my aggressive demand, but I knew that my much-improved state of mind was a by-product of our interaction.

With newfound hope, I lifted my head and prepared to stand. Instead, a fresh set of tears made their way down my cheeks.

There, sitting on the ground in front of me, sparkling in the artificial lighting that brightened the room, was an Austrian crystal.

Ready or Not...

There were two things that I knew immediately: one, that it was an Austrian crystal, and two, that it was the sign I had asked for.

With deep emotion, I cradled the crystal in my open palm. I'd never seen an Austrian crystal before, and I still didn't understand why it was required for our mission. But the specimen resting in my hand was a vision of multi-faceted perfection, and it further soothed my soul in that it linked John's prophetic insight to the supernatural that I'd experienced. It was confirmation that we were on the right track.

Girded with both Felix and the crystal, my two prized possessions, I searched the room for the rest of the group. The clock on the wall read 3:52...and we needed to launch by 4:30. I wasn't sure what Mr. Boothe considered dawn, and I didn't want to be around to find out.

Moments later, Amanda walked through the door. She immediately closed in on my splotchy face and worried.

"Selina? Is everything okay?"

"I'm fine," I assured her, voice carrying the strength to support my assertion.

Amanda hesitated for a moment, weighing my words with my disheveled appearance. Ultimately, she believed me—there wasn't time to spare, so if I said I was fine...well, I was fine.

"We have everything packed—a miracle in and of itself—even the things for Felix. We just looked at the items Boothe gave you for Felix and applied the same ratio to determine how much we might need," she explained, watching closely for my reaction.

I nodded to show that I understood and agreed with her logic.

"The one thing we couldn't find was the Austrian crystal. We looked pretty extensively, but I don't think there's one laying around. Max seemed to think we could do without it…our time is running low and we can't think of where else to look," Amanda explained.

My throat constricted with emotion; I swallowed my gratitude and smiled at Amanda as I opened my palm to reveal the crystal.

"How did you—where did you—" Amanda was at a loss for words, eyeing me with open surprise as she tried to work out how I might have come to possess the gem.

"I didn't go anywhere to get it," I answered. "It was in my conversation with the supernatural…I demanded a sign," I explained, faltering to find the right words. "And this crystal just appeared at my feet."

Amanda's mouth hung open. I could guess at the many questions she wanted to ask, but didn't. The voyage through outer space would be long, and there would be plenty of time for stories…especially when the stories were ones that everyone would want to hear.

"Have you checked in with the others?" I asked Amanda, growing itchy with anticipation now that I'd checked on the time.

"Marcus is confident he can fly the spacecraft, and he and Peyton worked out a way to communicate from the craft to Earth without anyone knowing. I don't get any of it, but Peyton, Marcus, and Max all agree that it will work, so….I'm hoping it will work," Amanda told me with a small smile.

"Oh, and Marcus already wiped all the surveillance footage, the back-up memory footage, and set a timer for surveillance to reinitiate in five hours' time. There shouldn't be any record of our dalliances," Amanda added. "Peyton just needs to make it back to the pods and look like she's been sleeping when Boothe comes for us."

As if on cue, the three walked into the room.

"It sounds like we're ready," I greeted them.

"As ready as we'll be," Max agreed. "I'm assuming Amanda filled you in? We were able to accomplish everything except find an Austrian crystal."

My smile grew as I was able to hold up the crystal for a second time. Like Amanda, Max opened his mouth to ask his question before nodding his understanding and moving to the next topic.

"We're ready to go," he told me directly.

"Then let's go," I announced, butterflies swarming in my stomach. "We don't want to encounter Boothe. And we're sure the surveillance has been wiped?"

"It's wiped, for sure," Marcus answered with confidence.

"And Peyton is going to be able to communicate with us and access the control room without trouble?" I confirmed.

"Well, it's going to be dangerous," Max admitted, "but there's no way we can get around that. We've discussed her alibi and how she can avoid being seen—those are the main things."

"And Marcus figured out a way to make it look like our spacecraft has gone rogue—The Organization won't be able to track our movement or even our path after we launch," Peyton added.

"So they won't be able to sabotage or abort our trajectory," Marcus explained. "I doubt we'll get away with launching without notice—the spacecraft makes a lot of noise, and the force is intense."

I nodded, body trembling with anticipation. We'd talked about it and prepared for it, but now that the moment had finally come, I found myself in disbelief. We were launching into space.

"Okay?" Amanda asked, pushing us forward and out of stupefied silence.

"Yes, ready," I stuttered, straightening up. "Marcus, lead the way."

"Good luck," Peyton said softly.

"See you later," I responded quickly, trying to set the tone for casual goodbyes that would not drain or distract us from the objective at hand.

"Make sure you get back into bed without the others noticing," Max cautioned.

"I will, I will," Peyton assured us. She bit her lower lip, gave a small wave, and then disappeared down the hallway and out of sight.

"Alright, Marcus—it's show time," Max announced.

"Does anyone need to use the restroom?" I blurted.

My question was met with raucous, genuine laughter.

"Do *you* need to use the restroom?" Amanda asked, thinking I was making a joke.

"Maybe," I answered honestly, cheeks turning red. I realized it sounded like a silly question to ask, but I knew what it looked like to go to the bathroom in space, and I knew without a doubt that it would be one of the things I'd miss most about Earth.

"It was a good suggestion," Max smiled at me, clearly amused. "We should all try. But quickly," he added seriously. "And we should stick together. We're getting close to daybreak, and I want to get out of here."

It's weird to say, but going to the bathroom was oddly fascinating, knowing that it would be the last time for a long time. I paid attention to the little things that would soon be relics of the past: sitting on an actual seat, watching the swirl of the water as it flushed, washing my hands with soap and water…

When it was done, the three of us (Felix nestled close to my chest) followed Marcus down new hallways to the spacecraft launching unit.

It was really just a long, dark tunnel with no light at all. I felt a bit like a mole as we burrowed farther and farther down towards the spacecraft. I fought the urge to question Marcus of whether or not he was sure we were headed in the right direction—he'd already visited our craft to ensure it was in working order, as had Max and Amanda as they'd helped to load the craft with all our necessities. Besides this, Marcus was about to take full responsibility for charting our passage to Heidel—if I questioned his ability to navigate us to the spacecraft in the first place, what did that say about my confidence in his ability to transport us through outer space?

Soon enough, the concrete flooring ended. Marcus guided us up one of the silver ramps and onto the craft that would be home for months and months to come.

My first impression of the craft was that it was sleek, sophisticated, and state-of-the-art. Soft lighting backlit the control panels that covered every last inch of the room we'd walked into. The temperature was cool but comfortable, and while the craft was small, the doorways on either side assured me that we wouldn't be sailing out of the Milky Way in a closet.

"Want a tour?" Marcus asked, unable to hold back a wide, boyish grin as he stepped up to the controls.

Amanda laughed out loud. "Is that all it takes to please you? A room full of buttons?" she teased.

"You're forgetting about my love affair with food," Marcus was quick to quip back.

"Ahhh, how could I forget," Amanda smiled.

I appreciated the good moods, but also worried that we weren't in the clear yet. Max must have been thinking the same: he shifted weight from side to side anxiously before speaking up.

"I think we need to suit up right away," he was direct in communicating. "It's inching closer to 5 AM."

"I'll double-check that all the supplies are where we left them," Amanda launched into no-nonsense mode, disappearing through one of the doorways.

"Roger, that," Marcus agreed. "I'll get her warmed up, then suit up. We should be able to take off in less than ten minutes," he estimated.

Max nodded but didn't relax. His shoulders were tense and his jawline tight. He noticed me eyeing him closely and didn't soften one bit—he was clearly *very* worked up.

"I'll help you get suited up," Max offered tersely before ushering me to a side cabinet. He pushed a flat, circular button and the paneling swept to one side to reveal a walk-in closet.

"Fancy," I couldn't help but comment as we walked inside the plush interior. Vanity lights came to life behind four alcoves outfitted with multiple space suits. Above each, a marquee flashed with the name of one of our space travelers.

"They'd already created all of our suits, custom-made to our measurements," Max explained. "Marcus programmed the marquee to light up with the correct names. They even made a suit for Felix," he added, a small smile creeping onto his face.

I restrained my delight and was quick to clothe Felix before stepping into my own uniform. Again, I was surprised by the lightweight, comfy material—not what I'd expected after hearing of the discomforts of past expeditions. Max seemed to guess at the many questions that rattled around in my head—he shook his head before nodding for me to step out of the closet.

"There's so much we'll need to talk about. In time," he promised.

As if on cue, a deafening alarm screamed throughout the spacecraft. A terrified Felix clawed at my spacesuit in an effort to hide at the same time that I looked to Max with horror. Then, just as abruptly as it had begun, the alarm ended.

My heart beat like a hammer and I followed quick on Max's heels as we rushed to find Marcus and Amanda.

"Get suited up," Max ordered grimly. Neither said a word as they disappeared into the closet.

Blood pounded in my ears; the suspense was killing me. I felt like a small child—I wanted to ask Max a dozen questions I knew he didn't have the answers to. None of us knew what was happening, but we could all guess—and it didn't bode well for us.

"This is not a drill," Mr. Boothe's voice came through the intercom system clear as a bell. "All staff is to report to the foyer immediately. Do not bring any belongings with you. I repeat, this is not a drill."

The nervous energy building in my body threatened to consume me; I had no outlet or way to release my anxiety, and I was way beyond breathing exercises.

"Marcus!" Max called once.

A frazzled Marcus burst out of the closet seconds later with a countenance of pure concentration. "Find your seats," he commanded before launching into action.

I followed Max and Amanda to the jumper seats and strapped in as I watched Marcus' fingers fly across the control panel to flip switches and press buttons.

"I think this one is for Felix," Amanda told me, pointing to a small carrier that strapped to the space just beneath my seat.

"I'm going to hold him," I determined, answering with less finesse than I would have under typical circumstances.

Amanda didn't say any more; I suspected we were all trying to stay calm and preoccupy ourselves from spiraling down into the apprehension of wondering what Mr. Boothe was working on and if we were in danger. There was no way to communicate with Peyton, and there was no surveillance of The Organization headquarters from the spacecraft (that I knew about). The very best we could do was wait, and hope.

"Boothe is shutting down all power," Marcus cried out, still in his switch-flipping frenzy.

"What does that mean?" Max called back, raising his voice to be heard over the growing noise of the motor.

"We can't wait for 100% charge before launching," Marcus yelled, wiping sweat from his brow as he kept his eyes trained on the screens in front of him. He turned around to make eye contact. "If we wait, we risk losing all power. I don't know if Boothe knows where we are or what we're up to, but he's shutting down all power in the headquarters."

"Bottom line, Marcus," Max shouted. "What are you saying?"

"We could be foiled any second—there's no way to know. We're at—" Marcus paused to glance at the control panel— "65% charge right now. We didn't work the models for less than 100% charge, and I doubt we can make it into the atmosphere at 65%."

The noise of the craft grew louder and louder at the same time that I was very aware that Boothe hadn't made any further announcements. If he hadn't already figured out what we were up to, he would find out in moments.

"We can't wait for 100%!" Marcus screamed, succinctly summarizing his major concern.

"Wait for 83%, and launch immediately," I heard myself yell.

I felt Max's and Amanda's eyes on me, but neither challenged my recommendation. We could make it on 83%, I just knew it. It wasn't an impression or obvious supernatural impression, but I was confident.

Marcus locked eyes with me and nodded with resolution before strapping himself into his own seat. His eyes didn't stray from the control panel.

Please, please—don't let Boothe power down before we can launch.

I still hadn't figured out how to communicate with the supernatural effectively, but my earlier pleas had garnered a response. I was hoping that the willpower and desperation behind my current appeal would be heard and honored.

"78!" Marcus bellowed for our benefit as our numbers drew close.

My head was bent between my knees in prayer and also to quell my nausea. I was holding onto Felix too tightly, but he made no protest.

"80!"

"Oh my God, please help us," Amanda begged, eyes squeezed tightly shut.

"81!"

"Get ready," Max warned us. "We never had the chance to go through the launch simulation—it's going to be rough."

"82!"

Even over the din of the engine and impending take-off, shouts could be heard. I bit my tongue—it was too late to change our launch number—and prayed that we would make it to 83.

Marcus never called out the final number.

Instead, there was a moment of complete stillness before my body rattled like a tambourine. I shook in place violently, arms wrapped around Felix in a vise-like grip, flesh slick and smelly with dour sweat.

There's something wrong with the craft, I worried. *We overlooked some detail...maybe the power was shut down...maybe 83 wasn't enough charge for us to launch.*

But then, the most dazzling sensation I've ever felt.

For all its shaking and trembling in preparation of our take-off, the spacecraft seemed to catapult through the atmosphere with power and purpose I hadn't thought possible. I was rooted to my seat, eyes closed— I couldn't care less that I was missing the view of a lifetime.

Survive. Survive. Survive. This was my supremely-optimistic mantra as I kept my head bowed and my eyes closed.

The feelings in my body kept changing: the rattling ceased, but then the tumbling began—our spacecraft seemed to be a yo-yo spinning through the atmosphere.

I'm going to die. My stomach flipped and I desperately wished for a reprieve in motion. Someone was dry-heaving...I wasn't the only one who felt miserable. How long this lasted, I don't know. But I didn't die, because the next thing I knew, the tumbling stopped.

I took a few deep breaths before I ventured to open my eyes. When I did, I first took inventory of the pasty, sickly-looking faces of my friends: it was clear none of us were feeling well, but we were all alive.

My gaze traveled beyond, then—to the glass paneling that lay just beyond Marcus and the control panel.

Black like I'd never seen before. Everywhere. In all directions. But also, dotting the atmosphere with no small measure of brilliance, snowy-white stars.

Someone gasped, and it took a second for me to realize that I was the one who had made the noise.

"We did it," Amanda whispered reverentially.

I nodded, struck speechless. We hadn't made it yet, but we'd successfully executed the first step. Ready or not, we were gliding through outer space towards Heidel.

Made in the USA
Columbia, SC
19 July 2019